A Very Corporate Affair
Book 5
Breaking the Bank

D A Latham

Copyright © 2016 D A Latham All rights reserved.
No part of this book may be reproduced, scanned or distributed in any printed or electronic format without permission.
Please do not participate in or encourage piracy of copyrighted materials in violation of the author's rights.

Disclaimer

This is a work of fiction, and all characters, names and situations are purely illustrative and are the product of the author's imagination.
Any resemblance to actual persons, living or dead, business establishments, events or locales is entirely coincidental.

DEDICATION

To my dearest darling Allan.

CONTENTS

Acknowledgments	i
Chapter One	1
Chapter Two	18
Chapter Three	44
Chapter Four	67
Chapter Five	87
Chapter Six	107
Chapter Seven	126
Chapter Eight	145
Chapter Nine	159
Chapter Ten	190
Chapter Eleven	206
Chapter Twelve	222
Chapter Thirteen	238
Chapter Fourteen	251
Chapter Fifteen	267
Chapter Sixteen	281
Chapter Seventeen	303
Chapter Eighteen	322
Chapter Nineteen	344
Chapter Twenty	359

ACKNOWLEDGMENTS

I'd like to thank Iris Winn for her unwavering support and enthusiasm
and
Brian Schell for his sense of humour and terrific pep-talks.

CHAPTER ONE

Oscar watched Lucy while she slept, the knowledge that she was second-best saddened him a little, but not enough to do the right thing and let her go and find a man for whom she'd be first choice. He knew he was a selfish man. She slept deeply, blissfully unaware of his torment. The false sense of security that Oscar had woven allowed her to believe he was unaffected by attending Elle and Ivan's wedding. A hint of a tropical breeze caused the white muslin curtains to flutter gently.

Oscar eased himself silently out of bed and padded out onto the balcony. He swept his hand along the marble balustrade and gazed out at the Caribbean Sea, glittering in the moonlight. He had an almost irresistible urge to run away, to escape this paradise and the knowledge that he'd just delivered the woman he loved into the arms of a man who had already damaged her.

He'd pretended to be enthusiastic, of course, even giving her away at the ceremony, covering up how he really felt. It was a novel experience for him, disguising his devotion. He didn't normally feel very much for women. He didn't feel that much for Lucy. He wished it'd been her he'd been delivering into Ivan's possession. He'd have been happy for them. Instead, Lucy was destined to be second-best for the rest of her life, which was a shame.

On paper, she was perfect. Well, nearly. Her father was big in shipping, wealthy and went by the title of 'Sir.' It wasn't quite the Dukedom his mother had wanted, but it was enough to appease her. They had a decent family fortune, a heraldic crest, and were Jewish, albeit not quite as pure a lineage as the Goldings. Lucy was also beautiful enough to be considered "a catch," and a far better option than Lucinda Rothschild, also affectionately known as Shrek.

He knew he'd have to propose soon. They'd been seeing each other some months, enough time to make a decision. He was fond of her, although her propensity for social media irritated him, and her large circle of friends seemed to have enormous influence and take up a lot of her time. He wondered if they'd still be around so much if he installed her at Conniscliffe full time. On the up-side, she would be described in their circles as a "gal," not a "girl," the distinction being that she knew what was expected of her within a marriage. She'd put on her wellies, roll up her sleeves and join in with life at the castle without complaint. His life wouldn't need to change too much.

She'd be a good hostess, exemplary corporate wife, and diligent mother, he felt. The arguments for making her Lady Golding were stacking up. He liked the fact that she was well educated. Until Elle, he'd always gone for the pretty-but-dim types. Elle had opened his eyes to how much fun a bright, intelligent woman could be.

Elle.

His heart had broken watching her say her vows on the beach, promising to love another man until "death us do part." She'd looked beautiful, of course, barefoot, young, and carefree, just as she should have done. Her hair had shone, glossy with the golden strands that permeated through it. She'd smiled all day long.

Oscar thought back to the last family wedding he'd attended, when one of his cousins had married a very minor European Royal. It had been a stiff, rather glum affair, with everybody in uncomfortable costumes and protocol dictating that all the guests sit for a three-hour ceremony, thus rendering the entire congregation desperate for the loo. His mother had been almost puce by the end. Only years of rigid discipline had prevented her from sneaking out to find the ladies' halfway through. The reception had been tedious too, with everyone frozen into their restrictive clothes, too hot and uncomfortable to enjoy themselves. The poor bride had barely been able to move all day, her dress had been so heavy, encrusted with glittering stones. It had been an effort for her to smile for the hours of photographs. At the end, she'd looked ready to burst into tears.

Oscar stepped back into the bedroom and padded past Lucy's sleeping form. He needed a drink. Downstairs, in the large kitchen, he began to relax as he pulled a beer out of the fridge and deftly opened the cap. Careful not to make any noise and wake her, he opened the door and stepped out onto the terrace. It was a hot night, the temperature hadn't dropped enough when the sun had gone in to cool it down enough for sleep. He hated air conditioning; the noise and the dryness. Most places cooled down when it got dark. He took a long swig, hoping that the beer would anaesthetise him as well as quench his thirst. He was more of a wine drinker, so beer was a little alien, but he liked it. It made a change.

Lucy woke as he slipped back into bed. "You ok?" She asked sleepily, putting Oscar on alert. He wondered if his inability to sleep had betrayed his feelings.

"I'm fine, was just thirsty and hot," he muttered quietly. She didn't answer. He heard the deep breathing associated with sleep. He relaxed and turned onto his side, determined to conquer the regrets that plagued him.

The following morning, Lucy sat by the pool enjoying the early morning sunshine. She'd let Oscar sleep in, as he'd not gone to bed until late the night before and had been restless. She sipped her freshly-squeezed orange juice and contemplated the previous day. She wasn't sure how she'd have felt about getting married on a beach with only two guests. Elle had been quite happy, she was sure of it, but the idea of letting a nouveau-riche Russian organise everything wouldn't have gone down well with her. Lucy fully expected her wedding day to be the biggest day of her life, eclipsing her degree and getting her first full contract. She wondered if attending the ceremony yesterday would make Oscar all romantic. He'd certainly seemed a little misty-eyed afterwards.

The butler interrupted her by placing a tray of tea beside her. She thanked him and watched him retreat back into the kitchen. She poured the tea from the little Villeroy and Bosch pot into the equally stylish teacup and added milk from the small jug that nestled in its crushed ice bed. Taking a small sip, she reflected on how lovely Mustique was, especially given that decent tea could be found. She liked the villa that Oscar had rented too, with its pristine pool and modern interior, which was a world away from the Golding holiday home in Tuscany.

Oscar pulled on a pair of shorts and a t-shirt before joining Lucy at the pool. He kissed her gently on the cheek before flopping down on the lounger next to her. "What would you like to do today?" He asked.

She smiled at him. "We could explore the island. Bunty McKendrick told me that Basil's Bar is a lot of fun."

"I thought you weren't meant to tell anyone you're here," he said, frowning.

"She's sworn to secrecy," Lucy replied, waving her hand airily. "I told her by text this morning. Thought the blackout was only pre-wedding?"

He grunted, not sure whether she was correct or not. Even so, he felt it wasn't unreasonable to expect her to keep quiet for a few days. He hoped nothing would come of her indiscretion, and they wouldn't have reporters swarming around on jet skis bearing long lenses.

They both enjoyed a long, boozy lunch at Basil's Bar, punctuated by Oscar being recognised by a shipping magnate he knew from London and bumping into yet another of Lucy's old school friends whose husband had a villa on the island. Not for the first time, he marvelled at the sheer number of friends she had, mainly, it seemed, due to her involvement with every single school sports team from her time at Marlborough school.

He sat back and observed her chatting to her friend, noting that she could be relied upon for effortless small talk. Lucy had a way of putting people at ease, of fitting into every social situation. The school friend's husband was a hedge-funder, richer than Croesus, yet Lucy chatted easily, unintimidated by extreme wealth. She'd also got along with his friends, the titled establishment, people who held positions of real power.

Even his mother had liked her from the moment she'd met her.

"I really, really like Mustique," she exclaimed when they were alone again. "We should totally look for a place here. I don't suppose the house we're staying in is up for sale?"

He shook his head, "I doubt it, besides, how often would we use it? I barely get over to Tuscany as it is." The thought of maintaining yet another house really didn't appeal to him. It seemed as though he spent most of his time marshalling builders as it was. Conniscliffe required so much care and attention that he couldn't bear the thought of taking on another property.

Lucy pouted prettily. "You don't take enough holiday." She was fully aware of the perks of his position at the bank. Being chairman, he didn't have the same restrictions as ordinary workers. Even his work at the Lords was flexible. It wasn't as though he had to show up every day like Pearson Hardwick demanded she did.

She enjoyed her job, she'd worked hard to get it, but working 9 to 5 had its drawbacks, the primary one being restricted holidays. The days of long, uninterrupted summer holidays, plus skiing in Klosters, as well as Christmas breaks in Barbados, were just a distant memory. She'd done a few years of the career thing and discovered it was nothing like Cosmopolitan magazine had promised. She was ready for a break, and Oscar could provide the best way out.

She, too, watched him in Basil's; the easy way he had with people, learned through years of public school and careful training. She loved the way people naturally looked up to him, his superiority stamped onto his face by the ingrained knowledge that he was born to rule. Lucy was informed enough to understand that the bankers did indeed run the world, regardless of what governments liked to pretend. Money and power were quite the aphrodisiac in her book, and she knew he was in need of a wife, Lady Golding had said as much.

That night, after a delicious dinner of curried red snapper and saffron rice, prepared by the villa's chef, they sat out by the pool enjoying the remainder of their bottle of wine. Lucy decided she needed to push things along a little as Oscar had been a little distant all that day. She drained her glass and excused herself for a minute. Back up in their room, she slipped off her clothes and found the underwear she'd packed specially. She'd discovered by accident that Oscar preferred her to be a little more traditionally attired when he'd turned up unannounced at her house and caught her wearing her "bigs" due to it being that time of the month. They'd had quite the profound effect on him. She slipped them on, followed by a rather matronly cotton bra which had broderie Anglais around the cups. Satisfied, she quickly text him *Can you come upstairs pls*.

A frisson raced through Oscar as he read her text. There was one area that Lucy excelled, and that was the bedroom. He finished his wine, gulping it down greedily, and set off upstairs. Opening the bedroom door, he could see the room was almost dark, just a side light cast a low glow over the large, white bed. Lucy was standing by the window in the shadow.

She stepped forward, revealing that she was just wearing bra and knickers. He cast an appreciative eye over her lean, lithe figure, clad only in white cotton. The way it hugged her derrière, concealing so much, yet teasing him with its innocent facade. "I've been a very naughty girl," Lucy whispered, "I texted Bunty when you told me not to." She held her hands behind her back as though she were cuffed. He swallowed noisily and walked into the room.

"You know what I'm going to do?" He asked. She nodded. Oscar sat down on the bed and beckoned her towards him. She sashayed over, crossing her long legs as she moved.

She was wearing red Laboutins, his favourites. His eyes swept her up and down, from head to toe, settling on her feet. She stopped just in front of him. "You know what to do," he said, a stern edge to his voice. She knelt at his feet and smiled at him before reaching to undo his shorts. He leaned back a little to give her better access as she freed his erection. Within moments, her tongue was caressing the head of his cock with lush, slow licks. Oscar stayed silent, just watching her as she worshiped him.

He let her carry on for a while, until she was sucking him hard. Without preamble, he thrust his hands under her arms and threw her onto the bed. She landed on her front, and before she could protest, Oscar's hands were roaming her cotton-clad derrière. "You dirty, naughty girl, pretending to be all innocent," he hissed. "I know what you want."

"I want your cock, sir," Lucy murmured, enjoying the game.

"Are you just a slutty girl with a greedy cunt?" He barked.

"Yes sir," she replied as his hands delved between her legs, feeling how saturated the cotton was. He tutted.

"I think you're dirtier than you're admitting. Sluts need a good spanking. Over my knee." He sat down on the edge of the bed while Lucy crawled over and draped herself over his lap. He stroked the cotton of her knickers before bringing his hand down with some force onto her buttocks. She squealed. It had hurt a bit, more than usual.

He smacked her again, the noise splitting the silence of the silent room. Lucy held her breath as his palm struck her again. "Bit hard, that one, Osc," she muttered.

"Then I'll fuck you instead," he told her, rolling her off his lap and laying her on her back on the edge of the bed. In one swift movement, he pulled her knickers down and lifted her legs so that her Laboutin-clad feet were on his shoulders, as he thrust into her. She yelped, surprised by the force with which he entered her. As he began to move, she placed her high heel near his mouth for him to suck on. Lucy knew his "quirks" and accepted them. She watched as he licked and sucked on the shoes, enjoying the fact that such a small, insignificant fetish made him as hard as steel and as wild as a lion. He slammed into her again and again, seemingly oblivious, as though he was in his own world, focused purely on the shoes.

As her orgasm hit, Lucy tried to curl her toes, tensing her calves in the process, which sent Oscar over the edge too. As he emptied himself into her, he gave the quivering shoes one final lick and turned his attention to the real-life woman laying in front of him. A post-orgasmic flush had turned her chest a most appealing shade of pink, he noted, which was perfectly framed by the white edge of her "nanny" bra. He smirked as he recalled the origin of that particular quirk; the secret observation of Nanny Jenkins undressing in the nursery bathroom. He'd found a little hole in the ceiling above while exploring the attics. As a seven-year-old boy, it had been almost impossible to resist shoving a pillow under his bed covers to make it appear as if he was fast asleep and creeping up to the attics to satisfy his burgeoning curiosity. Nobody had ever found out, and it had stopped when he'd been sent away to school.

Lucy sighed, breaking his reverie. She dropped her legs down and kicked off the shoes, separating their bodies. Sex was the only area where she felt that she had any sort of power over Oscar. She understood his quirks and accepted them, although she missed cunnilingus. She was trying to convince him to give it a go, but he wasn't keen. "That was... mmmm," she said, gazing up at him adoringly.

"Sure was, you sexy little minx. Are you trying to drive me crazy dressed like that?" His voice had a teasing tone. He flopped onto the bed next to her and traced his finger around the edge of her bra. He'd been glad of the diversion, and it had pulled him out of the funk he'd been in, if only for a little while.

"I don't want to go home tomorrow," Lucy whined. "Can't we stay a bit longer?"

"I thought you had to be back at work?" He asked. It had been the only reason he'd booked such a short stay, that and not wishing to be around during Elle and Ivan's honeymoon. He really didn't need Ivan's triumph rubbed in his face, which he knew was going to happen.

Lucy pouted. "I'm sick of only getting five weeks off a year. There's never enough time to relax properly." He kissed her pursed lips. Oscar wasn't stupid, he knew what she was angling for.

"Let's make the most of our last evening here then. Walk along the beach?"

She smiled. "We can walk up to that beach bar, see who's there."

"Sure." He masked his irritation. She didn't understand that sometimes he needed it to just be the two of them. After spending the afternoon rolling the idea of proposing around in his head, he needed a time and place to ask her, preferably without an audience. He already had a ring, one that had been in the family a long time, which his mother had deemed suitable for the woman he chose to be the brood mare for his children.

He felt surprisingly nervous as they strolled up the beach, not because he thought Lucy might decline his proposal, more the thought of the permanence of his decision. He told himself over and over in his head that Elle was gone. Marrying Lucy might take the sting out of his loss. It would be a new life to go with the new year, a time for fresh beginnings.

The bar was quiet that night, almost subdued, possibly because the raucous partying had taken place the previous night. They found a table and ordered a bottle of wine from the small list. Lucy scanned the terrace to see if there was anyone she knew. Staying off her phone and away from social media for a few days had killed her. She liked being connected to people and as lovely as Oscar was, he could be a bit quiet at times. "We should have asked Ivan and Elle to join us," she said, hoping that Oscar had brought his phone with him so he could give them a call.

"They're on honeymoon," he reminded her. "I should think they'll want to be alone." He didn't know if that was true or not, but he really couldn't face seeing them and having to put up with Ivan when he had that horrible smug look that he sometimes had. His mother had been correct when she'd called him Podunky. Just thinking about him made Oscar's blood pressure rise. He switched his attention back to Lucy. "Anyway, our last night here should be about us." It sounded more romantic than he'd really meant. Lucy beamed at him, her face bright and expectant.

He chickened out.

He'd fully intended to propose, but somehow his mouth wouldn't form the words. Instead he decided he needed to warn her. It was only fair. "I really like it here," he began, "away from all the pressures. Being chairman of the bank isn't all perks and privilege you know." She stayed silent. "There's a huge amount of duty too. Everything has to be done properly, according to protocol. I couldn't get married barefoot on a beach."

"I'm fully aware of the restrictions you face," Lucy said, thrilled at the way the conversation was going. She'd taken Lady Golding out for lunch at Claridge's just before Christmas, and had been fully briefed on the downsides of joining the ranks. She knew she'd be at Conniscliffe full time and would be expected to produce an heir immediately. Being a bit broody, it hadn't sounded bad at all, plus she had quite a few friends in Sussex, so she wouldn't be lonely.

Oscar looked around the bar. There was only a pair of old-timers seated on one of the rustic wood tables on the far side, not like the previous time they'd visited when it had been rammed. It struck him as a little odd that a place catering to such a wealthy clientele would be so basic, with its straw roof and rickety furnishings. They sold Cristal champagne though, he noted. "You seem very pre-occupied," Lucy said. "Is there something on your mind?"

"You need to understand what you're getting into," Oscar said, as if he'd already proposed and she'd already accepted. "I can give you a life free from worry, but it brings its own issues, namely the loss of your autonomy. If there's a function we have to attend, then there can't be any excuses. Just because you won't need to work doesn't mean you'd be free of duty."

"I know how it works," Lucy said. "Hugo was a Duke remember? I had plenty of practice."

He hated being reminded about her ex. In an ideal world, she'd have no dating history at all, but unless he was willing to settle for a spectacularly ugly but well-connected girl, there was always going to be that problem. He didn't really like very young women anyway, and Lucy was far too pretty to have not had other men chasing her. Idly, he wondered if their offspring would be tall and slender with golden skin and hair alongside an ox-like constitution. She was certainly gifted with good genes.

"Do you want to get married? It'd mean giving up an awful lot of the things you're used to, like your job, your freedom and your anonymity," he asked.

"Are you trying to propose?" She asked rather bluntly. He nodded, knowing that he'd fluffed it. "In that case, the answer's yes. I'll marry you." Lucy tried to conceal her eagerness but failed. "Am I allowed to tell people?"

"I think we need to tell our families first. I haven't formally asked your father's permission yet," Oscar reminded her. He smiled at Lucy's beaming face, pleased that he'd managed to make her so happy.

"I can't see that being a problem, my father thinks you're wonderful," she told him. Both her parents had thoroughly approved of him when she'd taken him to stay at their weekend house in the Cotswolds. Her family wasn't as grand as his, but her father had earned a knighthood for services to the shipping industry and her mother was on the boards of a couple of charities. The Elliots and the Goldings would merge quite nicely. "We can call them when we get back to the villa."

"It's the middle of the night back home," he reminded her. She pulled a face.

"My mother will want to know."

"So will mine," he said, grimacing. "She'll completely take over the wedding preparations, so be prepared."

Lucy laughed. "Your mother has impeccable taste, so I'm sure any interfering will be done with the very best of intentions, plus of course she's an expert on protocols, which I'm not." With just that answer, Lucy reminded

Oscar exactly why he'd known she'd be a good choice of wife. She understood exactly how the politics of the aristocracy worked, how allegiances were formed and when to acquiesce gracefully. Whether it was instinctive or from her education at a top public school, he didn't know, but in his heart of hearts he knew she'd fit into his world far better than Elle would've done.

They walked back to the villa along the beach. The evening had had a surreal quality for Oscar, from proposing in a ramshackle beach bar to finally admitting to himself that he'd truly lost the love of his life, none of it was what he'd envisaged for himself. In his inner daydreams, he'd have done a grand proposal at Conniscliffe in the white garden, to Elle, in May when the garden was at its best. He'd have been romantic and well-prepared. She'd have accepted, tearful with happiness at such a wonderful gesture. Instead, he'd been clumsy and awkward, having left the ring at home. It had been more like a business discussion than a love match, as though they were planning a merger rather than a life together.

Lucy, on the other hand, was ecstatic. Just the thought of becoming Lady Golding sent a thrill right through her. She genuinely adored Oscar, even when he was a bit distant or grumpy. She regarded him as a truly good man, handsome and refined. In the lottery of husband-catching, she'd hit the jackpot.

CHAPTER TWO

As Oscar fully expected, his life was thrown into a turmoil of activity back home once the announcement of his engagement was made in The Times newspaper. His mother had been delighted, and he was happy that he'd finally pleased her. Lucy's parents were overjoyed too. Her father had clapped him on the back and given his blessing immediately.

His heart had broken when Elle had called to congratulate him. She'd sounded pleased for them both. He wanted to hear a little crack of regret in her voice, but it wasn't forthcoming. He'd barely seen either her or Ivan since Mustique due to everyone being busy. There'd been so many articles written about the "new power couple" that it'd made Oscar want to puke.

"I've got some good news too," she told him.
"Oh?"

"I've given up my job. It's a bit of a long story, but I got passed over for promotion, then head-hunted by a rival firm, before being offered the same promotion by Ms Pearson. I turned it down and handed in my notice. They're gonna contact you to offer the bank another named co-ordinator. They put me on gardening leave last night."

"I see. Can I ask why?" A feeling of dread started forming in the pit of his stomach.

"We want to try and start a family."

He wanted to scream, to roar like the wounded animal that he was. Oscar regarded himself as a very flawed man. He knew it was his own fault that Elle had walked away from him and into Ivan's arms. He'd replayed that night's events countless times in his own mind as if wishing it had been different would have any bearing on what had happened.

He kept his voice even. "Well, good luck. Listen, I have to go. I'll speak to you soon." Elle barely had time to say goodbye before he replaced the receiver. It had taken every ounce of his self control not to point out that Ivan was just a thug who'd got lucky. He put his head in his hands and allowed himself to wallow for a few minutes before his PA came in with his schedule for the following week.

Lucy had loved the antique diamond ring Oscar had given her. She wore it consciously, aware of its weight on her finger as she tried to show it off at every opportunity. She'd been counselled by her mother not to give up her job until the wedding had actually gone ahead, just to be sure that Oscar wouldn't get cold feet at the last minute. It was good advice, plus Lucy was on best behaviour, aware of how men get bored with wedding preparations. Lady Golding was delighted to be involved, so joined Lucy and her mother at the atelier's studio to discuss styling.

The two mothers had met before, so greeted each other warmly before parking themselves on an ornate gilded sofa to pass judgement on the dress mock-ups that Lucy tried on. "Of course, with her lovely figure, anything she chooses will look wonderful," Lady Golding whispered to Penelope, Lucy's mother.

"Oh, to be young, tall and slender," agreed Penelope, thinking how delightful Lady Golding was, although she wondered why she didn't use her Christian name.

They gasped as Lucy emerged from the dressing room in a fitted gown, with modest three-quarter length sleeves and a fishtail hem to the skirt. It showed off her long, lean figure perfectly and was traditional enough for the Synagogue at the castle. The atelier fussed around, clipping fabric in at the back and arranging a veil to see the general shape. When she was satisfied, she led Lucy over to the large, full length mirror positioned on the wall. "Oh yes, that's exactly what I had in mind," she exclaimed. "What do you think?" She asked in the general direction of the sofa.

"Perfect," said Lady Golding. "What finish will you have? Do you think they'll have time to bead it?"

"Beading would be wonderful," agreed Penelope. "I'm not sure it's feasible in the time frame though."

"When is the wedding?" The atelier asked.

"July," Lucy said.

"It's doable; tight, but it can be done. We can call in extra workers."

"Cost isn't a consideration," said Penelope. The atelier went off to get samples of beadwork for them to peruse.

Two hours later, the three of them were ensconced in Claridge's restaurant having a spot of lunch before tackling the bridesmaid's and pageboy's outfits. Between the two families, there were fourteen little girls and eight boys who were of suitable age. Lady Golding was concerned that numbers would be cut on her side, which would mean having some very awkward conversations. She nervously passed the list of names to Lucy, cringing slightly.

"Would it be politically difficult to take any names off the list?" Lucy asked after they'd ordered their lunch. Lady Golding nodded.

"A little, yes. I do understand though that it's a lot, but we're a large family, and there's a certain expectation..." She trailed off. It was rare for her to be uncertain, but Lucy and Penelope had been so agreeable up until that point that Lady Golding was sure she'd have to make concessions somewhere.

"I'm sure it'll be fine," Lucy said. "Sometimes it's better just to accommodate rather than cause friction, don't you think?"

Relieved, Lady Golding nodded, marvelling at how easygoing Lucy was. Oscar had chosen well. "It would make things a little easier.."

"Then that's settled," Penelope said. "We'll go ahead and choose styles, then perhaps you can marshall the children to their fittings? Have you finished your guest list yet? Three hundred and fifty was quite tight for us, but I've whittled it down." The Synagogue held seven hundred guests and would be precisely split between both families. When she'd broached the subject of having the ceremony under a Chuppah in the white garden, Oscar had rejected the idea straightaway, displaying uncharacteristic anger at the suggestion. His grandfather had altered the old family chapel on the castle grounds, turning it into a private synagogue. Oscar was determined to use it.

"All done, ready to send out the invitations," Lady Golding confirmed. She'd enjoyed compiling her list, having been lobbied rather a lot for invites. She'd had ten lunches in town in the three weeks prior. It was going to be the society wedding of the year. "I've also ordered my outfit. I'm going for soft peach tones. I hope that doesn't clash with yours?" She asked Penelope.

"Mine's pale blue, almost a baby blue, bolero jacket over a blue patterned dress," Penelope confirmed.

"Sounds wonderful," Lady Golding said, "Blue's definitely your colour." She smiled, relieved that there were no battles to fight. In fact, there'd been no need for her legendary sarcasm at all with Lucy. After the horrific problem with Elle, Lady Golding had mellowed slightly and she was just relieved that Oscar had recovered from his broken heart. She'd worried about him after Elle had left him, and despite all her best efforts, hadn't returned. Lucy had seemed like manna from heaven, dropping into Oscar's life and making him smile again, if only a little bit.

Meanwhile, Oscar was having lunch with Ivan to discuss the mining operation Ivan had begun on his land in Odessa. It required a large investment in machinery, but promised enormous rewards once operational. "Would you take outside investors?" Oscar asked, as he spread lamb-liver pate on tiny rounds of toast.

Ivan shook his head. "I always retain ownership. If needs be, I'll raid the war chest, there's more than enough in there."

"I'd be interested in having a punt on it with you. If you'd rather keep your corporate raiding fund intact," Oscar told him. Ivan raised his eyebrows.

"You want to go into business with a Podunk Russian? What would the other lords say?"

Oscar laughed. "They'd probably be green with envy that they couldn't get a sniff. Ukrainian minerals and carbon deposits are pretty tied up these days, and their government doesn't grant exploration licenses to westerners. Quite rightly."

"Just the copper alone is worth a fortune, even without the coal seams," Ivan mused out loud.

"So why didn't Vlad explore it?" Oscar asked.

Ivan shrugged. "Didn't have time I think. Only purchased the land a few years ago. He probably had a good idea what was down there to have bought it. He really didn't want to share the real reason Vlad had bought it, namely to give smuggling gangs a bit of privacy and charge them a fortune for the privilege.

"Vlad never did anything without good reason," Oscar agreed.

"I need to invest about half a billion into getting the operation up and running," Ivan admitted. "I don't know what kind of investment you'd want to make. I mean, it's not small change." The idea of spreading the risk was quite appealing. He only had the preliminary drilling results back and the geologists report to go on. Mining wasn't his area of expertise.

"I'd be prepared to go halves," Oscar told him. Goldings getting a foothold in Ukrainian fuel production made a lot of sense, especially given the proximity to

Crimea, which had gone back to being under Russian protection. At the very least, it would give him more leverage over the Ukrainian politicians who'd been a bit bolshy as of late.

"I'll get Elle to set it up as a subsidiary company, then we can both funnel some cash in and take an equal share." Ivan was quite pleased to have Oscar on board and break his "own everything" rule, as he trusted him implicitly. He was also aware that Oscar made his investment decisions for political reasons rather than financial, so was happy to play a long game and not expect a return too quickly.

"How is Elle?" Oscar asked. He'd half expected her to join them for lunch.

"She's good, thanks. In court today fighting a patent case for us."

"Who's having a pop at you?"

"Not having a pop at me, we're having a pop at Samsung. The bastards copied the screen design of the Bel-Phone. They're trying to keep the proceedings under wraps in case we win and make them pull the handset off the market."

Oscar winced. "That'd be expensive for them."

"They should've thought of that before pinching our ideas. They know from our lawsuits with Apple that we always defend ourselves." He sat back in his seat while the waiter cleared away the plates.

"Elle tells me that you're planning to start a family."

"Certainly are. I want a lot of children. Elle does too. I suppose because neither of us have any family left. Elle said that Lucy found a dress for your wedding."

"You know more than me then," Oscar admitted.

"This morning apparently. Lucy called her during recess I think." He paused. "So it's all systems go for July?"

"I believe so. My mother is having the time of her life. There's swarms of workmen in the castle sorting out all the spare bedrooms and repainting the ballroom." Ivan noticed that Oscar didn't seem too happy about it. If anything, he seemed a bit down. He stayed silent as Oscar went on; "I'm sure it'll all be fine, and it's not as though I have to do anything more than get a suit made. The girls can fuss about which flowers to get and who should be invited."

"Don't you want to be involved?" Ivan was shocked, he'd enjoyed organising their surprise wedding. Oscar shook his head.

"There's a whole hen-house of women debating napkin colours and flower-girl outfits. I really don't need to have an opinion. Plus of course, they're all pissed at me for not giving them a year's notice. Apparently, July doesn't give them a lot of time to plan a wedding extravaganza, plus Lucy won't give her notice at work until after the wedding."

'So she doesn't trust you to go through with it,' thought Ivan. He didn't say anything. The waiter returned, carrying their main courses, which gave him time to turn the thought over in his mind. Ivan wasn't a huge fan of Lucy, only insofar as she irritated him with her public school accent and boundless enthusiasm for everything. He didn't believe her to be stupid though, especially as she'd completed a law degree and got herself a full contract at Pearson Hardwick. There was only so far a posh accent could take someone.

"Are you not looking forward to it?" Ivan asked after the waiter had left. He'd loved every moment of his own wedding, from first seeing Elle dressed in a white frock, right through to dancing on the beach with her as the sun went down.

Oscar pulled a face. "It's just so over-the-top. Mother's having the castle tarted up so everything probably stinks of paint, and Lucy's so busy I barely see her. I'll be glad when it's all over." Ivan stayed silent, debating with himself how he'd have felt about having a large, formal wedding. "I just wish women didn't make such a fuss over everything." The irritation was evident in his voice.

"July isn't a long way away. It'll be over soon enough," Ivan soothed. "In the meantime, you're in town during the week, no?"

"Thank God. At least I only get it at the weekends," admitted Oscar, as he took a forkful of his veal supreme. Ivan wondered exactly what his problem was. The truth was that Oscar hadn't even been to Sussex for a few weekends since before Mustique. Lucy had so much going on that it'd been easier to stay in town. "By the way, there's an opportunity for some land and a building plot just outside Derwent. You might want to take a look. It's on with Polkard and Bilcher, estate agents."

Back in his office, after offloading the shares in Samsung that the Golding investment fund held, Oscar pondered why he was so depressed. His life wouldn't really change, apart from having Lucy at Conniscliffe every weekend, which he quite enjoyed, as it made a change from just having his mother around. After much thought, he came to the conclusion that it was due to his fear of getting married. As wives went, Lucy was a good choice, well-suited and very well-liked in his circle. Even Darius had approved of her, having met her during a weekend house party, remarking that he found her easier to get along with than Elle. Darius didn't like clever or educated women as a rule. Arabella, his wife, was decidedly nice, but dim.

His thoughts led back to that terrible night. Darius hadn't pushed, but their code was always if Oscar served sticky toffee pudding for dessert, then he wanted a fix. "Oscar knows how to spoil me," Darius had told Elle when the butlers had brought it out. His innocent delivery of that line had just added to the subversion. Oscar's thoughts were abruptly interrupted by his secretary announcing the arrival of his mother and Lucy.

"Oscar, darling," said Lady Golding before holding her cheek out for a perfunctory kiss, "We've had a marvellous day. The dress is all sorted, and the bridesmaids and page-boys outfits have been chosen. We even had time to speak to the florist about dressing the synagogue and the ballroom."

"Sounds like a very productive day," he replied, trying to muster up some enthusiasm.

"Lots ticked off the list," beamed Lucy. "I don't suppose your secretary could rustle us up a pot of tea? I'm exhausted."

He pressed his intercom and asked Melanie, his PA, to bring drinks and three cups. Lucy, meanwhile was checking out the paintings on the walls, squinting at the signature of the Picasso. He'd brought it to his office, as it didn't really fit in at Conniscliffe. Plus it gave a slightly edgier vibe to his rather staid space. "Is this a real Picasso?" She asked.

He nodded while his mother piped up; "hideous thing. Looks better in here than it did in the long gallery."

"I rather like it," Oscar said, mainly to be awkward. She shot him a withering look. "How's the decorating going at home?" He asked, getting back onto safer ground. His mother had largely left the maintenance of the castle to him after his father had died, claiming to be too busy. With guests to impress, all of a sudden she was marshalling builders and revamping bathrooms. It amused him.

"Apart from a leak when one of the plumbers didn't seal a joint properly, it's going quite well," she said. "The ballroom will look tremendous when it's done. Are you coming down this weekend?"

"Yes, I've nothing planned up here." He knew he should've consulted Lucy, but was irritated by the way her weekends always seemed chock-full of friends and activities. He wanted to just relax by the fire in the snug and read.

"I'm gonna be in town until Sunday afternoon," Lucy said. "I'm playing badminton for the Fulham ladies team, then their annual dinner. Sunday morning, I promised I'd meet Tara for brunch. I'll drive down afterwards." Normally, such a schedule would have annoyed Oscar, but he let it pass without complaint. They were interrupted by Melanie bringing their tea. As she placed the silver tray on his desk, she gave Lucy a thin-lipped, rather tight smile.

"Is that everything?" She asked Oscar.

"Yes, thank you."

Lady Golding stood up to pour their tea, making Oscar's first, with milk added after the water, just as he liked it. "Perhaps we could have dinner together Saturday evening?" She said as she placed his cup and saucer in front of him.

"Sure." He noticed Lucy looking at him quizzically and decided he needed to put on a happier front. "So what decision did you make about the bridesmaids? Who are we going to disappoint?" he fully expected the list to have been pared down somewhat, twenty-two little ones would be a nightmare to control on the day. Even William and Kate hadn't had that many at the Royal nuptials.

"Nobody," Lucy said, smiling at Lady Golding. "It'll be a bit of a job getting them all rehearsed, but, well, I couldn't bear to say no to any of them. Besides, it'll look great in the photos."

"The invitations were delivered yesterday, So I can get the calligrapher to finish them off and get them posted tomorrow," Lady Golding chimed in. "Penelope is emailing me her list when she gets home." She was extremely proud of having learnt to email under Lucy's patient tutelage, considering herself quite the up-to-date dowager, especially after Oscar had given her an iPad and shown her how to check the weather on it.

"Sounds as though you have everything completely under control," said Oscar. He wished that they'd leave. His office normally felt like a powerful place. With his mother seated opposite his desk, he felt small, almost insignificant, as though he wasn't good at his job. He wondered why he felt that way when he'd almost reached his father's record for expanding the client base. His father had been at the helm for thirty-five years, Oscar just five. The shrill ringing of his phone jolted him. He picked it up.

"Hey Oscar, Ivan told me about the Odessa deal. I'm going to list a subsidiary company this afternoon with you and Ivan as equal shareholders. Is that correct?" There was no mistaking Elle's breathy voice, complete with pronounced glottal stop. In spite of himself, Oscar smiled.

"Hi. Elle. Yes that's all correct. I'm just here with Lucy and my mother."

"She said she had the day off. Tell them I said Hi. Have they both been having fun?"

"I believe so. Now do you need a meeting about that new company? Will there be things for me to sign?" He really wanted to see her, even though he knew there was no hope of her ever reciprocating, he liked being around her, even just for an hour. He missed her.

"No need. I'll set it up with myself as company secretary. Makes it all much easier. I'll let you know when the articles of association are done and a bank account required. Listen, I gotta go, the court's being recalled." The line went abruptly dead.

"Did I just hear that right, that you're doing a deal with Ivan?" Lucy sounded surprised.

"Yes. Do you have a problem with that?" He asked, frowning.

"Links to that part of the world could be highly advantageous," his mother told Lucy. "Fuel security is an issue of the future. It's very wise to get on top of it now, before it becomes impossible."

"How do you know all that stuff?" Lucy asked her, impressed by her knowledge of current affairs.

"Had lunch with the foreign secretary last week dear. He was lobbying for an invite. Interesting little man, I must say." She leaned forward, as if she might be overheard. "Terrible bad breath though, very noticeable. Nearly as bad as that Blair chap. His could kill a goat at twenty paces." She smirked as Lucy giggled.

"Quite," Oscar agreed, stifling a smile. "Ivan had some land which is very promising, so I jumped onboard before anyone else could. It's important to keep diversifying the Golding investment fund."

Lucy pulled a face.

"What?" Oscar asked.

"I'm not totally sure I'd trust him enough to do business with him. I know he's a friend of ours, but he's a bit…" She trailed off.

"He's a bit what?" Oscar demanded.

"Well, a bit rough around the edges if you know what I mean," she said. "Don't get me wrong, I love Elle, but they're both well-suited."

Lady Golding glanced at Oscar rather nervously. She knew how angry any hint of snobbery towards Elle made him. "I don't think Elle's integrity has ever been called into question, dear," she said, a warning tone enmeshed in her voice. The last thing Lady Golding wanted was any reason for Oscar to back out of the marriage. He didn't seem very happy to her, she'd seen him become withdrawn before, an episode which had rendered him susceptible to the temptation of the oblivion that cocaine had provided.

"I'm not saying it has. Just that she relies on intelligence rather than refinement."

Oscar kept quiet. He didn't want an argument, especially one where he might say more than was wise. Drawing in a deep breath, he turned his attention to the cup of tea in front of him and took a sip, wishing it was something stronger. "So, are you done for the day?" He asked nobody in particular.

"I'm dining with Viscount Trevelyon and his wife this evening," his mother told him, glad to change the subject.

"I thought they were already on the list?" Oscar said, frowning slightly.

"They are, they just don't know that yet," his mother said, smiling impishly. "I'll allow them to think their lobbying gained them an invite. They're taking me to the Gordon Ramsey at Hospital road."

"Anyone would think you're enjoying milking this," Oscar quipped. He was delighted that his mother was out having fun and socialising again. Since his father's death, she'd largely shut herself away at Conniscliffe, restricting herself to local causes and eschewing the wider world. It had narrowed both her world and her mind, to the point that her unhappiness had spilled over, poisoning her interactions with anyone unfortunate enough to stand in her path. Being busy with preparations had transformed her. She was more the mother he remembered from his childhood again. He could remember picnics in the gardens when he was a boy, his mother joining in with games of hide-and-seek, while his father went off to his job in the city every morning.

"Well, it's such fun trying out all this nouvelle cuisine. Far better than dining on my own every night, plus the Viscountess is a real hoot." She turned to Lucy, "She used to be a showgirl in Las Vegas back in the day. Met the Viscount at the roulette tables, and he swept her away to England and married her. Everyone thought it'd never last, but forty years later, here we are."

"How romantic," Lucy exclaimed, clapping her hands together. "I'm gonna need to go in a minute." She finished her tea.

"Where?" Oscar asked. He'd planned a quiet night in.

"I'm standing in for someone in the firm's quiz team. We're up against Penroth Westlake tonight and Henry Stanton is off sick. I know it's a bit last-minute, but I didn't want to let the company down, and Jonathan Olgilvy couldn't do it, as his wife's about to give birth in the Portland. Could you take my bags home please?" She pointed at the pile of cardboard carriers which bore names such as Chanel and Prada. His mother had left hers in the boot of the Bentley.

"Sure. Oh well, have a nice time," he said as she pecked his cheek before disappearing.

"Is everything alright?" His mother asked as soon as they were alone. "You seem a little distant?"

"I'm fine," he snapped. He really didn't want to admit to his mother that he was still pining for Elle, especially as she'd married another man.

"Alright, but please make sure you attend your meeting this week." With that, she pecked his cheek and left. Oscar sat back in his chair and mulled over the conversation. The only bright spot in his afternoon had been speaking to Elle, which had been torturously brief. He decided to visit his Narcotics Anonymous meeting after work that evening. He glanced at his watch. It was almost five. If he hurried, he'd make the five-thirty session in Victoria Dock.

There were at least twenty other people in the room when Oscar arrived, most of whom he recognised from the previous meetings he'd attended. He greeted them warmly, having heard their stories and knowing that they too struggled on a daily basis to stay clean. He regarded himself as a recovering addict, knowing that cocaine still had a hold over him. He could never again be in temptation's way. He would never not be an addict.

He took a seat and sat quietly, listening to the story of a new member, a young man who showed the signs of recent drug use. His poison of choice had been heroin, and he still bore the grey pallor and darkened eyes of the habitual user. He told the room that he'd just come out of rehab and was struggling to resist going back to his old ways. It seemed like the only thing that had stopped him was a lack of veins to inject.

Oscar recalled his own 'dark days,' when cocaine had him in its icy grip. How he'd bought it almost in bulk, not in tiny foil wraps at cut prices, purchased in a back alley and adulterated with substances designed to inflict maximum damage while increasing the dealer's profits. Oscar had sourced the best, most pure versions, the cost barely even noticeable due to his vast trust fund. He'd kidded himself that because it wasn't street drugs, he wasn't a junkie. As he listened to the poor wretch talk about his self-loathing and the destruction of his life, Oscar knew that in truth, he was no different.

His father had discovered him laying on the floor of his Mayfair apartment, naked and shaking after a seizure. His cold, unemotional father had cried in the private ambulance as they were whisked away, first to a private hospital to get him stabilised, and then to a rehabilitation centre on the Isle of Wight. It had been the only time he'd ever seen his father express any sort of emotion. It was also the only time he'd felt loved by him.

He'd expected the judgmental sigh of disapproval that he knew so well. He was fully aware that he'd let everybody down, most of all himself. He'd been groomed since birth to take over the family bank, to inherit a distinguished title, part of an edifice that was the Golding family dynasty. Instead, his father had shocked him by holding his hand and accompanying him to that godforsaken clinic off the south coast, displaying a compassion that had been invisible until that day.

When he came home, his father had sat with him in the white garden and talked. He'd opened up to Oscar, asked if he was the cause of his unhappiness and told him he was proud of the way Oscar had conquered his addiction. He also told Oscar that he loved him.

It was a game-changer. He never touched cocaine again, although he made sure he was never put in temptation's way. As he watched the young man cringe at the way he'd let his mother down, Oscar gave thanks that his father had lived long enough to see him turn his life around and become a rising star on the bank's board of directors.

He stayed for coffee and biscuits after the speaker had finished, as he had nothing to rush home for. He chatted with the young man, discovering that his name was Kyle, and he came from the Isle of Dogs, which was a rough part of town in the process of slowly being gentrified. Kyle's mother had been an alcoholic, and he didn't know who his father was. Oscar cringed inwardly at Kyle's revelation that his mother was in prison for theft, and he was living alone in her council flat, albeit without electricity as he had no money for the key meter.

His benefits hadn't been forthcoming and until they'd been paid, he couldn't afford even the most basic of life's essentials.

"I'll take you to the supermarket and get some food and charge your key thing up," Oscar heard himself say. He knew better than to just hand the young man some cash, which would risk his sobriety.

Kyle looked skeptical, "Why would you want to do that man?" He asked.

"Call it penance," Oscar replied. He took a last swig of his coffee, resisting the urge to pull a face at the synthetic flavour of the instant brew. "Come on," he said.

Kyle followed him out of the hall and into the car park where Oscar had left his Range Rover. They jumped in. "Wicked car, man," Kyle said, stroking the biscuit-coloured leather with great reverence.

"I like it," Oscar replied, easing the large car out of the parking space.

"I bet you were addicted to Charlie," Kyle said, "Rich buggers always are."

"Only Columbia's very finest," Oscar quipped. "Mind you, a drug is a drug, and a junkie is a junkie."

"Drugs are a great leveller," Kyle agreed. "I used to sell stuff to half the City. Those poncy traders and bankers were my best customers.

"If you were a dealer, how come you're not dripping in gold chains and driving your own flash car?" Oscar demanded. His dealer had driven a Porsche.

"The profits went up my nose or in my veins," Kyle said, quite cheerfully. "When you're shooting up, you don't tend to be too bothered about going to work. Before I knew it, the Russians had muscled in and taken over my patch. All I got left with was this crummy addiction and a bunch of flat veins."

They pulled up outside the nearby Tesco Metro, and Oscar dutifully followed Kyle around holding a basket for his purchases, which seemed to consist of mainly crisps and pot noodles. "Don't you want some proper meals?" He asked as they passed the aisle of ready-made microwave dinners. Kyle shook his head.

"The cooker doesn't work. I'm fine with kettle stuff." He felt embarrassed enough as it was, filling up a whole basket at a stranger's expense. Having to admit that his mother hadn't even had a working cooker made it worse. The store was full of other suited men, stocking up before returning home from work. Oscar didn't feel as though he stood out. Kyle did though, in his grey hoodie and ill-fitting jeans, his body thin and scrawny from years of abuse. Oscar guessed his age as somewhere in his early twenties.

Oscar paid at the checkout, and added a hundred quid's worth of electric onto his key. "Man, you sure?" Kyle exclaimed. He'd expected a twenty at the most. Oscar nodded.

"You'll be alright from here?" He really didn't want to drive into a dark estate.

"Course. Listen, if there's anything you need..."

"Thanks." Oscar didn't know why he was thanking him. He turned and walked out of the shop, straight to his car and drove home in a trance. He needed to be back in his own world. As he stepped into the lift, the thought struck him; this was what Elle's life had been like. Poverty, she'd called it. He'd never understood it before. He couldn't imagine her in a council flat, struggling to buy electric. He wondered where she'd got her poise from, how she'd dragged herself out.

He was already in bed when Lucy arrived home from her quiz night. He placed the book he'd been reading on the bedside table as she walked in bearing a big smile. "Did you win?" He asked. He'd already made the decision to appreciate her more, to make her happier.

She nodded. "It was a rout. Pearson Hardwick are still at the top of the league table."

"Excellent news."

She disappeared into the bathroom to brush her teeth, emerging a few minutes later. He watched as she began to strip off. "I really wish I didn't have to go to work tomorrow. Having today off has been so much fun."

"You know my answer to that one," he said. They'd already discussed Lucy giving up her job. He had no idea why she refused to submit her notice until after the wedding. With the amount she had to organise, it would've made her life much easier if she wasn't still trying to work nine to five during the week.

"I know," she replied. "It's tempting, but..." She trailed off, not wanting to say the words. She didn't really have to. Oscar knew that she worried about him changing his mind. He held his arms open.

"Come to bed. You must be shattered." She slid her naked body under the duvet and snuggled into him.

"So what did you do this evening?" She murmured, enjoying how strong and masculine he felt.

"Went to my Narcotics Anonymous meeting, then home. Nothing exciting. He didn't know why he found it easy to admit his addiction, but not his act of kindness. For some reason he wanted to keep it private, even though he knew she'd approve. Lucy was quite the sucker for a sob story, he thought, recalling her buying a homeless man a sandwich and a coffee once when they were out shopping. He knew she made a point of always having a little change in her pocket for Big Issue sellers and buskers.

She leaned over to kiss him, stretching her neck to reach his lips. She tasted of mint and wholesomeness as he softened into her. As he stroked the silky skin of her shoulder, she hummed with pleasure. Her breath caught as he moved his hand lower to caress her breast, gently kneading it in his palm. He wanted to pleasure her, to make amends for the way he felt inside, a sort of consolation prize. Her hand reached around his torso, holding him in a sensual grip. He felt her pushing him onto his back.

It didn't take much to turn Lucy on, just his proximity was usually enough. She loved his firm, masculine body, his long legs, and his mask of barely-restrained power. She slid her body over his and began to rub herself on his erection, letting him feel her arousal. When his eyes had closed, she sank down onto him, watching as his sculptured lips parted, letting out a deep breath. As she moved, he moved with her, their bodies totally in tune, moving faster, deeper as time went on. She heard his breathing become ragged and reached down to rub her clit, reaching the moment of no return only a split second before Oscar. His eyes sprung open to watch her as she came, her long, slender thighs tightening their grip on his torso as her body shuddered. Her orgasm salved his conscience. *At least she's having a good time*, was the thought that popped into his head, which was unfair, as he'd enjoyed it too.

CHAPTER THREE

Elle stacked the papers she'd printed off for the new company in a neat pile on her ridiculously enormous desk. It was so large that it resembled a small conference table. Ivan had given her a terrific corner office and fitted it out so lavishly that she couldn't help but smile whenever she walked in. Seated in her leather 'executive' chair, she swung round to gaze at the view of the river through the floor-to-ceiling windows. Even after seeing the same scene for the best part of a year, it didn't stop the little rush of excitement that ran through her belly. The river Thames was the lifeblood of London, and to everyone who loved the city as much as she did, it encapsulated the essence of what it was to be a Londoner. It was why apartments and offices with river views commanded such high premiums. The river was an ever-changing landscape that provided both a sense of permanency and a hypnotic drama to entertain for an hour. As she sat and gazed, she felt the familiar twinge of her period begin. A visit to her ensuite bathroom confirmed it. *Another month of no pregnancy*, she thought. She felt surprisingly bereft, even though they'd only been trying a month or so. Last month, Ivan had been sanguine about it, stating that it would take a while to get the contraceptive shot out of her system and her body ready to make a son. Back in her office, she picked up the phone and called his mobile. "No baby this month," she told him as soon as he picked up.

"Malyshka, there's plenty of time," he soothed. "It's only a few weeks. These things happen when they happen."

She wondered if she should send him to get his sperm count checked, then dismissed the idea. He was right, it was too soon. "Keep fingers crossed for next month," she said. "I've got the articles of association for the new subsidiary ready and the liability insurances. Would you like me to open the bank account and get some funds moved in?"

Marvelling at Elle's efficiency wasn't a new feeling for Ivan. At every turn she managed to surprise him with her abilities. She made the complex task of setting up companies look incredibly easy and straightforward. "Please. Can you speak to Oscar too? He needs to place his investment and sign the share documents."

"They're all prepared. I'll see if he wants to do lunch. If he can, will you be joining us?"

"Maybe. I'm waiting on Sergei. He needed to see me about the Talk'n'Walk shops in Manchester and Liverpool. He's on his way now, so depends on what time I finish, but I may need to lunch with him."

Oscar agreed immediately to joining Elle for lunch, telling his PA to contact Lord Bronstein and cancel the lunch he had arranged. "Just say that I had a matter which required my immediate attention," he instructed her, before checking his tie and slipping on his jacket. Melanie nodded and reached for the phone.

Elle was already waiting in the bistro on the ground floor, having secured a very private booth so that they could attend to business without nosy onlookers. Oscar noticed that her bodyguard was seated nearby, at the only table with a good view of hers. She stood to greet him, pecking his cheek warmly. "How are you?" She asked.

"Very well, thank you. You?"

"Good, thanks. Sorry it was such short notice, but I'm glad you could make it."

"Not a problem at all." There was no way he'd have ever admitted that he'd had to snub another peer at the last moment. Lunches with just Elle were a rare treat. "No Ivan today?" He held his breath.

She shook her head. "He's seeing his takeover manager. Apparently there's an issue with a couple of the shops up north." She opened her menu and began to peruse the options. She was starving.

"Oh? What sort of issue?"

"I think there's a fraud going on. Fake invoices, handsets going missing, that sort of thing. Sergei went up for a few days to check it all out. They've got no idea just how tightly Ivan sets these things up. The system threw up red flags straightaway. I think I'll have the sea bass."

"You don't get involved in frauds anymore, I trust?" He couldn't bear the thought of anything else happening to her. The night she'd been shot had been the worst of his life, especially having to sit at home and wait for news. He watched as she broke off a bit of breadstick.

"You honestly think Ivan would let me go into any more corporate fraud cases?" She grinned before popping a piece into her mouth. He shook his head, aware that Ivan had dropped everything to jump on a plane and get to her as fast as possible, as well as sitting by her bedside until she'd regained consciousness. In the meantime, he'd had to pace around and stop himself flying to New York, which his mother had advised would be a bad idea.

The waiter interrupted them to take their order. Oscar decided to have the same and ordered for both of them. There was something about his old-fashioned good manners and chivalry that Elle had always appreciated. It was what set him apart from other men. "I spoke to Mrs Restorick before I came down," she said. "The company is incorporated, and liability insurance in place. She set up the bank account. I'll funnel some cash in once we've got all the share documents signed. Do you want to do yours now or come up to the office after lunch?"

"I can do it now if you've brought them with you." She slid two files across the table. He opened them and began to read. "Forty-nine percent each?" He glanced up at her quizzically.

"Yep. Two percent to me. Gotta keep you two boys in check." She grinned impishly. Oscar realised she was putting a buffer between them, just in case there was any power play. Knowing it could work to his advantage, he decided to accept the loss of one percent. He pulled his fountain pen out of his jacket pocket and signed the contract.

"You really are a minx at times," he muttered, handing the files back.

"I don't know what you mean," she said, feigning innocence. "You and Ivan both get equal shares."

"With you holding the balance of power."

"As I said, gotta keep you both in check, Ivan in particular." Elle was under no illusions that Ivan was a gentleman when it came to business. In fact, she regarded him as a corporate shark who needed his megalomaniac tendencies kept firmly controlled so as not to cross too many lines. She was in love with the man, but not blind.

"Ivan wouldn't double cross me," Oscar said with confidence. "He might be a bit aggressive in business, but he's no fool." He had enough dirt on Ivan to ensure that he'd never try any raiding tactics, plus being chairman of the Beltan board gave him sufficient access to make sure there was nothing being hidden.

"No, I don't think he would, but with my name on the share register, he'll be more circumspect about risk levels."

"True. Well, we should drink a toast to our new venture together." Oscar raised his glass and clinked with hers, pleased that she'd be tied to him, if only in business. He took a sip of his wine, a particularly fine Sancerre. "Ivan tells me you're looking to start a family?"

Elle stared down at the table. "It's not happened yet, mind you, it's only been a little while."

"Won't you miss all this?"

She glanced up at him and smiled, "I suppose so, but even if I have a large brood, I can still exercise my brain. They don't give you a lobotomy when you give birth these days."

He laughed in spite of the alarm he felt at hearing of her plan for a large family. Somehow, he'd convinced himself that Elle had been too much of a career girl to have wanted to produce an abundance of babies. He felt the familiar spark of envy at Ivan's luck. "Large brood? I'm surprised."

She blushed slightly. "Both of us are orphans, both only-children. We don't want to inflict that on the next generation. Ivan wants a load of boys to carry on his empire. For obvious reasons, I'm not too fussy whether we have boys or girls." She paused. "Why are you surprised?"

He shrugged. "I don't know. Sometimes it feels like you're a different person with Ivan than you were with me I guess. I never thought you'd be amenable to having a lot of children." He took a bite of his sea bass. Elle placed her knife and fork down and thought for a moment.

"Are you still pissed at me for going back to Ivan?" Her light blue eyes held his with her impenetrable gaze. He shifted slightly in his chair, uncomfortable with her bluntness.

"No, not at all," he lied smoothly, rubbing his nose.

"Good. How's the wedding plans coming along?" She asked, glossing over the sadness she felt for him. Elle had studied body language in detail. He wasn't fooling her.

"Good I think. Lucy and my mother are having a wonderful time organising everything. I just wish she'd follow your example and drop the nine-to-five. It'd make her life much easier."

"I haven't stopped work," Elle said. "Law doesn't begin and end at Pearson Hardwick. If anything, I work as much for Beltan as I ever did in my old office."

"Yes, it's a shame Lucy didn't opt for corporate really. She could've joined Goldings." He didn't really mean it. The thought of working with Lucy all day horrified him. "By the way, speaking of Beltan, how did the case go with Samsung?"

"We won. They've had to pull the handset."

"I had shares, you could've warned me."

"That's called insider trading. Samsung insisted on secrecy, which was upheld by the judge. Did the share price fall much?"

Oscar shook his head. "I sold the shares after I lunched with Ivan. Got a good price too. Lucy thinks it was just a happy coincidence, so won't be blabbing and getting you into trouble."

"Has she moved into your apartment yet?"

He nodded. "We spent every evening together, so it made sense. She'll move to Conniscliffe full time after the wedding."

"Is she happy about that?" Elle tilted her head to the side, listening intently.

He sat back in his chair. "Of course she is. Why wouldn't she be?"

"Because she won't see you very much."

Her reasoning made sense in that he realised Elle would've only married for love. If he'd have married her, the thought of spending four days apart each week would've been torture. In truth, the thought of only seeing Lucy at weekends was fairly appealing. It gave him plenty of time for his business at the bank, plus his duties at the Lords without the need to fit in with anyone else.

He was hoping his life wouldn't change at all.

Back in his office that afternoon, he pondered why he felt so off-centre. Eventually, he gave up pretending to read the reports on his desk and stood to stare out of the window at the teeming concourse below. From his vantage point up high in the tower, the people were just tiny ants, scurrying about on the vast slab of concrete that made up Canada Square. Idly, he wondered how many of them had loved and lost.

He was still pondering the problem when Melanie announced that his afternoon meeting with the chairman of the Bank of England was scheduled for five minutes time and the chairman was waiting in the lobby. "Bring him in," Oscar said, pleased at the distraction. He greeted Mr Varnwell warmly and ordered a pot of tea.

"Just thought I'd give you a heads-up," Mr Varnwell said as he settled himself on the sofa, "We've been instructed to work on Basel four. All the merchant banks will have to hold higher levels of liquidity."

Oscar groaned. Basel referred to the banking regulations and seemed to get more complex and onerous with each re-write. "What level of liquidity are they looking for?"

"Ten percent. Higher percentages if there are riskier investments on your balance sheet."

"That's outrageous. Who decides if an investment is risky or not? Do they not think a healthy banking sector is important for the economy?"

"I agree. We warned the Chancellor. He's got a bit of a bee in his bonnet following the LIBOR scandal. I'm worried it'll wipe out Natwest and damage Lloyds almost fatally." He took the cup and saucer from Oscar and slurped his tea.

"Won't he take your advice on this?" The chairman shook his head. "I remember him from school. He was a proper little know-it-all back then," Oscar reminisced. "Ended up with a degree in art history if I recall correctly. Not as clever as he thought he was."

"He appears a little out of his depth," Mr Varnwell admitted. "Just won't accept that provoking another banking crisis could have the opposite effect of what he's trying hard to achieve."

"Which is?" Oscar enquired.

"He wishes to break up the banks into retail and investment entities. Unfortunately, he wants the retail parts to be run along the lines of the old building societies."

"That's ridiculous. He'd be sacrificing the entire British economy for an outdated ideology. The societies all merged or closed for a reason. Can you talk some sense into the man?"

"It's still in early stages, just embryonic really. You probably have more clout with him than I do," the chairman confessed. "It's why I wanted to rope you in, as it were, at this stage. There's still time to head it off at the pass."

"Leave it with me."

They chatted a little about Oscar's upcoming nuptials while finishing their tea. As soon as he'd gone, Oscar pulled out his mobile and dialled Darius.

"I have a problem," he said as soon as Darius answered.

"Makes a nice change from 'we' have a problem," he replied. Oscar rolled his eyes. Darius could be a real dick at times. "What's up?"

"The Chancellor is what's up."

"Oh dear, more regulation? Can't you take him out to dinner and persuade him to see the error of his ways?"

"Gideon Osbourne admit he's wrong?"

"Hmm, I see your point. Ok, but I'll want something in return..." A momentary silence hung in the air between them.

"I thought we agreed that we wouldn't indulge again?" Oscar felt the flame of excitement return, something he hadn't felt for a while.

"You miss it, don't you?" Darius purred the words. "You're a dirty little fucker who needs it badly. Don't think I don't know." He could hear Oscar's breathing deepen. "Why don't I meet you this evening at the Tower Bridge Hotel? We can discuss this in more privacy."

After the incident with Elle, he'd sworn that he'd never succumb again, but the lure, the excitement... the sheer degradation... He needed it. "Ok. Seven o'clock, in the bar."

"I'll make the arrangements."

That was it. He was back in the grip of an addiction. It was that easy.

Two floors up, Ivan said goodbye to Sergei and went in search of Elle. He found her in front of her computer, concentrating intently as she typed furiously. She stopped as soon as she saw him and beamed a smile. "Malyshka, sorry I didn't make lunch. Did Oscar agree to those terms?"

"Yep, all signed and done. I moved our funds into the account. Oscar'll do the same this afternoon. Was the problem with the stores sorted out?"

"Of course. Sergei discovered that both managers were working together. Both have been sacked. The fools should've known they'd get found out."

"Are you prosecuting?" Elle asked. She knew he hated being stolen from. For Ivan it was far worse than being lied to or misrepresented. He actually admired anyone bright enough to get one over on him.

He nodded. "Of course. We have to send a message to the rest of the workforce."

"I'm sorry I didn't get pregnant," she said. She needed his reassurance. Having made the decision to have a family, she was predictably single minded in that pursuit. Elle could never be half-hearted once she'd made her mind up. Seeing her sad expression, Ivan scooted around the desk and perched in front of her, wrapping his arms around her shoulders.

"It'll happen. There's no point getting stressed about it."

"If I couldn't..." She paused, "You wouldn't leave me would you?"

He held her a little tighter. "My darling, I couldn't function if I loved you any more than I do. There's no way I'd leave you. If it didn't happen naturally, we'd find the best doctors or even adopt. It's only been a little while, these things take time."

"You're such a good husband," she teased before pursing her lips for a kiss.

"I do my best." In his wildest daydreams, he'd never thought he'd fall so completely in love with another person the way he had with Elle. He thanked the gods every morning when he woke up to hear her chatting to the dogs or pounding the treadmill. He planted a kiss on her upturned mouth, then let her go. He tried his best not to be overly demonstrative when they were at work.

He took a cheeky swig of her tea, wincing at the lack of sugar, then opened the file laying on the desk. He examined the share certificates, smiling at the way she signed 'Elle Porenski,' wondering if he'd ever get used to it. "Was Oscar in agreement about you having two percent?" He asked.

"Thought it was a great idea, didn't quibble at all," she said absently, having turned her attention back to the screen.

"He seemed a little.." He trailed off. Elle glanced up at him.

"A little what?"

"Depressed maybe? He doesn't seem too excited about his wedding."

She waved her hand airily. "Seemed fine to me. Oscar doesn't show emotion very much." She kept her eyes firmly glued to her screen. She really didn't want to discuss the clues she'd picked up that all was not well. "What's the plan for this evening?"

"We're out with the Ukrainian Ambassador tonight. They want a little something in return for allowing us mining licenses."

Elle stopped typing and looked up. "Such as?"

He shrugged. "Probably a donation to Party funds. If it was a direct bribe, it would be the minister himself. They might want some infrastructure built or reassurance that we'll use local companies for supply."

"That sounds suitably corrupt," she began.

He interrupted her, "It's the way it's done. The machinery arrives in the next couple of weeks, so Kristov has put a militia together to protect it. We're depending on the Ukrainians to allow that, hence the need to keep them on side." He omitted to tell her that he'd allowed Kristov to keep a safe passage through the perimeter of the site for his smuggling operation. He liked being owed.

"How does Kristov find these militias?" She asked. Ivan had already confessed the mafia connection, so she was under no illusion as to Kristov's background.

He shrugged. "Prisoners, peasant men, ex-military I suppose. I really don't know." The mini army guarding the Russian mining operations were a rather rag-tag bunch, but they did their job efficiently. There'd been no more problems there.

After another kiss goodbye, he left as she had work to do. As he made his way back to his own office, he passed the open-plan part of the Beltan offices and watched the hive of activity. Beltan was now far larger than he'd originally envisaged when he first set up Retinski, which was now just a subsidiary. The worker bees buzzed busily as they flitted from desk to desk, doing the minutiae jobs that a large conglomerate required. Telecoms, engineering, technology, media, mining, chemicals, recruitment, the list was endless. He'd had to become expert in so many areas so quickly, yet he felt calmer and worked less than in the days when it was only Retinski.

Further down the corridor were banks of offices dedicated to the accountants and lawyers, under the stewardship of Elle, who were squeezed in four to an office. They were running out of room, and were negotiating to take over the floor above, swapping the space for offices a few floors down currently used by their recruitment arm. The four companies upstairs were proving difficult, demanding their new space be re-fitted, plus sweeteners for the hassle involved in moving. In a lot of ways, Ivan had preferred it when his company was smaller, his offices quiet and peaceful. Even with soundproofing, he could hear the steady drone of voices permeating into his sanctum. He ached for the solitude of Sussex, where the only noise was birdsong and the gentle rustling of the trees. He quickly emailed Elle to see if she'd mind driving down that evening after dinner, rather than waiting for the morning.

He didn't have to wait long for a reply as she wandered into his office a few minutes later. "We can go tonight, I don't mind. Is something wrong?" She asked.

"Nothing's wrong, it's just noisy. I just thought it'd be nice to wake up on the estate. Nico can bring the girls when he picks us up from the restaurant. I want the whole weekend alone with you."

An involuntary shiver ran up her spine. Elle loved their weekends just as much as Ivan. "And the plan is?" She asked, fluttering her eyelashes seductively. Ivan laughed at her coquettish display.

"I'm already seduced, Malyshka, I've already made plans to make wild, passionate love to you all weekend."

"Wrong time of the month remember?"

He shrugged. It wouldn't stop him. "A good orgasm will help with any stomach pains." He had no idea if that was true or not, being rather uninformed about such things. He fervently hoped it was the case.

"Yes, I've read that somewhere before," she agreed, "we can see if it works."

Ivan silently congratulated himself. "I'll inform Nico about the change of plan. We're meeting the Ambassador at seven. Galina booked a table at some new restaurant that she read about in the Times."

"Ooo, a restaurant? Bit chancy, isn't it?" Normally meetings were held in their conference room.

"Their private dining room," he corrected. "Nico's gone over to sweep it and install some bugging devices." He searched her face for signs of disapproval. Like a good poker player, she didn't react. She was quickly getting used to the 'Russian way,' the brutality and sly practices that were the norm in that part of the world. She was also getting used to the restrictions that were part and parcel of living a billionaire lifestyle, such as not being able to speak freely unless they were at home, safe in the knowledge that they weren't being listened to. Very occasionally, she longed to just have a day of anonymity, to be able to shop in the high street or take a tube. It was outweighed by the enormous benefits of personal shoppers, first class service, and of course, her marriage to Ivan. Even if he was poor, she was sure that she'd still love him just the same.

The Ambassador and his wife were charming company. They enjoyed a lavish four-course meal seated in a private room, away from the hubbub of the main restaurant. During coffee, and happy that Ivan was well-oiled enough from a few bottles of Krug, the Ambassador began revealing the list of requirements from his government.

"The mayor asked for some new roads, proper asphalted ones, linking the port with the two nearest towns," he began.

"I can certainly look at that," Ivan said, not revealing that he'd already seen the plans his team had drawn up with that infrastructure included. He had to get the ore out somehow.

"Perhaps you could also look at upgrading the tenements in Teplodar. I can sell them to you for a 'nominal' amount, I take it you need to house your workforce?"

"I'd be very interested," Ivan told him. "I take it the authorities are favouring my application?"

"I think if you promised those roads, bought the tenements, and spent a little of the money you plan to invest in this venture, then they'll wave it through. What's the total investment for your plan?"

He peered at Ivan over the top of his little glasses, having put him on the spot. "Initial investment is half a billion GDP," Ivan said casually. He knew the Ukrainians would cream over that amount flowing into the country, especially as their banking sector was fairly precarious. "Over the long term, the benefit to the people and government of Ukraine will be many multiples of that." It wasn't true, as the profits would head straight to Beltan and Goldings, but he didn't need to spell that out. The Ambassador didn't need to know that Elle had set everything up so that all their profits went offshore, out of reach of any national tax authorities. He knew from previous conversations with Oscar that his family investment trust was based in the Cayman Islands.

The Ambassador sat back in his chair and smiled at his wife, who hadn't taken her eyes off Ivan all evening, knowing that he'd be delivering the best possible news to his superiors. He would spin it that he himself had persuaded Ivan to mine the land, and would claim that he'd played hardball to get the best possible deal for the region. With a coup like that on his record, he'd be able to take his pick of positions. He quite fancied the New York Embassy, although his wife had a yearning for somewhere hot for a change.

In the docklands, Oscar was driving home in a trance. He didn't feel ashamed of himself, in fact he didn't feel anything much at all.

Numb.

Sated.

All the edginess and irritability of the previous few weeks had melted away. Like a heroin addict after a fix, his feelings were deliciously blunted. Darius had made it especially degrading by forcing him to wear a silk neglige while telling him how ridiculous he looked. It had been a relief to finally let go, to slip out of being Oscar Golding, bank chairman and peer of the realm, and let Darius reduce him to the dirty pleasure-seeker that he knew in his secret reveries that he truly was.

Lucy was chatting on the phone when he got in, perky and happy that she'd finally got all the bridesmaids organised for measurements that Saturday. She smiled at the sight of him, noticing how cheerful he appeared. "Did you eat?" She called out as he disappeared into the kitchen.

"Yes, I ate with Darius," he said. He didn't need to lie or conceal, it was perfectly fine for him to spend an evening with his old friend, the fellow who'd be his best man and accompany him in the ceremony. He poured two glasses of wine and took them out into the lounge, placing Lucy's in front of her while she finished the call to her mother.

"Good day?" She asked.

"Yes, did the deal with Ivan, that's all signed and sealed. I think they're meeting the Ukrainian Ambassador this evening. Apart from that, just dinner and a catch-up with Darius."

"Was Arabella there?" She asked. He shook his head and picked up the TV remote to flick the channel. Newsnight was about to start, and he liked to keep up-to-date with political developments. He flung his arm around Lucy's shoulder and sat back while the credits rolled. "It'll be all about that sex scandal with the Chancellor," Lucy mused. Oscar's face whipped around to look at her.

"What sex scandal?" He'd not had the radio on during the drive home, preferring instead to listen to his Amy Winehouse CD. It had suited his mood better.

"Osbourne. Apparently caught snorting cocaine off some prostitute's body." She told him. "I suspect he'll resign. Shh, look it's starting."

"Tonight we go straight to number eleven Downing Street to hear the Chancellor's response regarding the revelations in the press that broke this evening," the presenter began. Oscar felt his heart rate rise. It didn't matter how often Darius did that type of hatchet job, it still felt pretty shocking to witness just how much power he had. Oscar turned the sound up.

"Chancellor, what do you say to these allegations?" The presenter asked, his face twisted aggressively, as though he was personally angered by the situation. Oscar watched as Osbourne squirmed slightly on the brocade-covered chair on which he was perched uncomfortably on the edge.

"I had a life before politics and did the normal student stuff. I don't do it now and haven't since I've been in office, so I believe it to be a private matter," he said, rather primly.

"Rubbish!" Oscar shouted at the Telly, making Lucy jump.

"So, Chancellor, do you advocate the use of illegal drugs and sex workers?" Evan Davies pressed him. The Chancellor laughed.

A Corporate Affair Book 5

"Goodness no, but, hey, I was a young man having a mis-spent youth. I'm sure the public won't judge me for having lived a bit. Far better than a career politician who's never had any life experience."

"Bastard," shouted Oscar. "He's the original career politician. He's never even had a proper job in his life."

"So will you be tendering your resignation to the Prime Minister in the morning?" Evan Davies was clearly no fan either.

Gideon shook his head. "No. The Prime Minister and I have already spoken, and I have his full support, given the task we need to perform getting the country's finances back on track, and the banks under control. That's what's important, not whether or not I partied a bit during the holidays at uni."

Oscar switched the program off in disgust. Darius would just have to come up with something else.

"You seem a bit cross about him," Lucy ventured. She was no fan of the chancellor after he'd gone out with one of her friends and behaved like a total arse, cheating on her with another friend, causing a lot of bad feeling all round. It had happened a long time ago, but the rift it had caused had lingered.

"He's an idiot, not fit for his job and only got there due to his friendship with the Prime Minister," Oscar told her. "The sooner he's out of office, the better." He noticed that Lucy looked a little tired. "Anyway, enough of that, how was your day?"

She smiled, her blue eyes crinkling slightly. "Mostly good. Between your mother and I, we've organised all the bridesmaids for next Saturday morning, for measurements."

"Good... and the not-so-good?"

"I'm working on a difficult divorce. The father claims his ex-wife is abusive to their children and wants custody. The wife is blocking all attempts to get information and is making unreasonable financial demands. The poor children in the middle are the ones suffering."

She took a large gulp of her wine. In truth, it'd been harrowing, seeing the poor man so fearful for the safety of his kids. She'd had to make an emergency case to the judge to try and get the children out, asking for an interim care order to place them with other family members. The mother, predictably, had gone nuts. She was nuts at the best of times, claiming she should have all the matrimonial assets, plus at least seventy-five percent of the man's income for life. Lucy couldn't wait for the toxic woman to be demolished by the court. The judge left the children with her.

Oscar squeezed her shoulder. "Come on, let's get some sleep. Have you got a heavy day tomorrow?"

She was so relieved it was the weekend, that she wouldn't have to face the case for another two days. "Badminton, then the team annual dinner. I did tell you about it all," she reminded him.

"Of course, then brunch Sunday morning. Sorry, it all went out of my head. I'm driving down first thing, I can check on the progress mother's making with the building work. We'll earmark Sunday afternoon for some relaxation. I think you'll need it."

Lucy gave him a grateful kiss, happy that he seemed a bit more like his old self.

CHAPTER FOUR

Oscar was in good spirits as he drove down to Sussex the following morning. Lucy had skipped off happily to her badminton tournament, delighted that he'd brought her tea and toast in bed and had made love to her slowly and lovingly. She put his recent grumpiness firmly down to work pressures and was pleased that he seemed more relaxed again. He hummed along to the radio as he manoeuvred his Range Rover down the country lanes which led to the large gates that protected his castle.

He flicked the remote control and sat patiently as the gates whirred, then slowly opened, revealing the magnificent tree-lined vista ahead of him. It didn't matter how many times he'd seen that same view, it still made his heart soar, while simultaneously relaxing him. He felt the last vestiges of tension leave his shoulders.

Jones opened the large front door exactly on cue as Oscar bounded up the steps. He'd already noticed the multitude of white vans parked outside on the drive. "Welcome home sir," Jones said, as Oscar strode into the hall. "Your mother is in the west wing, supervising the decorators."

Oscar discovered Lady Golding standing in what was once the taxidermy-filled sitting room, wearing slacks, a loose, practical top, and with her newly blonded hair wrapped in a scarf. A team of men were busily hanging wallpaper, which appeared to be hand-painted birds on a pale cream silk background.

"Hello darling, do you like the new decor?" She asked, airily waving her hand at one wall which had already been completed. He pecked her cheek before walking over to check it out.

"Very nice. Why are they working on a Saturday though?"

"Lots to do and a very tight deadline," she replied. "The plumbers are only halfway through the bathrooms, although goodness knows what will happen if all the guests take a shower at the same time." She was clearly enjoying herself, fussing over furnishings, relishing the thought of the castle full to capacity again. It had been a long time since they'd had a lot of guests stay over.

"You'd better take me on the tour," Oscar teased, pleased that she seemed so animated. She instructed the paper hangers to continue, and they set off up the large staircase to check out the freshly refurbished bedrooms.

"We'll have at least a hundred of the rooms completed by July," she told him. "If the men can manage more, they will. Maybe over lunch we could run through the guest list and work out how many people will need accommodation. That is, if you're not planning anything else."

"We can do that. I haven't made any plans for this weekend, and Lucy won't get here till tomorrow, so I'm at your service all today." For the first time in years, the idea of spending a day with his mother was quite appealing. She chattered happily as they inspected the myriad bedrooms which were in various stages of redecoration. It amused Oscar to see the way the builders and plumbers gently ribbed her, clearly comfortable in her company. She was a totally different person to the angry, uptight, and stifled person that she'd allowed herself to become.

The ballroom redecoration was well underway. The gilding on the ornate plasterwork gleamed with fresh gold leaf and the wallpaper was now a rich cream silk, in keeping with Lucy's colour scheme for the wedding. "The round tables we had in storage were a little scruffy, so they're with the French polisher," she said, "and the chairs are being covered in cream fabric with white bows. The wedding co-ordinator has organised that."

"Wonderful," Oscar said. He meant it. The ballroom was already looking fabulous, even before the decorators had finished. The floor needed re-polishing, which he assumed would be done last, once the rest had been completed. Seeing the castle come to life after it had been effectively mothballed for so many years was just marvellous.

"Are there any changes you'd like to make?" His mother asked him. He shook his head, he had no desire to rain on her parade.

"I think you're doing a tremendous job," he said warmly, which prompted a big smile. "Are the works running to time?" He hoped that she'd done proper plans. He wished he'd taken a bit more notice when he last spoke to her, but he'd been wrapped up in his bad mood and hadn't visited since before Mustique.

"Ahead by two weeks. I have spent rather a lot though, I should warn you."

He didn't care. Money was one problem that Oscar didn't have. He could refurbish the castle every year for the rest of his life and not touch the family fortune. "Not a problem," he told her. "Spend whatever you want."

"All the receipts are in your study, plus the plans and schedules. I didn't know whether you wanted to have a look," she ventured.

"Great. Yes, I will." The upkeep of Conniscliffe was a responsibility that Oscar took very seriously. Fully aware that he was merely a custodian for the duration of his lifetime, he made sure never to skimp or delay repairs and upgrades. He liked to think that he preserved Conniscliffe far better than the National Trust would have done, especially as he hadn't had to open it to the public or install a tacky gift shop, the likes of which were the usual way in which historically important houses paid their way.

Jones brought him a pot of tea while he perused the invoices and receipts his mother had left in a neat pile on his large mahogany desk. Just the new bathrooms alone were projected to cost a small fortune. She'd also engaged several interior designers to assist in getting the rooms finished to the standard required for entertaining the various heads of state who'd be attending in July.

He flicked through the rest of his post, which was mainly junk, before tossing it all aside and heading out into the garden. He needed some fresh air to clear the smell of paint from his lungs. He found himself drawn to the white garden, a space he knew he'd forever associate with Elle. It was too early in the year for much to look at, but even just green, it soothed his soul a little. In his mind's eye, he could still see her sitting on the little bench, declaring that she was in paradise. He was glad that the garden had finished flowering by the time Lucy had come into his life. She was happy taking long, muddy walks through the countryside in her Hunter wellies and practical Barbour jacket. He liked the way her cheeks glowed rosy after a long trek in the wind and rain, her hair tied into a ponytail. For such a pretty girl, Lucy was remarkably low-maintenance.

Over lunch, Oscar and his mother went over the guest list, making a note of who would require overnight accommodation, coming to the conclusion that they'd be approximately five completed bedrooms short. Lady Golding made copious notes and decided to engage yet another interior designer to ensure that the rooms would be ready on time. "I could always ask Ivan and Elle to put people up at their place," Oscar ventured. "I'm sure some of the politicians would be delighted at being in close proximity."

"I'll bear that in mind if I can't get all the rooms ready on time, or if there's any last minute extras," Lady Golding told him. "How many bedrooms does he have at that carbuncle of his?"

Oscar shrugged. "No idea, must have at least five though."

"I thought it was bigger than that. Only five?"

"I don't know, it might be more. I've never had the official tour."

"Hmm," she replied, "I imagine it's like the lair of a Bond villain, full of gadgets and control rooms for his world domination plans."

Oscar laughed. "Not that I've seen. I doubt if Blofeld had squashy sofas and a pair of badly behaved, madcap spaniels. Ivan's place is surprisingly comfortable. He doesn't like antiques, and the colour schemes are pretty tasteful. It's nothing like Vlad's old place. If you'd have seen that, your nose would have been so far up in the air you'd have fallen backwards."

Lady Golding laughed. "I'm sure it can't have been that bad, although he was a particularly odious little man. I only met him a few times, when your father financed some of his business activities. I always felt uncomfortable around him, as if there was something 'off' about him."

"His house was a shrine to gold leaf and purple silk," Oscar told her. "It was a ghastly as he was. I gather Ivan rented it out to an Arab, who thought it was fabulous." His mother shook her head, smirking.

**

"I'm glad we came down last night," Ivan said as he placed a plate of scrambled eggs on toast in front of Elle. She poured herself another cup of tea from the pot and watched as he blew on two pieces of sausage before holding them out for Bella and Tania, who inhaled them straight away. "Chew darlings," he admonished them as they wagged their tails, begging for more.

"What was bothering you yesterday? You seemed edgy," Elle said, as she cut into her breakfast.

"It was just noisy and busy, plus I had little to do, so I almost felt like a spare part," he admitted. "I guess I'm more used to doing all of it myself. It takes some adjusting."

"Control freak," she teased, before popping a forkful of eggs into her mouth.

"It's who I am," he said.

She swallowed. "The company is far too big for you to manage with just the small Retinski team. It's quadrupled in size in just six months. Stands to reason that it's four times the staff. Anyway, the board are there to take the load off you. It's important to let them do their jobs. All you need to do is oversee them and count your dosh."

He laughed. "Our dosh," he corrected her, mimicking her South London slang. "Gail Heywood pretty much takes care of that for me." He liked her routine of preparing a report every Friday showing the cash position and liabilities. Fridays were the highlight of his week. He thought back to the first time he'd shown Elle a Friday report, soon after they'd married. She'd actually gasped at the final figure, which had pleased him. The cash figures didn't even include property or any other fixed or intellectual assets. The recruitment company had been a particularly good cash generator.

"So what have you planned for today?" Elle interrupted his thoughts.

"Today, my darling, I thought I'd be a good husband," he told her.

"You're almost always a good husband," she reminded him. "Apart from when you're a tosser."

He smiled at her. It was time to reveal the surprise he'd been keeping all that week. "We have an appointment. It's not far away, but not until this afternoon. We've got time to walk the girls first."

Elle frowned. "What sort of appointment?"

"A nice surprise for you."

"I love surprises," she told him.

They walked the dogs after breakfast, meandering down the path through the woods, the girls at their feet, sniffing everything they could find. Elle watched as Ivan relaxed, his shoulders dropping and his hands unclenching as the forest worked its magic. By the time they'd had lunch, he was fully back to normal, singing along to the radio as he cleared their plates.

At first, Elle had found it odd that they had no staff at the weekend. She'd broached the subject once, after experiencing the way the staff at Conniscliffe unobtrusively catered to Oscar's needs. Ivan had explained that he enjoyed looking after himself, it gave him a break from managing people, besides, there were people available in the staff property, and the security were twenty-four-seven. He also pointed out that Oscar didn't have a household of staff during the week at his apartment, whereas Ivan did.

After lunch, Ivan called for the Bentley to be brought round and set about getting the girls ready, putting on their diamante collars and filling up their water flask. "They're coming too?" Elle asked.

"Oh yes. Their opinion is very important," he said, his inscrutable expression not giving anything away.

They set off through the gates and down the lane, a route that Elle hadn't been down before as it led away from both Conniscliffe and London. She watched through the tinted windows as the fields rolled by, catching occasional glimpses of early lambs. "Where are we going?" She asked as they drove through a wooded area, the lane narrowing to only one car wide. It felt as though they'd gone in a wide circle.

"Wait and see. We're nearly there," he replied. The lane came to an end with a pair of large wrought iron gates in front of them, which were open. They drove through and along a tree-lined driveway, which ended at a rather ramshackle old mansion. A Mercedes was already parked.

They stepped out of the car and took in the view. Fields rolled away below them, culminating in acres of woodland, as far as the eye could see.

"Like the view?" Ivan asked.

"Gorgeous." She replied.

"Good. It's up for sale. I'd like to build us a house."

Her head whipped round to stare at him. "Build?" He nodded.

"We could make it perfect. Design it from scratch exactly to our specifications. Don't get me wrong, I love the house we have, but it's got no indoor pool, the gym is a little small, and there might not be enough room if we have a lot of children." His sapphire eyes probed hers for a reaction.

"Would you get planning permission?" She asked, eyeing up the old house, which had seen better days, appearing to have had extension upon extension tacked on to it over the years.

"Its already got outline for a country house," he said. "There'd be some changes I'd want to make to the plans that were submitted, but not too much."

A tall, slim man strode out of the house. "Mr and Mrs Porenski? I'm Gary Butler. It's quite an estate, isn't it? A thousand acres in total. The woodland is broad-leaf deciduous and bordered by streams." He held out his hand to shake Ivan's. "Please, come into the house so you can see the view properly." They followed him into a very dated hallway, which had stained floral wallpaper and a threadbare, dark red carpet. The house smelt musty. The dog's noses worked overtime, twitching madly at the abundance of new smells.

"The plans that were approved have the new property situated in the same place as this one," Mr Butler said as he shepherded them through to a large lounge. "It makes sense with the view, plus it's all relatively flat here. Easier to build."

"I understand that the house that was approved was twenty-five thousand square feet," said Ivan. "Is that correct?"

Elle was already standing at the large, picture window, drinking in the view. It was bucolic perfection, with a long, large lawn stretching away from the house, leading down to the woods.

"Yes, that's correct. If there are changes to the internal layout, as long as you stick to that size, you won't need additional planning," Mr Butler confirmed. "Plots like this, with planning in place and the total privacy that this location affords, well, they're like hen's teeth."

Ivan looked at him quizzically. "It means that they're rare," Elle clarified. She was getting used to having to explain some of the 'Britishisms' that weren't quite clear. Ivan's English was good, but not infallible. He nodded, before picking up Bella and showing her the view through the window. Tania immediately begged Elle to pick her up too. "How long will it take to build?" Elle asked, struggling to lift her one-armed. Her shoulder was still weak from the shooting, and while Tania was slimmer than the rather rotund little Bella, she still weighed rather a lot. Eventually, she managed to get her into position on her hip.

Ivan shrugged. "A couple of years? Maybe not even that long." He knew full well that if the babies started coming, he'd move Heaven and Earth to get it finished. "Just think, a house built to our exact specifications, with everything brand new."

"What about the house in Windsor?" Elle had always thought that they'd use it once they had a family as it was big enough to accommodate a large brood, plus it satisfied Ivan's obsessive need for security.

"I don't want to live there," he replied. He didn't want to expand on that. He didn't want to explain that he'd felt strange in there, as though Vlad would walk in at any moment. It was too full of ghosts for him to relax there. "Anyway, I prefer Sussex. I feel more at home here."

"The boundary to your land would be that far tree-line over there," Mr Butler pointed out. "Beyond that are the outer grounds of Conniscliffe Castle, so you'll have quiet neighbours. This plot is unusual in that there are no rights-of-way running through it. It's always been a private estate."

"Who lived here before?" Elle asked.

"The Bonnington-Carter family. There are no heirs as such and the estate was left to charity. They've obtained the planning to make it more saleable. Thankfully, the council wouldn't approve a large housing estate, so they settled on one new house."

"That was probably Oscar's doing," Ivan said. "He was the one that alerted me to this."

They followed the agent upstairs and into an empty but large room that bore the hallmarks of being previously a bedroom, with dirty pink carpet and hideous floral wallpaper that was streaked with stains from damp. It all smelt musty and dank. "You can really appreciate the view properly from up here," the agent said. He'd already shown a few people around, so knew that it was the vista that attracted buyers. He stood back to allow them access to the window. Elle could just see one of the ramparts of the castle several miles away.

"How would you secure this though?" She asked Ivan.

"The border with Conniscliffe is already secured with a fence. In fact, the entire estate is fenced. The gates secure the north boundary, which is the only access road in and out," Mr Butler interjected.

"The same as we have now," Ivan said. "We'd have surveillance, laser wire, you know, all the stuff we currently use. If it's already fenced, half the work is already done." He could sense that Elle was overwhelmed. She was naturally cautious when it came to spending money, whereas the idea of creating the perfect home, chock full of gizmos and gadgets as well as the most beautiful furnishings that money could buy was inordinately appealing to him.

"It'd be so much work," she said quietly, as though they'd be rolling up their sleeves and building it themselves.

"Not really. We'd employ the best architects, designers and builders," Ivan said. "We'd have so much fun picking out what we wanted. It'd be our house, rather than a house I made before we met." She gazed up at his face, his expression was so sincere that she needed to hug him. Unfortunately, they were still holding the dogs, which meant she couldn't.

"Such a good husband," she murmured. He'd managed to surprise her at every turn. She looked at the view again, in her mind's eye imagining children racing down the enormous lawn, heading into the woods to play. "It's perfect," she announced.

"Good. I'll put an offer in straightaway," he said to a rather startled Mr Butler. "Get onto the vendor and offer sixteen-and-a-half million please. I'll want a fast sale." He turned to Elle. "It's up for twenty five, but I looked up the two charities concerned and discovered that both are strapped for cash." He turned back to the agent, "Tell them I want a quick sale. Ten days max."

CHAPTER FIVE

Lucy was exhausted by the time she pulled into the driveway at the castle. She'd had a frantic weekend, stuffed full of activities, friends, and socialising. Her dinner the previous night had been fun, although it had gone on longer than expected, and she hadn't gotten back home until nearly two in the morning. Her brunch had entailed even more alcohol, although she'd limited it, knowing that she'd have to make the drive down to Sussex. She fervently hoped that Oscar wasn't going to expect her to be bouncy and alert. She parked her Mini on the drive and grabbed her handbag. Before she'd even had time to reach for the door handle, Jones had opened the car door and was waiting for her to step out. "Lord Golding is in his study ma'am," Jones said, rather formally.

"Thank you," Lucy trilled, before handing him her car keys and trotting up the steps to the large front door. She found Oscar poring over the schedule of works his mother had left for him. "Hey you, had a good weekend?" She asked, before kissing his cheek.

"Not bad. Better now that you're here," he replied. "How did your match go?"

She pulled a face. "Not great. A couple of the team had off days. We came second in the league."

He pulled her onto his lap and wrapped his arms around her. "Mother's made great progress with the ballroom, and we think there'll be enough bedrooms ready to accommodate everyone." He showed her the schedule, which she read through quickly.

"She's done jolly well to get all that done on time already. I bet she'll be exhausted by the time the wedding comes around," She said. "I can't wait to see the ballroom."

"Let's order a pot of tea for when we get back," Oscar said. He'd noticed how tired she looked. Her eyes were rimmed with red from lack of sleep. They headed off to the ballroom, pausing only for Oscar to poke his head around the kitchen door and ask for some refreshments to be placed in the snug.

"It's beautiful," Lucy squealed as he led her into the enormous room.

"It's not finished yet," he told her, gratified by her initial response. For once, her unwavering enthusiasm wasn't irritating. "It'll look even better once the floor's freshly polished and the tables all set up. He recalled past events in the grandiose room, parties and balls that his parents had thrown. Oscar recalled peeking through the spindles in the staircase as a small boy, watching all the glamorous ladies and their penguin-suited menfolk arrive to dance and drink. He'd been allowed to attend when he was fourteen, and had been fitted for his first dinner suit.

They'd been heady days, when his mother had been young and fun, and his father had cut a powerful figure. The castle had been a meeting point for tycoons, politicians, and royalty. It had been a place for them to relax, party, and form alliances. They hadn't hosted a ball there in over ten years.

Lucy wandered around the vast room, taking in the details. The low winter sun shone through the large arched windows, making the gilding covering the plasterwork glow with an iridescence that lit the room.

"The chandeliers are still being cleaned," Oscar said, interrupting her thoughts.

"I hadn't noticed they were missing," Lucy admitted. She glanced up at the ornate, painted ceiling, to see just bare wires hanging down where the three enormous chandeliers usually hung.

"Are you ok?" He asked, concerned.

"I feel exhausted," she admitted. "Last night turned into a late one, so I probably drank a bit more than usual. I'm sorry." She wished that she'd been more effusive about the ballroom. She knew how much the castle meant to Oscar.

"Come on, back to the snug," he said, taking her hand. "We can have some tea, relax in front of the telly, or you can have a nap." She let him guide her back down the corridors, through the gallery, and back to the room Oscar reserved for relaxing. Lucy was pleased to see that Jones had left a tea tray, complete with some little sandwiches and tiny cakes.

Oscar settled her on the sofa, poured her a tea, and loaded a plate full of sandwiches for her. "Thank you," she said gratefully. She loved it when Oscar took care of her. He always seemed like a different person when they were at Conniscliffe than when they were anywhere else, more relaxed and attentive. She kicked off her ballet flats and tucked her feet under one of the sofa cushions.

"All I've organised for next weekend is the bridesmaids' measurements on Saturday morning," she ventured after a sip of tea. She felt guilty for being absent so much of the weekend and leaving Oscar alone with just his mother and the workmen for company.

"That'll take a while. Twenty-two little ones who won't stand still for more than five minutes," he pointed out, "I bet the atelier's looking forward to it." He was glad he hadn't been roped in to attend. He wasn't great with children, although he expected to be fine with his own, especially if they had a similar upbringing to the one he'd experienced. He'd been a page boy at age five for his aunt and had been forced to endure a whole day wearing tights, britches, and a stiff, uncomfortable velvet coat. It had been an unseasonably hot day, and the sun had shone directly on him through the large windows of the synagogue, rendering him a hot, sweaty mess, close to collapse. Despite that, he hadn't dared leave his post standing behind the happy couple, nor had he cried or otherwise made a fuss. He hoped the bridesmaids and page boys that his mother and Lucy had picked would be similarly disciplined.

"I'm sure it'll all be fine," Lucy said, "although the Prost-Winston children can be quite a handful. Marina doesn't believe in discipline, says it stifles their creativity."

"They'd better not play up at the ceremony," Oscar warned. "The Rabbi won't stand for children running around during all the different parts of the service. You might need to warn Marina that they'll be expected to play their parts quietly and respectfully, especially when we're in the synagogue.

"I already told her. She just brushed me off saying that the children will have a wonderful time and that was all that mattered. I didn't have the energy to argue." She sighed loudly. "I'll see how they are at the studio on Saturday. If they behave like feral monsters, I'll just have to face up to telling Marina that they can't be part of it."

"I'll tell her if you can't face it," he offered. Marina was an old friend who had embraced the 'Earth mother' concept a bit too much. Her children, while wildly photogenic, were hideously behaved and dramatically over-entitled. They'd run amok the last time they'd visited the castle, almost knocking Jones over while he had a tea-tray in his hands and spilling squash on the Aubusson carpet. Oscar was certain his own children, when they came, wouldn't be so ill-mannered.

"Might take you up on that," she said, a weak smile playing on her lips. When it came to her job, Lucy was perfectly capable of being assertive, yet the idea of tackling a tricky social situation left her with clammy hands and a large dose of anxiety.

They'd just finished their tea, when Lady Golding came in to say hello. "The ballroom looks marvellous," Lucy told her, "The bedrooms too. You've been busy."

"Still a lot more to do yet," she trilled. "Now that I've got you both together, the Rabbi needs to meet you both and talk you through the service and marriage rituals." She looked at them both expectantly.

"I've been to enough weddings to know how it all goes," Oscar said.

"So have I. Half my family are Orthodox, so I've attended some very devout ones," Lucy added.

"I'm sure you have," Lady Golding soothed, "but the Rabbi insists on it. Now, if you're both here next weekend, I'll invite him down. We can get it over with."

"Lucy's out Saturday morning, but I'll be here," Oscar said. The last thing he wanted was to attend the bridesmaids' measuring. Even entertaining the Rabbi would be infinitely better. "I might even come down on Friday."

"Super. Well, I'll leave you two to it. I take it you're leaving early in the morning?"

"We'll be gone by seven. Lucy's got to be in work by nine-thirty and the traffic might be bad." As soon as he'd said it, he noticed Lucy's shoulders lift and the now familiar look of tension creep across her face. When his mother had left, he asked; "Are you having a rough time at work?"

She nodded. "It's that case, Penfold versus Penfold. The woman's deranged and the judge wouldn't listen to the father's fears regarding the children. I'm back on it tomorrow."

Oscar patted her hand and planted a soft kiss on her forehead. She may not have been the great love of his life, but he was fond of Lucy and hated to see her natural exuberance and happiness stifled. At that moment, he swore to himself that he would never be the one to cause that look of anxiety. It was like seeing a small, happy child told off in public, hanging their head, the joy beaten out of them.

The next morning came way too fast for both of them. Lucy sighed as the Range Rover passed through the gates, away from the sanctuary of Conniscliffe. She remained silent during the journey, mentally counting down the days until she could live full time at the castle and start planning her family. She really hoped that the Penfold case would be over by then. "You ok?" Oscar asked, concerned by how quiet she was. He noticed that she hadn't even glanced at her phone, which she was normally glued to. He suspected that she'd switched it off.

"I'll be fine," she said. "It's nothing you've done, it's just work," she added, worried that he might think he'd upset her.

"I know that," he replied, amused that she felt the need to explain herself.

"It's ninety-one days till I live at Conniscliffe," she blurted out. "I can barely wait."

He glanced at her and smiled. "You can move there any time you like. Just say the word." It made him happy to hear how much she was looking he forward to married life. A lot of girls would've been horrified at the thought of living full time in an old castle, with just his mother for company throughout the week.

Eventually the trees turned to buildings, and they got closer and closer to London. Oscar leaned over to switch off the CD they were listening to and put the radio on. He wanted to hear the eight o'clock news. The press had quietened down about the chancellor, and Oscar wondered what else Darius would pull out of the bag. They listened in silence to the presenter reading out the usual tales of fires, murders, and robberies that epitomised life in a busy capital city. Each event got barely a line read out, just a line for a life snuffed out, the main worry being the place and if it would affect traffic flow.

Oscar dropped her off outside her building in the city and headed over to the docklands to begin his week. Outside the grey-fronted building which housed the ancient law firm, Lucy took a deep breath, before steeling her shoulders and striding into the lobby. She greeted Roger, the security guard who stood like a sentinel in the lobby, and made her way up to her floor.

Gingerly, she switched on her computer and clicked onto the mail logo. She perused the list of unopened emails, scanning for anything ominous. When it became clear that there wasn't anything from either Mr Penfold or his ex-wife's lawyer, she breathed an audible sound of relief before working her way through the list. The only matter that required her immediate attention was an email from an elderly client who wished to add another charity to the long list of beneficiaries in her will. Lucy quickly typed a reply, inviting her to come in and review everything. As Monday mornings went, it was a promising start.

Unfortunately, the calm didn't last long. The phone on her desk began to ring. Even the sound it made was ominous and gave her a chill of foreboding. It was a rather hysterical Mr Penfold. "The children aren't in school today," he yelled. "She's done something to them, I just know it. They were both fine yesterday."

"Have you called the school?" Lucy asked, her spine prickling. "They might be unwell or something."

"They've not heard a thing. She's not answering her phone either," he babbled, "besides, it wouldn't be both of them at the same time."

"Have you informed the police?" She asked.

"I didn't know if I should," he said.

"Yes, I think you should. They can go round there and check up on them." Lucy sounded more decisive than she felt.

"I went past the house just now. There's lights on and the car is in the driveway. This bloody court order… I could have knocked and made sure they were alright," he said.

"You can't," she soothed. "It would be contempt of court to visit on any day apart from the court-appointed Sunday session. If you're in prison, you can't be a father." It was harsh, but true, and Lucy needed to remind him that there'd be consequences for marching up to the house he used to own and knocking on the front door. "Let me make some enquiries, and I'll call the police if needed. I need you to stay out of this," she said sternly.

The first thing she did was call the school to find out if the mother had been in touch. She spoke to a sympathetic receptionist who confirmed that no, the children hadn't arrived, and Mrs Penfold hadn't phoned in to say what was wrong. Lucy then called Mrs Penfold's lawyer, a strident, feminazi-type of woman who, if she had her way, would have Mr Penfold castrated as part of the deal.

"I've not heard anything," she snapped. "Besides, it's none of your client's business if my client makes decisions for the children. She's no longer beholden to him and his hysterical anxieties. We still maintain that he's suffering from mental illness."

"He's their father," Lucy snapped back. "As a co-parent, he should be kept informed of any matter that pertains to the children, or have you forgotten how the law works? Anyway, in the absence of any meaningful insights from you, I'll go ahead and call the police." She slammed the phone down and took a few deep breaths. Just dealing with Jessica Sandown, Mrs Penfold's lawyer, made her heart rate rise to heart-attack levels. There was something about the woman's sneering voice and arrogant demeanour, as well as the ridiculous demands that rubbed Lucy up the wrong way.

An hour later, two policemen knocked on the shiny, black-painted front door of Mrs Penfold's home in Kensington. After a few minutes, she answered, looking a touch harassed. "Can we come in please madam?" The first policeman asked. "There's a matter we need to discuss with you."

She stepped aside to let them in. They wiped their feet on the mat and followed her into the hall. "Please tell me there's been an accident and my ex-husbands dead," she said brightly.

"No madam, we've been instructed to find out where your two children are. Apparently, they didn't go to school today and you're not answering your phone."

He watched her crumple.

"He took them to school this morning," she whispered.

"Who did?"

"Antony. My ex-husband," she clarified. "I was looking for my phone before you knocked. I couldn't find it." Her skin turned pale with fear. "He came yesterday, said he wanted to make peace for the sake of the children. I wasn't keen at first, but he promised me he'd changed... calmed down." She was babbling. The policeman, who's name was Colin, sat her down at the kitchen table, while the other one went back out into the hall to speak into his radio. Within twenty minutes, all ports and airports would be on alert.

Colin was taking notes, asking where the ex was living, did he have a car, descriptions of the children, and the like. Pete, his partner, relayed information to the control centre to get a car sent out to the father's place.

"Was your husband a violent man?" Colin asked.

She nodded. "Only to me though, not to the kids. Well, he only punished me physically. He'd verbally abuse the children though. It's why I'm divorcing him. They're only babies, they can't take his temper."

"Have you got a recent photograph of them?" Colin asked. She thought for a moment.

"Only on my phone," she said, realisation dawning. "He took all the photographs when he moved out. Said that I saw the children every day. I tried to object, but..." She trailed off.

"Are there any on your social media?" Colin asked.

"Yes! Oh, good thinking," she exclaimed. She jumped up and went into a study room, which, Colin noticed was largely bare except for an IKEA desk and an old Dell desktop. Marks on the walls denoted places where pictures had been recently removed. They had to wait a few minutes for the computer to boot up. When it finally sprung to life, Mrs Penrose logged into her Facebook and Colin saw picture upon picture of two cherubic blonde children.

"This one was taken about a week ago," she said, a photo of a girl and a boy dressed in party outfits filled the screen. "It was their friend Curtis's birthday party."

"They're very close in age?" It was more a statement than a question.

"Only a year between them. Sebastian is five, Emily four." She gazed lovingly at the photograph. They were interrupted by the crackle of Pete's radio. He went back into the hallway. All Colin could make out was "bodies found." His spine prickled. He'd dealt with a child murder before.

Lucy's phone rang approximately an hour later. She answered as she always did. "Hello, Lucy Elliot speaking," even though it was a bit redundant given that the switchboard knew who they were putting the call through to.

"Jessica Sandown is on the line," came the disembodied voice of the switchboard. Lucy's heart sank.

"Are you sitting down?" Ms Sandown began. "The bodies of two children have just been found at your client's address, along with your client and a knife covered in blood. I'm sure you'll get a call from him soon, as he'll need someone to represent him on his murder charge."

She felt sick. Bile rose in Lucy's throat as she tried to take in what Jessica had just told her. "He called me this morning," she muttered.

"I'm on my way to Notting Hill station to assist Mrs Penfold," Jessica spat. "I suggest you contact them as well seeing as you're a witness. Did you really not realise the man was a sociopath?" She was scathing. "Mrs Penfold and I did our utmost to keep him away from those kids, but you fought a dirty game to get him back in there. Hope you're happy now."

"Perhaps if your ridiculous demands had been a bit more realistic, this highly-adversarial divorce would have been settled a lot more amicably and maybe this wouldn't have happened," Lucy shouted. The line went dead.

She let out a loud sob, then threw up in her waste paper bin. Shaking, she dialled through to her supervisor. "Something terrible has happened and I need some help," she said. Within a few moments, the head of family law was in her office. He took one look at her and pulled up a chair, before sending a trainee out for some strong tea.

Taking big gulps, Lucy recounted the events of that morning. "Did you record the calls?" Evan, her supervisor, asked. She nodded before finding them on her system and pressing play. Even with the benefit of hindsight, there was nothing in his voice to suggest he'd just committed murder. Evan nodded at the point where Lucy had told him to stay away from the house. "There's nothing there that could've alerted you," he said after the recording had finished.

"I know, but still," she said quietly. "What if he calls to ask us to represent him?" She wondered if he'd already killed his kids by the time he'd called her.

"Then we pass him to a criminal defence lawyer," Evan said.

"I just can't believe I didn't spot this," she said quietly. "Am I really that bad a judge of character?"

Evan regarded her carefully before speaking. "I think you expect others to be as honest as you. Perhaps you could have been more circumspect, less willing to believe everything you were told."

The phone began to ring. Lucy picked it up rather gingerly. "Hello, Lucy Elliot speaking.

"Hello Lucy, it's Antony Penfold. I seem to be having a spot of bother after saving my children from that woman. Could you nip down to the station and sort it out for me please? They won't listen to me." His voice was chillingly cold, as though he was asking her to get him off a speeding ticket. There was no emotion in his voice. She put him on speakerphone so that Evan could hear.

"I'm afraid I can't help you, I'm not a criminal defence lawyer. I practice family law," she said.

"Oh. I just thought that you could speak to the policeman, tell them how awful my wife was and sort this mess out. It's just a misunderstanding."

"Mr Penfold, did you murder your children this morning?" Lucy asked. She glanced nervously at Evan.

"I saved my children," he insisted. "She's a nutcase. They were in terrible danger staying with her. At least now she can't hurt them." His voice was smooth, silky, almost seductive. If you took away what he was saying, he would've sounded plausible.

"Mr Penfold, I'm Evan Williams, Ms Elliot's supervisor and head of Family Law. I'm afraid we can no longer assist you. I suggest you ask the police for a duty solicitor." He pressed the button to end the call.

It was at that precise moment that Lucy decided that she didn't want to carry on as a lawyer. As soon as she was alone, she called Oscar. Just his calm, soft voice soothing her as she tearfully recounted the events of that morning made her realise that she had options. Remaining at work until after the wedding may have been the wisest thing to do, but knowing that she'd assisted a child murderer hung heavy on her conscience.

When the police arrived at her office to take a statement and a copy of the call recordings, she was more in control and able to assist them as much as she could.

When the sombre policeman had left, she sat and typed up her resignation letter. She prayed that Miss Pearson would take pity on her and place her on gardening leave. If nothing else, she'd have to get her doctor to sign her off work for the notice period. All she knew was that she didn't intend working so much as another day.

At four o'clock, she placed her letter on Ms Pearson's desk and stood while she read it. "Evan told me what had happened this morning," she said, "you really shouldn't blame yourself."

"I should have spotted that the man was unhinged," Lucy pointed out. "I really don't want to handle his divorce or deal with that Jessica Sandown again."

"I quite understand. It must have been a dreadful shock. What did the police say?"

"They've charged him with the murder of his children. He's being held in the psychiatric wing at Pentonville for evaluation. I've given a statement, plus copies of the calls he made to me."

"If you need to speak to someone about this, the company will pay for professional trauma counselling." Ms Pearson looked sympathetic.

"I just want to go. This really isn't for me. I'm sorry." Lucy began to cry. Large tears slipped down her face. In another life, crying in front of the boss would be horrifying. At that precise moment, Lucy couldn't have cared less. All she could think about was those two little ones, how scared they must have been. How hard she'd fought to get him access. How much she'd treated his ex-wife as an adversary to be beaten. Winning had been the most important issue, and she'd been so blinkered that she'd ignored the warnings his ex-wife had given.

"I think you need to give this some thought and consideration," Ms Pearson began. Lucy interrupted her.

"No. I want to go. Now. If you don't allow me to, I'll go sick for the remainder of my contract."

"Lucy, this is just an incident. You cannot allow it to dictate the rest of your career." Ms Pearson took off her glasses and stared at her. In normal circumstances, Lucy would have said she was right.

"I want to leave today," she repeated. She was unusually immovable. There was no sign of the fluid, persuadable Lucy who could often be convinced to change her mind by reasoned argument.

"As you wish. I'll put you on garden leave with immediate effect and we'll meet again in two weeks to discuss a way forward."

"Thank you," Lucy said, before turning and walking out. She made her way straight to her office where she filled a bag with the personal detritus she'd accumulated over the three years she'd been there. She felt shocked, numb. Whether from the news of the children's deaths or from walking away from her career, she wasn't sure. As soon as she stepped outside, she called Oscar to tell him she was on her way home.

Oscar was contemplating attending a Narcotics Anonymous meeting that evening, when his phone rang. After speaking to Lucy, he decided that he needed to go home and be around to listen and soothe her. As he waited for the lift, it struck him that he wanted to be there for her, even though he knew she'd be a tearful mess. It was progress, he felt.

All the way home in the taxi, Lucy held it together. Years of training that the upper classes receive from nursery school onwards kicked in. Looking back, she was horrified at her behaviour in Ms Pearson's office, making demands and refusing to compromise. As soon as she exited the cab outside their building, it was as though the floodgates opened. Great heaving sobs broke free, echoing in the mirrored lift up to the twelfth floor. Oscar was in the lounge when she arrived, hauling her heavy bag through the hall. He jumped up to take it from her, carefully peeling the strap off her shoulder, where it had left a deep indent. "I could've picked you up," he said in an accusing tone.

"I didn't think… I just wanted to get out of there..." She wondered if she'd upset him too. He pulled her into a hug. Lucy rested her head on his shoulder and breathed in his wonderful scent. It reminded her of home, of safety. He felt strong and steadfast as he held her tight, as though he could absorb her pain. Eventually he let her go.

"Have you eaten?" He asked, his voice quiet and serious. She shook her head. "Fatima left some steaks. I'll throw them under the grill."

"I can do it," she protested. She wasn't hungry, but regarded it as her job to prepare and cook food for them, at least when they were in town.

"I want you to relax, have a glass of wine and tell me what happened," he said as he led her into the kitchen and pulled out one of the stools which was tucked under the lip of the island. Obediently, Lucy perched herself on it and watched as he pulled the biggest two glasses out of the cupboard and expertly opened a bottle of red. He poured her a huge glass, nearly half a bottle's worth. Lucy hoped it wasn't a Petrus, or something similarly expensive as she needed to glug it.

While Oscar was tending to the grill, Lucy described the events of the day. As she recounted the call telling her about the children's bodies being found, fresh tears began to fall, landing heavily on the cream marble in front of her. She took a large slurp of wine, and seeing how Oscar narrowed his eyes, decided that it was probably some rare, exquisite vintage that should be sipped and savoured. She took a more ladylike mouthful.

"As upsetting as the situation is, I can't see how you could've prevented it, or done anything differently," Oscar said when she'd finished talking. "You couldn't possibly have known he suffered from mental illness, given that he had a good job. His employers didn't spot it."

"True. He was a fund manager, pretty successful given how much he was earning." She took another sip. "Maybe he wasn't mentally ill, just a psychopath."

"Sounds that way," Oscar said absently as he concentrated on their steaks, prodding them to see if they were done. Satisfied, he pulled two plates out of the cupboard and split a ready-made salad between them, before flipping the meat on top. He placed it in front of Lucy. "There you go. You'll feel better once you've eaten."

Despite her earlier protestations about not being hungry, the smell of the steak made Lucy's mouth water. She picked up her steak knife and cut into the meltingly soft Wagyu beef. Oscar pulled out another stool, perched himself on it, and began to eat. "Have you spoken to your mother yet?" He asked.

Lucy swallowed. "Yes, I called her earlier. She was sympathetic, more understanding than I expected."

"Really? What did you expect?"

"She kept saying I shouldn't give up work until after the wedding. I thought she'd be cross with me."

"Hardly like you gave it up for fun, is it?" She shook her head. "So are you going to stay in London this week or head down to Conniscliffe?"

Lucy thought about it for a moment. She had nothing pressing until the bridesmaid's meeting on Saturday. The thought of the safety and peace at the castle was appealing. She could help Oscar's mother with the redecoration too. "Unless you need me here, I'd quite like to drive down tomorrow," she said.

"I'll call my mother after we've eaten and let her know," Oscar said. He genuinely felt sad for her, for the shock she'd had. Her career, which had begun so promising, had fallen in flames. "Why did the father alert you to the fact that the children were missing?" He asked. It was bothering him.

Lucy shrugged. "I suppose he thought that if the police were looking at her, they wouldn't be looking at him. I don't know really." She paused. "Why would a man murder his own children? Hardly the actions of a sane, rational individual."

"Yet he was managing a large investment fund? Figures," Oscar muttered. He had scant regard for the city boys. In times gone by they'd been drawn from the quick-witted but sly barrow-boys of the East End, as well as the well-heeled aristocrats in need of something to do with their time, who fronted the institutions, giving the impression that it was a chummy boy's club. Nowadays it was all rocket scientists and maths nerds, drawn from the top universities. They could write a trading algorithm, but didn't have the natural cunning of their predecessors. It was relatively easy for a well-trained financier, such as

Oscar, to get one over on them, except for the psychopaths he'd encountered, usually tasked with running the big funds. They were prized for their lack of emotion, their cold, fearless approach to investing and the analytical way they viewed the world. Oscar had met many Antony Penfolds in his time at the bank. The men with sharp, inhuman eyes, who noted every detail to try and use it against you at a later date. He shuddered at the thought of Lucy near a man like that.

Oscar called his mother after dinner to let her know that Lucy would arrive in the morning. His mother sounded shocked at the turn of events, but promised to keep Lucy busy and her mind off of her problems. He spent the rest of the evening half-watching TV while Lucy relayed the sorry tale to multiple friends, her phone glued to her ear. One of those friends was Elle, who listened quietly, tutting at the appropriate moments, before agreeing that family law was totally harrowing.

"Someone at Mishcon had a similar thing happen if I remember rightly. Fought for access only to have the dad kill the three little boys. Mind you, in that case the father at least had the decency to off himself afterwards," Elle said. "I can't believe your one was mad enough to think it was a 'misunderstanding'."

"I wish I'd worked a bit harder and gone into corporate now," said Lucy.

Elle was silent for a moment. "Are you forgetting I got shot in New York? It's not all shiny offices and well-mannered clients, you know."

Lucy gasped, "I'm so sorry, I wasn't thinking." She was relieved when Elle giggled. "Touché."

"Well, at least we'll be neighbours down in deepest, darkest Sussex," Elle said, "Ivan's had his offer accepted on the estate on the other side of Conniscliffe. The architects are coming over this evening to discuss preliminary ideas."

"Super," Lucy exclaimed, "will it be a modern glass cube?"

"No idea. I don't know if Ivan even knows yet. I know it won't be a fake Tudorbethan monstrosity, but that's about it. I doubt it'd be a glass box either, given how obsessive His Nibs is about privacy. All I know is that it'll be big."

Ivan strode into the room announcing the imminent arrival of the architects, before noticing that she was on the phone. "Sounds like you're needed," said Lucy. "We'll speak again soon."

Nico brought the two architects into the penthouse. They were very clearly brothers and introduced themselves as Oliver and Christian Allan, from the famous Allan partnership. "We design and build legacy houses," Oliver explained as they were invited into the drawing room. Christian glanced around the room.

"I like your style," he commented. Elle smiled at him, before offering them a drink. Oliver, the more serious of the two, asked for water, while Christian happily accepted a glass of the wine that Ivan had just opened.

Elle listened as Ivan outlined the project, describing the land, the view, and the access. She quickly worked out that Oliver took care of the technical aspects while Christian was the more creative of the two. He threw in ideas that neither she or Ivan had even thought of, such as excavating a large basement for both wine and staff quarters as well as a security hub and bunker.

"Far more effective than just a panic room," Oliver chimed in. "We can even make it thick enough to withstand a nuclear attack, if that's what you want."

They looked at the drawings the council had granted planning on, which Ivan spread out over the dining table. "These are pretty good," said Oliver, "but you'll find the pool house way too hot facing due south with a glass roof. We need to put that on the West side of the house. No point having the cinema room on the south side either. That can go on the north." he sat back and sipped his water. "It just needs a bit of tweaking, nothing major. When do you complete on the purchase?"

"A few days time," Ivan replied. "How long would a house like this take to build?"

"That depends on your budget," Christian answered, "and the type of finish you require." Elle looked quizzical. "It takes longer to lay marble than it does carpet or tiles," he explained. "Depending on accessibility to the site, demolition of the existing house, and the shell of the new one would be around nine months. The interior fitting has too many variables to guess on a timescale."

Ivan decided he liked Christian's honesty. "It would be ultra-high end fittings. No expense spared."

CHAPTER SIX

The first thing that Lucy did at Conniscliffe was to accept the role of 'assistant' to Lady Golding. It was a relief to just be a gofer, with no real responsibility, but also busy enough to keep her from dwelling too much on past events. She was glad she'd escaped down to Sussex as the Penfold case had attracted much media attention. If she'd remained in London, the press would've been ambushing her at every opportunity. She'd seen them outside the Pearson Hardwick head office on the evening news. Thankfully, the company press office had handled it, and the reporters seemed to have got bored trying to get a reaction from the firm.

The police had phoned her twice, for clarifications as to the timeline, but apart from that, she nestled in the bosom of the castle, fetching fabric samples and carrying Lady Golding's checklists. Meanwhile, Oscar carried on as usual in London, visiting the Lords, dining with colleagues, and chivvying support for voting down the upcoming banking bill, which wasn't an easy task. The only high point of his week was a visit to Narcotics Anonymous, where he was pleased to see Kyle still on the wagon and looking a touch healthier. After the talk, he sought him out. "You're looking well," Oscar said as he shook his hand.

"Thanks. It's amazing what some food can do," Kyle replied, "My benefits came through this morning, so I can pay you back some of what I owe..."

"Nonsense, keep it. I don't expect reimbursement," Oscar said a little stiffly. "I'm just pleased that things are looking up for you."

"Yeah," Kyle said, a little distracted. "Can I ask you something?"

"Of course," said Oscar, wondering what he was going to request.

A flush worked its way over Kyle's cheeks. "How do people get jobs? I mean, I know about the job centre, but they only have local stuff, cleaning work mainly. I just wondered how people moved away." He paused. "You look like you're successful." For all his bravado and street-smart demeanour, so much of the world remained a mystery to Kyle. He had no idea how to learn to drive, how to vote, or how to escape the destructive influences around him.

"What sort of job would you be looking for?" Oscar asked, frowning slightly.

Kyle shrugged. "I don't know. Something outside. When I was a kid, I wanted to be a parks gardener. You know, the ones that make all the bedding displays. I asked my probation officer how to find out about jobs, but she said the council wouldn't employ anyone with a record."

"I see, would you excuse me a moment?" Oscar said, before heading off in the direction of the toilets. Once out of sight, he called his mother to enquire whether they were still looking for apprentice gardeners. "There's no way he could be trusted in the house though," he warned her.

"So why do you want to help him?" Lady Golding asked. Oscar thought for a moment.

"Kid deserves a break." It was largely true, and Oscar didn't want to go into the deeper truths of his penance for betraying Elle, his previous snobbery towards people like her, or just the fact that he felt sorry for Kyle because of the rotten hand life had dealt him.

"Ok, send him down in the morning. He can stay in the gardener's accommodation. Tell him it's only a room though. I'll let Fred know he's got a new apprentice. He'll be delighted at the prospect of some more help." She paused, "I'm glad you found time for your meeting."

"So am I. Anyway, better go." It was only after he'd prodded the phone to end the call, that he realised he hadn't asked how Lucy was. A pang of guilt hit.

Back in the hall, he found Kyle pouring out a cup of tea. "Were you serious about moving away?" Oscar asked him.

He nodded, "I'm just not sure how it works. Do you have to tell the council?"

"Well, I have a job opening for an apprentice gardener in Sussex, just outside Derwent. It's a live-in position, but you only get a room. Meals and bills are included."

Kyle's eyes widened. "Really? Like, straight up? You're not having me on are you?" Oscar shook his head. "You won't regret it, I'll never let you down," Kyle promised.

After giving him directions, plus twenty quid for the fare, Oscar set off home to give Lucy a call, mainly out of guilt. As predicted, she sounded happier, caught up in the loveliness of wedding planning and getting intimately acquainted with the castle. He'd wrestled with himself as to what to tell her about Kyle, before deciding that honesty was the best policy. Rather surprising to him, Lucy was delighted at his benevolence, promising to make Kyle feel welcome when he arrived the next day. When she put the phone down after their conversation, she smiled at the thought of her more liberal ideals rubbing off on him.

**

Every evening that week, and some of the day times too, Ivan and Elle met with the architects to thrash out details which would normally take a few months. In typical Ivan fashion, according to Elle, he wanted the demolition to begin the day after they completed the purchase. "I just don't see the hurry," she'd said, as they disagreed on the number of bedrooms they'd require. She'd wanted five, but Ivan had insisted on ten.

"You could get pregnant any moment," he'd pointed out, before turning back to the plans and the lists of requirements he was formulating.

"I won't unless you put those plans down and come over here," she purred, smiling seductively.

"They'll be here in less than half an hour," Ivan reminded her.

"A quickie then."

He strode over to the sofa and held out his hand. "Bedroom," he muttered. She placed her hand in his and stood, before allowing him to lead her down the hallway into the master bedroom. "A quickie you say?" He asked. She nodded, her skin flushing at the thought of what was to come.

He lifted up the skirt of her dress, sliding his hands over her thighs as he searched for the waistband of her thong. He yanked it down, the roughness of his movement betraying his own eagerness as he leaned her forward, over the end of the bed. She felt his fingers dip inside her, testing her own arousal as he struggled to free himself one-handed.

She felt his fingers move to her clit, pressing a little firmer as he rubbed tiny circles over her most sensitive spot, before he thrust into her, causing the air to leave her lungs as his large, rock-hard cock filled every inch of her.

Elle braced herself against the end of the bed as he began to move, slamming into her at a punishing pace, each thrust taking her further and further towards her personal oblivion. As he slammed into her, his mobile chirped, the tri-tone that indicated that their visitors were on their way up. Both desperate to come, Ivan sped up his already frenzied pace as he felt the familiar quivering of her orgasm begin.

"You need to come now baby," he commanded in his 'sex' voice.

It was enough to push her over the edge. Elle plunged into her orgasm, only just aware of Ivan pressing in deep and letting go. She was also vaguely aware to the front door opening and Nico's voice calling out for them.

"Two minutes," Ivan called out, concerned that Nico could walk in on them. Elle giggled at the sheer naughtiness of getting caught having a quickie. Ivan was flustered as he grabbed a flannel from the ensuite and cleaned himself up before tucking himself away and zipping up his fly.

A few minutes later, they strolled out into the lounge, noting that Bella and Tania had made themselves at home on the Allan's laps. Christian was happily fussing Tania, whereas Oliver looked less comfortable, trying to ignore Bella, who was on her back, presenting her fat tummy for some rubs. If the brothers noticed Elle's post-orgasmic flush, or her overly bright eyes, they didn't mention anything.

"Good evening gentlemen,"Ivan said. "I have good news. We'll be completing the purchase tomorrow. The searches came back today and everything is as expected." Elle's face whipped round.

"You didn't tell me. Didn't you want me to check over the searches first?" There was a hint of annoyance in her voice.

"You were busy, besides, Anatoly checked them over for me."

"But it's going to be my home too."

Ivan sighed. "Did you conveyance this apartment when you bought it?"

"Well no. It was easier to use a specialist from my firm." As soon as she admitted it, she realised she was on a losing argument. Anatoly, her deputy in the legal department, was also overqualified to read a local authority search document. He also regularly handled the property acquisitions and disposals for the company.

Ivan turned to the architects. "Is the demolition company ready to start? Did you get that quote from the ground works team?"

"Yes and yes," said Oliver, still ignoring Bella, who wiggled to let him know that she was still there and hadn't had her tummy scratched yet. "Ground works can't finalise the quote until the plans are finished. Have you given any more thought yet as to the layouts I gave you?"

"Yes. We're going with ten bedrooms," said Ivan confidently.

"We didn't decide that," Elle butted in. "We didn't make a decision." She was starting to get annoyed. Ivan had a habit of taking over their decisions, often to the point that she felt railroaded. Just the day before, he'd announced that he'd ordered her a new Bentley, as she liked his. He'd not even let her choose what colour to have, going full steam ahead with ordering a top-of-the range bulletproof one in silver. She'd wanted to object, but caught herself and decided it sounded bratty and ungrateful to complain.

"The choice was five enormous suites or ten bedrooms with smaller bathrooms. Any more than four kids and we'd run out of room," Ivan pointed out.

"I know," she said in a small voice. The whole thing just seemed to rub her nose in the fact that it was Ivan's money paying for everything, Ivan's choice. She just couldn't shake off the ratty mood she'd been in for the past week. Even the orgasm hadn't cheered her up. She couldn't work it out, it was like PMT, but she wasn't due her period for another ten days.

"What is eating you?" He asked as soon as the two men had left. "Don't you want this house? Don't you like the plot? Tell me. I can still pull out." He threw his hands up.

She stared down at Bella, who was sprawled out on the rug. "I don't know what's wrong," she said, not meeting his eyes. "Maybe it's because it's all such a lot of money," she said eventually.

"Oh don't give me that," Ivan was scathing. "It's a fraction of our net worth. Don't patronise me by pretending that I'm stupid. It's something else, and I need to know." He was starting to lose his temper.

Silence.

Elle just couldn't put her feelings into words.

He slammed his hand down on the table. "This is my Conniscliffe. Don't you understand? The home I want to build for you, for us. The least you could do is pretend to be enthusiastic."

"I am," she said weakly. "I'm sorry." She stood up and wandered over to the kitchen, burying her nose in the enormous fridge. Mrs Watton had left some cooked sausages for the dogs. She took one and bit into it, before assembling a plateful of cheese, biscuits and some grapes. She was starving, even after having a large roast dinner earlier. "Want some cheese?" She asked. "We have Brie, Stilton too."

"You're hungry?" Said Ivan, incredulous. He regarded her intently. She nodded, before stuffing a sliver of Brie and a biscuit into her mouth. Both dogs immediately woke up and positioned themselves at her feet, just in case she dropped anything. "You want me to make you a snack tray?"

She nodded. Ivan made wonderful bed picnics. "You don't mind having a fat wife do you?" She joked, as she popped the last bit of cheese in her mouth. He smiled widely.

"Not at all, in fact I'm counting on it." He set about pulling food out of the fridge, deftly making up a large tray containing sausage rolls, caviar and blini, pate, and found some maltesers, baklava, and the remains of a fruit cake that James had dropped round earlier in the week. He carried it all into the bedroom, where Elle and the dogs had already made themselves comfortable in the enormous bed, the spaniels sprawled over his side. "Girls, you gotta let me have more than an inch of space," he admonished.

"This looks lovely," Elle said, eyeing the tray. "Hope I can stay awake long enough to eat it."

"So you're hungrier than normal and tired?" Ivan asked, grinning at her.

She clicked.

"You think I'm pregnant, don't you?"

He nodded. "Don't want to get too excited yet, but, well, maybe." He noted that she seemed a little pale too.

As they watched the news, sharing the snacks, Ivan wondered what Elle would be like with a bump. He snuck a look sideways at her. Radiant, he decided. He couldn't imagine her becoming one of those women who waddled around like a beached whale. She was too strong and fit for that. Rather clueless, he decided she would wear her bump neat and high and stay elegant and fragrant while she incubated their first son. Even if she did become fat and cumbersome, he was sure her figure would snap back into shape quite quickly, at least for the first few babies.

**

At eight the following morning, with a shaky finger, Kyle pressed the intercom on the pillar of the huge iron gates. He'd left home at five, just to be sure of getting there. Sussex might as well have been Timbuktu, a foreign place. The only other time Kyle had left London was when he was in prison in Wakefield. He'd been driven there though.

A disembodied voice made him jump. "Conniscliffe Castle. Can I help you?"

"I'm... I'm Kyle, I was told to come here for a job," he stuttered.

"Oh yes, Lord Golding told us to expect you. Are you in a vehicle or on foot?" The voice took on a kinder tone.

"On foot."

"Proceed through the smaller gate to the side. Make your way down the driveway. The Head Gardener will pick you up in a golf buggy." The side gate clicked. With some trepidation, Kyle pushed through it and began walking. Five minutes later, a ruddy-faced, rather jolly man, who introduced himself as Fred, picked him up. As they trundled back to the castle, Kyle took in the magnificent gardens, which to him, resembled an enormous park.

"This place is amazing," he said.

"These are just the outer gardens. Wait till you see what's nearer the house. As part of your apprenticeship, you'll learn lawn care. By the time you've mown and aerated this lot, you won't be quite so fond of it."

Fred showed Kyle his new living quarters in the staff block, which was far grander than it sounded. Even though it was just a room, it was clean and furnished. There was a communal kitchen, plus a lounge, with a TV, a pool table, and comfortable sofas. It was a world away from the squalor of his mother's flat.

He followed Fred around all morning, marvelling at the size, scope, and sheer perfection of the Conniscliffe grounds. The other apprentices and under-gardeners seemed alright, all meeting for lunch in the staff dining room, where a hearty stew, vegetables, and fresh bread was served.

The first task he was given was edging the lawns. It was an easy, but time-consuming job, which none of the others liked doing. Kyle was quite happy though, carefully following Fred's instructions and applying all his concentration to make it as neat and perfect as possible. When the light faded at five, Fred commented on what a good job he'd done and that they were finished for the day.

Kyle wondered if he'd died and gone to Heaven.

Meanwhile, Lucy had just stopped a decorator making the terrible mistake of hanging a thousand-pound-a-roll hand-painted wallpaper upside down, noticing at the last moment some tiny birds appeared to be dangling off branches, as opposed to perching on them. Lady Golding, on hearing about it, had breathed a prayer of thanks that Lucy had been there. She wouldn't have noticed until it was too late, unless she'd had her glasses on. Rather embarrassingly, it had already happened in one of the bedrooms, where a fleur-de-lys pattern was now pointing downwards. Lady Golding had already decided to allocate that room to one of the Scottish ministers, whom she figured wouldn't notice.

The two of them made quite a good team, with Lucy happy to follow Lady Golding's instructions, lending her boundless energy and good nature to the task at hand. It also helped take her mind off the Penfold case, which was the main story on every news channel. She'd been largely insulated from the press by both Pearson Hardwick, which had taken the flack, and by the high, deep walls of Conniscliffe. She'd seen on the BBC that Mr Penfold had been sectioned though.

"Did you ever feel threatened by him?" Lady Golding had asked her, when they watched the news that night. Lucy shook her head.

"The only person in this that unnerved me was the wife's solicitor. Antony seemed alright, a very articulate and charming man, really."

"I met a few psychopaths in my time. They often rise up to positions of power. My husband used to say that all politicians had something wrong with them. To want that much power and control usually indicates a character defect." She took a sip of her cognac.

"Oscar isn't though," Lucy countered.

"He was born into it dear. If he hadn't been, well, I doubt if he'd have had the ruthlessness or drive to climb his way up the commons."

Lucy had to agree. "So who have you met lately that you think is suspect?" She asked, genuinely interested. Lady Golding seemed to her a rather good judge of character.

"That Home Secretary is rather suspect," she confided. "The Health Minister too. Way too cold about how patients should be treated. There's lots of them in Westminster really. Lots of Maggie's cabinet had that cold-eyed look, but that's all before your time." She decided not to mention Darius, who, in her opinion, was a sociopath.

"What about Ivan? I never know if I should trust him or not." Lucy asked.

"His father-in-law, mentor, whatever you want to call him, Vlad, now that was a man who was evil personified. My late husband was convinced he was the devil himself." She paused, "Ivan's a greedy man, but it's plain to see that the only thing that drives him is fear. Elle's the same. I think both are terrified of going back to where they came from."

"Hmm. I think you're right," Lucy agreed. "Elle used to be really nervous about her accent when we did our training contract together. Worked unbelievably hard, way more than anyone else."

"Fear is a great motivator," Lady Golding said. "Talking of which, did you update the spreadsheet today? I'm hoping we're still on schedule."

"I did," Lucy beamed. "Oscar'll be so pleased when he arrives tomorrow. All major works are running to time, with the plumbers and the painters slightly ahead. The only issue is the fabric for those curtains in the Great Hall. I'll chase it in the morning. If it really can't be done, I'll see if I can source something similar from elsewhere."

"Super. Yes, a twenty-week lead time for a bit of damask is ridiculous," she agreed.

"Would you be able to come with me on Saturday morning, help marshall the little ones? I'm a bit worried they'll all run amok and the atelier won't be able to get their measurements properly."

"I shall put on my best child-catcher expression and terrify the Prost-Winston tearaways, if that's what you're asking," Lady Golding said with a smile. "Their mother's worse than useless. Almost encourages them to be little savages."

The following day dawned bright and sunny. One of those crisp days of spring that lays promise of more glorious ones to come. Lucy woke early and bounced out of bed, having decided to go for an early morning run around the grounds. She pulled on her jogging bottoms, a sweatshirt, and her trainers before heading down to the kitchen to grab a quick coffee and a banana. Within twenty minutes, she was outside, trotting down the path that led to the kitchen gardens, which in turn would lead her to the outer grounds and the more open vistas which were better for a good, fast pace. She was surprised to see Kyle carefully edging out all the vegetable beds, not that she remembered his name. None of the other gardeners were ever out that early. She waved and wished him good morning as she ran past, not seeing how he stared at her as she disappeared into the distance.

Kyle decided that he loved early mornings, when the air was clean and fresh and the gardens deserted. As he worked carefully on the edges, he could allow himself to daydream that it was his garden, his life.

He'd been surprised at just how many people worked at Conniscliffe and wondered how on earth Oscar managed to pay all their wages every month, let alone all the bills for the place. The heating bill for just the staff rooms must cost a bomb, he figured, and all the rooms in the castle had to be kept warm too. His mother's old flat had got mould when it wasn't kept warm whilst they were both in prison. He'd been glad to close it up and leave, although he was cross about leaving so much money unused on the electric key.

By the time Lucy had done a complete circuit of the grounds, sweat was pouring from her face and her legs felt pleasantly jellied. She decided on a quick, perfunctory shower before breakfast, as she would need to shower again before Oscar arrived that evening, along with the Rabbi. Although it had only been four days, she'd missed him terribly and couldn't wait to see him.

Oscar was seated in a comfortable wing-back chair in the House of Commons tea room when Osbourne walked in. He saw him look around for an empty seat and spotting that the one opposite Oscar was unoccupied, made a beeline for it. "Hello Golding, long time no see. Mind if I join you?" He asked as he plonked his skinny behind in the chair. "So what brings you here? We don't often see you slumming it with us commoners."

"Just had coffee with the Honourable Member for Harrogate West," said Oscar. "He's just left, sitting on the select committee this afternoon."

"Oh yes, something to do with foreign affairs isn't it?" Osbourne said. "Would you like another coffee? I wanted to ask for your input on my new banking bill." He waved down the waitress and ordered more coffees. "I'm under pressure to instigate Basel four. Something needs to be done, especially after the LIBOR scandal and the bailouts."

"Why?" Oscar asked. "The bailouts were years ago now, and the people fixing the interbank rates are in court soon."

"The public feel that there were no sanctions against the bankers," Osbourne explained. "We've got an election in a couple of years, and the arguments are still knocking about."

"So prosecute the chairmen who were in place at that time. This Basel four sounds like a dangerous game to me."

"Ah, so you have heard about it then. I did wonder, but I know what you banker types are like. It's all deals in dark rooms with you lot."

Oscar's eyebrows shot up. "Pot calling kettle black? For your information, I was approached because some people are rather worried. It won't affect me, our capitalisation is above what the regulations will require, but it could tip the retail banks over."

"Ripe for takeover then?" Osbourne's eyes gleamed, seemingly delighted at the prospect.

"Ripe for failing," Oscar corrected him. "Politically, is it really a good idea to provoke another banking crisis on your watch?"

"Well, nobody stays in politics forever," he said cryptically, taking a swig of his coffee. "Goldman's and Morgan Stanley would love to get their hands on a major retail operation. I take it Goldings would want a piece of the action too? Oscar stayed silent. "So if I pushed the legislation through, there'd be a potential bonanza..." He looked expectantly at Oscar.

"You'd want a large payoff to split the carcasses between us?" Oscar said.

"I'd have to clear the way through the monopolies commission for you too, don't forget that," Osbourne reminded him.

"So how much are Goldman's and Morgan Stanley dangling in front of you to make this happen?" Oscar asked. Osbourne leaned in even closer.

"A billion each. Citibank are interested too." He sat back.

Oscar leaned in. "Here's the problem. You're gonna crash the whole economy, rob the entire electorate, and you're gonna do all that for a few billion pounds? You'll send your party into the political wilderness for an entire generation."

The Chancellor stood up. "Think it over. Let me know if you're in, because it's gonna happen with your backing or without it. The people are way too stupid to know what even hit them. Nobody even questions why we owe so much right now. We just tell 'em we spent too much on single mothers and they swallow it hook, line, and sinker. The electorate are as dumb as dirt."

Oscar watched as he wandered out, greeting people and clapping backs as he went. When he was sure the Chancellor had gone, he pulled out his phone and called Darius to relay the conversation.

For all his faults and foibles, Oscar was at heart a decent man in the way that only someone born into great wealth can be. A couple of billion pounds as a bribe to ruin millions of families' lives seemed a stupidly unfair transaction. Despite the fact that he'd owe Darius yet another favour, he knew that he needed to stop Osbourne by whatever means possible.

CHAPTER SEVEN

Elle never quite understood why their fellow billionaires' wives found quite so much to complain about. She loved having stylists and image consultants on tap, courtesy of Joan at Vogue. She was immensely flattered that so many of the top designers wanted her to be seen wearing their latest creations, and she thanked her lucky stars every day that she wasn't still living in Lovell Avenue. With all that in mind, she dutifully purchased a selection of pregnancy tests to try and work out why she was so off-centre and ratty. Poor Roger had held the basket as she'd toured Boots that afternoon, checking out the best one to buy.

Ivan had a late meeting with the mining experts, so didn't get home until eight. It was the first 'night off' they'd had alone since he'd made the decision to purchase Maytrees, which had completed that day. She'd placed a bottle of champagne in the fridge, as she knew he'd want to celebrate, figuring that she'd have her glass before doing the test, as she knew Ivan wouldn't allow her to drink if the result was positive.

The girls seemed to know that something was up, as they followed her around the apartment like two little shadows, resting their muzzles up against her legs at every opportunity. She'd got home quite early, and Mrs Watton had grassed them up for bad behaviour, describing how Tania had somehow managed to steal the steaks meant for dinner from the kitchen island while she'd been putting the dry cleaning away. She'd discovered them both fighting over the last morsels of a hideously expensive chateaubriand. Both dogs appeared unrepentant and had even had the gall to ask for their dinner. Due to Ivan's late meeting, there was enough time to roast a chicken, so it wasn't a complete disaster.

"Those architects not coming tonight?" Mrs Watton asked Elle.

She shook her head. "They said they had to meet with another client. It'll be a while before ours even begins being built, so there's plenty of time."

"It must be very exciting?" She asked as she expertly peeled potatoes into perfect ovals.

"It is, but confusing too. There's so many choices to make, decisions to take. Visualising in three dimensions isn't something I'm particularly good at, but Ivan seems to have it all under control."

"I'm sure he knows exactly what he wants," the housekeeper agreed. She glanced down at the pregnancy tests on the island. "So you think you might be expecting?"

"Ivan thinks so. I'm not so sure. We haven't been trying long."

Mrs Watton smiled her benevolent smile. "My eldest son's wife has just announced that they're having their second. I do love babies in the family. Let's just hope your children are better behaved than these two delinquents," she nodded towards the spaniels. Bella responded by starting to heave, eventually throwing up all the stolen beef onto the kitchen floor. "Too rich for you, wasn't it?" She chided as she grabbed the kitchen roll to clean it up before Tania had the chance to be really gross by eating it secondhand.

By the time Ivan got in, Elle was antsy and nervous. "I bought some pregnancy tests today," she blurted as he walked through the door.

"Excellent." He said, before kissing her softly on the lips. He always loved it when she was home before him. "We can do it now?"

She shook her head. "Dinner's ready. Let's eat first. We're celebrating, remember."

"Yes. Maytrees is ours. Demolition starts on Monday morning. It won't be ready in just nine months though, which is a pity."

She pulled a face. "Hardly short of space are we?"

He grinned and kissed her nose. "That, Malyshka is very true. Did you know that it was normal in Russia for babies to sleep in a drawer? Nobody could afford cots. Besides, there was very little space in the bedroom."

"I'll get the violin out later," she said, "your food is ready." She pulled out the plates of roast chicken that Mrs Watton had left in the warming drawer and placed Ivan's in front of him, before fetching the champagne from the fridge and handing it to him to open.

"To our new home," he raised his glass, "and hopefully to filling it." They clinked, and Elle took a sip. It tasted strangely metallic.

"Does your drink taste funny?" She asked, alarmed. Ivan looked quizzical and took another sip of his.

"No, tastes fine. You think it's off or been tampered with?"

"It tastes of metal."

Ivan picked up his phone and summoned Nico, who was there as quick as a flash. "Elle thinks this tastes odd. Can you test it please?" Nico picked up her glass and sniffed it. He shrugged before taking a sip himself.

"Tastes fine to me. I'll swab the glass and send a sample of the champagne off, just to check. It came from our usual supplier though."

"I'll open a different bottle," Ivan said, disappearing into the pantry. He picked out a bottle of Merlot, not strictly right with chicken, but he had no time to chill anything. Besides, he'd had the Merlot a while, so knew that the consignment had been fine. He opened it and let it breathe for a moment while he rinsed two glasses to make sure they were completely clean. "Try that one," he said, placing the glass in front of Elle. She took a sip and pulled a face.

"Tastes revolting, like iron fillings," she announced. Ivan and Nico glanced at each other.

"I don't think there's anything wrong with the champagne," Ivan said to him.

"No sir," Nico agreed. "Shall I take it, just to be sure?" He was partial to a drop of champagne. Ivan nodded, noting that Elle had almost finished her large plate of food, having been unable to wait. He began to eat.

Bella and Tania looked on mournfully as Elle cleared her plate, used to finishing off leftovers. "You had yours earlier," she reminded them as Bella rested her chin on Elle's knee and gaze up at her with reproachful eyes.

"It's ok, girls. You can have some of mine," Ivan said. "I went out for lunch with Ranenkiov," he explained before cutting the remainder up into small pieces and placing his plate on the floor. "How was it at Conde Naste?"

"All fine. Advertising revenues are up on last month. Joan has increased sales by five percent in the last three months. They want to do another piece on us though. Apparently, that 'at home' article was extremely popular."

"Enough about work. Are we gonna do this?" He felt nervous. Up until that point, pregnancy, family and creating his dynasty had been an abstract concept. He stood and held out his hand to help her up.

"You're not watching me wee on a stick," she told him. "I'd like a bit of privacy for that bit."

He laughed. "Alright, I'll wait outside." She picked up the pregnancy test and followed him through to their ensuite, shutting the door firmly in his face.

As she held the little contraption underneath her, her heart rate rose. Latent monsters raised their ugly heads, reminding her of how badly her mother had struggled. As the stream of urine dwindled, she let her eyes wander around her luxurious surroundings, the marble-covered walls, the thick, monogrammed towels draped over an enormous heated rail. This wasn't her mother's life.

"I'm done," she said as she opened the door to find Ivan leaning against the jamb. He followed her in and together they sat on the edge of the bath, side by side, both staring at the little plastic tester.

Two minutes can seem like a very long time. The spaniels even came in to see what was happening.

Pregnant.

"We did it," Ivan yelled, displaying none of his usual restraint. He grabbed her hand. "We started a dynasty." They both grinned at each other. "I knew it! I said you were pregnant." He looked down at the spaniels, "Girls, we're having a baby. What do you think about that then?" They both wagged their tails, as if on cue, which made them both laugh. He wrapped his arm around Elle's shoulder and squeezed her, which made her wince.

"I'm sorry," her said, releasing her. "Did I squash your shoulder or was it pregnancy pain?"

"My bad shoulder, you big oaf," Elle laughed. "It's way too early for pregnancy pain."

"Sorry. Anyway, come sit on the sofa, or should you be in bed?" Anxiety washed over him. He'd felt different when they'd married. Elle being his wife had given him an intimacy he'd never had before. The fact that she was carrying his child brought out even more of his protective instincts. The thought loops would drive him mad, he decided.

"It's very early to be going to bed. It's not even nine yet. Besides, I want to watch White Collar." She wandered out to the lounge and sat down on the large sectional sofa before picking up the remote control.

"Aren't you going to tell anyone?" Ivan asked, puzzled. To him it had seemed momentous, and he wanted to tell the whole world.

"It's very early. We should wait until the three-month point."

"No way. How can I keep quiet for another two months? I'm gonna have a son and heir."

Elle rolled her eyes. "I'm sure you'll be very 'Lion King' when it's born. Until then, don't tempt fate. Now, changing the subject, is there any chance of a coffee?"

"No, it's bad for you. I'll make you a green tea." He sounded petulant. She just rolled her eyes at him and sat back to watch her program. A few minutes later, Ivan appeared carrying a large stack of books, which he placed on the coffee table in front of her. "Pregnancy books. I bought them a while back. I don't have to hide them now."

"You are funny sometimes," Elle teased.

"That top one. Page 38 it tells you that pregnant women should avoid caffeine. It raises the blood pressure. You can laugh at me, but I don't want my son coming out with a funny-shaped head or six toes if it can be avoided."

She pressed the Sky Plus button before turning down the sound. "If we had an imperfect baby, it would still be perfect to both of us. If anything, you'd be even more protective, and I don't think a cup of coffee would make it grow an extra toe. Those sort of things are genetic, not caused by external factors, so scram and get that coffee on, otherwise I'll hold my breath until it becomes a girl."

He huffed a bit, but did as he was told. The thought of a tiny little girl was terrifying. He'd never sleep soundly again.

A few minutes later, he placed a decaf latte in front of her and a glass of Merlot for himself onto the coffee table. "What shall we call him?" He asked, as he flopped down beside her, patting the seat next to him for the girls to jump up and get their ears rubbed.

"At the moment, he or she's just a bundle of cells. The unisex term 'baby' is probably ok," Elle said. Clearly Ivan wanted to talk. He rifled through the pile of books.

"Baby names," he announced, holding one aloft. "An English name or a Russian one?"

"I don't know, a hybrid maybe? It's gotta go with our surname. Anyway, it's a bit early to choose. We don't know whether it'll be a boy or a girl."

"It'll be a boy," Ivan said confidently. "Put your feet up. Don't leave them dangling like that." He nodded towards her feet.

"Are you gonna be a tosser for the next eight months?" Elle asked.

"Yep." He grinned at her before flicking through the pages.

"Great," she groaned.

Laying in bed that night, Elle was just dozing off amid the cacophony of dog snores, when she was rudely woken up. "What do you think of the name Peter? You know, as in Peter The Great?" Ivan asked. He'd lain awake, turning over the events of the evening in his mind.

"Old-fashioned," Elle muttered. "Go to sleep, you can be a tosser in the morning."

The next day, Ivan walked into his office "Morning Galina. Great news, Elle and I are expecting our first son."

"Congratulations. That's wonderful news. When's it due?" She clasped her hands in front of her chest.

"January. Block my diary out for the whole of that month."

"Will do. Do you need me to book the Portland or anything?" She swiped at her tablet and opened a page for notes.

"Yes. Plus you need to find the best doctors for me too. Roger is making sure that Elle works as little as possible, also that she eats regularly. Research and print out a list of the things she mustn't eat for him."

Galina tapped away at her tablet.

"Source organic, free-range foodstuffs, and have them sent to both our homes. Inform the housekeepers of the new regime."

"Does Elle need any supplements?" Galina asked.

"Nico's just gone down to the ground floor to purchase Folic acid capsules," Ivan replied. He knew he was being over-the-top and would probably annoy Elle, who seemed remarkably calm about the whole thing, but being in control, planning in advance, and being organised helped quell the rising panic in his gut. He almost wanted to email Karl for some support, someone who would reassure him that he'd be a good father, that he could raise children as successfully as he could run companies.

"It's exciting isn't it?" Galina brought him back to the present. "Joan will know all the best baby-clothes designers. Will you need the number of your usual interior decorator to get the nursery ready?"

"Yes to all of that. Call Joan. And diarise a meeting for the nursery." He sat back and sipped his coffee while Galina scurried away to make a start. Still smiling, he picked up the phone and called Oscar.

"Hello Ivan, what can I do for you?" Oscar asked, fully expecting a long, boring conversation about mining equipment.

"Thought you'd like to be among the first to congratulate Elle and I. We're expecting our first son. Found out last night." He smiled as he waited for Oscar's reaction.

"Congratulations. Great news," Oscar managed to force out. His voice sounded tight, which Ivan noticed.

"The first of many," Ivan said, a note of triumph showing in his voice. "Anyway, I'd better go, lots of people to tell, planning to do."

As soon as he came off the phone, Oscar sat for a moment with his head in his hands, his heart beating wildly. It had started off as a good day. The sun shone on his short walk to the office, Melanie was in a good mood, and he was scheduled to meet a fellow peer, a good friend, for a long, boozy lunch in The Grill at the Dorchester. He was a huge fan of their blue lobster chowder. He'd planned a helicopter to take him down to Conniscliffe, so that he wasn't late for dinner with the Rabbi.

Elle was pregnant.

He'd thought it painful watching her marry, but somehow that paled into impermanent insignificance against the news that she would have Ivan's child forever. He wanted to scream, howl at the unfairness of it all. Again, he ran through the events of that terrible night in his mind. If there was anything he could've said, done, to change things. It should've been him calling people, crowing about impregnating her. It should've been Elle by his side at dinner with the Rabbi.

His pity-party was interrupted by his phone ringing. He lifted his head from the desk and picked it up. "You owe me big time," said Darius. "Put the news on." Obediently, Oscar picked up the remote control and pressed the button. The screen opposite his desk sprang to life, pre-programmed to the BBC news channel.

"Tributes have been paid to the late Chancellor Gideon Osbourne, who died of a heart attack early this morning." He read out the banner on the screen. "Heart attack? How did you pull that one off?"

"Easy. No point waiting until he'd crashed the economy. Best to get rid of traitors before they get the chance to do any damage." Darius was startlingly matter-of-fact.

"Very true. Rather drastic though. Couldn't you have uncovered a rent-boy scandal or something?" He didn't like being reminded of his oldest, closest friend's ruthless streak, even though he'd utilised it frequently over the years. Darius wasn't as squeamish as Oscar. His job as head of the intelligence service suited him very well.

Darius chuckled. "Nowadays a rent-boy scandal just makes politicians more popular. Gideon would've played it as a more edgy, Bohemian way to get votes from the LGBT tribe. Remember when we let it out about Cameron and the pig's head? Everyone liked him just a bit more after that."

"True," agreed Oscar.

"Just don't forget that you owe me. Are you free next week?"

"During the week, yes."

"Wednesday night at the Tower Bridge Hotel. I'll book dinner for seven." The phone went dead.

Lunch was a far more sombre affair than was originally planned. Oscar was in a sour mood, not helped by copious amounts of alcohol. His friend, Henry, put it down to upset over the news of the Chancellor's demise and simply kept Oscar's glass topped up while regaling him with stories of bad behaviour, including infidelity during a parliamentary fact-finding trip to Rio de Janeiro.

Even hearing that a rather crusty, overweight old goat, a fairly elderly peer of the realm, had been thoroughly serviced by one of the Lib-Dem lot, a middle-aged, rather bookish blue-stocking, who everyone assumed was either asexual or a lesbian, failed to amuse Oscar to the extent that such salacious gossip would normally have done.

The Chief Rabbi was a warm, kindly man, who was well liked by his congregation and held in very high esteem by his colleagues. He'd been to Conniscliffe many times, presiding over the late Lord Golding's funeral as well as attending social functions at the castle. He was delighted to be asked to officiate at Oscar's wedding, having been the one to perform both his Brit Milah and his Bar Mitzvah. It was even more fortuitous that he knew Lucy's parents too, although he hadn't officiated at any ceremonies for them.

Lady Golding loved to entertain, even if it was only one guest. She supervised the table decorations in the small dining room, watching as Jones checked the place settings with his ruler, making sure that everything was straight and the correct distance from the edge of the table. She'd also planned the menu carefully to ensure no meat and milk were mixed. Normally they didn't bother, but she didn't want the Rabbi to know that.

Oscar hopped out of the helicopter to find Lucy waiting for him, her hair whipping around her face from the downdraft of the rotor blades. She looked rested, happier than she'd been the last time he'd seen her. Her cheeks had a rosiness that only the Sussex countryside could produce. She flung her arms around his neck and pressed a warm kiss onto his lips. "I missed you so much," she said, as they hurried away from the noise.

He always felt better at Conniscliffe. Whatever London threw at him, he could take as long as he could escape to the comfort and safety of the ancient, thick walls of his ancestral home. Jones was serving tea in the drawing room, and Lady Golding and the Rabbi were both already ensconced on the formal, damask-covered seats. It was at that moment that Oscar realised that Lucy was now part of that concept of 'home.' She might not be Elle, but she was his, and hopefully he'd be the next person announcing his impending children. As he shook hands with the Rabbi, he wondered if he'd have as many regrets if he lost Lucy too. Watching her charm the elderly Rabbi, he decided that he would.

"Terrible news about Gideon Osbourne, isn't it?" Said his mother as he sat down.

"Yes, dreadful," he agreed, accepting a cup of tea from Jones. "A real shock."

"So young too," Lucy said.

"Did you know him well?" Asked the Rabbi.

"Not terribly well," said Oscar. "Mansion House dinners, that sort of thing. We didn't socialise."

He was glad when the conversation moved on to their impending nuptials. Given that both Lucy and he were Jewish, understood the meaning of marriage, and had wide experience of the ceremony, it was a straightforward conversation, which didn't take up too much time during dinner. At ten, Oscar and Lucy said goodnight and retired, leaving Lady Golding and the Rabbi in the drawing room, reminiscing over old times.

"I need to bury myself in you," Oscar said the moment they were alone together in his room. "I need to rip your clothes off, put a pair of heels on you and fuck you senseless," he said quietly. He wondered if she'd object, seeing as the Rabbi was downstairs. She didn't.

Lucy stood in the centre of the room as Oscar stalked up to her. He seemed needy somehow. He'd clearly been distracted since he'd returned. She shivered with excitement as he pulled the zip of her dress down, feeling his warm hand graze the skin of her back. He pushed the dress off her shoulders and let it fall to the floor. Without another word, he unclasped her bra and pushed that off too. Lucy stood, wearing just pink, lacy knickers and her sandals.

"Get the rest off," Oscar ordered her, in an authoritative tone. Lucy complied, hastily undoing the little straps around her ankles and kicking off the rather sensible low-heeled shoes before sliding her knickers down her legs. Meanwhile, Oscar had pulled off his tie and untucked his shirt. "Lay on the bed," he ordered.

He carefully removed his cufflinks, laying them neatly in the leather gentlemen's organiser on the bedside cabinet before shedding the rest of his clothes quickly and unceremoniously. Naked and already aroused, he strode over to the wardrobe and picked out a pair of cherry red, impossibly-high Choos.

He placed them carefully on her feet and gazed down at her, wanton and horny, waiting for him to make his move. His cock was straining, ready for some relief, but he decided to delay until he could lose his mind alongside his control. He began to kiss and lick the shoes, feeling the glossy leather against his lips, tracing the spiked heel with his tongue. Lucy lay on her back, her legs pointing up to the ceiling, giving him access to the shoes, but closed, cutting him off from that most intimate part of her.

He reached down to play with her nipple, palming her breast before using his thumb to lengthen and excite the sensitive pink bud. He heard her moan softly as the sensation travelled down to her groin. He smiled against the side of the shoe. For some reason, hearing her moaning for him pleased him. He opened his eyes to see her mouth slightly open, her eyes closed, and a look of pure pleasure on her face. He bent down and cupped her face, kissing her deeply as her eyes sprang open in surprise, before fluttering closed again as she enjoyed the kiss.

He slipped into the cradle between her legs and thrust his way inside her, gratified to feel how turned on she was. Being inside her was like a velvet hug, all comforting and safe. He began to move, slowly at first, making sure the position was right, testing the angle to make sure it was comfortable, then he began to pound, hard, fast, the most aggressive fuck he'd ever given. He poured every ounce of his frustration, his disappointment, and his anger into every thrust. Their bodies crashed together, skin slapping loudly as he fucked her like a rag doll, holding her hips down as he slammed himself into her.

"I need to fuck your cunt so hard," he said.

"Oh yes," she whispered. "Hard, do it harder."

He bucked into her, grasping her shoulders to prevent her moving. It was angry, animalistic sex, with Lucy matching him at every step. Sweat poured off him, splashing onto her. "Give it to me," she growled. "Give me everything you've fucking got, you savage bastard."

He fell over the edge, into his release. It felt as though he was shooting a bucketful of cum into her as he let go. He felt her come too, powerful contractions which milked his cock of every drop.

"Oh, God," he gasped as they both shuddered together.

As their orgasms subsided, he lay his head on her chest, nested between her breasts, as he attempted to get his breath back and gather his thoughts. "I've missed you this week," he admitted.

"Me too. Not just because of what happened on Monday," Lucy replied, "and at least I've kept myself busy here." She paused. "So you missed me?"

He nodded.

"Are you upset about Osbourne? I know that he was more than just an acquaintance."

"No, not really. By the way, how's that chap I sent down doing? Has Fred said anything?" He'd almost forgotten about Kyle.

"Very pleased, I think. He seems quite a good little worker."

Oscar nestled in a little more. He felt Lucy wriggle slightly. "I need you to move," she said, "You're heavy. Besides, I need to clean up." Reluctantly, he rolled off her and watched as she disappeared into the bathroom. A few minutes later she reappeared and snuggled in beside him. "So, anything else happen this week?" She asked.

"Ivan called to tell me that Elle's expecting," he said. "Oh, and I met with Henry DuPont for lunch today."

A pang smacked Lucy square between the eyes. She realised that he was bothered about Ivan's announcement. "Are you broody for a baby too?" She enquired.

He shrugged. She took that as a yes.

"It'll soon be our turn," she said.

Lucy lay awake listening to Oscar's breathing as he fell asleep, his arm and one leg casually thrown over her, possessive even in sleep. She decided to come off the pill before the wedding, hopefully so she'd conceive on honeymoon.

CHAPTER EIGHT

Ivan held Elle's hair back from her face as she threw up, rubbing her spine gently. When she finally came up for air, he dampened a washcloth and handed it to her to wipe her face. "Oh God, three months of this," she whined. "I'll be a withered little husk." She gingerly stood up, every movement causing a wave of nausea to wash over her. "No more coffee," she said weakly. It had been the smell of the latte that Ivan had made her that had set her off.

"Poor Malyshka," he soothed. "I'll make you a green tea. Mrs Watton bought you some ginger snaps to eat when you're sick. I'll get those too." He disappeared to fetch them. Elle examined her face in the mirror, she looked grey. Her hair hung limp around her face and she had the beginnings of a spot on her chin. Within a few days of finding out that she was pregnant, the symptoms had hit with a vengeance.

"Your boobs are bigger," Ivan remarked as he returned with two steaming mugs of what looked like hot water, and a plate of brown biscuits. He placed them down on the vanity unit.

"They hurt like hell," Elle told him, "Why are you having manky herbal tea as well?" She peered at the two cups.

"Keeping you company," he replied, as he began to lather up his face for a shave. "It's not fair for me to drink coffee if the smell makes you sick."

"Such a good husband," she teased.

"Not really, I'll have a latte at the office. I have a few hours until our appointment." He began to shave his face, drawing the razor over his strong jawline in long, confident strokes. Elle preferred him with his weekend stubble, but for weekdays, he liked to be clean-shaven.

"I really should go in too. I want to check on the purchase contract for Lonier Communications and read up on that intellectual property case we're launching on Telefonix."

He felt his blood pressure rising. "You've just been sick. You're pale, tired, and need to rest. I'll pick you up at eleven for our appointment."

Elle could hear the edge to his voice. She tried to figure out why it meant so much to her to carry on working. It wasn't as though they needed the money, or even the status. Her career was really the last thing she needed to worry about. Beltan was running as well as a large conglomerate possibly could. In reality, she was just a cog in its giant wheel. Anatoly would be perfectly fine taking over her workload.

All debate was forgotten as another wave of nausea washed over her, rendering her helpless again, bent over the toilet.

By their time Ivan arrived back at the apartment to pick her up, she'd just about managed to shower and get dressed. She knew she looked a wreck-her hair was scraped into a ponytail, and she had dark circles around her eyes, but Ivan didn't comment. Instead, he just fussed the girls as he waited for Elle to put on her coat.

The Portland wasn't quite what Elle had expected. She'd envisaged a five-star hotel with midwives on hand. Instead, there was a hospital smell and the birthing suites were decidedly wipe-clean. The doctor was a kindly, middle-aged woman, with a sleek, chestnut bob and a soothing disposition. It wasn't the first time that Elle had experienced the gulf between private, paid-for medicine, and the off-hand, surly care the NHS dished out. Tests were done, forms filled out, and appointments made.

"When do we have the first scan?" Ivan had asked. He'd brought a sheet of neatly-typed questions along with him, which had made Elle cringe a little when he'd pulled it out and started grilling the doctor. She'd made it seem as though such behaviour was perfectly normal.

"A few weeks. There's not much to see yet. I can see from the urine test that your wife is indeed pregnant, but calculating it from the date of her last period, she's not very far along yet." The answer seemed to satisfy him, and he moved on to the next question on his list, which was about the security of the building.

As they headed back to the docklands, Ivan beamed with satisfaction. He flung his arm around Elle's shoulder and planted a wet kiss on her cheek. "How're you feeling?" He asked.

"Happier for having seen a doctor," she replied. "Not that I was worried before, but it's always nice when someone reassures you that you're normal, isn't it?"

"You're young, healthy, fit, perfect for childbirth," he said. "I just worry..." He tailed off.

"About what?" She turned to look at him.

Ivan wrestled with what he wanted to say, for the first time in years struggling to find the right words in English. Her baby-blue eyes penetrated his sapphire ones. Eventually he said; "I just worry because you don't seem very happy."

"Of course I am," she protested. "I just keep thinking about my mum, how hard it made her life, you know, having me." She paused. "I keep reminding myself that I don't have her life, that I'll never be hiding behind the sofa from the rent man, or struggling to feed anyone."

"Poverty always leaves its scars on the souls of the people it touches," Ivan said, glancing out of the window of the Bentley. "I've gone through those same thoughts myself. I keep thinking how my father must have felt, not being able to feed us properly."

"I keep telling myself that ordinary people have children too, not just mad billionaires. They cope without all the trappings we have." Elle laid her hand on his chest, over his heart. "I'm scared of not working, which is irrational, stupid even. I want to go into the office, even though I feel like death, simply because I'm scared to not be part of it all, as if it'll all disappear in a puff of smoke unless I'm tending to it." A tear rolled down her cheek, which broke Ivan's heart. He gently wiped it away with his thumb.

"I was worth thirty billion or so when I married you," he told her. "It won't disappear. If it did, I'd just make it all over again. Never be scared Malyshka. I'll be scared for both of us. I want you to feel secure, happy, joyous that we've been blessed with a son."

"So quickly too, Mr Fertile," Elle teased, the mood lightened a little.

"Well, yes, that goes without saying," he preened slightly, secretly extremely proud of the fact that he'd got her knocked up so fast. *Russian sperm*, he thought, *the best swimmers in the world.*

They were interrupted by Elle's phone ringing. She pulled it out of her bag and looked at the screen before answering it. "Hi Joan, how's things?"

"Super. Firstly, I'd like to congratulate you both on behalf of everyone at Conde Nast. Secondly, a few of our favourite designers have offered to provide you with maternity wear. Thirdly, both Chloe, Marc Jacobs, and

Burberry would like to dress the baby. I thought we should delay the 'At Home' article we're going to do until you're a bit more pregnant."

"Thank you, but how did you know I was pregnant?" Elle asked, glancing over at Ivan.

"Ivan sent an announcement around the company on the intranet this morning," Joan said, "Didn't he tell you?"

"Must've slipped his mind," Elle replied, shooting Ivan a daggers look. He had the grace to blush. "It's very kind of everyone. I agree about the editorial piece."

"Super. Well, I'll get everything shipped over to you once it comes in. I know Ivan said it would be a boy, but, well, let's hedge our bets and stick to neutrals shall we?"

"Good idea," Elle said weakly. They ended the call. She turned to Ivan. "So you told everyone?" He nodded, wary of her reaction.

"I was excited."

"We've got half a hundredweight of designer Babygros arriving. You better get that nursery sorted out," she growled.

"Ok," he said, staring straight ahead.

She struggled to stay cross with him. "Tosser."

"Yep, that's me," he quipped, gracing her with his glorious smile. She couldn't help but grin back at him.

**

Lucy and Lady Golding arrived at Atelier Boucheire at precisely ten o'clock the following day, to be greeted by the noise levels of a rock concert and what could only be described as scenes of mutiny, led, it seemed by the Prost-Winston children, who were bouncing on the cream silk sofas wearing their outdoor shoes. The mothers stood in a gaggle gossiping, while Madame Boucheire and her assistant looked as though they were about to have a nervous breakdown.

"WHAT IS GOING ON HERE?" Lady Golding's voice boomed out, making Lucy jump.

Silence prevailed.

"Get off the sofa," she ordered the eldest Prost-Winston boy. He jumped down immediately. Lady Golding walked further into the room. The children all stared at her, some with slack jaws. "You are all here today to be measured by the greatest atelier in London. I expect you to be silent, stand still, and do exactly as you're told. Is that clear?"

"Yes miss," they chorused as one.

"They're just having fun," Marina objected. Lady Golding shot her such a withering stare that she visibly shrank.

"Damaging fine furnishings is not 'fun,' nor is behaving like a football hooligan." She turned back to the children. "Line up, smallest to biggest. Everyone who stands up straight and does what they're told will get an ice-cream sundae once we're finished," she announced.

The children scrambled to get in place, a tiny little-blonde haired moppet was pushed to the front.

"Rory is on lactose-free," Marina called out, determined to put Lady Golding in her place for ordering her darlings around. They looked positively meek standing in their line.

"I'm sure Fortnums caters for weak tummies and mental mothers," Lady Golding snapped. The other mothers tittered.

"Thank you," Lucy whispered as the staff got on with measuring everyone.

"I hope this outfit will be cotton. Amelia is allergic to man-made fibres," Marina said to the atelier when it was her daughter's turn to be measured.

"Her dress will be silk, she'll be fine," Lucy said. She really didn't like Marina much. She felt braver with Lady Golding by her side. Marina turned back to her daughter, whose measurements had been completed. Lucy couldn't help but notice that the child was wearing a polyester top.

"All done? Now go and play. See if you can teach all the other children your song and dance routine. There's a big space in-between those mannequins." Marina said before she turned back to her conversation. The little girl stood, lost.

"I don't want to," she said quietly. "I want to be good, like everyone else."

Lady Golding's heart broke for her. She bent down to her and said; "If you want to be quiet and just watch everyone, then that's absolutely fine. Come sit with me." The little girl's face broke into a wide smile, and she hopped onto the cream silk sofa next to Lady Golding. Lucy watched as her future mother-in-law said something that made the little girl laugh.

Later that afternoon, after having treated everyone to ice-cream sundaes in Fortnums, Lucy asked Lady Golding how she managed to control children quite so effectively. Seeing her marshall twenty-two small children like a cross between the Pied Piper and Mary Poppins had been quite a masterclass.

"Children are like puppies, all they want to do is gain praise and affection. They want to do the right thing and appreciate it when you show them how to," she said. "No child wants to be scolded, they respond far better to firm boundaries and lots of kindness. Works a treat every time."

Back at Conniscliffe, Oscar bumped into Kyle on the driveway. Kyle had been at a bit of a loss as to what to do with himself, so decided to walk into Derwent. He had to find out where the probation office was, as he was being transferred there for the rest of his supervision period. The other apprentices had invited him out that night for a drink in the Derwent Tavern, which he was looking forward to, so he wanted to make sure he knew exactly where it was. There was a girl, Amber, who was on the same course, that he rather liked the look of. She'd been quite chatty when they'd planted out the rows of beans together. He hoped she'd like to take things further, figuring that going out for a drink was probably the best way to scope her out.

He also needed to find a Narcotics Anonymous meeting, although he didn't think that Derwent would be awash with heroin, so the temptation wouldn't be put in front of him. Even so, he wanted to stay strong and not muck up the chance he'd been given.

"Hi Kyle, how was your first week?" Oscar asked, noticing how much healthier he looked. His cheeks were pink from being outside and he seemed... stronger, sturdier somehow.

"It's been great, thanks. Fred's terrific, really knows his stuff doesn't he?"

"He's been working here since before I was born. Settled in alright? It's a big change from London isn't it?"

Kyle nodded. "Good though. No sirens, no gangs... I actually found it difficult to sleep the first few nights because it was so quiet."

Oscar smiled. "You get used to it. Off out?"

"Yea. Gonna walk into Derwent. Gotta find the probation office and where they hold the NA meetings."

"Oh, those are held at the back of the working man's club, just on the high street. There's an alley up the side that leads to the door. It's not hard to find."

Kyle shifted slightly, momentarily uncomfortable. "Does anyone else know, you know, how we met?" Oscar shook his head. "Do they know you were a junkie?"

Oscar grinned. "Oh yes, it's no secret. Conniscliffe is like a family though, we don't blab our secrets to outsiders. I stayed here when I came out of rehab, so all the staff saw the state I was in. It never made it outside the castle walls though. The papers never got to hear about it."

"Bit like Narcotics Anonymous then," Kyle said. When he'd joined, it had been impressed on him that he was never to disclose who had attended meetings. "Anyway, I'm off into Derwent. Enjoy the rest of your day."

"You too," Oscar said, as he started off in the direction of the synagogue. The Rabbi wanted to check it over, make sure all was well before the wedding. In truth, Oscar hadn't been inside since his father's funeral, so it was probably a good idea to have a look.

It had been converted a few generations previously from an old chapel from the time that the castle had been built. It was an atmospheric old building, large and imposing, with high windows and thick stone walls. Within the family, they still called it The Chapel, it was only when Rabbis visited was it referred to as the Synagogue.

The Rabbi was wandering down the path just as Oscar arrived, having said goodbye to Lucy and Lady Golding over breakfast, as they left for London. Oscar opened the heavy oak doors and they stepped inside. The cleaning staff had been in recently, Oscar could tell by the way that the pews gleamed and the ornate menorah shone in the sunlight coming through the large, arched windows. Like the rest of the castle, no expense had been spared, and the synagogue was as lavish in its decor as any major place of worship, having taken inspiration from the great synagogues of Jerusalem for its fittings. A vast chandelier, made in the shape of the Star of David, hung from the centre. Oscar had always thought it was the most beautiful building in Conniscliffe.

"I've always loved it here," said the Rabbi. "Only seems like yesterday that I was here last. I remember your father's funeral, how packed it was."

"Indeed," said Oscar. He really didn't want to be reminded.

"Lucy seems to be a great choice of wife," said the Rabbi. "Your father would've been pleased. I know your mother likes her very much." He stared intently at Oscar, as though searching his face for signs that Oscar wasn't so convinced.

"Mother is a good judge of character," Oscar said smoothly. "She hasn't liked many of the women I've introduced her to over the years." Except Elle, he thought. "Lucy will fit in exceptionally well, she's keen to start a family."

"Yes, your mother said. It'll be wonderful to be called on to welcome new life into the faith." He paused. "She's not expecting already, is she?"

"No, not yet. We're waiting until we're married. It's important to both of us that our children are legitimate."

"Yes, good, good," said the Rabbi, as he wandered up the aisle and inspected the pulpit.

Half an hour later, Oscar waved him off as he headed back to London. As soon as he'd gone, Oscar made his way out to the white garden to sit and think.

The garden was still green at that time of year, apart from some white tulips and some very late white daffodils. Another month or so would see the start of the Wisteria and the early Clematis, when it would all look more familiar. He sat himself on the bench and remembered the day he'd sat there with Elle beside him. He recalled her hesitantly confessing that she came from a poverty-stricken background, that her mother had been a single parent. He, of course, had been shocked and a little put-off by her revelation, as if being poor had been a choice she'd made. Seeing her now, living a billionaire lifestyle with grace and aplomb really slammed his own prejudices into his face.

He plucked a bud of leaves from the Wisteria covering the seat and crumbled it between his fingers, wondering if he would curse himself for the rest of his days. There'd been a time, before Elle, when it had all seemed so simple, so cut-and-dried. You stayed within your own tribe, the people you grew up with, understood and trusted. People like Lucy, who could be relied upon do and say the right thing, behave the right way, smooth the path through life for anyone in their orbit.

He'd always thought it was ironic that the upper echelons of banking, of which he was one, placed so much store by good manners, good breeding, and gentlemanly behaviour, given the dark arts of finance and politics which they all practiced. Oscar knew that he'd financed warlords, crooks, and gangsters. It was an unspoken truth that the people on the top of the pyramid never discussed. Even Ivan knew that he was responsible for slave labour, preferring to ignore the fact and concentrate on extracting even better profits each year. He wondered how Elle reconciled it in her mind, knowing that she came from the enslaved class, who neither himself nor Ivan would have given a second thought to exploiting, if it meant bigger profits.

His thoughts turned to Lucy, how much happier she seemed after just a week at the castle. Having observed her making small talk with the Rabbi, he knew he'd made the right choice. He'd look forward to coming home to her every weekend.

CHAPTER NINE

With July fast approaching, wedding preparations went into overdrive. The catering kitchen was scrubbed down and readied for the catering company to cook for both the wedding breakfast and the banquet that was planned for the evening. Dress fittings came and went for everyone involved and the chandeliers were finally re-hung in the ballroom, taking it from a nicely-decorated room to something exquisite. The wedding planner was an extremely effeminate man called Ashley, who used his camp mannerisms and faux sweetness as cover for ruthless efficiency and an attention to detail that could only be described as obsessive. Lady Golding adored him.

As the days wore on, he bullied, cajoled, and downright ordered the entire wedding entourage into as many preparations as possible, forcing Marina Prost-Winston to get all three children's hair cut by declaring that their 'ends looked like rats had chewed them' as loudly and publicly as possible. When the time had come to start rehearsals, he'd stood with his clipboard, like a general ordering his troops into battle formation, as they took their places in the chapel. Oscar had to admit, he was terribly impressed by the way the skinny little chap took charge, choreographing the whole thing, and Ashley's copious spreadsheets seemed to cover every eventuality.

As the day approached, Lucy became more nervous, while Oscar began to allow himself to feel excited, more at the prospect of having the castle full of people and dancing again, but also for Lucy, the next Lady Golding, to give her the security that he knew she needed.

He'd kept away from Ivan and Elle, which had been a good thing. They'd been busy with work, their new building project, and life in general, and Oscar had kept himself busy at the Lords, ratifying legislation before the summer break, when Parliament would be in recess. With no new banking legislation on the horizon, his work at the bank was pretty steady, mainly limited to the odd meeting and some socialising. It wasn't exactly a hard life.

"It's gonna be a struggle being properly devout in front of everyone for a whole weekend," Lucy said to Lady Golding, who laughed.

"Don't let the Rabbi catch you eating bacon for breakfast," she teased. "You'll have to keep your wits about you. Oscar too, as we'll be serving everything as normal. Very few of our guests are of the faith."

"No point having a full on wedding in the Synagogue smelling of bacon is there?" Lucy giggled. She was glad that Oscar's family were like her own, only Jewish at weddings, Bris or Zeved Habat and funerals. She'd eaten pork at school, to fit in, and had liked it. The same thing had happened to Oscar at Eton.

**

Ivan decided that morning dress was the most ridiculous outfit that the British had ever invented. He'd had his made, of course, by his usual tailor, who'd assured him that every detail was correct for a society wedding. "I'm gonna melt wearing this," he complained to Elle as he buttoned up the front of the jacket. The coat-tails felt long and alien, brushing the back of his legs. He doubted very much that Conniscliffe had air conditioning. It was a blisteringly hot day already, and it was only eleven o'clock. "Why do Brits think it's a good idea to wear three layers on a hot day in July?" He grumbled.

Elle looked cool and summery in a pale lilac dress, loosely fitted over her little bump, with a floaty navy blue bolero, with a navy and lilac wide-brimmed hat and navy sandals and clutch. Her hair had been freshly blow-dried into soft waves, and her makeup was kept soft and smudgy. Ivan eyed her, partly proud of how perfect she was, partly envious of her more practical outfit. "You look very smart," she assured him. "I'm sure you'll be able to take your jacket off later."

"I might have to come back here for a swim to cool down," he huffed. He was starting to perspire already.

"I think we're stuck there all day," Elle said. I'm hoping I'll be able to kick off my shoes at some point. My ankles'll get so swollen it'll look like I've got my legs on upside down."

"I went to a Catholic wedding once where just the service was three hours long," Ivan said, "I hope this isn't gonna be like that. Have you ever been to a Jewish one?" Elle shook her head. "I didn't really even realise that Lucy and Oscar were devout," he said.

Elle pulled a face. "They're not, as far as I know. I think it's just a family thing." She picked up her clutch. "Anyway, let's count ourselves lucky that we haven't had to stay all weekend like some of the guests. At least we can come back here tonight and throw ourselves in the pool if need be."

They set off downstairs to say goodbye to the dogs, who were flopped out on a shady bit of the patio sucking on chicken-flavoured ice lollies, while Viktor sat nearby watching over them, wearing just his swim shorts, his gun on the table beside him. "You be good girls for Viktor," said Ivan, wondering if he should tell Viktor to go put on his suit, before dismissing the notion as just envy that he got a Sunday at home with the girls by the pool, while he had to sit in a church wearing a penguin suit.

"Which car do you want to take?" Nico asked as they stepped outside. On the drive were two identical silver Bentleys. Despite not being given a choice of colour, Elle had been delighted with hers.

"Doesn't matter," Ivan said, walking to the nearest one, which happened to be his. "Nico, put your chauffeur's hat on, oh-- and turn the air conditioning up as high as it'll go."

The mood at the castle that morning was celebratory, with people and staff milling about. It gave everything a festive air. People had arrived the evening before, by helicopter, car, and taxi. Kyle had been tasked with assisting the pilots in parking on the great lawn on the outskirts of the estate. A row of choppers sat waiting for their esteemed passengers who'd require them early Monday morning, when everyone would be leaving.

Lady Golding was in her element. The castle was full to the brim with fun, interesting people and she hosted a dinner on the Saturday evening in the large dining room, which had required the two long tables to be set side-by-side to accommodate everyone. She held court, changing tables through the courses, so as to be able to chat with as many people as possible. Both Oscar and Lucy had watched her in astonishment, wondering where she got all her energy from.

The two of them had taken a table each, welcoming their guests and introducing them to others at the party. It had been a good icebreaker having a dinner the night before.

"Did you have a hen party?" An elderly viscountess asked.

"Oh yes," Lucy replied. "A whole group of us went to Barcelona for the weekend a few weeks ago. It was a riot, so much fun."

"Nobody got into trouble, I hope?" The old lady asked, a twinkle in her eye.

Lucy grinned. "Bunty McKendrick got drunk and fell in a fountain, then took all her clothes off, but it was ok. Arabella made Darius get her out of jail."

"She always was a pickle that one," chortled the Viscountess, before raising her glass to Bunty, her god-daughter, who was sitting further down the table.

"Nobody took any pictures, so no harm done," said Lucy, taking a tiny sip of her champagne, determined to make her one glass last all evening. She was under strict instructions from Ashley to go to bed early and apply plenty of miracle night cream, not that she was particularly looking forward to sleeping in a single bed in Lady Golding's apartment.

Oscar sat next to his sister, Stella, who had arrived that day with her 'friend' Paulina. Lady Golding had graciously welcomed them both warmly and hadn't commented when Stella had announced that they were quite happy to share a room, if the castle was full. "Mother seems happy," Stella had whispered to Oscar as their mother greeted another old friend with pecks on the cheeks and a big smile.

"She is. Getting all this organised has kept her too busy to be miserable. She's better with people around her."

"Last time I saw her, she looked like she'd been sucking a lemon. It's good to see her perked up." Stella paused, "It's good to see you happy too. You look well."

"Thank you, I feel it. Mind you, the last time you saw me was just after father's funeral. I hadn't been out of rehab long. I'm not all tanned like you though, well, not until I've had a couple of weeks out in Tuscany."

"When do you fly out?" Stella asked.

" Monday. It's gonna be a long enough day as it is tomorrow without trying to travel to Italy as well. How long are you staying for?"

"Depends how mother is with Paulina really. If she's like this, on best behaviour, we'll stay a week. Jones said that all the guests staying in my apartment here are leaving Monday morning, so I might use the opportunity to show her around a bit. I've missed Conniscliffe."

"I'm sure she'll be fine. She's mellowed a lot recently. Are things still good out in Italy?"

She smiled and nodded. "The villas are all mostly booked for the whole summer, thanks to some good TripAdviser reviews. It's hard work, but good. It's important for Paulina that it's a success because she doesn't want to live off my trust fund."

Oscar glance over at Paulina, who, like Stella, had her hair cut short and wore a smart pantsuit as opposed to a dress. They were both striking women, well-suited and had made a life together, despite the opposition his parents had placed on their relationship.

"Lucy seems lovely," Stella said. "Very much your type. Was Mommy-dearest a bitch to her when you brought her home for the first time?"

Oscar laughed. "Not really. Mother had the Gorgon knocked out of her by the time Lucy came along. Think she was just pleased to see me settled." Stella tilted her head, questioning. Oscar went on; "I brought a girl home who was more than a match for her, a lawyer whom I'd met at work. It's a long, boring story, but let's just say that mother was delighted when the sweet, gentle Lucy came on the scene."

"Didn't Lucy tell me that she was a lawyer too?" Stella asked.

Oscar nodded. "Family law. Elle was a corporate lawyer, the sharpest I've ever met. She ran circles round mother. You'll meet her tomorrow, she's coming with her husband."

"She was a married woman?" Stella gasped. "Oscar, what were you thinking?"

He laughed, "she wasn't married when I met her. I lost her to him. My own stupid fault. As I said, long story. I met Lucy through her. They did their training together."

"I can't wait to meet this Elle tomorrow," Stella said, just as Lady Golding sat next to her.

"Elle? Lovely girl, sharp as a tack. Her husband, well, put it this way, he'd even turn your head," Lady Golding joked. Stella laughed in spite of herself.

"Doubt it mother, but you can live in hope. Good-looking is he, then?"

"I hate to say it, but probably one of the most handsome men I've ever seen. Even gives me a little shiver," she said.

"Mother!" Oscar chided her jokingly. "Don't let Elle hear you talk like that."

Laughing, Lady Golding went off to chat to the Emir.

"She's had too much to drink do you think?" Stella asked. Oscar shook his head. "Well, looks like I'm staying for the week then."

Lucy was up ridiculously early the following morning, having heeded Ashley's warning to be in bed by ten, plus the single bed had been extremely uncomfortable, given that she was used to a super kingsize bed with Oscar's warm body next to her.

It was her wedding day, the day she'd been waiting for.

She pulled on her dressing gown and opened the curtains. Sunlight flooded in, the strong, bright light of a perfect summers day. The sky was cornflower blue, with just a couple of tiny, white, fluffy clouds, just enough to be picturesque. The first smile of the day was entirely natural as she gazed out at the gardens, which had been primped and preened into utter perfection.

A knock at the door interrupted her. "Come in," she called out. Lady Golding walked in, followed by Jones, who was bearing a large trolley full of breakfast goodies.

"Morning Lucy. How are you feeling? Thought you might like your breakfast in privacy, you know, no need to forgo your protein."

"Wonderful," Lucy said, eyeing the trolley. The smell of bacon filled the room. Lady Golding poured out two cups of tea and took one with her as she sat on the small sofa opposite the bed.

"It'll be a bit of a bunfight in the breakfast room. Jones is taking Oscar something too. Has Ashley given you your schedule?"

"Oh yes. I'm early though, I don't need to shower and wash my hair for another hour and a half, plenty of time for tea and breakfast. Are you on schedule?"

"Oh yes. I checked with the kitchens earlier. Breakfasts are all being served from seven. Traditionally, the bride and groom aren't meant to eat until after the ceremony, but I don't want either of you passing out on me."

"So you sneaked some up?" Lucy said. "Very wise. I get dizzy if I don't eat, and Oscar gets grumpy, neither of which would be particularly welcome."

"There's also something I'd like to give you; well, to pass down really. It was given to me on my wedding day, by Oscar's grandmother. She said it would bring me luck. I thought it could be your 'something old.' You don't have to wear it if you don't want to." She reached down to a box which was on the lower shelf of the trolley and handed it to Lucy.

It was a leather-covered box, too large for a piece of jewellery, but the weight and feel of it indicated something of value would be inside. Lucy opened the lid. Inside, on a bed of purple velvet was a diamond tiara. It was exquisite. She pulled it out of the box and turned it over in her hands.

"Rumour was that it first belonged to Catherine Parr, worn when she married Henry the eighth. I'm not entirely sure how it came to be in our family, as the acquisition is a little murky, but it brought me good luck."

"Brought her good luck too, it would seem," quipped Lucy. She tried it on her head, it felt reassuringly heavy.

"I told Ashley I'd be surprising you with it, so the hairstylist already knows," she added, "I didn't want him pitching a fit at a change being made."

Lucy threw her arms around her and hugged her. "Thank you so much... for everything."

"You too. I know you make my son happy, and that makes me happy," she replied. "Now, eat up before it all gets cold. I'll go back downstairs and make sure everyone's getting fed. What time are your parents arriving?"

"About eleven."

"I'll make sure Jones is on alert for them."

Oscar and Darius decided to take a walk through the grounds, primarily to get out of the way as teams of hairdressers and makeup people began to arrive. They walked side-by-side until they were out of the gardens and walking the huge lawns of the outer grounds. "It's not too late for me to spring you out of here you know," Darius joked. "What's on the other side of that wall?"

"Porenski's estate," Oscar replied, "and he's got laser wire all along it. We'd probably get shot."

"Thought he bought the Bonnington-Carter estate over the other side?"

"Yes, that too. He owns the land on both sides. He's just demolished the old mansion that was there. Think he's going to build a vast hi-tech monstrosity."

"You're surrounded by the Russian mafia," Darius said melodramatically. Oscar laughed.

"He's not a bad neighbour. His estates are so huge that I never even see him."

"That's not so bad then," Darius said. "So you're entirely sure about this marriage?" It was the same question that Oscar had asked when he'd been Darius' best man.

"As sure as I'll ever be."

"And what's that supposed to mean?" Darius demanded.

"She's not THE love of my life, but she's the best choice as a wife," Oscar said, rather cryptically. Darius was probably the only person he could admit that to.

"You mean she's not Elle, don't you?"

Oscar nodded.

"Elle's gone, married. You could hang around for the rest of your life hoping that she'll ditch the Ruskie. in the meantime, you'll have wasted your life waiting." Darius was surprisingly fierce.

"I know," Oscar muttered.

"Lucy's a good girl. She'll be a good wife. This… infatuation… you have with Elle, it's time to let it go, she's not for you."

Oscar sighed. He knew Darius was right. He was just glad that Elle had proved true to her word and never disclosed what had happened that night. He'd had a hell of a job convincing Darius not to bump her off. Even so, he was nervy about her, especially given who she'd married.

"Ok, but I don't need an escape plan, just so you know. By the way, has Arabella checked your speech?"

"Oh yes, mind you, she left in that funny story about how I dragged you out of that Paris brothel at the last minute, wearing just your underpants."

"No she didn't. Arabella's way too prim to let you tell that story. It places you in that brothel too remember."

"Oh yea. I'd better go back and re-write it then."

They both laughed as they headed up the path back to the house.

Inside the castle was a hive of activity. The staff, mostly employed by the caterers for the day, were setting up tables laden with champagne flutes and ice buckets in the grand hallway, where guests would be greeted by Lady Golding and Mr and Mrs Elliot. Ashley fluttered around with his clipboard, checking details and barking orders. From the reception hall, they'd be led out, through the blue drawing room, out into the grounds and through the sculpture garden to the Synagogue where the ushers would show them to their seats. The guests who had stayed at the castle the night before had already been briefed during breakfast as to timings and seating. Ashley was determined it would all run like clockwork. He'd even scolded the Prost-Winston children for running around during breakfast, calling them 'savages.'

As Ivan and Elle arrived, flanked by Nico and Roger, Elle was surprised to see the hallway all decked out with massive displays of cream and white roses. "This must've cost a fortune," she whispered to Ivan as they made their way through to the gardens, following the other guests.

He nodded, taking it all in.

They admired the sculptures dotted around the garden as they sipped their champagne, which for Elle would be the first of only two glasses she'd allow herself. Ivan made a bee-line for the shade of a large copper-beech, where he could observe quietly. Unfortunately it wasn't long before he was recognised by the Foreign Minister and was forced to make small talk.

At half-twelve, a man in black morning suit banged a small gong to get everyone's attention. "Ladies and gentlemen, your presence is requested in the synagogue please." Dutifully, everyone began to troop in.

They were seated several rows back from the front, in the middle of the row, with Roger and Nico put at the back, alongside the other security men who were guarding the various heads of state who were present. Ivan wasn't too worried, guessing correctly that a full security risk assessment and sweep would've been done before the Chancellor of Germany, the Sultans of Brunei and Saudi Arabia, and the American Secretary of State had arrived.

Elle looked around. She'd never seen inside the synagogue, wrongly assuming it was just an old family chapel. She'd expected dusty old pews and a bare stone floor. "This really is a show of wealth isn't it?" She whispered.

"Should we have one built in our house then?" Ivan asked, confused. he'd rather show his wealth in the house itself, rather than locked away and used rarely. Elle shook her head, amused.

"I'd rather spend our money on a fuck-off indoor pool," she whispered. He flashed his film-star smile.

"Agreed," he said, pleased that they were in agreement. He was also delighted that she'd called it 'our money' for a change, rather than 'his,' as she usually did. He looked around the room, watching as the great and good of society arrived to take their places. The thought struck him that he was now part of it, recognised by the people around him, some of whom smiled and waved as they spotted him.

Part of the British Establishment. Not bad for a poor boy from the slums of West Biryulevo, he thought.

His eyes were drawn to a display cabinet behind the canopy thing that had been set up at the front. Six eggs glistened with gilding and enamelling, lit up rather cleverly from above. In amongst all the artworks and artefacts surrounding them, the six, small eggs shone out. He wished he could get closer for a better look. He nudged Elle and pointed towards them.

"Oh, I thought they were meant to be a secret," she said. Ivan's head whipped round to face her.

"Secret? Are they what I think they are?"

"Yes. They normally live in the garden room. Oscar showed them to me on a tour once. The middle one, the purple one, that's my favourite."

"He's got six of them? How? They never come on the market." He was starting to get agitated. In his opinion, Fabergé eggs should be in Russian hands. They were part of the Russian heritage, examples of the great craftsmanship of the motherland.

"He told me that his grandfather had bought them off Lenin, when they were strapped for cash after the revolution," Elle told him. She could see he was becoming agitated. She placed her hand on his knee, which always calmed him down. "He won't sell them, there's no point in asking, and I think they're kept very secure here," she warned him.

"I'm not gonna steal them," Ivan hissed, "What do you take me for? I'm wondering if he'd sell them."

"I can tell you right now that he won't," she hissed in reply. She wondered why they were out on show, especially after she'd been asked to keep their existence secret from Ivan. She didn't know that it was Lady Golding who'd thought that they'd add to the opulence of the synagogue, and had forgotten to mention it to Oscar.

When all the seats were filled, Oscar and Darius appeared, striding down the aisle to take their places at the front, underneath the canopy. Oscar looked around the room, smiling to several people. He caught sight of Elle and Ivan, which made his heart lurch. "Forget her," whispered Darius. "And who put your pretty eggs out on display? There must be at least half a dozen people in here plotting how to nick them."

Oscar followed Darius' gaze. *Dammit*, he thought. "Must've been mother."

Seeing the two of them together made Elle's heart sink. She'd assumed that their 'friendship' had cooled after that terrible night, but watching their body language, seeing the way they leaned towards each other and how comfortable they were together, she was certain that nothing had changed. It was too late to warn Lucy, Elle realised, and a horrible sense of sadness washed over her.

"You look wonderful my darling girl," Said Lucy's father as she emerged from her room. Her hair was curled into soft waves, with the front pinned up around the diamond tiara, with the veil cascading over it and down to the floor. Her slender, lithe figure was wrapped in a form-fitted column dress, encrusted with tiny seed pearls and crystals. She looked every inch the perfect bride.

"It's time to assemble everyone outside the synagogue," said Ashley, checking his watch. "Five minutes to go." He stood watching as the bridesmaids and pageboys trooped past, straightening ties and tweaking sashes as they went.

Michael, Lucy's father, offered his arm and led her down the wide, sweeping staircase with Ashley holding onto her veil to make sure it didn't get trodden on.

"Are you certain?" Her father asked as they stood on the steps of the synagogue while Ashley marshalled the children into their positions before making sure that her veil was perfectly in place.

"Absolutely certain daddy," Lucy replied, almost overcome with the emotion of the last time her daddy would be looking after her.

Ashley spoke into his earpiece and the organist began to play Mendelssohn's Wedding March. As the sound filled the room, Lucy and her father began to walk down the aisle. Every head turned as they made their way to the ornately decorated chuppah to join Oscar and Darius.

Elle had never seen a Jewish wedding before, so struggled to follow proceedings. She didn't understand the significance of the betrothal with the wine, nor the Rabbi saying; "Behold, you are betrothed unto me with this ring, according to the law of Moses and Israel."

Ivan began to fidget during the reading of the marriage contract, which seemed to take forever, and when they disappeared into the vestry with Darius and Lucy's brother to witness the signing of the contract, Ivan wondered if it meant it was all over and they'd just crept out the back.

When they came back in for the seven blessings and the breaking of the glass, by Oscar stamping on it, Ivan whispered that it was probably the last time Oscar would ever be able to put his foot down again, which made Elle snigger. She was grateful to Ivan for lightening the heavy heart she had, watching her friend marry a man with such a dark secret.

To Oscar, the whole ceremony had felt surreal, as though it was happening to somebody else and he was just an observer. He'd said and done all the right things at the correct times, of course, even with the rising sense of panic he'd felt in his gut.

Lucy wondered if anyone else had ever felt as happy and filled with joy as she felt during the ceremony. Oscar had looked so handsome in his morning suit, with his lifelong friend by his side, that she was fit to burst.

As they made their way back down the aisle, Lucy couldn't help herself beaming. She stole a glance at Oscar, who seemed to have a rather fixed smile on his face, which she put down to nerves.

The photographs seemed to Oscar to take forever. The photographer had chosen the long borders as the main backdrop, with some out on the large lawns of the outer garden. He even wanted to take a load of snaps near the lake, which meant a bit of a trek.

After the guests had posed for the group shots, the ushers marshalled them all into the ballroom to get them seated ready for the wedding breakfast. An hour later, Oscar, Lucy and both sets of parents arrived back, with all the bridesmaids and pageboys in tow, looking rather hot and bothered.

"This is really gonna be a long day," Ivan grumbled as they waited for Lady Golding to stop yapping and take her seat so that the food could begin being served. He was starving hungry, given that it was already three o'clock and they hadn't eaten since breakfast.

The servers began to bring out the starter, meltingly soft scallops, cooked in butter and served with caviar and a tiny salad. It was gorgeous, and Elle wished that she wasn't so hungry, so that she could savour it slowly, rather than demolish it in two bites. Luckily the main course was served quickly, a rack of lamb with duchesse potatoes, fresh green beans and a cauliflower veloute. It was a spectacular meal, especially when the servers brought up the dessert, gold leaf-topped chocolate mousses with little tulles formed in the shape of the Golding coat of arms.

"Oscar sure knows how to organise a function," Ivan said, taking it all in. He cast an appraising eye around the ballroom, checking out the chandeliers and the tasteful gilded plasterwork and made a mental note to talk to the Allans about having something similar at Maytrees.

"Ladies and gentlemen, could I have your attention please?" Darius' voice boomed out. "As best man, it's my duty to make a speech. I'll make it pleasantly short, so as not to delay the smokers racing out into the garden too long." There was a titter. "The day I met Lord Oscar

Golding was the first of September nineteen eighty-eight. We were seven years old and had just been dropped off at St Dunstan's prep by our parents, which I'd found quite a traumatic experience. Oscar came up to me and told me to keep my chin up, assuring me that we would, in due course, formulate an escape plan.

We decided to make our getaway in the dead of night, by jumping over the wall. Now in reality, it was probably only about ten p.m., but at seven years old, with an eight o'clock lights out, it seemed very late.

What I discovered that night was that Oscar was indeed very good at escaping, managing to make it over without too much difficulty. Unfortunately, I didn't, being shorter and less... athletic... than he was. So there I was, scraping my knees trying to struggle over the wall, when we heard the voice of our housemaster in the darkness. Now Oscar could've kept quiet, or run away by himself, but he didn't. He stayed, clambering back over the wall to take his punishment alongside me. He became my best friend, and I've never been able to shake the old devil off ever since." He waited for the polite laughter to die down.

"Every scrape I got into, every madcap idea, every major event, Oscar has either instigated it or egged me on. He was behind my arrest in Bombay, the reason we got chased across Brazil, and is single-handedly responsible for having made my life a thousand times more fun, more interesting and more exciting than it would've ever been without him. My hope for Lucy is that he does the same for her, minus the 'getting arrested' bit of course, and together they can bring out the very best in each other. So please, everyone, raise your glasses to Lucy and Oscar, Lord and Lady Golding."

Applause rang out, filling the ballroom. "Who's he?" Ivan asked Elle.

"Darius Cavendish, Oscar's best friend. Works in the intelligence services." As soon as she'd said it, she regretted it.

"Your secret contact?" Ivan stated. "Figures."

Elle tried to listen to the rest of Darius' speech, but struggled to concentrate, acutely aware of Ivan's irritation at her revelation. A few moments later, Ivan leaned in and whispered; "He got me out from that kidnapping didn't he?"

Elle ignored him.

"Thought so," he said. She dug her elbows into his ribs to shut him up, before picking up her glass again for Darius' toast to all the parents.

When the speeches were all finished, a string quartet struck up and people began to stand up and mill around, chatting to old friends and visit the loos. After waiting in the queue, accompanied by Roger, for fifteen minutes, Elle was finally comfortable and able to mingle. Back out in the ballroom, she spotted that Ivan was chatting with someone, a woman, with long, brunette hair trailing down her back in curls. As she approached, the woman turned slightly so that Elle could see her face.

Penny. Bloody. Harrison.

She stopped in her tracks.

Ivan looked happy, animated as he spoke to her, Elle watched as she laughed at something he said. She looked impossibly glamorous in a bright, Mediterranean-blue chiffon dress which skimmed her tiny waist, showing off her tall, lithe figure.

Rather than interrupt them and have to stand next to Penny, feeling fat and dumpy, Elle scanned the room for anyone she knew. Darius was nearby, having just taken another glass of champagne from one of the servers. "Loved your speech," Elle said as she wandered up to him.

"Thank you. It was heavily edited by Arabella, so much so that it was really her speech. She wouldn't let me tell all the really funny stories about Osc." He paused. "So how have you been?"

"Blooming," Elle said, smiling at him. "Getting fatter each week."

"Yes, congratulations, Oscar did tell me that you were expecting. Wonderful news. I bet your husband's thrilled?"

"Very much so. He wants an enormous family. I think it's a Russian thing."

"Oh, I don't know, I think Oscar's hoping that Lucy fills this place up with small Goldings. He's hoping for a honeymoon baby. I'm still trying to convince Arabella that we've had enough time as just 'us' and we need to get cracking. She only wants two though."

"Lucy will be a wonderful mother," Elle said.

"Oh yes, I agree. She's such a warm, gentle person, perfect for Oscar. They met through you didn't they?" It was a subtle insult, but wasn't lost on Elle.

"Yes, they did. Well, I'd invited Lucy to the Law Awards, and Oscar was invited by our firm. We all shared a car, and, well, let's just say the rest is history." She smiled at Darius to disarm him.

"Very fortuitous, also very helpful in repairing his broken heart. Poor man was really suffering. It was lucky that Lucy came along." Darius was unemotional as he spoke, which only served to accentuate the meaning of his words. Elle shifted uncomfortably.

"I'd better get back to Ivan. Nice to see you again, especially under such happy circumstances." She slipped in a sly dig of her own before hurrying back over to Ivan. Roger, who'd heard the whole exchange, frowned slightly.

Ivan had been mildly perturbed when Penny had touched his arm, making him jump, just as Elle had disappeared to the loo. He'd not seen her since the night he'd kicked her out of his house to go and rescue Elle. It turned out that she was there as somebody's plus one, a much older gentleman who was a financier, and knew Oscar through work.

"I missed you," Penny said to him.

"Well, things move on," Ivan replied. "I'm a married man now." he paused. "I hope you're keeping well?"

She pulled a face. "A seventy-year old billionaire? Yeah, I'm doing alright I suppose."

"The pool of billionaires is rather small," Ivan said, which made her laugh.

"I should go to Silicon Valley really, plenty of them there."

"Bit younger too," said Ivan. She laughed again.

"Well yes, I must admit," she leaned in close and whispered in his ear, "nobody can fuck as hard as you can. Nobody."

He laughed. "You really are the devil in disguise. You know my wife is here with me today?"

Penny sniggered. "Says the man with eyes darker than midnight in Moscow. You can admit it, we had great sex together, didn't we?"

"We did. However, we won't again. My wife is far more a tiger than you, both in and out of the bedroom. I take my vows very seriously." He was starting to get alarmed and didn't want to give her any false hope, as she'd been enough of a pain to get rid of the previous time he'd seen her. He graced her with his film-star smile and spotted Elle making her way through the crowd. "And here she is, my beautiful wife." He stressed the word 'wife,' just in case Penny was too stupid to understand that he was committed.

"She's expecting?" Penny said as she followed his gaze. "That was quick."

"I have fast swimmers," Ivan boasted.

"Clearly," Penny purred, before turning and walking away, giving him a dismissive wave over her shoulder as she departed.

"Was that who I think it was?" Demanded Elle.

Ivan nodded. "Nobody of consequence. She's here with her boyfriend, a very elderly billionaire."

"Figures," said Elle. "An eighty-year old billionaire with a bad cough'd be right up her street," she added, rather bitchily.

"Maybe her acting career stalled?" Ivan said, smiling at her scowling face. He loved it when Elle got jealous. "She is getting older."

Lucy flitted from group to group, greeting everyone, agreeing that the speeches had been marvellous and the lunch had been divine. Darius' speech had actually bought a tear to her eye, so heartfelt and full of love and admiration for his best friend. Her father's speech had been wonderful too, making her smile with stories of her as a little girl and how delighted he was to welcome Oscar into the family.

"You ok, beautiful wife?" Oscar made her jump as he came up behind her, laying his hand on her shoulder. She softened into his touch.

"Wonderful, thank you, handsome husband," she replied, kissing him softly on the cheek. "I'm trying to savour the day as much as I can. It's just going so fast. The ceremony seemed as though it was over in a flash."

"Hmm," Oscar was non-committal. "It's almost six. Last time I looked at my watch it was five to two. Another hour and dinner will start being served. Have you managed to speak to everyone yet?"

"Almost. I'm working my way around the room. You?"

Oscar shook his head. "I got cornered by the Duchess of Tewksbury and couldn't get away for at least twenty minutes. My mother had to pretty much prise her off. She wanted to give me 'marriage advice,' which consisted of me mostly saying 'yes dear' to everything."

Lucy laughed. "She means well."

"Yes dear."

They were interrupted by one of the Prost-Winston boys running around, his arms outstretched, making airplane noises. Oscar grabbed him by the arm just in time to prevent him running into a server who was bearing a tray full of champagne glasses.

"Enough!" Oscar barked at him, before delivering him out to where his parents were smoking in the garden. By the time he was back under the care of Marina and Hugo, he was sullen, having been roundly told off.

Lucy spotted Elle and waved to catch her attention before pushing her way through the throngs of people to go and say hello. "You look amazing, really beautiful," Elle gushed as she kissed her cheek.

"A very beautiful bride," Ivan added when it was his turn to peck her. "Oscar is a very lucky man."

"Thank you," Lucy said, as she sat down at their table. Like Elle, she needed to sit for a moment. Her shoes were starting to hurt, and her dress weighed a ton.

"Lovely service," Elle said. "I didn't know that you were Jewish." Lucy nodded.

"Jewish family, we're not devout though, a bit like how Oscar is, it's more a tradition thing. I thought that the synagogue was beautiful though."

They were joined by Oscar, who flopped down gratefully onto the chair next to Lucy. "We were just complimenting Lucy on the wedding," said Elle. "Doesn't she look gorgeous?"

"Very," agreed Oscar, "now, does anyone need more drinks?" He asked, glancing at their empty glasses. He waved over a waiter.

"A soft drink for me please," Elle said.

Oscar ordered a glass of apple and elderflower fizz for Elle and took glasses of champagne for the rest of them. "Your cellars will be a bit depleted after this," Ivan said, sipping his drink. He deduced, correctly, that it was a vintage champagne.

"Have you seen how much is down there? We could throw parties like this every day for a year and not get through it all," Oscar said.

Ivan laughed. "I was most impressed with the synagogue. I had no idea it was as lavish as it is."

"Ah, that was mainly my great-grandfather's doing. He was far more devout than subsequent generations."

"Impressive," said Ivan, "although I couldn't help but admire the eggs. I had no idea you had a collection."

"Yes, my grandfather bought them. I gather Lenin needed some liquidity in a hurry. I have no idea who he stole them from. We don't normally have them out on show."

"That's a shame," said Ivan smoothly. "They deserve to be admired. You know that if you ever want to sell them..."

Oscar cut him off. "I'll never sell them. They're the centrepiece of the Golding collection. I'm always on the lookout for more, but sadly they never come onto the market these days."

"I know," said Ivan, "and if one ever did, you'd be fighting me for it. They should be in Russian hands, as they were when they were first created."

Oscar laughed and clapped Ivan on the back. "I'm not sure that any are still in Russia these days. The Tsar and Tsarinas should have been more careful with them."

"I agree," Ivan said. "But that doesn't preclude them being owned by the sons of the Motherland." He paused. "Would you mind if I took a closer look at them? Another time of course."

"Not at all. When we get back from honeymoon."

With that, Oscar and Lucy moved on to greet the Sultan of Brunei, who was seated at the next table, with his wife and eldest son, whom Oscar had gone to school with.

That night, as Ivan and Elle lay in bed talking about the festivities, he surprised her by stating; "I really, really want to own a Fabergé egg. I'd give it a beautiful room of its own in Maytrees."

Elle thought about it for a moment. "Why? It's just a pretty egg," she said, thinking of Darius' assessment of them.

"It's my heritage," Ivan said, "and my children's. They'll grow up not knowing the Motherland, being English, not Russian. It's important that they know and understand the Russian ways."

"Okay," Elle replied, "keep looking out for one. There's nothing stopping you taking them to Russia on holidays though, show them the Hermitage and stuff." She didn't really understand why Ivan would be bothered about such a thing, given that he'd run away from the place in terror.

"Hmm, maybe. Depends how safe it is."

He could hear Elle's breathing deepen. "I'm glad we had our wedding the way we did." He said quietly, not sure if she could hear him. He'd enjoyed the day, but couldn't have been bothered with all the people, the organisation that a wedding like that had required. By the end of it, both Lucy and Oscar had looked tired out from the endless small talk and smiling.

"Me too," she managed to mumble, just before she dropped off.

CHAPTER TEN

Lucy rubbed some sun-cream on Oscar's back as he lay dozing by the pool. She dabbed a bit more on her nose and settled herself down on the sun-lounger beside him to read her book. Her thoughts kept drifting back to the wedding. She smiled at the memory of their first dance, Oscar leading her across the floor to 'All of me,' her favourite song. He'd made her feel so elegant as they swept across the centre of the ballroom, marred only by the little Prost-Winston brat skidding past on his knees and Lady Golding dragging him away by his ear.

The party had carried on into the small hours, with snacks served at midnight out on the terrace. With the Rabbi long gone, everyone had been able to openly enjoy the buffet, including the sausages.

With so many people staying at the castle, the breakfast next morning had been almost as festive as the party the night before, and far more relaxed than it had been the previous morning, even though it had been 'all hands on deck' for the resident cooks, as they had no outside caterers to help.

The guests had cheered when Oscar and Lucy had appeared, probably thinking they'd spent their wedding night doing something other than drop into bed exhausted. They'd saved that for when they'd arrived at the villa that night.

Lucy smiled to herself at the conversation between Stella and Lady Golding at the breakfast table. They'd been talking about Ivan. Lady Golding herself had introduced her to him and Elle during the reception, and had stood chatting to Elle for quite a while.

"So, what did you think of the Russian chap?" Lady Golding had asked her, before nibbling on a croissant.

"Good-looking, I'd agree. Not my type though," Stella had said.

"Well, obviously," her mother teased. Stella laughed.

"The funniest bit was watching you come over all unnecessary around him. You're quite the cougar, mother."

"Am I?" She said. Lady Golding looked around the table. "What's a cougar?"

"I do believe it's an older lady who likes younger men in the bedroom," said an impossibly posh Dowager

Duchess in her cut-glass accent, which had made Minty Darlington laugh like a drain.

Lady Golding looked impish. "Hmm, well, guilty as charged," she said, making the whole table laugh. Oscar had laughed along with everyone else, enjoying seeing his mother so happy and also watching her and Stella get along so well. He told Lucy it had caused a huge rift in the family when Stella had come out, shortly after she'd met Paulina. Their mother had been particularly vile to both of them, as though they could choose who they fell in love with. Oscar had said that he admired Stella for sticking by her partner through all the pressure. He didn't blame her one bit for running off to Italy, and although he hadn't visited her out there, it sounded as though she and Paulina had made a good life for themselves.

He was a good, kind man, Lucy thought as she picked up the glass of fresh orange juice that the butler had brought out. It was icy cold and naturally sweet, just the tonic for clearing the system after so much excess. They'd arrived at the villa the previous evening, only to find that the staff had laid on another feast to keep the celebrations going. She'd eaten more in the past three days than she'd normally have in a week. She was certain that she'd stretched her stomach as it seemed as though she was still hungry. She glanced at her phone, it was only eleven, another two hours till lunch.

As she sat and debated whether or not to go down to the kitchen and grab a snack, Oscar woke up and stretched. "I put more lotion on you," Lucy told him. The sun was fierce, even before mid-day. Tuscany was having the mother of all heatwaves.

"Thank you," he said. He still felt sleepy. The combination of a couple of late nights and the heat had made him more tired than he'd been in a long time. He struggled onto his elbows to help him flip over onto his back, and noticed that a cold juice was on the table beside him, condensation dripping tantalisingly down the sides of the glass. He picked it up and chugged it down, before replacing the glass and picking up the suntan lotion. "Come here, let me put some more on your back." Obediently, Lucy shifted and sat perched on the edge of his lounger. Tenderly and carefully, he applied more cream, taking care to cover her skin completely. Somehow, he felt differently about her since the wedding. She'd given herself to him, become his to take care of. Even when they'd made love for the first time after the ceremony, it'd been different, more loving.

As he rubbed in the cream, Oscar wondered if he'd have felt the same if it had been Lucinda Rothschild, but quickly dismissed the idea. Lucy had beautiful, silky, honey-coloured skin and a tall, slender figure. He wondered if the act of getting wed had been the solution to getting Elle out of his system once and for all. he'd barely thought about her since the reception. Even then, Lucy had shone out next to her.

"Are you hungry?" Lucy asked him.

He shook his head. "No. We only had breakfast a couple of hours ago. Why? Are you peckish?"

She nodded. "A little. I'm not sure why. Maybe I've just got used to eating too much."

"I'll go see if there are any of those breakfast pastries left." Oscar stood up and strode towards the kitchen. As he stepped inside, his eyes took a moment to adjust to the dim light. He spotted a plate of croissants and pain au chocolat.

"Mr Oscar, you want something fresh?" The cook called out from the pantry.

"These are fine," he called back, before taking them out to a grateful Lucy, who scoffed them down surprisingly quickly. From then on, every time the butler brought them out drinks, there'd be biscuits, nachos, or a sandwich to accompany it. The amaretti were particularly good.

"Did you enjoy the wedding?" Lucy asked during dinner that night, sitting outside on the stone terrace. Oscar thought about it for a moment.

"More than I expected, really. I felt a bit strange during the ceremony, but apart from that, yes. Did you?"

"Loved every moment of it. I think our parents enjoyed it too. Your mother was in her element." She reached for another piece of bread.

"Yes, she loves a party. Let's just hope she carries on entertaining, especially after spending all that time and money redecorating the place." He reached for his glass and took a sip. Icy cold Chianti always tasted different in Tuscany; he couldn't work out why. It was the reason he rarely drank it back home.

"We should entertain more," Lucy said. "I love throwing parties. We can make use of all the space too. In fact it'd be a shame not to." It was her subtle way of making sure that she had plenty to do once she got back. Her days had been spent first on the redecoration, then as that had drawn to its conclusion, organising the wedding itself. When they returned from honeymoon, she'd be at a loose end.

"And very good at it you are too," said Oscar before leaning over to plant a soft kiss on her lips. She glowed with his compliment.

"Remember the first time you brought me here?" She flirted.

"When I lured you here under the guise of offering you a lift on my plane you mean?" He laughed. "I remember it well. Inviting you over to look at the frieze in the drawing room, hoping I'd get lucky." He smiled at the memory.

"I still don't think I've done more than barely glance at it," she replied. "I really must have a proper look tomorrow. In fact, I've never even had a proper tour of this place."

"Tomorrow," he promised. "At least you're intimately acquainted with Conniscliffe now. It's a fascinating place isn't it? Did mother show you the secret passages?"

"A couple of them. Quite useful for getting from the East Wing to the drawing room in a hurry," she said, "although I'm sure there's plenty I haven't seen."

"I'm still convinced there's places I've not discovered yet, and I'd like to think I covered every inch of that place when I was growing up. With this old place, my father almost took it back to its bones before rebuilding it, so I doubt if there are any bricked-up rooms or hidden attics."

"This is a beautiful old place," Lucy said. She gazed around the old stone terrace with its arched pillars and shuttered windows. The thought struck her that this was her life now, an existence of unimaginable luxury, staff, and almost unlimited wealth. She'd been brought up around money, but not on that scale. Watching Lady Golding spend had been an education. Her own mother had always been quite frugal in comparison. Mind you, her parents didn't own a bank.

"You're in a world of your own," said Oscar, leaning over to put his face in front of her. "What are you thinking?" it was a question he rarely asked, normally he wasn't in the least bit curious as to what thoughts might be passing through another person's head.

"Just, well, how different my life will be when we get back," she confessed.

"Well, yes, but you already knew that," Oscar pointed out. "The moment you agreed to become my wife, you knew you'd become Lady Golding, doyenne of Conniscliffe castle and this place." He waved his hand airily to denote the villa.

"I didn't really mean that," Lucy said quietly. Oscar tilted his head, questioning. "I just couldn't help notice how much your mother spent. Is that normal for your family?"

Oscar laughed. "Oh yes, she likes to spend. I didn't mind at all because it was all spent on Conniscliffe. I'd been meaning to get the redecoration done for years, but, well it wasn't a priority and there was always so many other things to take care of and not enough time."

"She spent upwards of twenty million. Didn't that bother you?" Lucy asked. They'd never really had the conversation about Oscar's net worth, but now, as his wife, she thought that she should know.

"Why would it bother me?" Oscar asked, slightly perplexed. "It's only money."

"But it's a lot… I take it you have plenty?"

"Oh I see, oh yes. I have a family trust, which I use, along with my salary for day-to-day expenses. Stella has one too, although she does also get dividends from her shareholding. I'm also the majority shareholder of Golding's Bank as well as its investment funds. Don't worry, mother could spend that every year and not make a dent."

Lucy stayed silent. She couldn't work out how much that all added up to. "Don't ever think that money equals power," Oscar said quietly. "When I was being instructed in the ways of the family firm, my father always used to tell me that money was just a confidence trick that the rich played on the poor. There is no scarcity of money, it's just created by people like me in the form of loans. We keep it scarce, so as to give value to the commodities that people want." He went on. "If I wanted to give you a billion pounds, say, I'd just make a loan, with say, a hundred pounds a year repayment plan. That way, you'd have the money you wanted, and I'd have power over you. It's why all the governments are in our pockets. If they don't do what we want, we up the repayments. He paused to close Lucy's jaw with his index finger after it dropped open. "So to answer your question, the truth is there is no figure. I mean, we could work out how much Conniscliffe is worth and how much my shareholding is worth, but there really is no figure for how much I have access to. Let's just say that we won't go short."

"I had no idea..." She murmured. Her mind was racing. Unlimited money was one thing, but power was something Lucy had never craved. She realised how little she knew Oscar. "This power... How do you use it?" She asked.

He shrugged. "Depends. I tend to stick mainly to business. My father financed the overthrow of communism in Russia by backing all the capitalists who became the oligarchs..."

"Ivan?" Lucy butted in.

"Yes. He financed Ivan's takeover of the telecoms sector. That was how Ivan started out. I financed some of his acquisitions since then, but not all of them. He's so cash-rich nowadays that he can pay for his own adventures."

"Wars?" Lucy asked quietly, unsure as to whether or not she wanted to hear the answer. Oscar shook his head.

"I leave that to the Rothschild lot. They still own all the central banks. Golding's is a commercial merchant bank. Don't get me wrong, we've done our share of political manipulation, but generally we do it through the corporations that we finance. How do you think China equipped itself for mass manufacturing? Or the Middle East paid for all its oil wells?"

"So what's the next thing?" She asked.

"Security. With the population expanding, fuel security, food security, and military security are big issues that need to be tackled." He really didn't want to spend the entire evening talking shop, as he had other, more fun activities on his mind. "So how about we retire to our chamber and continue our plans for world domination up there?" He teased.

"It's kind of sexy," she admitted, before standing up and throwing her linen napkin down on the table.

He followed her up the sweeping stone staircase, mesmerised by her swaying hips and long, lean legs, coloured golden by the sun and shown off perfectly by her short, fitted white dress. His only issue was that she was wearing roman-style sandals, flat, with laces around her ankles. He liked her in heels that stretched her calves and showed off her feet to their best advantage.

Their bedroom was a masterpiece of cool, pale shades of grey, white, and taupe, dominated by an enormous four-poster bed, which, legend had it, had once belonged to an Italian nobleman, who was famed for his Lothario-like conquests. Pale grey silk drapes hung from the carved mahogany posts, giving it a slightly ethereal appearance.

"What would you like to do tonight?" Lucy asked coquettishly. She loved Oscar's slightly kinky side and encouraged him to explore it. "You could tie me up."

"Strip, then put on some heels," Oscar barked, before looking around the room for something to tie her up with. He spotted the curtain tie-backs, which would be perfect. Taking the twisted silk ropes from their hooks, the grey silk curtains fell shut.

Lucy had fully expected him to tie her hands to the bedposts, but Oscar ordered her to clasp her hands behind her back. Deftly, he tied her wrists together. "Lay face-down on the bed," he ordered her, as he slipped out of his shorts and shirt, freeing his already impressive erection. He always got turned on seeing Lucy naked, except for heels. She'd chosen a pair of black Laboutins, which were his favourites. There was something about the red soles that sent him a little bit crazy.

With Lucy face-down, her bottom in the air, Oscar took his time worshipping the shoes. He liked to lick and suck on the heel as well as press his lips on the cool, glossy patent leather. Everything from the smell of the leather to the feel of the rigid heel flicked a switch in his mind, one that controlled his arousal. He could get turned on without the shoes, but they took it up to another level.

With Lucy in that position, it was easy to reach up and caress her sex. "Dirty little bitch, getting all wet like that," Oscar chastised her. He smacked her buttocks with his palm. She jumped, mainly due to the surprise.

"Yes, I'm a dirty whore," she said. "I need spanking. Hard."

His hand landed again on her buttock. He loved seeing her writhing. Parting her pussy lips, he could see her glistening skin. He wanted to lick it, to see what that would do to her. He'd never done it before, due to Darius' description of cunnilingus being like licking a raw chicken.

Taking a deep breath, Oscar leaned forward and ever-so-lightly touched the tip of his tongue on Lucy's clitoris. She jumped slightly, before relaxing, purring; "You dirty, disgusting boy."

He touched it again, pressing firmer this time, then he licked it. It was nothing like chicken. He pressed his thumb inside her and licked her again, feeling the effect as her wetness flooded his hand. "Oh my God," she cried out as he began to lick her repeatedly.

His cock was as hard as stone. Just tasting her arousal sent him into the stratosphere. He smacked her again. "Have you seen what you've done to my cock, dirty whore? What are you going to do about it?" He demanded. He shuffled up the bed to show her his rock-hard dick. Her head was turned awkwardly on the pillow, so he couldn't fuck her mouth.

"I'm sorry. I didn't mean it," she protested, secretly delighted to have broken his fear of going down on her, especially as he seemed to like it. He smacked her again.

"I'm gonna have to fuck you. Don't come. Got that dirty bitch?"

He positioned himself behind her, the tip of his cock poised to slam into her. Lucy held her breath, trying to calm down the intense sensations in her core which threatened to overwhelm her as soon as he pushed into her.

She wondered why he was waiting.

He smacked her again, then thrust into her, the sensations assaulting her all at once. She yelped as he powered into her again and again, over and over until she couldn't control the pleasure any longer. "I'm coming," she screamed.

He felt every ripple, every contractions as though it was his own. As she pulsed around him, he let go, shooting his load into her with a ferocity that even took him by surprise. Sweat dripped off him, onto her back as he slumped over her.

A few moments later, he untied her hands as he slipped out of her. They lay side-by-side, getting their breath back.

Lucy rolled towards him. "That was an unexpected treat," she said, planting a warm kiss on his shoulder. He turned towards her and grinned.

"I'm not sure what came over me. It was an irresistible urge," he told her. He didn't really understand it himself.

"Maybe because it's yours now," Lucy suggested. He planted a kiss on her lips.

"Maybe."

"It wasn't so bad was it?" She had to ask.

He shook his head. "It was nothing like licking a chicken."

She burst out laughing. "What? Was that what you thought... why?"

Oscar grabbed the pillow and hugged it. "That lying bastard Darius. He was always the first to try everything."

"Go on," she urged, trying to keep a straight face. She liked it when Oscar opened up.

"When we were around fourteen, he got this girlfriend. I think her name was Louise. Well, he claimed to have tried it with her, when he lost his virginity to her. Naturally, I wanted to know what it was like, so he made me lick a raw chicken, with the skin on, and said it was just like that. Of course, I got food poisoning and was ill for a week. It put me right off."

Lucy tried hard not to let her face crack, but she couldn't help it.

"It's not that funny," he huffed.

"Yeah, it is," she replied through her giggles.

"I must admit, I'm as dry as a bone after having my tongue out like that," he confessed, before picking up the phone and asking for a trolley to be left outside with some water and another bottle of cold Chianti. A few minutes later, there was a knock on the door to let him know it was there. He slipped on a robe and went out to get it.

"Is there anything to eat on there?" Lucy asked as he wheeled it in. He checked under a silver-domed cover.

"Sandwiches. You can't be hungry again?"

"Starving. I've worked up quite an appetite since dinner," Lucy told him. He set the plate beside her on the bed and chugged the water before pouring them each a glass of Chianti.

"To my beautiful wife," he said, raising his glass, "and may married life always be as good as this." They clinked glasses and drank, the icy cool wine slipping down easily in the heat of the evening.

Oscar slept better that night than usual, especially given the heat. One thing his father hadn't installed in the villa was air-conditioning, and he always found portable units too noisy, so they made do with open windows and a ceiling fan. He woke up to sunlight streaming through the chinks in the curtains. Lucy was still asleep beside him, her long blonde hair fanned out over her pillow and her honeyed limbs splayed out on the silky white sheets. He yawned and stretched, before glancing at the bedside clock to discover that they'd slept in until nine. He slid his feet out of bed and found a pair of swim shorts to pull on. He left her sleeping and went downstairs in search of coffee.

He was on his second latte when Lucy finally appeared. She'd already put on a bikini and had thrown a sheer dress over it. "Have you had breakfast yet?" She asked.

Oscar shook his head. "I was waiting for you. You were out cold," he said with an indulgent smile. "It's all laid out and ready," he nodded to the end of the terrace where tureens and plates of food were set on the tables.

A little later, he was settled on a sun lounger, dozing again after a large breakfast of bacon, eggs, and a selection of the wonderful Italian pastries. He could hear Lucy yapping on the phone to one of her friends, chatting about the wedding, thanking whoever it was for all the compliments. As he lay in the sun, Oscar decided that he liked married life.

CHAPTER ELEVEN

It was quite shocking seeing a big hole where the house at Maytrees used to be, Elle decided as Ivan and she donned hard hats and ventured over for a look on Saturday morning, several weeks after the wedding. The site was dry and dusty and full of diggers, which were busy gouging their basement and bunker out of the hillside. There'd been loads more meetings with the Allan brothers, with what seemed like thousands of decisions to make regarding layout. The meetings had now moved on to interiors and finishes, even though the house had yet to be built. She wondered how this vast hole full of dust was ever going to turn into their dream home.

"I'm thinking, keep the formal and kitchen gardens to the sides and rear of the property, along with the outdoor pool and tennis court, leaving the vista down the hill intact as it is," Christian said, pointing to the front of the hole. "We can make a start on those while the shell is being built as there'll be quite a lot of earthworks involved and we'll already have the machinery on site," he shouted above the noise of the dumper truck busily ferrying a load of earth past.

"Good idea. We'll go over the plans next time we meet, which, if I remember correctly, is Tuesday evening," Ivan said. Elle's heart sank at the thought of yet more meetings. At five months pregnant, she was finding it hard to keep her eyes open past nine o'clock in the evening.

They peered into the vast hole. "The wine cellar is over there, the bunker straight down here and the plant room on that side," said Christian, gesturing as they went. "We really want to get the concrete base poured before the weather turns. The actual walls will go up quite fast, as long as it stays dry."

"I'll pray for an Indian summer then," Elle said, before wandering over to gaze at the view. The trees, while not yet bearing the rich colours of autumn, had taken on the tired appearance of late summer, their leaves tattier, less fresh than they'd been at the start of the season. As she stood gazing, she spotted a clay being fired into the air. It was followed by a loud shot, which shattered it into tiny pieces. She wondered if it was Oscar who'd fired it.

As the shot rang out, she felt herself dragged to the ground, landing on Viktor, who quickly rolled his body to cover hers.

"Get off me," she spluttered. "It's only clay pigeons." She glanced over to see Ivan in a similar position, with Nico on top of him. "It's ok," she called out. "It's only Oscar having a shooting party."

Nico rolled off and stood up. "Nearly gave me a heart attack," he muttered, angry. "Why is he shooting?"

"They do it for fun. Watch," she said, pointing as another clay was launched, then shattered as a shot rang out.

"Where's the fun in that?" Nico said, sounding disgruntled. "They should be able to hit that easily. I could get that with just a handgun." He was immensely proud of his abilities with a gun. He helped Ivan up, who appeared quite shaken.

"They shoot quite often," Elle pointed out. "Haven't you heard them before?" Ivan shook his head.

"Maybe they've done it when I've not been down here," he said. "Either that, or it's not as loud on the other side."

She shrugged and wandered back to the hole, noticing that steel spikes were in place on the far end, ready for the base to be poured. It was genuinely quite exciting, she thought, as she brushed the dust off her shorts.

**

Lucy was in her element, hosting a weekend house party for twenty of their closest friends. It was important to her that both sets of friends met and mixed together well, and given that they all discovered connections to each other via schools or family, it was all going swimmingly well.

They'd arrived early Friday evening, along with Oscar, and had enjoyed a lavish formal dinner in the grand dining room. Lady Golding had helped plan the menu and the seating and had been in good form as she'd sat at the other head of the table, opposite Oscar.

It had turned out that Arabella, Darius' wife, knew Lucy's friends Giles and Polly quite well from the Polo club, which meant they had lots to chat about from the start. Minty had had a passing acquaintance with another of Lucy's pals from her badminton league, so greeted her enthusiastically and introduced her to the others.

They'd decided to shoot on Saturday morning, as the weather report predicted rain that afternoon, so hasty arrangements were made to bring the timing forward. Kyle didn't mind working on a Saturday morning, loading up the clays before launching them into the air. It also meant he got an extra forty pounds for his trouble, which he could add to the savings he'd started since arriving at Conniscliffe.

He watched the 'toffs' in action, with their expensive guns and upper-class accents. It amused him the way they all competed for what was essentially a pointless accolade. Being able to destroy lumps of clay wasn't, in his mind, a particularly useful skill.

The women in the group fascinated him, especially Lucy, who he thought was the most beautiful woman he'd ever seen. He loved it when she came down to the kitchen garden, where he was mostly based, asking questions as to what was ready and what would be available in the following few weeks. She always spoke to him as though he was a real person, he thought, not a scum-rat junkie, as most beautiful women had... in the past.

He needed to find out which perfume she wore, so he could buy some for Amber for her birthday in October. Things had been progressing well with her. She might not have been an ethereal beauty like Lucy, but she was pretty in a more solid, outdoorsy sort of way.

"Great job Kyle," Oscar called out as he strode over at the end of the shoot. "You got the hang of that straightaway."

"Thank you," Kyle replied. "It wasn't exactly difficult. It'll be more of a job clearing it all up on Monday." He cast his eyes across the great lawn, which was covered in fragments of clays. Some of the ones which had been missed, or only partially damaged, would bugger up the lawnmower blades if left on the ground.

"Did you go to your NA meeting this week?" Oscar asked, out of earshot of the others.

Kyle nodded. "Yes. You?"

"Yes, I went to the one in town." He paused. "Good work, keep going."

He strode back to the house for his coffee and cake, unsure as to why he cared so much about Kyle. All he knew was that he felt extraordinarily proud of the change in him. Within just a few months, he'd been transformed into a strapping young man, with a friendly manner, and a formidable work ethic. Fred was delighted with his progress.

Back at the castle, people had gathered in the morning room, where the cook had laid out pots of coffee and a selection of cakes. Oscar poured himself a cup and grabbed a couple of slices of cherry almond, which was his favourite, and went in search of Lucy. She was in the far corner, talking animatedly to her friend 'Kipper,' so-called because her mother had always served kippers for breakfast on their yacht, which various school friends had stayed on during the holidays.

"You need to tell him," Kipper had told Lucy.

"When I'm three months, I will," Lucy replied, "I don't want to get his hopes up, till I know it's safe." She'd calculated that the three month point would be the following week.

"Hey Luce, you want more coffee?" Oscar asked as he made his way over. She shook her head, before helping herself to a slice of the cake he'd piled up on his plate. "You'll get fat," he teased. Oscar had noticed that Lucy wasn't quite as thin as she used to be, but put it down to not having to diet herself into her wedding dress any longer. He wasn't the most observant of men.

"Tell him," hissed Kipper.

"Tell me what?" Oscar asked.

Lucy guided him out of the room, into the sitting room next door. He looked at her expectantly. "I wasn't going to say anything until after this weekend," she began.

His heart sunk. Naturally, he expected it to be something bad.

"We're having a baby," she told him, before holding her breath waiting for his reaction. A broad grin spread across his face.

"That's amazing news, why the secret?"

"I'm not three months gone until next week," she said. he did a rough mental calculation.

"You were pregnant when we got married?"

She nodded. "I didn't know though. I didn't find out until just recently. I wanted to wait until the risk of miscarriage had passed." She felt foolish for keeping it secret from him.

"Well, it's wonderful news. I think we should announce it now, to all our friends," he said, pulling her into a hug. "Does my mother know?"

"Yes. She was the one who advised me to wait before I told anyone."

"I see." A pang of pain pierced his gut. He'd been excluded from the initial excitement. He knew Ivan had known the moment their pregnancy had shown up on an early test. It seemed to Oscar that everyone had known about his impending child but him. He wondered if Lucy had been afraid of his reaction.

"Don't look like that," she said, smacking his arm. "I didn't want to get your hopes up until it was safe, that was all." She gazed into his eyes. "You are happy… aren't you?"

"I'm... delighted," he assured her. "Come on, let's announce it."

He led her into the morning room and rapped a teaspoon against a cup to get everyone's attention. "I have an announcement to make," he began. "My darling wife, Lucy and I are happy to tell you that we are expecting our first child together."

Applause and cheers filled the room. Lucy blushed a deep pink at being the centre of attention, with people congratulating her and kissing her cheeks.

Lady Golding stood in the corner of the room, pleased for them both. Babies were her favourite things in the world, and she couldn't wait to welcome her first grandchild. She should have been watching the way Oscar beamed with pride and happiness as his friends congratulated him. Instead, she was quietly observing Darius, who stood with a face like thunder, unable to bring himself to say anything at all to the happy couple. His wife hadn't noticed, being too busy chatting excitedly to Lucy. Lady Golding shivered, the chill of Darius' sociopathic stare sending her nerves into meltdown. He'd always hated Oscar going first, or blazing a trail, only happy when he did everything first. He'd been that way since they were children. Unfortunately, Oscar couldn't see it, blinded to Darius' foibles by their shared experiences and friendship.

Eventually, Oscar made his way over to Darius. Lady Golding watched the mask slip back on and Darius clap Oscar on the back. She also saw him whisper something in Oscar's ear, which had momentarily shocked Oscar, but he'd quickly recovered and carried on working his way around the room.

"Synagogue, one a.m.," Darius had whispered in Oscar's ear. A shiver ran through him. Another fix.

Lucy liked Darius a lot. She'd loved his best man's speech at their wedding and the way he and Oscar had stuck together all through both their schooldays and beyond. He sat next to her at dinner that night, listening to the reason she'd given up work in such a hurry. The Penfold case had been headline news, so he was familiar with it. He was also extremely sympathetic, murmuring platitudes all through desert, which was sticky toffee pudding.

**

At quarter-to-two the next morning, Ivan was awakened by the shrill ring of his bedside phone. Groggily, he picked it up. "Yes?" He slurred.

"We have Lucy Golding at the main gates, asking to be let in. She wants to see Elle," Roger said. He was on duty that night.

"Let her in," Ivan said.

"What's happened?" Elle asked. The phone had woken her up.

"Lucy's outside," Ivan said, switching on the bedside light, which made them both squint. He swung his legs out of bed and pulled on a robe, before throwing Elle's over to her to slip on. Together they padded down the stairs, to see Lucy throw herself in the front door the moment Roger opened it. Tear-stains streaked her cheeks, and her hair stuck to her head, as though it had not long been flattened by sleep. She was wearing just pyjamas and a pair of slippers.

"Are you alright?" Elle asked, alarmed. It was a bit of a daft question, considering.

"No. I'm gonna ruin him," she spat. "I caught him having sex. Pair of Judas bastards."

"Come, I'll make you a tea," Elle said. She wanted to shut Lucy up before Ivan found out what Elle suspected had happened.

"Having sex with who?" Ivan asked, his voice soft and silky smooth.

"Darius. A fucking bloke. Can you believe it? I couldn't believe what I was seeing."

Elle cringed. "Oscar?" Asked Ivan. "You are talking about Oscar?"

"Of course I am," Lucy said. "I'm gonna ruin him, take him for every sodding penny. Lying, cheating bastard." Tears started running down her face again. Elle pulled her into a hug.

"Come on, let's get you a cup of tea." She looked over Lucy's shoulder to see Ivan staring at her, realisation had dawned.

Lucy's hands shook as she picked up the mug and took a sip. The three of them were sitting around the huge granite-topped island in the kitchen. "I feel such a fool," Lucy sobbed. "I mean, how come I didn't know? Didn't realise he was gay?"

"I don't think you can beat yourself up over something that was deliberately concealed from you," Ivan said, looking pointedly at Elle. She gave him a rather fierce hard stare back, willing him to keep quiet about her own experience. She felt wretched enough for not being truthful to Lucy from the start. Elle handed her another tissue. Neither of them noticed Ivan slide his phone out of the pocket of his robe and, hidden by the lip of the island, he pressed 'record.'

"So what exactly happened?" Ivan asked.

Lucy took another sip of tea. "He got out of bed about one, maybe just before. I was just dozing really, so he didn't realise I woke up. I didn't think much of it, figured he was getting a drink or going to the loo, but then I heard the door to the kitchen slam."

"It has been quite windy tonight," Elle said.

"I looked out of the bedroom window and saw him head down to the synagogue. Well, I wasn't sure if it was

Oscar or not, but I pulled on my pyjamas and followed him."

"Why did you follow him?" Ivan asked. Lucy's face crumpled again.

"I told him I was pregnant today. I thought he might be upset about it, that he'd gone to pray or something. I wanted to reassure him."

"You're pregnant too? That's wonderful news," Elle said.

"Oscar seemed OK with it too," Lucy went on, "but as the evening wore on, he seemed nervous, jumpy almost. He kept asking if I was tired, suggesting I go to bed early. Anyway, I followed him; I was about ten minutes behind him." She blew her nose again. "I crept up to the doorway, but couldn't see anything, so I slipped in quietly and crept through the lobby bit. They were on the altar."

"What do you mean 'on the altar'?" Asked Ivan. Elle shot him her 'be quiet' stare.

"Oscar was bent over the altar, Darius was fucking him from behind," Lucy stated simply. "Darius was calling him a slut, whore, that kind of thing. It was beyond gross." Ivan's eyebrows shot up.

"Do they know you saw them?" Elle asked.

"Oh God, yeah. I screamed the place down. You never saw that little fat troll Darius move so fast. I told them I'd tell the world, ruin them both."

"That wasn't wise." Elle said. "Darius is pretty powerful."

"So is Oscar," Lucy said. "They've both got plenty to lose. They should have thought about that before they did what they did."

"So you left," Ivan said, ignoring Elle. "Do they know you're here?"

Lucy shook her head. "I told them I was going back to London to stay at my brother's, well, my old house. Oscar did try and stop me, but I outran him and got to my car before he could grab me. I didn't want to hear his pathetic excuses. I'm sick of being taken for a fool."

Oscar was sitting on his bed, his head in his hands, cursing himself for being such a weak, stupid idiot. When he heard a soft knock on his bedroom door, his stomach lurched. He wondered if it was Lucy, coming back to talk things over, accept his apology and his promise that it would never happen again. This time he'd mean it.

"Come in," he called out. The door opened and in walked Darius. "What do you want?" Oscar demanded.

"Bad news. She's at Porenski's place. I'm tracking her phone. She didn't go up to Chelsea after all. That means he probably knows by now." He paused. "We're in deep shit, Osc."

"You think I don't know?" Oscar said, scrubbing at his face.

"I did tell you to dope her, like I do with Bella, especially after the last time," Darius said. "Thing is, Lucy isn't gonna disappear quietly. You need to think about that, what you've got to lose here, especially if Porenski's involved."

Oscar closed his eyes in despair. Even if the board would overlook his sexual misdemeanours, every deal, every investment he'd made with Ivan would come under intense scrutiny. He thought about the Conde Nast money he'd funnelled secretly through Switzerland and the massive investment he'd made in the mining company. He'd left himself wide open to claims that he'd been blackmailed. He knew he'd lose his position at the bank, possibly triggering a massive crisis. "What do you suggest?" He asked.

"Let me clean this mess up. No arguments this time, there's too much at stake." Darius stared at him with his cold, dark eyes. Oscar knew exactly what he meant.

"She's pregnant with my child. I can't," he said quietly. "I just can't sanction that." Darius stayed silent. He wasn't asking for Oscar's permission. He already had operatives making their way down to Sussex. He'd already ordered the kidnap of Sophie Penfold.

"You're going to need to think about it logically," Darius told him. "Get some sleep and give it some thought. We'll talk in the morning." With that, he left.

Oscar paced around the remainder of the night. At five, he went into his mother's apartment. She was fast asleep. He shook her arm. "Mum, wake up, please." She woke with a start. As soon as she saw Oscar's face, she knew something was terribly wrong and could hazard a guess at what it was.

"Not again?" She asked him. He nodded.

"I'm sorry."

"And it was such a happy evening," she said. Her heart broke for him. She held out her arms. He lay down beside her. She began to stroke his hair, like she used to when he was a boy.

"I think Darius is going to hurt her," he said quietly. "She's gone to Elle and Ivan's place. Darius is freaking out."

"Maybe Elle can convince her to keep quiet too," his mother soothed. "Lucy's a gentle soul and she loves you very deeply. Give her a chance. I'll talk to Elle as well, see how the land lies. At least at their place, Lucy hasn't shouted it around London."

"Hmm," murmured Oscar. He wanted to believe she could smooth it all out.

**

Lucy fell asleep on the sofa in the kitchen at about five in the morning, overwhelmed by the drama of the night. Elle placed a throw over her and followed Ivan up to bed. They were both exhausted, but he was too wired to sleep.

"That was what he did to you, wasn't it?" Ivan asked the moment their bedroom door was closed. Tania lifted her head off the bed for a moment, annoyed at being woken up. "It's the hold you have over them, isn't it?" He demanded. Elle nodded, sad that the secret was out. "Then why the fuck did you let her marry him? You must've known he batted for the home team."

"He told me it was a one-off, that he'd never do it again. I believed him, but couldn't have gone back to him," she said quietly. She really didn't want to discuss it with Lucy in the house, just in case they were overheard. She pushed Bella into the middle of the bed and squeezed onto the edge. Her eyes were stinging with the lack of sleep.

She woke up at eight, late for her, but still early considering she'd only had a few hours. She padded downstairs, ready to counsel Lucy to stay silent and accept a large payoff in return for her loyalty. As she wandered into the kitchen, she saw immediately that Lucy was gone. The blanket was neatly folded and placed on the sofa with a note on top. 'Have gone back to London. Thanks for listening last night. Much love, Lucy'.

Elle sighed and threw the note onto the island. She filled the kettle and set it to boil. As she waited, she pulled her phone from her bag and called Lucy's number. It went straight to voicemail. She cursed and picked up the house phone. "Hi Roger, what time did Lucy leave?" She asked.

"Six fifty-one," he replied. "Is everything alright?"

"Yes fine," she said, before replacing the receiver.

CHAPTER TWELVE

Lucy didn't even make it out of Tuppence Lane, the single-track road between Ivan's house and the main 'A' road, which would have led her through Derwent and towards London. She'd seen the Nissan four-by-four as soon as she rounded the bend in her Mini convertible. She slowed down as a stressed-looking woman flagged her down. "We've broken down," she said, "and my phone battery is flat. I don't suppose you have a mobile I could use?"

It wasn't the first time that Lucy's innate kindness had been used against her. She leaned over to fumble in her bag for her phone. She certainly didn't see the woman whip out the hypodermic syringe that she had behind her back. In fact, the first she realised anything was wrong was when she felt it plunge into her arm. "Hey!" She managed to yell before the world went black.

It took no more than a minute to bundle her into the boot of the Nissan. There was no CCTV and nobody watching, the operatives had made sure of that. The woman shook out her long, blonde hair and sat in the driver's seat of the Mini. After one last look around to make sure that nobody was about, she set off after the Nissan. Her job was to make sure that the cameras in London caught sight of a blonde-haired woman driving the car. Easy.

Lucy was taken to a safe house in Streatham, South London, where Sophie Penfold, also drugged, was being held after being taken from her home in the early hours. Both women were placed side-by-side on the floor of what should have been the living room, on plastic sheets. "Ok, we need to get plenty of DNA transfer," said the driver of the Nissan, a nondescript, brown-haired man who blended into almost any setting and had been recruited for his psychopathic disorder. Two operatives were already there, having been the ones tasked with getting Mrs Penfold. Together, they staged a mock-fight between the two women, scraping Lucy's fingernails across Sophie's face, adding tufts of Sophie's hair to Lucy's clothes. They then carefully wrapped Mrs Penfold's hands around a large kitchen knife so there'd be plenty of prints. Mr Nondescript wondered vaguely why such a pretty woman needed to be 'removed' in that way. He told himself it wasn't his job to question, just to carry out orders as cleanly and clinically as possible.

"Right, I think that's it," Mr Nondescript said. "I've just been told the scene is to be the killer's house, as though Mrs Golding went there. They carefully carried both women into the back of a van, which had replaced the Nissan in the garage of the house.

Lucy's Mini had just parked in the driveway of the Penfold residence when the van pulled up outside. Two large rugs were carried in, while the blonde driver hopped into the back of the van. With both women out cold, they were held in position while the operatives used Mrs Penfold like a puppet to drive the knife directly into Lucy's heart. She never felt a thing. They let her fall as blood spurted out, giving the blood spray a natural effect. She lay crumpled on the floor, her slender, honey-coloured limbs splayed out across what was formerly a cream carpet.

When it was over, another shot was given to Mrs Penfold, which would bring her round from her slumber in around twenty minutes. No trace of anything would be found in either of their bodies. They checked the scene and took off their plastic coveralls before they left. It was still only half-nine. Not bad going for such a sophisticated hit.

By ten o'clock, Sophie Penfold was staring at the scene of carnage in her lounge, wondering what on Earth had happened. Her heart started pounding as she stared at the woman laying dead on the floor in front of her. She couldn't recall her arriving at all. She glanced at the bottle of pills on the side table, prescribed for her by her GP and wondered if they'd made her black out. She turned her attention back to the body on the floor. It looked like Anthony's solicitor, the woman who'd given him access. Noticing the knife in her hand, she ran screaming from the house, covered in Lucy's blood, causing an elderly lady out on the street to faint at the sight of her. By five past ten, there were police swarming into the area. Confused and broken, Sophie Penfold had given herself up.

**

"Lucy had to go into town, said there'd been an emergency. One of her friends, I think," Oscar had told everyone at breakfast. They seemed to accept that, although Kipper asked a couple of times which friend it was, and what the emergency could be. "I don't know," Oscar said. "I was asleep." He forced down some eggs on toast, even though the last thing he wanted to do was eat.

"Oscar, can I have a word," his mother popped her head round the door. He jumped up, avoiding Darius' stare and went out into the corridor. "I just phoned Elle. Lucy left there before seven this morning. Apparently, she left a note saying she was heading back to London. Her phone's off though." Lady Golding was genuinely concerned. "Elle agreed that Lucy needed to show restraint, talk it through, maybe taken a payoff rather than exercise the nuclear option."

"Does Ivan know what happened?" He asked.

She nodded. "Lucy told him."

"Shit!" He spat. "Ok. Thank you."

He headed back into the dining room and poured another coffee.

Darius' phone buzzed in his pocket. He excused himself and went to the loo. Alone, he opened the text and read it. *Done* was all it said. He deleted the text and went back out, pleased with himself. It had been a complex plan, cobbled together in a hurry while Oscar had been crying to his mother. It had been an enormous stroke of luck that Lucy had left the Russian's place as early as she had.

He finished his bacon and eggs, then announced that they'd hit the road, knowing that it wouldn't be long before the shit hit the fan. The others followed his lead and began to get bags ready and say their goodbyes to Lady Golding and Oscar.

"Do say thank you to Lucy for me, when she gets back," Kipper said. "Tell her I hope everything's alright."

"Will do," Oscar replied, pecking her cheek. He wanted everybody gone so that he could keep trying Lucy's phone. It was still going straight to answerphone. "Where the hell is she?" He implored his mother.

Approximately half an hour after everyone had left, the police arrived.

Oscar felt as though it was the worst day of his life from that moment on. "Are you sure it's her?" He'd demanded as the policemen sat in the drawing room, bearing their sad faces, the ones they used to convey bad news.

"Yes, we're sure. She had her bag with her driving licence and credit cards in. Her car was parked on the drive outside. We've located her brother who has agreed to identify the body," PC Wilmot explained. "The suspect has already identified the deceased as the lawyer who gave her ex-husband access to murder their children," she told him.

"I don't understand why she went there," Oscar said.

"Talk me through last night," PC Wilmot said, pulling out her notebook.

"We had a party here, about twenty people. We announced that Lucy was expecting our first child. It was a happy night," Oscar said. "Although we had an argument at around half-one and she stormed out."

"What did you argue about?" The policewoman asked.

"Nothing really, stupid," Oscar said. "She went over to our friend Elle's house, just down Tuppence lane. Elle said to Mother this morning that Lucy had left before seven, leaving a note saying she was heading up to London, but nothing more. Her phone was off," he added.

"How does this Elle know she left before seven?" The PC asked, wrinkling her nose.

"They have security guards. I suppose one of them must have let her out of the gates," Oscar said. He scrubbed at his face. "This can't be happening. It's got to be a mistake."

They were interrupted by a visibly shaken Jones, who'd been listening outside, bearing a trolley of tea cups and a teapot.

Lady Golding was as white as a sheet as she stood up to pour, her hands shaking as she tried to lift the teapot. "Let me do that ma'am," PC Wilmot said, taking the pot from her. Lady Golding flopped back down onto the sofa, her usual ramrod back melted into jelly.

"That poor, poor girl," she said. "She came here to escape the fallout from that case. Why on Earth did she visit that woman?"

"The press went crazy, as you're probably aware," Oscar clarified. "That was why Lucy stayed here while it was all going on. She said she felt safer here."

"Did she think her life was in danger then?" Asked the other policewoman.

"She thought the Penfold woman was unhinged," Lady Golding interjected. "It's why I don't understand why she went to see her."

"We're going to need to establish a timeline and witnesses," PC Wilmot said. "It can wait, we don't need to do it now."

"I can give you a list of everyone that was here. We were all here all night, and I saw everyone at breakfast," Oscar said. "I didn't admit we'd had a row though. I told them Lucy had a call from a friend and had been called up to London for an emergency." He paused. "It was a bit embarrassing."

"I understand," PC Wilmot said, sympathy evident in her voice. She hated having to tell people that their loved ones had died. It was surprising how often it happened after an argument or fight.

**

Elle and Ivan were wandering through the woods with the girls when Elle's phone rang. She didn't normally take it out with her, but she was waiting for news from Lucy, so had it in her pocket. She pulled it out and glanced at the screen. "Hi, Oscar," she said. Ivan frowned.

"The police are on their way over to see you," Oscar said. "I have some terrible news. Lucy went up to London to see that Penfold woman, who stabbed her."

"Oh my God," Elle exclaimed, "Is she alright?" Her spine prickled.

Oscar's voice cracked as he told her; "No, I'm sorry, she's not. She was murdered."

A cold shower drenched Elle's nerves. "Oh Oscar," she said softly, "I'm so sorry." She noticed Ivan staring at her intently as tears began to roll down her cheeks.

"The police will tell you more... I just... can't. One thing though, I said Lucy and I had a row, that she stormed out and came to you. I didn't tell them why we rowed."

"I understand," Elle said.

"I don't know what to do," Oscar said, his voice cracking. "I'm hoping against hope that it's all a mistake, that it was someone else."

"They're sure?" Elle asked.

"Yes."

They were interrupted by Nico jogging down the path, a perplexed expression on his face. "The police are here. They won't say why," he said. Police showing up unexpectedly was generally cause for alarm in his book. He had a natural distrust for them.

"They're here. I'll call you later," Elle said. She turned to Nico. "Would you show them into the lounge please?"

As they walked back, she told Ivan what she knew, and that he wasn't to say what the row between Oscar and Lucy had been about. His only comment on the news that Lucy was dead had been; "How convenient."

PC Wilmot gazed around the sumptuous living room as she waited for the house inhabitants to return from their walk. Their security guy had asked if they wanted a drink in his heavy, Russian accent, which had made it sound far more sinister than it needed to be. She glanced at the obviously expensive furnishings and deduced that she was in the wrong job. "This is quite some place, even nicer than that castle," her partner,

Juliet, whispered, just before Ivan and Elle walked in, followed by two rather grubby spaniels.

"Have you spoken to Oscar Golding this morning?" PC Wilmot asked, after introductions were made.

"Just now, I'm sorry, we're both a bit in shock," Elle said. "Are you certain it's Lucy?" The policewomen both nodded. Elle tried to pull herself together. She grasped Ivan's hand.

"We are. I'm sorry. Now, her husband says she came here last night after storming off. Can you tell me what time she arrived and how did she seem?"

"It was quarter to two. Roger, one of our security guards, phoned up to tell us she was at the gates. There'll be a log of that, and the time she left."

"And how did she seem?"

"Angry, upset. She said she'd had a row with Oscar, she wouldn't say what it was about," Elle said. "We had a cup of tea, and she fell asleep on the sofa out in the kitchen. I covered her with a blanket, and we went up to bed. When I woke up, she'd gone. The blanket was folded up and placed on the sofa, with a note on top, saying she'd gone up to London."

"Do you still have it?" PC Wilmot asked.

"It's on the kitchen island," Elle said. Ivan jumped up to get it, asking if anyone wanted a coffee.

"Did she say anything about going to see Mrs Penfold?" Juliet asked. Elle shook her head.

"Not a word. To be honest, it's surprising that she did. The case affected her very badly, she pretty much ran away to Conniscliffe after those children were murdered. I know that she really struggled with the part she'd played in it, but her colleagues would know more about that than I do."

"Was she depressed?" PC Wilmot asked.

Elle shook her head. "I don't think so. I don't know, but she told us last night that she was pregnant."

Roger came in, having been woken by Ivan. "I was on duty last night," he told the coppers. "She arrived at one-forty-five a.m., and left at six-fifty-one in a blue Mini convertible."

"Was anyone else around? Any strange cars?"

"Not that I heard or saw, until a load of cars came past just before ten, from the castle I think. They have to come up Tuppence lane to get to the A road." He paused. "We have CCTV footage of her arriving and departing. I can email it to you if you give me the address."

"Great, thank you," Juliet said, ripping a page from her notebook to scribble down down her email. She handed it to Roger, who left, promising to do it straightaway. Nico followed him out.

"So you have private security here?" She asked Ivan.

"Naturally," He replied. "We take our safety and security very seriously."

"I would too, if I lived in somewhere like this," Juliet said, rather insensitively. They stood up to leave. "If you think of anything else, please do contact me." She held out her card to Ivan, who took it without a word.

When they left, he was silent until they were sure they were alone. "I bet she was bumped off by that friend of Oscar's."

"I can't see how," Elle said, "I mean, it was too quick, too slick. They'd never have had time to get it all organised. I think it was how it appeared, that she went to see that mad woman, who flipped out, maybe if she found out Lucy was pregnant, and stabbed her."

"Hmm." Ivan wasn't convinced. "We need to up our security. I have a bad feeling about this. I saw how quickly Oscar managed to get Dascha and Vlad assassinated. The British intelligence services don't mess about." He was worried that Lucy had just painted a large target on their backs.

"Now you're just getting paranoid," Elle pointed out. "Anyway, I'm gonna call Oscar and tell him what we told the cops."

She sat outside on the terrace to call him, relaying the conversation she'd had. He told her that he'd just come off the phone to Lucy's parents, who were on holiday at their villa. They were understandably devastated. Lucy had been the light of their lives. Her mother had been hysterical with grief. He'd also had the news that her poor brother had identified her body and was being consoled in the local police station.

"Was it Darius that did this?" Elle asked him.

"I don't know. I don't see how," Oscar said. "I just don't get why she went to see that woman."

"Neither do I," Elle agreed.

"So..." He paused, "Ivan knows?"

"Yes, he knows. Lucy told him."

"Damn. Has he figured out the same thing happened with you?"

"Yes. He's not stupid. He also figured out it was why you and Darius were both so keen to help me, keep me on side."

"Shit."

"I'll keep him quiet, don't worry. It won't get out," Elle said quietly. "Ivan has as much reason to keep quiet as you, the amount of money you've laundered for him in the past. I'll remind him of that."

"I appreciate that," Oscar said, hoping that Darius would see things the same way. He hadn't been able to face talking to him, instead calling Arabella and telling her the news. She promised to ring all the others for him, to save him having to tell the story over and over.

While Elle was outside on the phone, Ivan carefully transferred the recording he'd made onto a USB stick, which he placed at the back of the safe. He also called Kristov and booked some more bodyguards to arrive at his office the following day. "Are you under threat?" Kristov asked.

"I'm not sure. Maybe, possibly Elle as well. Her friend was murdered this morning."

"I saw on the news, Lady Golding was it? Though she was stabbed by a nutter?"

"I'm not certain all is what it seems," Ivan said. "It's why I want more security."

After the call to Elle, Oscar wandered down the corridor towards the kitchen to grab a bottle of water. As he passed the drawing room, he heard his mother crying. It stopped him in his tracks. His mother never cried. As he listened to her sobs, he closed his eyes and drew in a deep breath. He wondered if he'd ever forgive himself for the terrible event which had led to Lucy's death.

He turned around and retraced his steps back to the garden room, past the collection of eggs, now back in their rightful place, and out through the French doors into the gardens. He needed to collect his thoughts. He was drawn, as he always was in times of crisis, to the White garden, where he could sit quietly and think more clearly. He wandered around the flower beds for a few minutes, checking out the late summer daisies that dominated at that time of year, before settling himself down on the Wisteria bench, where he allowed himself to cry.

Big, fat tears rolled down his face as he thought of Lucy, with her gentle, fun nature. He allowed himself to imagine how their child would have been, visualising a tiny, fair-haired boy who would have raced around the gardens and ridden his toy car along the corridors, just as he had done.

He remembered their honeymoon, how happy they'd been, how he'd been convinced that he'd married the right woman. More tears fell as he remembered her in her wedding dress, bursting with happiness as they'd danced together in the ballroom.

All gone.

"I heard man. I'm so sorry." he glanced up to see Kyle standing in front of him holding a trowel. He hadn't even heard him approach. Kyle sat himself down on the bench next to Oscar without waiting to be asked.

"She was always too good for me," Oscar told him. "I'm just a junkie at heart."

"Most people are really," said Kyle. "When I was in prison, my therapist said that everyone masks their pain somehow. Some people smoke, some drink, some eat, and some stuff Charlie up their nose or H into their veins. Whatever it is, we all do something." He patted Oscar's hand rather awkwardly.

"Lucy didn't deserve what was done to her," he said, sniffing loudly.

"No, she didn't," Kyle agreed. "But then the good ones never do. Only the evil bastards ever seem to get away with stuff, good people pay the price." He stood up, unsure as to what to do. "If you ever need to talk, I'm, you know, here. For the record, I think you did deserve her. You're a decent man, you know, after what you did for me."

"Thank you, but I assure you, I'm just a no-good addict." Oscar wished he could tell Kyle the truth, but he knew that if he unburdened himself, he'd only burden Kyle, and he didn't want anyone else suffering any more than they needed to.

Kyle stood up, anxious not to outstay his welcome. "I'll be around if you need me. Stay strong." With that, he hurried back to the kitchen garden to get on with harvesting the beans.

Oscar watched him go, glad to have some solitude, especially since Kyle's presence at the estate was mainly down to his own feelings of guilt at the way he treated Elle. Kyle was the embodiment of his need to atone for his own weaknesses, ones which both Elle and Lucy had paid a heavy price for. He made a decision then and there to cut Darius adrift, both as a friend as well as a henchman. In the future, he would fight his own battles.

His thoughts were interrupted by the police calling to tell him that Sophie Penfold had admitted killing Lucy Golding, claiming that she must've blacked out while doing it. She'd been sent to a secure mental institution to be assessed.

CHAPTER THIRTEEN

Two operatives dug for hours to create a hole underneath the wall of Ivan's estate big enough to wriggle through. they'd cursed the iron-hard ground which had been baked solid by the late summer sun. Alerted by Darius to the presence of laser wire along the top, they'd correctly worked out that the only way in was to go under.

Both dressed in black, they kept in the shadows, working out where the cameras were pointed. Their target was the magnificent silver Bentley parked to the side of the house, in front of the bank of garages. Silently, they crept along the wall until it was just six feet in front. One would keep lookout, while the other rolled under the car to do the business that they'd come for. It wasn't the first time they'd carried out such an operation.

"Camera above second window," whispered Luke. "It's not trained on the car though." He stayed by the wall, while his partner, Mike, rolled neatly under the Bentley.

Silence. Nobody came out.

Mike positioned himself under where the driver's seat would be. He pulled out a tiny hand-cranked drill and carefully made a hole into the car above, hidden underneath the seat. With practiced ease, he attached the cassette-shaped device to the bottom of the car, first feeding its little hose through into the interior. It was so small and so discreet, not one police examination had ever discovered one, especially as it was well-disguised to look like part of the car.

Inside the device was two cartridges of gas. The first one, primed to start pumping its contents into the car at fifty miles an hour, thanks to a motion sensor embedded in it, would make the inhabitants euphoric, happy, and reckless. When the car hit eighty, the second chamber would be emptied, a high-tech derivative of Zyklon B, the gas that had been used during the holocaust. The new version left no trace, either in the car, or the bodies of those it killed at high speed. It was one of their most effective tools.

Happy that it was securely attached, Mike rolled back out and slithered back to the wall. Within a few moments, he and Luke were back out and filling in the hole they'd dug. Viktor, who was on duty that night, never saw a thing.

Elle woke early. She'd had a terrible night, laying in bed going over and over the events of the previous day in her mind, wondering if there was anything she could've said or done to stop Lucy leaving and going where she went. She was almost certain that Lucy hadn't mentioned anything about going to see that Penfold woman. It didn't stop her from running their conversation through her mind repeatedly until she'd dropped off from sheer exhaustion. She glanced at the clock, it was only half-five. She turned her head to see Bella laying beside her, nestled against Ivan's body, his arm around her, making an extremely comfortable dog cradle. She suspected that Tania might be in a similar position on the other side of him, judging by the snores emanating from that direction. She reached over to give Bella's ear a little rub, prompting her to give a contented sigh.

Ivan was out cold, his face relaxed and boyish as it always was when he was asleep. Elle took a moment to admire his masculine beauty. He had sexy weekend stubble, which simply served to make him more handsome, if that was at all possible. His soft, full lips were parted allowing a glimpse of his white, perfect teeth.

Elle smiled at him before slipping her feet out of bed and padding silently across the expanse of cream carpet to their bathroom, where she switched on the powerful shower and stood underneath, lathering herself up. She jumped as Ivan appeared beside the glass, her eyes dropping to his impressive morning erection. "Well, good morning to you too," she purred.

"Can I scrub your back?" He asked, his erection twitching in her direction. He stepped into the shower and stood behind her. She turned around to face him, a sexy smirk on her face.

"You can do more than that." She watched as he picked up the body wash and squeezed some into his hands. As he swept the lather over her skin, he set nerve endings alight across her body. She loved Ivan's touch, always gentle, but firm as though he didn't believe her to be made of glass.

His hands worked their way down lower, across her bump, which he loved to stroke, culminating in his fingers dipping in-between her legs. She sucked in a breath and let him play a while, enjoying his expert ministrations, while the sweet scent of her vanilla body wash filled the steamy enclosure.

"I need you inside me," she begged, as his talented fingers took her almost to the edge. Carefully, he lifted her and braced her back against the cool tiled wall. Gently and slowly, he eased himself into her, while her legs hung limp over his arms, trusting him totally to bear her weight. Ivan closed his eyes as he moved, sliding in and out rhythmically, just enjoying the closeness of their bodies. Truth be known, Lucy's death had caused a loop to form in his overactive mind, taunting him how easy it was to lose a wife. He couldn't even begin to imagine what Oscar was going through.

He needed to feel Elle, taste her, smell her sweet scent, remind himself that she was real, alive, and totally his. He became aware of her hand sliding off his shoulder, between them, to her clit. He leaned forward and kissed her, pressing his tongue against hers, exploring her mouth. He wanted to be inside her in every possible way.

He swallowed her cries as she came, her entire body pulsating with the sensations he was inflicting on her. He felt his cock flooded with her wetness. it tipped him over the edge and he came too.

They both stayed joined for a minute, hot water pouring over them as they simply needed closeness, to feel that the other was real. Eventually, Ivan softened and slipped out of her. He set her down gently. "Thank you," he said. "I needed that." He brushed the water from his face. Elle smiled as she saw his eyelashes had gone spiky, as though he'd used mascara. They framed his deep, sapphire eyes beautifully. She sensed his sadness.

"I struggled to sleep. Yesterday was just… such a shock. Her poor family," Elle said. Ivan pushed her wet hair back from her face.

"I know Malyshka, if anything happened to you…" he paused. "My life would be over. I keep running it like a tape through my mind."

She kissed his nose. "You need to keep busy, too busy to have thought loops."

"You're right. What's your schedule today?" He began to lather his body. Elle would've quite happily just stood and watched. She pulled herself together.

"Meeting my personal shopper at the penthouse. I did tell you on Friday. After that, I'll pop into the office, I've got some paperwork I want to clear up. You?"

"I'm meeting Kristov first thing in my office. He's bringing some extra guards for us. I want to up our security details for a while."

"You think Darius had something to do with Lucy's murder, don't you?" She challenged. He shrugged. He didn't know how they could've pulled it off so quickly. It was just a gut feeling. "I don't know, but it doesn't hurt to have more security."

"Kristov always sends Russians though," Elle whined. It wasn't that she minded having burly guards trailing around after her, she'd had to get used to it, it was more the fact that it was impossible to chat to them, to get to know them as she had with Roger.

"Indulge me," he implored. "I'll see if Kristov can find you some non-Russians, but for now we just put up with whoever he finds."

Elle sighed. "Alright, but you'll ask him, promise?"

He kissed her lips. "I promise. You'll take the girls with you, yes?"

"Of course."

They dried off and dressed, Ivan in a navy suit, Elle in a comfortable wrap dress, before heading downstairs to the kitchen, where Ivan made coffee and Elle put some bread in the toaster. She'd lost her appetite somewhat after the shock of the day before, but knew she had to keep her strength up. She quickly took the girls outside while the toast was doing.

At half-seven, Ivan called Nico to tell him they'd be ready to leave shortly. He filled the girl's water bottles before fixing their collars, kissing each one on the nose as he did up the buckle. "You're going to be good girls again this week. Don't forget your lessons," he reminded them.

"They'll still play up when Mrs Watton looks after them, she indulges them too much," Elle said as they stepped out of the front door.

The two Bentleys were parked side-by-side on the large, gravel driveway, Nico having got the other one out of the garage, ready. "See you at the office this afternoon," Elle said, as she shepherded the two spaniels into the back, then hopped in. Roger closed the door and got into the driver's seat.

"See you later," Ivan said, blowing her a kiss as he walked round to the other one. Nico hurried to hold the door open.

"Am I expected to wear that ridiculous chauffeur's hat again?" He asked in Russian. Ivan grinned at him.

"That's a great idea," he teased. "Oh hold on, I forgot the files I need for that meeting later. I won't be a minute." He disappeared back into the house as Elle was driven through the gates. He jogged through to the study and found the offending files on his desk, he gathered them up and was just heading back out when Jo arrived. "Good morning," he said pleasantly.

"Morning," she replied, "are you just off? I heard about your friend over at the castle. Terrible business wasn't it?"

"Dreadful," Ivan agreed. "Yes, just off. The organic regime seemed to have worked well? The food this weekend was superb."

"There's a couple of organic farms nearby. I sourced the beef from one of them. I'm pleased you enjoyed it."

"We did. Anyway, I'd better be off. See you soon." He stepped outside, closing the door behind him and jumped into the car.

Ivan quite liked it when it was just him and Nico. They could speak in Russian, and Nico always had a funny story to share from his days off. He maintained a small apartment in London and seemed to spend his downtime getting into drunken scrapes with his louche mates and various gangster groupie women, tales of which he entertained Ivan with whenever they did a long drive alone.

As Elle and Roger passed through Derwent towards the A road, they didn't see the black Audi parked in a side street. "That's them," Luke exclaimed as the Bentley sped past. "Mission accomplished." He started the engine and pulled out the opposite way. They'd decided not to follow the Bentley, in case it drew attention. The device had never failed. As they drove towards Brighton, Mike called Darius to let him know the mission had been successful.

Darius had gotten into his office early, which wasn't unusual. Arabella always knew never to object or ask for an explanation as to why he needed to set off in the early hours. He'd been almost jumpy sitting by his phone, waiting for the call. After he'd replaced the receiver, he immediately dialled Oscar.

Oscar saw Darius' number flash up on the screen of his mobile. He debated whether or not to answer it, his thumb hovering over the 'accept' button. In the end, he reasoned that Darius would simply call his landline instead, so he took a deep breath and pressed the green button. "Hi." He said rather flatly.

"Good news. All threats are neutralised. You can relax now," Darius said brightly.

"What?" Oscar asked, "I don't know what you're talking about."

Darius sighed. "The Ruskie. We rigged his car. Should have crashed by now."

Cold terror raced through Oscar's nervous system. "Elle,' he croaked, unable to get his words out.

"Collateral damage, I'm afraid," Darius said cheerfully.

The phone went dead. "Ungrateful bastard," Darius said to the silent phone.

Oscar was in an almost blind panic. With shaking hands, he scrolled through his phone to find Elle's number. He pressed it. It seemed to take ages to connect. He cursed the mobile reception in Sussex. Eventually, it began to ring.

He closed his eyes and prayed. One ring.

It rang again. He hoped that she was fumbling around in her bag for her phone.

Third ring. he prayed that she wasn't laying in the remnants of a crushed Bentley, that it wasn't too late.

She answered. "Hello Oscar, how's--"

He cut her off, "Get out of the car," he yelled. "The car's rigged. Get out."

He shouted so loudly that Roger heard him and screeched to a halt on the hard shoulder of the A21. Cars shot by going past, as he jumped out of the driver's door and raced around to the passenger side to get the dogs out.

"I'm fine though," said Elle, bewildered. Then realisation hit. She cut him off. "Ivan's in the other car." She prodded her phone and dialled Ivan, although Roger was already calling Nico. Her heart thudded in her chest as she waited for him to pick up.

"Hey baby, what's up?" He slurred, when he eventually picked up. By that point Elle was frantic.

"Get out of the car. The car's rigged. Get out," she screamed.

"Chill baby, we're good. Nico's gonna open this monster up, see what she can do," he slurred.

"Stop the car and get out NOW," she shouted. She noticed that Roger was yelling into his phone too, turned away from her. He couldn't bear to look at her.

Ivan's car began to nudge almost eighty miles an hour. "We better stop, see what she's moaning about," Elle heard Ivan say to Nico as his foot pressed down on the accelerator.

"Spoilsport," she heard Nico say as he began to brake. It was too late. The gas began its insidious journey into the car. The smell of almonds alerted Nico, who stamped on the brake.

"Look," Roger called out as the Bentley came into view, skidding around the dual carriageway. Elle could hear the screech of brakes as the car shot past. She watched helplessly as it skidded off the road and hit a tree, before bursting into flames.

It seemed to Elle as though it happened in slow motion. She heard herself scream as Roger thrust the dog's leads into her hands. She dropped her phone as she held on tight to the girls, who were barking loudly.

Running towards a burning car went against every bit of both instinct and training that Roger had ever had. He was paid handsomely to take a bullet for his boss, he reasoned as he raced towards the wreckage. It was the only chance he would ever have to pull Ivan out alive.

He could smell petrol as he approached, acrid in his lungs, the heat from the fire singeing his nostrils. He grabbed the rear door, ignoring the pain of the skin of his hands burning. Ivan was slumped in the seat, his phone still in his hands.

Roger didn't bother to check if he was still alive, just unclipped his seat belt then grabbed him under his arms and hauled him out. He was heavy, a dead weight. The fire burned stronger, licking across the roof of the car, across the floor, melting the cream carpet as it went. Adrenaline kicked in. With almost superhuman strength, Roger threw Ivan over his shoulder and ran towards Elle and the dogs.

He'd made about twenty paces when the car blew, the flames having reached the petrol tank. The force of the blast knocked him over. He landed face-down on the Tarmac with Ivan a crumpled heap on top of him. Elle was crouched over the dogs, shielding them from the debris raining down on them all. Nico never stood a chance. For a few minutes there was silence as both Elle and the onlookers tried to take in what had just happened.

Sirens were in the distance, blue lights racing towards them, called by the drivers who were stopped on the carriageway, having seen the crash. Traffic began to tail back, causing the emergency services to switch to the hard shoulder. A middle-aged lady got out of her car and ran over to Elle. "Are you ok, my love? The ambulance is on its way." She could make out the blue lights behind the queues of traffic forming. She picked up Elle's phone and bag from the ground and tucked the phone in the front pocket for her.

"My husband," was all Elle could say, turning her head towards where Ivan and Roger lay. She could see that neither of them were moving. She became aware of the dogs whimpering.

"Are you alright?" Asked the woman, checking Elle over. "and what about these two lovelies?" She bent down to stroke Tania, who was cowed underneath Elle. Bella barked and tried to dart out towards Ivan. Luckily, Elle had the leads in a vice-like grip. "Come on, sit down and keep hold of those two doggies," the woman said, helping Elle into a sitting position on the ground. "My name's Donna. I think you're going into shock." She'd noticed Elle was as white as a sheet.

Other people had started getting out of their cars. Someone ran over to Ivan and Roger. "They look dead to me," Elle heard him say to someone else. She closed her eyes, willing herself to wake up in their enormous bed, with the spaniels snoring beside them.

"Paramedics are here," she heard Donna say before she passed out.

CHAPTER FOURTEEN

Elle came round on the way to hospital. She was strapped onto a stretcher in the back of an ambulance. She could hear the siren wailing as they drove. She woke with a start from what was effectively a faint. "I'm ok," she said to the paramedic sitting beside her. "Where's Ivan? My husband?" She could see that she was alone.

"They've taken two men by air ambulance," the paramedic said. "I'm afraid the driver of the car didn't make it." He paused. "Which one was your husband?"

"He was on the floor. Roger pulled him out. Where are our dogs?" She began to panic as it all came flooding back to her.

"The police have taken them to be checked over by a vet, then they'll be kept securely in the police kennels."

"Is Ivan still alive?" She asked. "The one in the navy suit with dark hair?"

"I don't know. I wasn't dealing with him. All I know is that they're taking him to Sussex General. He'll probably be there by now, the helicopters are very quick."

"Are we going there?" Elle asked.

"Yes, we are. We'll be there in about ten minutes. Try to lay still," the paramedic soothed. "We'll get you checked over as soon as we can."

"I'm alright," Elle protested.

"You were unconscious when we arrived. We don't know if you were hit by debris. It won't take long to get you looked over by a doctor," he said.

Elle sat up and looked around the ambulance for her bag. She was relieved to see it on the chair opposite. The thought struck her that for everything she possessed, all the homes, clothes, and shoes, she was so pleased to see her bag at that moment. "Is my phone in there?" She asked, pointing to her handbag with her chin. The paramedic jumped up and picked up her bag.

"Yes, in the front pocket. Looks like the screen's broken though." He held it up for her to see. A large crack ran across the sapphire screen. "Very fancy phone, I must say," he said as he tucked it back in. "My daughter likes everything covered in diamanté too, she'd love it," he carried on, blissfully unaware that it was real diamonds adorning her limited-edition mobile. Ivan had bought it for her to celebrate the launch of the Bel-Phone.

"I need to make a call," Elle told him. He handed her the bag.

"We're not meant to, because of the equipment in here."

She ignored him and scrolled through her contacts. There was only one person she needed. She found the number and pressed call. He picked up on the first ring. "Elle," he said, "what can I do for you?"

"They got him, Kristov. I need your help. I'm on my way to Sussex General. Ivan's already there."

"I'm on my way."

It went dead. She lay back, ignoring the shocked stare of the paramedic. Her mind raced through the events. Any doubt she had about Lucy dissolved like sugar in hot water. Darius had shown his hand, and Oscar was involved as well. Posh-boy bastards might think she was just a stupid little pauper, but Elle knew she was a fighter. She'd fought back against the system her whole life. Those fucked-up public schoolboys wouldn't know what hit them.

Oscar tuned in to Radio Sussex, just in time to hear that the A21 had been closed due to a major incident. The number of casualties unknown, but it was reported that at least two people were dead, possibly more after a car had crashed and exploded into a fireball. He threw his cup across his study, where it crashed against the bookcase and dripped tea down Churchill's biography. He felt sick.

his mother came running in to see what the noise had been. Since Lucy, she'd remained nearby, watching closely to make sure he didn't relapse. Her worst fear was that he'd return to his old ways, finding solace in a foil wrap. "What's the matter?" She demanded. She stood in the doorway.

"Elle and Ivan. He got them," Oscar said, his voice cracking as he spoke. She stepped into the room and closed the door.

"What do you mean?" She asked.

"Darius. He called me this morning to tell me he'd rigged their car. It's on the news. They crashed on the A21. I tried to warn Elle, but she cut me off."

Lady Golding's hand flew up to cover her mouth.

"I know," said Oscar. "He was so happy about it too. Called me this morning all pleased with himself, saying that he'd 'neutralised' the threat."

"Please tell me this isn't true," she gasped. "He's gone even more crazy than normal. He's a dangerous man at the best of times."

"Both women that I loved," Oscar murmured. "Couldn't even spare one of them, the bastard." He too had realised that Darius was behind Lucy's murder.

"He's always been behind every problem you ever had," his mother pointed out. "The only person who couldn't see it was you. He's a sociopath, a classic, evil sociopath, with no respect for life, people, or God's creatures. You were just too blinded by the bonds of childhood to see that he's manipulated you your whole life." She'd always blamed him for Oscar's drug addiction, especially when her late husband had discovered that Darius had found Oscar's supplier for him and was helping himself to a cut of the dealer's profits. "You must stay away from him. Don't let on that you know he was behind Lucy's death. If you challenge him, he'll come after you. It's best to just cut him off."

"I couldn't bear to be in a room with him," Oscar said, his head in his hands. "I need some air." He left his mother in the study and strode out into the garden, drawn, as always, to the White garden. He sat on the Wisteria bench and let his tears leak out. The thought of Elle dying was unbearable enough, that she should die in such a terrible way was beyond his comprehension. She'd been so beautiful, so alive, as she'd she'd joined him for a dance at his wedding. Even pregnant with Ivan's child, she'd been fun and effervescent. She was a person who sparkled with life.

She'd been snuffed out because of him, he knew, because of his weakness, his addiction. The guilt threatened to crush him. He wiped away his tears and gazed, unthinking at his surroundings. Elle had described it as 'paradise.' He spotted Fred sauntering past pushing a wheelbarrow. He called out to him and sat as Fred made his way over. "I want this garden ripped out," Oscar said, "I don't care if you turf it, pave it, what you do, but I want it gone."

"I see," said Fred. "I won't be able to do anything for a couple of days. Let me know if you change your mind." He tipped his cap at Oscar and went on his way, praying that whatever was eating his lordship would pass. The White garden was his personal favourite.

Nobody seemed to be able to tell Elle anything. All they'd said was that both Ivan and Roger had been taken into the crash rooms in the large, noisy A&E department. She'd been instructed to lay on a bed in a bay while she waited for a doctor to arrive. She wanted to scream with frustration. Eventually, a nurse told her that both Roger and Ivan had been admitted, Roger had a severe concussion and burns, while Ivan's condition was more serious. "But he's alive, right?" Elle demanded.

"Well, yes, but his situation is described as critical," the nurse said gently. "They think he may have inhaled a lot of smoke or something. He's on full life support." She paused. "Are you his next of kin?"

Elle nodded. They were all each other had, neither had another soul on Earth who would care for them. "The doctor will be here soon," the nurse assured her. She didn't think it was the right moment to ask if Elle wanted to keep her husband on life support or not. She'd leave that question for someone else.

The doctor eventually looked her over, checked her eyes, and read her notes listing her blood pressure and temperature and declared her to be well enough to leave. She hopped off the bed and slipped her shoes back on. "You must take it easy. If you have any bleeding or pain, come straight back," he warned, looking pointedly at her bump.

"I'll feel better once I've found Ivan," she muttered. She headed back out to the waiting room to speak to the receptionist, who would know where Roger and Ivan had been taken. As soon as she went through the double doors, she saw Kristov, seated in a chair, a row of black-suited men in the row behind him, which gave him a rather menacing air.

"Mrs Porenski," he said, standing to shake her hand. "Terrible business. I've taken the liberty of stationing guards around Ivan and also around the hospital. You seemed to suggest this wasn't an accident?" He spoke softly, his voice gentle.

"Have you seen Ivan?" She asked. He nodded.

"Only through a door. He's alive, just. He has some burns and a head injury as well as some difficulties breathing. He's in good hands. His guard has a concussion and some burns, mainly to his hands."

"He pulled Ivan out of the car before it blew up. They told me in the ambulance that Nico didn't make it."

"Nico Sokolov?" He asked sharply. Elle nodded. She watched as Kristov crumpled. "Nico came to work for Vlad when he was just a boy, a bit like Ivan really. I watched him grow up. Mafia life wasn't for him. He loved fiddling around with electronics, devising security systems. Being Ivan's head of security was his dream job."

"I'm sorry," she said, placing her hand gently on his arm.

He nodded, then gathered himself together. "You go see Ivan, then we'll get a tea and you can tell me what you know. My men will keep the press away. Be careful what you tell the police, not many are straight and most are easily bought," he warned. "Ivan is in the third room down that corridor. Daichi will accompany you. Make sure you're never alone. I'll be out here."

With a lot of trepidation, Elle pushed through the double doors and into the corridor, closely followed by a tall, be-suited man who wore an earpiece, and she suspected, a gun. On the wall outside the room was a whiteboard, with the words "RTA this morning 7.50am." She wanted to write his name on it, which probably wasn't a good idea. She caught a glimpse of him through the glass of the door. He was hooked up to an array of machines, so many that she could barely see his face. She pushed her way in, not even noticing the guards standing outside the room in the corridor. Daichi followed her in, and satisfied that there wasn't anyone else present, announced in decent English that he too would wait outside.

"Ivan?" Elle called out, her voice hesitant. The machines bleeped back. She saw that he had a ventilator pipe going down his throat. His sapphire eyes were firmly shut, and he had a pad and bandage around his head. His face looked dirty. Smuts from the smoke had settled on his golden complexion, giving him the appearance of a beautiful urchin. Ivan never got dirty. "I'm here," she said. "The baby and I are ok. I'm gonna take care of this for you."

Nothing. No reaction at all.

She wandered down the bed and picked up the notes. Unable to make head nor tail of most of it, she set it down again.

A doctor came striding in. "Oh, hello, who are you?" She asked.

"I'm his wife, Elle Porenski," Elle replied. "You are?"

"Doctor Mullins. I'm a trauma specialist. We're going to be moving him shortly to ICU. It's a bit of a strange one, as his blood work has come back showing a problem with his cellular respiration, as though he inhaled something before the crash knocked him out." She was frowning.

"Smoke?" Elle asked.

The doctor shook her head. "Smoke wouldn't bind proteins to his blood in that way. It's definitely an odd one. We may try a blood transfusion, see if that helps."

"He's blood group O," Elle told her.

She watched as the doctor examined him and checked on the machines. "How's Roger?" She asked.

"It's nice to know their names at last," said the doctor. "He's ok. Well, he'll have a hell of a headache, and he has some quite serious burns to his hands, but we're confident he'll be ok."

"And Ivan?" Elle asked. The doctor sighed.

"I don't know. That's the truth. We can treat his trauma wounds easily enough. He took a bang to the head and has some burns to his lower legs. It's his respiratory injury that's more of a worry."

"Are there any consultants, specialists you can call on? Money is no object," Elle told her.

The penny dropped.

"He's that Russian billionaire isn't he? The one that's always in the news. I wondered why all those fellas stationed themselves outside the room."

Elle nodded. She hadn't looked in any mirrors, but she could guess that she didn't look like a billionaire's wife in her dusty dress and laddered tights.

"Let me ring around, see what advice I can find." With that she left. A few minutes later, a nurse and an administrator came in to get details for both Ivan and Roger. by the time all the forms were taken care of, Elle was itching to talk to Kristov. She also needed to call the office and speak to Ranenkiov, one of the directors. He was always a good ally during a crisis. He would handle things from that end. She glanced at her watch. It was still only eleven o'clock.

"There's been a car crash," she told Ranenkiov. "Ivan will be out of action a while. In the meantime, I'll take over the day to day. I'll be in tomorrow if necessary, otherwise Wednesday. Can you take care of things till then?"

"I wondered why the press kept calling," he said. "Is Ivan alright?"

"He's so-so," Elle said, trying to keep her voice light. "Don't talk to the press. Make sure nobody else does either. I want a total news blackout. Pull strings."

"Will do, and send him my best wishes," he said before Elle rang off. She leaned over to kiss Ivan's cheek. "I'll be back soon. Keep fighting," she said.

Nothing.

She stepped outside the room where Daichi was waiting patiently for her. She addressed the three guards standing beside him. "I want a full record of anyone who goes in or out of this room," she said. "Check their name tags, keep a log. Does everybody speak English?"

"We do," one of them confirmed.

"Good. They'll be moving him to ICU. Keep constant watch over him." They nodded.

Back out in the waiting room, Kristov stood up as soon as he saw Elle. "How is he?" He asked.

"Not sure. I'll tell you in the car. We need to go and spring the spaniels from prison."

"I've secured a way out via the back exit. There are press out the front," Kristov told her. "The staff are under strict instructions, but it's an NHS hospital, we can't close it down."

She followed him through a staff area and out to the rear of the car park where his blacked out Mercedes was waiting. It all felt like a bad dream. She sat back in the soft grey leather and told him in almost forensic detail what had happened, including what had happened to Lucy. The only bit she left out was why she'd rowed with Oscar and Darius. He listened to her account of how Roger had run towards the burning car. He was impressed that Ivan had inspired such devotion in his staff.

"Why do I know the name Darius Cavendish?" Kristov mused. He dredged through his memory. "MI5! I remember now. Odious man."

"Ivan always thought he was behind Vlad and Dascha's deaths," Elle said, "and it's exactly the same modus operandi."

"But this Oscar Golding, he called you to warn you?"

"Yes. I'm not sure why," Elle admitted.

"What I'd suggest is that we hit Mr Cavendish, but send a warning to his accomplice, Mr Golding," Kristov said. "I know a man who would take on such a job, it's complicated as I'm sure you appreciate. The establishment look after their own. A normal hitman would shy away from a job like that, knowing that they'd pull out all the stops to find him."

"So who?" Elle asked. it wasn't a conversation that she ever in a million years dreamed that she'd be having.

"I have someone. He's unknown to the authorities. There is no record of him anywhere, even in Russia. He's not cheap, but I happen to know that he's currently in London."

"How much?" Elle asked.

"Five million."

"Well there's no point in having fuck-off amounts of money if you never use it to tell someone to fuck off," she mused.

"I will order it. I will also fire a warning shot over Oscar Golding's head."

"Ok," she said, not really understanding what that meant. "So how do we do this? Do I need to get cash together?"

"I will see to it. We will sort money after its done." He patted her arm. "Ivan was very good to me after Vlad died. The very least I can do is assist in his safety and look after his wife. It's the Russian way." He didn't want to mention the fact that he was still operating smuggling routes across their land. It was a conversation he would only need to have if Ivan died.

Kristov stayed in the car when they arrived at Derwent police station. Elle walked up to the desk, surprised to see the officer who'd been to her house on Sunday.

"Hello, I think my spaniels were brought here after an accident this morning," she said.

"Oh, hello again Mrs Porenski. I heard about the crash this morning. My condolences for your loss."

"Thanks. Nico will be sorely missed. He'd been working for Ivan for years," she replied. She wanted to cry. As annoying as Nico could be at times, she was used to him. She flexed her steel backbone. "Are the dogs ok?"

"They're fine. We had the vet check them over. Apart from being severely overweight, they're fighting fit. They wouldn't eat anything though, refused point blank. One of the PC's even went down to the shop and got them some pedigree chum. Still turned their noses up." She rang through to ask someone to bring them out.

"We're going to need to interview you about the crash. It doesn't need to be today," she said.

"I'm going back up the hospital after I've taken the dogs home. I've got no idea when I'll be back. Can I give you my number? Call me when you need me and I'll either come here or meet you at the house." She scribbled her number on a sheet of paper.

"Is your husband badly hurt?" The policewoman asked. Elle nodded.

"They call it 'critical,' whatever that means. It's why I'm keen to get back there as quickly as I can. Did you tow the cars?"

"They were removed by Derwent salvage. They'll be in their yard. They'll write to you."

"Thank you," Elle said as they heard familiar yapping. The two spaniels practically did backflips the moment they saw Elle, attempting to jump into her arms at the same time, which resulted in a sort of dog crash. "Hey, girls, girls, calm down. You only just got out of prison, you don't want to go back there," she said as they licked her face enthusiastically. She reasoned that she looked a state anyway, so a bit of dog spit wouldn't make any difference."

After thanking the police again, she led them out to the car. Kristov seemed less than happy at them jumping on to the butter-soft leather car seats, but to his credit, he kept quiet, just muttering in Russian to his driver to book a valet clean. As they drove towards the house, he murmured "it's done. The unknown man is in play."

Jo and Viktor were shocked at the state of Elle, the news of the crash, Nico's death, and the fact that Ivan was laying unconscious. "Why didn't you call us?" Jo asked.

"Viktor was on nights, and I didn't really get much chance," Elle said weakly. "I've only come back here to drop the dogs off and get changed, then I'm going back to the hospital." She turned to Viktor, "Can you sort my car? It was taken by Derwent salvage." He nodded. She ran upstairs to take off the ruined dress and slip on a comfy tracksuit.

"You want me to take you to the hospital first?" Viktor asked when she came back down.

"You can take my car," Jo volunteered.

"Then I'll go back up to town," Kristov said, before his phone rang. He spoke briefly in Russian, then listened intently."

"They tunnelled under the wall to get in. My driver was checking around." Viktor jumped up and followed Kristov outside where his driver pointed out the freshly moved earth. "It's easy to get in when you know how," Kristov remarked dryly before kissing Elle goodbye with the promise that he'd call her later and would put patrols in place around the perimeter of their land. He also had people already scoping out Conniscliffe Castle, which he didn't mention.

"I'll call you if there's any news," Elle promised as she hopped into Jo's little Mini, with Viktor, who was well over six-foot-three, shoehorned into the driver's seat, and Daichi, who was also a big fella, squashed into the tiny rear bench seat. Viktor looked quite ridiculous driving the tiny car, but none of them wanted to trust the Mercedes which were parked in the garages, in case they too had been tampered with.

CHAPTER FIFTEEN

Ivan had been taken to the ICU while Elle was away, accompanied by various doctors, nurses, some orderlies, and a slew of black-suited men wearing earpieces. It was a strange procession. Once they had him moved and ensconced on a bed in the specialist unit, more blood was taken. Dr Mullins had ordered tests to be taken every hour. She'd never seen anything quite like the fury that was raging in Ivan's system. She'd called her former tutor, an expert in respiratory failure, to come down and take a look for her. He was in a taxi, having been assured that the patient's wife would pay for both his private consultation rates and his transport down to Sussex and back.

Ivan had been given a blood transfusion. She was debating the timing of another when both Elle and Professor Bernstein both arrived, almost together. "How is he?" Elle demanded as soon as she walked in.

"So this is the patient?" Professor Bernstein asked, standing behind her, motioning to Ivan.

"Glad you're both here. My office is this way, please follow me." They trooped behind Dr Mullins into her office, which was surprisingly small for a consultant's space. She pulled up some images on her screen. "This was the red blood cells when he was brought in." She swivelled the screen so that they could both see. Elle had no real idea what she was looking at.

"Strange," said the professor.

"I agree. This is how they look an hour ago, just before we gave him a transfusion." She clicked her mouse. Another image loaded. "I have no idea what this is, or how to treat it," she admitted.

"I've seen this before, but only in a textbook," the professor ventured. "It's a poison consisting of Hydrogen Cyanide and Diatomaceous Earth. It looks as though it's dissipated though, just leaving the damaged cells behind."

The doctor cocked her head to one side. "Are you saying what I think you are?"

"Ced," the professor said.

"Will someone explain what's going on please?" Elle butted in.

"It would appear that your husband breathed in the same substance that was used in the gas chambers to kill six million Jews," Dr Mullins explained. "It's commonly called Zyklon B. Now that you've pointed it out, it makes sense, although I didn't think it dissipated like this."

"A modern version perhaps? Maybe one designed not to show up in an autopsy," said the professor. "Now, how do you treat it? That's more difficult." Neither of them seemed to notice the look of sheer horror on Elle's face.

"Well, the good news is that it can't have been a large dose, otherwise he'd be dead by now," the professor pointed out. "A two-minute exposure is normally all it takes."

"When I spoke to him, just before the crash, he was slurring his words, he sounded drunk," Elle volunteered.

"I can't explain it," Dr Mullins said, shaking her head. "It's unlikely to have been any of the fixtures in the car burning, they're all tested nowadays." She turned back to the professor. "Is there an effective treatment regime?"

"Oxygen therapy via ventilator, daily transfusions, and Cobalamin, but via intra-dermal patch or injection rather than orally. You need to bypass the digestive system completely." He paused. "I can't promise that it'll work, but it's probably the best shot he's got."

Elle tuned out as they began to discuss dosages and timings. The full horror of the day hit her hard as she processed the revelation that they'd been targeted by a sophisticated hit. They'd have expected her to be with him in the car, with her own precious cargo, as well as the two dogs. If they'd travelled together, as they usually did, they'd have all been killed. She began to shake. "I'm gonna go sit with Ivan," she said. She stumbled out of the office and back down the corridor to the unit. Viktor was standing at the end of Ivan's bed, a stoic expression on his face. As soon as he saw her, he pulled up a plastic chair and set it beside the bed for her.

"Can I get you anything? Food, a drink?" he asked.

"Just some water please," Elle said. "Actually, a cup of tea if you can find one." He nodded and left. She leaned over Ivan's sleeping form. "I'm back," she said, kissing his cheek. It still felt familiar. She still had the sense of safety, just being near him, which she found faintly ridiculous given the circumstances. She caught a whiff of his aftershave. He even smelt the same, like home. She just couldn't contemplate losing him.

She recalled a conversation with Oscar, how he'd warned her that her life would always be in danger if she chose Ivan. At the time, it had been an abstract concept; Ivan had talked about known threats and unknown ones. He'd impressed upon her the need for constant security, for always being vigilant. Seeing how easily they'd managed to get to them had slammed it home to her that they would never be truly safe.

Dr Mullins and Professor Bernstein came in and examined Ivan again, checking his notes and peeling back his eyelids to check his pupils, before injecting him with something and fiddling around with the ventilator machine. "He looks a little pinker," Elle had said.

"We gave him a blood transfusion earlier," Dr Mullins explained. "We'll do another one tomorrow. It normally makes patients appear healthier, especially when their own red cells have been compromised." She turned to the Professor and thanked him profusely for his help.

"My invoice will be in the post," he said. "Where should I send it?"

For a moment, Elle was confused, but quickly realised what he meant. She fished around in her bag for a business card. "Send it to this address. My PA will take care of it, and thank you for all your help." He slipped her card in his pocket and bade them goodbye and good luck.

"You must be exhausted," Dr Mullins said. "I have one bit of good news though, Roger, the man brought in with your husband, he's woken up. You can go see him if you like, he's in room four."

When Viktor returned with a cup of boiling hot tea in a polystyrene cup, Elle left him by Ivan's bed and went to see Roger, who was sitting up in bed with his hands bandaged up. "How's Ivan?" He demanded as soon as she walked in.

"He's still alive, thanks to you," Elle said. "He's critical though. They gassed them in the car." Roger's eyes widened in horror.

"Nico?"

She shook her head.

"Damn. How'd they get to the car?"

"They tunnelled under the wall into the front garden," Elle said, "I called Kristov. One of his men spotted it."

"I see. Are the dogs alright?"

"Yes, they're fine. I sprung them from prison earlier. The police took them, tried to feed them dog food, then wondered why they turned their noses up."

"Little brats." He smiled weakly. "Do you know who did this?"

She nodded. "Kristov's taking care of it for me. He's put a load of extra security around us too." She paused. "Your hands sore?"

"Yeah. I burnt them on the car door. It was like pulling a tin out of the oven without gloves on. We were just lucky that the door opened. Mind you, that car was built like a tank." He paused. "And how are you holding up? Have you eaten?"

"I'm ok. I feel tired, that's all. It's been a hell of a day. There's still a lot to take care of. At the moment we have a press blackout, I'm gonna have to address that tomorrow, but knowing we were subject to a professional hit, I feel safer with everyone assuming that we're dead right now," she admitted.

"They said I've got to stay in overnight, mainly because the wallop I got when I hit the ground with your husband on top of me," Roger said, "but I can sign myself out..."

"No, do what the doctors tell you," Elle told him. "Viktor is here with me and Kristov will have the house and grounds crawling with his men. With your hands all bandaged up like that, there's not much you can do. I'll get one of the guards to fetch you a newspaper and some food."

"Alright. I just feel a bit useless laying here," he said, glancing around the featureless room. In some ways he hoped he'd be moved to a ward. At least there'd be a telly to watch. Elle stood up.

"You saved his life, no matter what happens now. If you hadn't got him out of that car, he'd be dead. Take it easy for a night." With that, she disappeared back to the ICU to sit with Ivan and drink her cooled-down tea, which resembled dishwater so much that it made her wince.

Elle had switched off her phone, as instructed, in case the signal interfered with the delicate equipment in the unit. She knew she had a truckload of stuff to attend to, but she couldn't bear the thought of leaving Ivan any more than she genuinely had to. The baby was kicking hard too, no doubt wondering why she'd failed to eat properly that day. She sat in the hard, plastic seat and rested her hand on her bump. If Ivan died, she'd be a single mother, albeit a wealthy one, but alone just the same. It had always been her worst fear.

Back in Derwent, a Russian man walked into Derwent Salvage and told them he was from the forensic service. "Thought you were coming tomorrow," the Gaffer said.

"We'll collect the wreck tomorrow as planned, I'm here to give it a quick examination," he explained. The Gaffer nodded over towards the wreck of the Bentley.

"Bloody shame that. It must've been a hell of a car."

"Identical to the one next to it," the Russian replied. He strolled over to the wreck and began to examine the twisted metal. He checked over the seats, what was left of the dashboard, then worked his way down to the floor. He ran his hand under the seat, straightaway feeling the tiny hose. Frowning, he edged himself under the chassis and found the small black box affixed to the metal. He pulled out his penknife and prised it off, before checking the other Bentley in the same place. Satisfied that he'd found what he was looking for, he bade farewell to the Gaffer, who was in the engine bay stripping down a Vauxhall Astra. On his way back to London, he called Kristov to tell him what he'd found.

"Bring it here, I want to see this for myself," Kristov had said. Getting hold of a sophisticated device like that was a major coup. Besides, it was better that the police didn't find it. He replaced the receiver on his desk phone and turned his attention back to the man seated opposite him. "His name is Darius Cavendish, he's the head of MI5. He used his position to kill one eminent Oligarch and he just used the same method on another. We need him eliminated." He looked expectantly at the man in front of him.

"I can do that. You have intel on him?"

"Of course," Kristov said. "I have a very full report on his habits, address, car, etcetera." He pushed a file across his very ornate desk, which had been sneakily liberated from Vlad's office after his death. The man opened the file and read slowly and carefully the information it contained. He spent a long time staring at the photographs of Darius that Kristov had gleaned.

"I will need the CCTV system disabled for five minutes at six o'clock," he told Kristov, "Just so that I can make a clean getaway. London is a bitch for these kind of jobs. My fee is as usual, five mil, up front."

Kristov pulled open a drawer in his desk and took out a carrier bag. "It's all there," he said, handing it to him. The man tucked it into the front of his motorbike leathers, zipping the money in securely.

"Consider it done."

Kristov watched the man's swagger as he left his office. As the door closed behind him, Kristov took a deep breath. He had an almost overwhelming urge to open a window and get some air. There weren't many men on Earth who could spook the old mafia boss, but the man with no name, just cold, dead eyes, was one of them.

There'd been no mention of the crash on the early evening news. Oscar had even searched online and found very little. The only information he'd come across had been in relation to the A21 being closed all morning due to a 'fatal crash.' He wondered how the board at Beltan would handle the announcement that their CEO and legal director were both dead. They seemed to be keeping very quiet.

He knew he should have gone up to London, but following Lucy's death, he'd informed Melanie that he would need the week off. He wanted to be in the bosom of the castle, it's thick, strong walls providing a substantial shield against the outside world.

A world without Elle.

He switched off the TV and headed back outside for a walk, needing to get away from his mother, who was hovering around him constantly, no doubt worried. He debated going up to his London apartment, but dismissed the idea knowing that he'd go stir crazy in its confines, plus he wanted to be as far away from Darius as possible. The idea of seeing his smug face, all pleased with himself made Oscar feel an almost volcanic rage. He didn't trust himself not to punch the bastard's lights out.

Kristov's men watched the comings and goings at the castle all afternoon and evening. They watched Fred trim back the bushes in the outer grounds, assisted by Kyle. They observed Jones the butler arrive at the front gate in a golf buggy to collect a parcel from a courier, and they watched a couple of women leave for the day at six o'clock.

"The gardeners are possibly our best bet, or the butler," Yegor said to his partner Ilya. They'd been tasked with a hit by Kristov, the idea being to frighten Oscar and send a message. They had strict instructions to make sure that they didn't target Oscar himself. Kristov had even sent them a picture to make sure that they didn't get the wrong person.

"The old one?" Ilya asked.

"Doesn't matter, any of them will do," Yegor replied. He was quite looking forward to it, he liked a bit of gore and prided himself on his brutality. He wasn't in the same league as the man with no name, but was a relatively effective hitman all the same. "Bloody shame it doesn't get dark until late. It would've been quicker in winter."

"And we'd have been freezing our nuts off sitting here in this bush," Ilya reminded him. Yegor laughed.

"You've got no blood. Are you sure you're from the Motherland? An English winter is like midsummer in Siberia."

"I'm from the South, remember?" Ilya reminded him. He was sick of Yegor's constant tales of hardship in the Siberian wastelands. The bastard had lived in London for over twenty years and was, in Ilya's opinion, as soft as shite.

Oscar wandered around the gardens until he found Kyle. "How's things?" Kyle asked. Oscar just shook his head.

"Bad, had more bad news today."

"Sorry to hear that," Kyle said, at a bit of a loss as what was the right thing to say. Oscar looked dreadful, his skin was pale and his eyes had red rims around them.

"I need something," Oscar said. "Something to help me sleep. I don't suppose you know anyone local?"

Kyle sighed. "It's not the answer. We both know that," he said.

"I know," Oscar agreed, but you know…" he trailed off. "I wouldn't normally ask."

"There's a guy in the Derwent Tavern who sells blow," Kyle said. "I don't think he sells anything stronger." He really didn't want Oscar to go back to coke.

"Some blow would help," Oscar admitted. "Would you get me some?"

"Oh, man, I don't know..." Kyle threw his hands up. He really didn't want to be the person responsible if Oscar fell off the wagon.

Oscar pulled some money out of his pocket and thrust it into Kyle's hands. "There's enough there, keep the rest. Just get me something to take the edge off. I lost a dear friend today."

Kyle stared at the money he was holding. He didn't want to count it in front of Oscar, but could feel that it was quite a wedge. "Alright. I'll get it tonight. I'll drop it in to you when I get back." He tucked the notes into his back pocket and carried on trimming back the lilac.

**

Darius left his office at six o'clock, as usual. He stepped out onto the pavement, planning to hail a taxi to take him over to Whitehall for a quick meeting before going home. He'd promised Arabella faithfully that he'd be home by half-seven as they were having friends over for dinner at eight. The motorbike parked on the pavement didn't even register. Couriers around London often left their bikes parked oddly when delivering documents and packages. He didn't even spot the rider, as he was busy scanning the street for a taxi with its light on. He certainly didn't see the man put a gun to his head and pull the trigger.

As passers-by began to scream, the man coolly got back on his bike, tucked the gun down the front of his leathers, and drove off. Nobody tried any heroic challenges. It was an utterly audacious, perfectly performed, gangland hit. When Kristov's hackers stopped jamming the CCTV network at five past, Kristov could see on his own screen that a man was on the floor, surrounded by people. He smiled. It was one all.

**

Lady Golding answered the phone when it rang. Oscar was nowhere to be seen, having announced earlier that he was going for another walk. "Hello, Conniscliffe Castle," Lady Golding said.

"Is Oscar there? Demanded Arabella, with none of her usual niceties.

"He's out. Is something the matter?" Lady Golding asked.

"It's Darius," Arabella let out a huge sob. "Someone shot him..." She dissolved into more sobs.

"Is he ok?"

"No," Arabella said in a small voice. "He's... he's... dead. At the scene. The police are here. I don't know what to do."

One part of Lady Golding wanted to punch the air with joy, but she couldn't ignore the feeling of dread in her gut. "Try and stay calm. Tell the police everything that you know," which she didn't expect would be much, "and I'll see if I can find Oscar."

"Thank you," Arabella managed to splutter. Lady Golding felt sorry for her. She'd always rather liked Arabella, it wasn't her fault that her husband was an evil psycho. The only sin Arabella had ever committed was being a bit dim.

She went outside onto the grounds to look for Oscar. She tried the White garden, the Sculpture garden, and even the kitchen garden. Getting cross, she walked up to the gate, calling out his name.

"What about her?" Ilya asked as she came into view.

"It's not dark enough yet," Yegor said, "If she's still around in an hour or so's time."

CHAPTER SIXTEEN

Lady Golding eventually found Oscar sitting on a bench at the far end of the long borders. "I've been looking everywhere for you," she said, huffing slightly.

"You don't need to be constantly on my tail," Oscar told her, getting annoyed. She'd been like that when he'd got out of rehab, not letting him out of her sight. It had been stifling.

"I think we have a very serious problem," she said. "We need to get back inside the castle straightaway."

"Why?" He asked.

"Darius has just been assassinated."

"Fuck," Oscar exclaimed.

"Language!" His mother chided.

Some things never changed, Oscar thought.

"Arabella just called, she's in a dreadful state." Oscar stood and followed her back into the morning room, locking the doors behind them.

"Are all the doors secured?" His mother nodded. "It could be over something else. Darius had his fingers in a lot of pies," Oscar mused.

"Maybe. I hope for our sakes it is. It does seem rather a coincidence though. You need to ring Arabella back."

When Oscar returned from his study where'd he'd made the call, he was as white as a sheet. His mother's stomach sank when she saw him.

"Well?" She asked.

"He was shot in the head at point blank range just outside the MI5 building by a fella on a motorbike," Oscar said. His mother gasped. "Oh, it gets worse," Oscar told her. "At the exact time, the CCTV across the whole of London went down, a problem which has been attributed to Russian hackers."

"How the hell did they know it was him?" Lady Golding asked. Oscar shrugged.

"Someone must've blabbed, either that or it's taken them this long to work out that he was the person behind Vlad's assassination."

Lady Golding frowned. "I thought that was a car crash?" Oscar shook his head.

"Like Elle and Ivan's was just a car crash?" He paused. "These people aren't stupid mother. They know when their own are being bumped off. Both Vlad and, I suspect, Ivan paid a lot of money to them for protection. Darius killed their golden goose. No wonder they're pissed." He was glad they had six foot of castle walls protecting them. He'd have to collect the gear off Kyle the following day, he thought, annoyed, as he poured himself a large cognac instead.

At ten o'clock, Kyle wandered down the lane towards the gate, with an ounce of blow and three hundred quid profit in his pocket. The fella in the Derwent tavern had insisted on having a drink while they did the deal, and Kyle wasn't a big drinker, so was swaying slightly as he walked. He planned to drop the blow into his boss, then see if Amber was around as he was feeling a little amorous.

Yegor and Ilya couldn't believe their good fortune. One shot to the chest was all it took. One small thud from Ilya's silenced handgun. "We need to make it a bit more dramatic," Yegor said, pulling his large hunting knife from it's sheath. "We're meant to be sending a message, remember."

By the time he'd finished, Kyle's body was lain up against the gates, with his head impaled on one of the imperial-looking spikes at the top. When they finished, they scarpered up the lane and back to their car, which was hidden behind a tree line on the Bonnington-Carter estate.

All hell was let loose at half-five the following morning when the gruesome remains were found by the milkman as he made the usual delivery. Oscar was awakened by Jones, who was still in his pyjamas, to tell him that police had been called and were on their way. He took a golf buggy up to the gates, where the police were already staring at the corpse and speaking into their walky-talkies.

Oscar thought he was going to faint when he first saw Kyle's remains. He closed his eyes and prayed to God that it wasn't real, that he was simply having a bad dream. Unfortunately when he opened his eyes, Kyle was still there. "Sir," a voice interrupted, "Sir, are you Lord Golding?" The policeman was calling him. "Could you let us in the side gate please?"

Oscar gave him the four digit code to open the smaller gate to the side of where Kyle lay. "Is this man known to you?" The policeman asked.

"Yes, he was one of the apprentice gardeners," Oscar replied, "His name was Kyle. Fred, the head gardener will have all his paperwork."

"Thank you sir. I don't suppose you'd know, but was the young man in any sort of trouble?" The policeman asked.

Oscar spotted his opportunity. He hated doing it, but it was better than the truth. "He was an ex-offender, not long out of prison for drug dealing. I suppose an old adversary may have hunted him down."

"Looks like that sort of thing sir," agreed the copper. "These drug types can be brutal, not that we see much of it down here."

"Oh, he was from London," Oscar said. "The Docklands. He recently moved here to take the apprenticeship. His probation officer can probably tell you more."

"Thank you sir, I'm sorry you've had this happen, especially so soon after losing your wife under such tragic circumstances. We'll take it from here so as not to inconvenience you any further." The policeman was so deferential that he almost tugged his forelock. Oscar took one last, long look at Kyle's body and hopped back into the buggy to get back to the castle. He needed to face his mother and tell her that the Russians had made it to the castle gates.

Elle had sat beside Ivan's bed all night, in amongst the bleeping machines, whose noises she could almost predict. She wondered how on earth the nurses put up with it. She'd dozed off a few times, but had been periodically woken when they'd come to do his vitals, taking his temperature and blood pressure as well as the frequent blood tests they'd done every hour. Kristov's guards had changed after eight hours, with new ones stationed outside the unit when she visited the loo at three in the morning. She couldn't wait for Viktor to get back, she wanted a familiar face, someone to trust. He'd gone over to pick up her Bentley the previous evening and was in charge of the team that Kristov had placed around the grounds.

"Would you like a cup of tea?" Asked a pretty, lilac-haired nurse, who'd just come on duty. She smiled at Elle.

"Yes please." Elle glanced at her watch, it was nearly eight. She felt disoriented and unsure how long she'd been there.

"Are you alright?" The nurse asked as she set a cup and saucer down on the table next to the bed. She could see that Elle was pregnant.

"Yeah, I'll survive," Elle said. "When our guard gets back I'll see if I can find somewhere to get some breakfast."

"There's a cafe downstairs on the basement floor. They do stuff there," The nurse said. She turned her attention to Ivan. "So, how's handsome today?" She asked his sleeping form as she expertly lifted his head and plumped his pillows.

"Out cold still," Elle said.

"Well, we don't know that," said the nurse, "Sometimes they can hear us, even if they can't respond."

"Hooray," thought Ivan, *"someone realises."*

"I understand he was the reason all those press turned up yesterday," the nurse said. "They soon got bored of being told 'no comment,' and disappeared by the afternoon. It was pandemonium with them all out there. An ambulance had trouble bringing someone in."

"Sorry about that," Elle said. "I came in and out the back way. We're keeping it all under wraps for now, for business reasons," she explained.

"Well there was nothing on the news last night," the nurse said as she took his blood pressure and noted it down. She unclipped a bottle under his bed and lifted it up to see how much was in there. "Well, we know his bladder's working just fine," she said, noting down the amount and clipping a fresh pouch onto the stand.

"Jesus Christ," Ivan thought, as he willed his body to respond. Nothing. He couldn't work out why.

"Hmm, no bowel movement yet," the nurse said brightly. Ivan began to panic slightly. "Right, well, that's him done for the moment. I'll be nearby if you need me, otherwise I'll be back at ten to give him a wash down and change the dressings on his legs." She nodded towards the cage keeping the blanket off of his burnt legs.

Elle watched as her lilac ponytail bobbed as she skipped off to her next patient. She leaned over to whisper in Ivan's ear; "If you can hear me, you need to bloody well wake up. I can't have you dying on me. You can't just check out without ever meeting your son, you hear me? You cannot let these bastards win."

Nothing.

Ivan had tried to move. He could hear the pain in her voice. He wanted so badly to comfort her, but nothing would move. He wondered if he was already dead, then dismissed the idea. Dead people didn't hear the living, didn't feel the pain of not being able to signal their awareness. As he lay there, he heard Viktor arrive, heard him say that the dogs were fine. Ivan relaxed a little at that piece of news. He heard Elle say that she was gonna find some breakfast and heard her chair scrape as she stood up. Knowing that she wasn't around, he allowed himself to drift off again. He just felt so tired.

Elle took one of the new guards down to the cafe with her. He stood as she waited in line at the food bar to choose from rubbery scrambled eggs, or slimy, undercooked fried ones, cremated bacon and barely grilled sausages. it was all a bit grim, but Elle mentally slapped herself and picked out scrambled eggs and some toast as well as a pot of tea. She found a table in the corner and rolled her eyes at the rather menacing guard, who insisted on standing in front of the table, blocking her off from the rest of the room, which simply served to draw more attention. She pulled her phone out of her bag and switched it on, before taking a forkful of egg. She was starving.

Ninety-seven missed calls and forty texts. She blinked. She wasn't expecting any at all, thinking that most people thought she'd been frazzled in the crash. Scrolling through, she was relieved to see that most of them were from Jo, Kristov, and Ranenkiov. She pressed the button to call Jo, needing to speak to someone normal, who wasn't a mad billionaire or a Russian hitman.

"Elle! How is he?" Jo asked as she picked up.

"He's still unconscious," She replied. "How are the dogs?"

"Oh they're fine, although when Bella refused to go out for her wee this morning, I told her she'd be sent back to prison. I've never seen her move so fast. I stayed here last night. I hope you don't mind?"

"Not at all, I'm grateful that the dogs weren't left with just their guards," Elle told her.

"Well, the guards are eating us out of house and home. The place is crawling with them. Your car's back by the way, it's been checked, and it's fine."

"Good. Any other news?"

"Not really. I just wondered how you were holding up."

"I'm ok. I'm getting quite practiced at this worrying about Ivan lark. Roger should be released today, although his hands are bandaged up," Elle said.

"Hmm, how's he gonna *wipe*, you know," Jo asked.

"I hadn't thought of that," Elle admitted. "I might need to organise a nurse for him. I do need you to dig him out some clothes and get them sent over for him, but that's all." They both sniggered. It felt good to talk to someone normal, Elle thought, as she listened to Jo moaning about the mad Russians who were patrolling the grounds, and how they expected Russian food, which in rural Sussex was a bit of a challenge.

"Nico ate English though, didn't he?" Elle asked.

"Yes, although I used to get a few bits for him from Ocado. They do herrings and pickled cabbage." She paused, "I'm gonna miss Nico. He was a decent bloke, easy to get along with, you know."

"Yeah. I'm gonna miss him too," Elle admitted. For as long as Ivan and her had been together, it had always been Nico and Roger in charge. With neither of them around, she felt vulnerable and a bit lonely.

She ate her toast before calling Kristov, wondering if it was too early for him to be in his office. Yet again she had to repeat the same update, that Ivan was still out cold. She hated saying it.

"I have good news," Kristov told her. "Mr Cavendish was killed yesterday evening. It was on the news, but I doubt if you've watched it. Mr Golding has been warned. I think you can consider yourselves relatively safe going forward."

A weight fell off Elle's shoulders. "Thank you. I know when Ivan wakes up he'll be grateful for everything you've done."

"It's nothing, just what any friend would have done. We look after our own Elle, you should know by now that it's the Russian way."

After speaking to Kristov, she sat back and mused on what he'd told her. Darius was dead. She'd commissioned a hit. Her, a lawyer from Welling had actually ordered somebody's death. She shuddered at what she'd become. In the heat of the moment, it had seemed the right thing to do. Under the harsh fluorescent lights of an English hospital, she felt as though she'd become a monster. Ordering a hit was a prison sentence if she got caught, she realised. For the very first time, she was glad that her mother wasn't around to see who'd she'd become.

Speaking to Ranenkiov cheered her up a little. He was part of her world, a world she understood and felt comfortable in. He'd managed to keep a complete news blackout going and assured her that she wasn't needed that week at all, that Galina had sorted both their schedules.

"Make sure nobody on the board tries to vote through extra bonuses," she told him, in reference to what happened when Ivan went missing in Russia and she'd been left in charge.

He laughed, "You honestly think they'd try that trick again? They're more scared of you than they ever were of Ivan." He paused. "Seriously though, if any rumours start flying around that both you and Ivan are dead, it might be wise for you to do a press conference to assure the world that nothing has changed, that Beltan is still running just the same."

"Will do, just let me know. I'll check my phone whenever I come out of the unit."

"And Elle? Don't worry about us here, we'll cope just fine. Galina was asking what injuries Ivan has?"

"Oh, he took a bit of a bump to the head, nothing too serious, his legs got a bit burnt too, looks like he has bad sunburn really," Elle told him. It was going to be the party line, she'd decided. She didn't want the world to know that he'd been gassed, or that it had been an attempted hit.

"She's terribly upset about Nico, think she had quite the crush on him," Ranenkiov mused.

"Really?" Elle was surprised. Galina was a dumpy forty-something with a 'sensible' haircut and wore frumpy outfits. The idea of her and the rather slick, flash, and frankly perverted Nico would have been hilarious if the circumstances had been less sombre. "Poor Galina, give her my best wishes."

As Elle walked back into the unit, Dr Mullins was injecting Ivan with a large hypodermic. Instantly, Elle began to panic, imagining that the contents could be anything, it could be poison. Dr Mullins could be a plant, sent to finish him off. She took a deep breath, trying not to let such an irrational paranoia take hold. "Good morning," Dr Mullins said, oblivious to the internal argument Elle was having with herself. "The blood work from earlier is back. There seems to be some recovery at a cellular level, which is good news."

"How long before he wakes up?" Elle asked.

"Oh we can't predict that I'm afraid. Bear in mind that it was only less than twenty-four hours ago that I was preparing to ask you if you wanted his life support switched off. I think we have a long road ahead."

"I see," Elle said.

"You need to prepare yourself in case he's suffered brain damage, or becomes permanently disabled. We're in uncharted territory with this particular poison," Dr Mullins explained. She was wearing her 'sympathy' face, the one she reserved for telling families bad news.

Poison? Fucking poison? I'll get better so that I can fuck over the person who did this, thought Ivan. *I'll get better, I'm Russian, built to last.*

"His finger moved!" Elle exclaimed. She'd seen it, his forefinger had lifted off the sheet for a moment. It had been fleeting, but was real. She leaned over him, "Do it again if you can hear me," she said. They both stared at his hands.

He lifted his finger. It seemed to take all his strength, but he needed to send a sign to Elle that he was with her.

"So he can hear and understand," the doctor pointed out. "That's extremely good news. We'll continue with the next transfusion, as it seems to be working." She peeled his eyelids open and shone her light in each of his eyes in turn. "Some movement. Ivan, move your finger if you saw or felt me do that" she instructed.

Course I felt that you daft cow. Bloody blinded me too for good measure, Ivan thought as he obediently lifted his finger again.

"Excellent," Dr Mullins declared. "Let's hope he continues to improve. Now, I need to check those burns on his legs." She lifted the sheet off the cage keeping the bedcovers away from his skin. Elle could see that his legs were largely devoid of hair and the skin was tight and shiny. When the doctor gently touched the skin to open his legs a little, Elle saw his finger move again.

"Does that hurt?" She asked him. His finger lifted.

"It will be quite sore," Dr Mullins confirmed. "He was lucky that his trousers were wool and didn't melt into his skin, that's when we see the real damage." She moved on to his head wound, which was a cut on his forehead, which had strips across it to hold it closed. The skin around it was also tight and shiny. "Burnt skin with a cut in it," the doctor explained, "not a great combination, I'm afraid, in terms of pain." She peered closely at it. "All looks nice and clean. Hopefully it won't leave too much of a scar."

Dr Mullins went off to deal with her next patient, leaving Elle sitting by Ivan's bed. She laced her fingers through his, gratified to feel some movement from him as he curled his finger around hers. "You need to come back," she whispered. "You've gotta teach our son the Russian way. I can't do it by myself." She laid her head down on the edge of the bed and kissed his fingers. She felt exhaustion wash over her as she watched the rest of the unit, people with their own dramas going on. In the bay opposite was a young woman, hooked up to machines the same as Ivan. It struck Elle that she hadn't had any visitors since she'd been brought in during the early hours.

That would be me, she thought, painfully aware that she had almost nobody in the world. She decided to give James a call. "I won't be long," she whispered as she stood up. Ivan had drifted off again, soothed by her touch.

"Hey little Elle, how's it going?" James asked. "I've been experimenting with different flavour gelato, I'll bring some next time I'm over." Elle smiled at the sound of his voice.

"Ivan was in a car crash, he's in Sussex General," she told him, "I'm here with him."

"Oh God, when did that happen? Is he alright?"

"Yesterday morning. He's starting to respond to treatment, but it was touch and go for a while. He's not fully out of the woods yet," she said.

"You should've called me," James said, "I could've come down and sat with you." He paused. "So does that affect the launch of 'Frogs Agogo'?" Which was his new game.

"No, Ivan wouldn't be doing the launch himself, I thought it wasn't going live till next month?"

"It's not, but if he's out of action, he can't talk to those fellas who want to buy all the data it generates," James said. "It's not the end of the world, it can go onto the App Store anyway."

"It's the data generation that's gonna make you the money though," Elle said. "If needs be, I'll negotiate on your behalf. Who's buying it?" It was a game where players had to go out and find the frogs which were placed in locations via GPS technology.

"Datatrax, I think they use it to work out which businesses the gogo players go near and flog them advertising, at least that was what they told me," he added. "Anyway, that's not important. Do you want me to come over? I can get an Uber."

She thought about it for a moment, then dismissed the idea. "I'm fine, just tired and need to sleep."

"Make sure you eat regularly," James instructed. "I know what you're like, forgetting meal times when you're busy. That baby can't feed itself just yet."

"I know," she sighed. "It kicks like a donkey when I forget to eat."

"Well, if you need me to come over and take care of you, just holler."

"Will do," Elle replied, glad she'd called him. James was like a best friend and brother all rolled into one. He'd be horrified if he knew she'd turned into the type of person who orders somebody's death, she reasoned. James just quietly dreamed up games, the sort of games that went viral and made headlines as well as pots of cash. His daft, Furious Frogs had driven sales of the Bel-Phone through the roof. Who knew that angry amphibians would prove so popular?

Back in the unit, Elle sat back down beside Ivan. The unit was full, every bed taken and surrounded by equipment which bleeped with annoying regularity. She wondered how any of the patients got a moment's sleep with the noise and bustle. The lilac-haired nurse zipped around, seemingly in five places at once, never taking a break or even slowing down as she checked machines, scribbled down notes, and took vitals. Elle watched her, impressed at her devotion and work ethic.

She lay her head on the edge of Ivan's bed and laced her fingers through his. "I know you can hear me. Please come back, I need you." She paused a moment. "I want our life back, our walks in the woods, our Sunday breakfasts, our giggling in the office when someone says something pompous or stupid. I want our bed picnics with the dogs, watching the news. I want to go back to planning our Conniscliffe, with your silly ideas about kitchen gardens and greenhouses. I want the dynasty, the huge brood of children that we planned, all racing around and making you do that Russian swearing thing that you do when you're cross." She kissed his fingers. "I want our rocking sex life, with it's hard fucks against the wall. I want that face you pull when you know that someone's bullshitting. I just want to be 'us' again, the Porenskis, two people in love that nobody can rip apart because we're the ones who dance on beaches at night under the stars. You need to come back to me baby, we aren't finished yet. We still have the rest of the world for you to own, you're only halfway there." She felt his fingers curl around hers. When she turned her head to see his beautiful face, his eyes were open. She never thought she'd be so happy to see his sapphire eyes again, although her joy was tinged with sadness at having to break the news of Nico's death.

Oscar sat opposite his mother in the breakfast room nursing a cup of black coffee. He couldn't force himself to eat. He noticed that his mother had barely touched her Eggs Benedict. "Are the police going to need to speak to you again?" She asked. He shrugged.

"No idea. They think Kyle was hunted down by someone from his past." It was a lie, and he knew it, but it was a convenient way of keeping that whole thing under wraps. It felt to him as though the Russian mafia had declared war, that they knew of his involvement in Ivan and Elle's assassination. He wondered who'd blabbed, who else knew what Darius and himself had needed to cover up.

"Maybe you need to speak to the Prime Minister," his mother suggested. Oscar shook his head. He didn't want it spreading any further. The more people involved, the more risk there was of someone connecting the dots, working out that the murders all linked back to him.

"I'm hoping that this is the end of it," he said. "Ivan and Elle's deaths have been paid back. That's how those people work, an eye for an eye and all that."

"That doesn't account for Vlad and his daughter," Lady Golding pointed out. "Although I believe they were killed to keep Elle safe. He was still one of them though."

"I don't think anyone minded Vlad being bumped off," Oscar replied. "If anything, I think they were all quite pleased. Ivan was a different story though."

"Hmm, I remember the fuss everyone made when he got kidnapped," Lady Golding said. "Every night on the news it was the headline feature. I think he was somewhat of a poster boy for slum dog Russian made good. It's strange that there's been nothing on the news yet about his death."

"I think the firm are keeping it all under wraps for now until they can figure out what to do. I'm surprised that nobody from Beltan has called me though. They must need a board meeting."

"It's only been a day or two, give them a chance," she replied. "They're probably panicking right now, wondering who inherits. I'm sure you'll get a call in due course."

Oscar had taken to sleeping in one of the other bedrooms as he felt safer being in Stella's apartment. Although all the apartments were interlinked and had connecting doors, he felt insulated against anyone finding him quickly. There was also no trace of Lucy in the large, rather soul-less room. He braced himself to visit his own bedroom. He needed to organise Jones to clear out her clothes and stuff. It was a job that he'd been putting off, but as her parents were coming over for her funeral, he needed to check to see if there was anything he needed to return to them.

His room was comfortingly familiar, it was the same room he'd slept in since he was a teenager, although he'd changed the decor over the years. He closed the door behind himself and opened the first of three enormous wardrobes. Lucy's clothes hung next to his suits, their bright colours contrasting with the dull, muddy colours of his formal wear. He worked methodically, pulling all her dresses off their hangers and folding them into a neat pile. There were too many memories attached to some of the frocks, of places they'd been together, good times they'd had. In particular, the silk Grecian-style dress she wore when he first met her. He lingered on that one, sniffing it to see if it still carried her perfume, before adding it to the pile.

When he'd finished the wardrobes, he moved on to the drawers. Lucy's makeup and skincare were unceremoniously dumped onto the floor, followed by her socks, tights and bras. He lingered over her knickers, finding the large, soft cotton ones that he'd found so appealing. He recalled her amusement at finding out about that particular fetish and her willingness to indulge him.

He was dreading opening her shoe cabinet. Rows of heels stared back at him, mocking him with their red soles and shiny leather. He slammed the door shut, unable to bring himself to touch them.

He was interrupted by Jones, who announced that the police were downstairs in the drawing room. He pulled himself together and followed his butler down. As he strode in, the two policemen stood. Oscar recognised the one with whom he'd spoken to the previous morning when Kyle's body had been found.

"Good morning sir, sorry to interrupt you," he said, "Just an update really. The autopsy on the body was done last night. It showed that he was killed by a single gunshot to the heart. He was already dead by the time he was beheaded."

Oscar bowed his head. It would have been over quickly. It was a small mercy.

"He was carrying some 'skunk,' which is a type of strong cannabis, in his pocket, as well as a substantial amount of cash. We checked his bank records, which showed that he withdrew very little of his wages. He was clearly living on something, so the conclusion we've come to was that he was dealing drugs again." The policeman paused. "I'm sorry that this happened sir. I know you thought you were giving him a second chance, giving him a job and a new home…" He tailed off.

"No good deed goes unpunished," Oscar said. He felt incredibly guilty, allowing Kyle's memory be trashed just so that nobody asked awkward questions.

"Yes, quite," agreed the pc, who had come to the conclusion that Oscar was one of those daft liberals who thought that crooks just needed more hugs and mollycoddling. "Anyway, forensics have finished with your gates, so we've sent in a specialist cleaning company. They're up there now," he said, nodding towards the driveway.

"Thank you," Oscar said. "By the way, I heard about that crash on the A21 on Monday. Dreadful business with all those people killed. Did you discover what caused it?"

"Driver speeding I believe," the copper replied. "Thankfully only one person killed and that was the driver himself." He shook his head. "Could so easily have been carnage that time of the morning, all those people travelling to work. Still, better be getting back to the station, lots of paperwork to do."

Oscar was barely aware of them leaving, his mind working overtime with the revelation that Elle was still alive. He briefly toyed with the idea that Ivan could have been the driver, but dismissed it. Ivan rarely drove himself and would've needed his drivers up in London with him. Ivan being alive would explain Darius' assassination and Kyle's death, which could have been a warning that the Russians meant business. He hurried over to his mother's apartment to share the news with her.

CHAPTER SEVENTEEN

The doctors wasted no time in removing Ivan's breathing tube. Once it was out, he tried to speak, but only a hoarse little squeak came out at first. It was still an effort to move, but at least he could see. He gazed at Elle and thanked the Russian Gods that she was ok, not even a scratch on her pretty face. She'd stood to show him that her bump was still alright and lifted his hand to place it on there so that he could feel the baby kick.

The next event was a move to a more secluded side room. Elle organised a room in the small, private wing, which was normally used for people having paid-for hip replacements in order to escape the inevitable long NHS waiting lists. It still stank of disinfectant, but was at least quieter and had better food. Elle had her first proper meal in over three days.

They'd just got settled when Roger turned up, his hands still swathed in bandages and sporting a black eye. "How's he doing?"

"He's awake," Elle said. "Not saying much as yet, but at least he can breathe on his own. How are you feeling?"

"I'm ok," Roger told her. "Still got a bit of a headache and it's bloody awkward with these on." He held up his hands. "I had a devil of a job finding you in here. Reception didn't seem to know where you were."

"Press blackout," Elle said. "I'll fill you in on everything later on at home. One of the goons can drop you off, it'll give them something to do." She tipped her head towards the door, where the corridor outside was lined with black-suited Russians.

"That was how I found you," Roger said, his eyes twinkling with mirth. "I just followed the bodyguards."

"Think Kristov went a bit overboard," Elle agreed. "Still, after what happened, I can't say as I blame him." She looked pointedly at his bandages, "Now, do we need to organise a nurse at home for you?"

"No, why?" Roger asked. Elle just raised her eyebrows. The penny dropped. "I'll be fine," he snapped.

"Ok, your call," Elle said, "The offer's there."

When Roger had gone, she went outside to call Ranenkiov and tell him the good news that Ivan had woken up. "That's a relief," he'd said when she'd relayed the information, "I was starting to worry. The press don't appear to have got hold of anything yet, but it was only a matter of time."

"The hospital has been pretty good too," Elle said. "They haven't broadcast that we're here at all. He's in the private wing now, so it's quieter and more comfortable."

"When is he allowed to go home?" Ranenkiov asked.

"I think we're a way off that decision," Elle warned. The doctor had examined him when he'd woken up and although she was pleased with his progress, she was still warning of the possibility of permanent damage. Until he could speak, it was tricky to assess.

"Ok. Well, I'd suggest we just carry on as normal. If anything blows up, we can address it, but all the while it's quiet, I'd suggest we enjoy the peace." He was right, Elle thought.

As she walked back towards Ivan's room, Dr Mullins approached. "I've been looking for you," she said. Elle tensed up straightaway. "Nothing bad, just wanted a chat." They fell into step as they walked the long corridor. "I should really alert the police about the substance that your husband breathed in. I'm worried that it may have been something within the car interior that didn't conform to the British Standard," she said, "What type of car was it?"

"A Bentley," Elle replied. "I'd rather it wasn't reported. I don't think it was a bit of dodgy foam."

"Oh?" The doctor asked, "and you think it was?"

"We know what it was, you told us." She paused. "Ivan is a highly prominent businessman, the Russian version of Bill Gates or Mark Zuckerberg if you will. There will always be people targeting us. It's something we live with and we're well protected. This time they got lucky. We know how they got to us, what they used, and how we need to protect ourselves from the same thing in future. So having clumsy Sussex Bobbies poking around, telling us to lock our windows really won't do a lot of good when we already live in a place with laser wire and a nuclear bunker. At best it'll be a nuisance, at worst there'll be an international incident."

Dr Mullins listened, then thought for a moment. "I'll say it was smoke inhalation on the official report, but, and it's a big but, if he has long-term health problems because of this, he must disclose what happened to whoever is treating him."

"He will. I have to ask, is there any record of the Zyklon B inhalation anywhere else?"

"Just his hospital record, which I'll take care of," she said. "I can't alter it, but I can seal it, citing privacy concerns. My colleagues won't divulge anything regarding Ivan's health, treatment, or care to the press."

"Good."

"So was this an assassination attempt?" Dr Mullins asked.

Elle just shrugged. She never liked to confirm or deny.

When they reached the room, Ivan was awake. He smiled at the sight of Elle. "Hi," he croaked.

"Hey you," she replied, glad to hear his voice.

"I'm going to test your cognitive abilities Ivan," said Dr Mullins, "What's two and two?"

"Four," Ivan muttered. Elle laughed.

"What's twenty-four percent of four-point-seven-five million?" She butted in.

"One million, one hundred and forty thousand," Ivan rasped.

"He's fine," Elle said. Dr Mullins' mouth had dropped open.

"Is that correct?" She eventually asked. "I don't have my calculator."

"Oh yes, it's correct," Elle said, amused.

"Can you get this tube out of my dick now please?" Ivan croaked. Out of everything, it was the thing bothering him the most. The thought of a big tube going down his pee-hole made him feel quite queasy, let alone the horror of having a bag of pee by the side of the bed for all to see.

"I'll do it after your injection," she told him, pulling out a syringe and a bottle of the stuff they were injecting him with. He lay back and let her do it, then ordered Elle out of the room when it came to the catheter removal. He really didn't want her watching that.

"Are you hungry?" She asked, just before she left. He nodded. "I'll see what I can find."

When she returned, she was carrying a plastic bag. She began to lay the contents out on his wheely-table. There were yoghurts, bars of chocolate, pots of jelly, and some cake. She'd also bought him a coffee from the coffee shop in the reception hall, and a straw.

"Did it hurt?" She asked when she sat down on the chair. He gave her a quizzical look. "Your pee hole? Is it permanently stretched?"

"Bloody hope not," he muttered, assessing the haul on the table in front of him. It was really warm in the room and the yoghurt would be cold. He tried to reach over to it, but his arms were weak and wouldn't lift that high.

"Here, let me," Elle said, taking the yoghurt and peeling back the lid. Tenderly and carefully, she spooned it into his mouth. It tasted wonderful.

"You're a good wife," he told her after she'd wiped his mouth.

"You might not say that when you've found out what I've done," she murmured. He turned his head towards her. "I ordered a hit on Darius," she confessed. "Kristov found someone to do it. It cost five million." She cringed waiting for his croaky anger to ensue.

"That's actually kind of sexy," he admitted. "Naughty, illegal, but yeah, sexy." He paused. "Is it done?"

She nodded. "He also said he'd fire a warning over Oscar's head. I don't know really what he meant, but I'm assuming we'll have to pay for that too."

Ivan blinked. "It means they kill someone close to Oscar, to frighten him into thinking that he's next." Elle's jaw dropped open.

"I hope it wasn't his mother, or Jones, his butler," she said, horrified. "I'm sorry, I really didn't know. I thought they'd put a horse's head in his bed or something. It'd be ok if it was that miserable bitch of a PA he has."

"I'm sure Kristov will tell you," Ivan said. "They're the Russian mafia, Elle, they really don't mess about with horses heads. That's for the Sicilian pussies." He sank back into his pillow, "I bet Kristov's been having a great time, he loves a good scrap."

Elle was appalled. "Ivan, this wasn't a 'scrap,' this was a sophisticated attempt to assassinate us both, which caused Nico's death, your near death, Roger's burnt and took a bash to the head, and the dogs ended up in prison, not to mention Lucy being killed and that poor unfortunate woman being framed for her murder." Her voice rose in pitch as she became more and more indignant. "It was a horrible chain of events that wouldn't have stopped until either we were both dead or Darius was."

"You know, you're magnificent when you're angry," he rasped. "So you know that Lucy was murdered then?" She nodded. "Wondered when you'd work it out," he murmured.

"So how are you feeling?" Elle asked, mainly to change the subject.

"I feel as though I've been burnt from the inside out," Ivan confessed. He wasn't certain whether his raw and painful throat was from the smoke or the poison that they'd spoken about, but it was as though a fire had raged in his lungs, leaving behind molten lava. He also really, really needed five minutes alone to go sit on the loo. "It doesn't hurt as much as it did yesterday," he told her. "My legs prickle from the burns still."

"You sound very hoarse," Elle pointed out. She pulled the lid off the jelly and began to eat it. He sat back and watched her, thinking how amazingly well she could adapt to any situation. In any crisis, he'd rather have Elle beside him rather than any man, except maybe Roger, or Nico (God rest his soul).

"You should go home for a while, get some sleep and some proper food," he suggested, "See to the dogs as well, they'll be wondering what's going on." He was getting a little desperate.

"Hmm, if you're sure?" She asked, concerned that he'd be all alone. The idea of a hot shower and her bed was tempting.

"I'm sure. Don't worry, I'll just sleep. It's hard to do with you here."

She grinned, kissed him on the cheek and skipped off. He breathed a sigh of relief, before calling Viktor to get one of the others and help him get to the bathroom.

He almost shouted in pain as his feet hit the floor, but confined himself to muttering some choice swear words in Russian. Viktor wheeled his drip as he propped Ivan up under his armpit, the other side supported by one of Kristov's men, as they made their way into the ensuite shower room. As he finally let go, Ivan looked around the white-tiled, rather stark room and felt homesick. He wondered how long he'd be in hospital, how long it would be until he felt normal again. It scared him that the simple act of wiping his own arse seemed like climbing Mount Everest in terms of effort required. He really was as weak as a kitten, although he did feel a whole lot better for spending five minutes on the loo. As Viktor and his friend helped him back to bed, his anger at Oscar began to burn almost as fiercely as the fire in his Bentley.

Oscar wasn't sure whether or not to be elated at the news that Elle was alive, or terrified that she was clearly now a powerful adversary with a good reason to bear him a massive grudge. Strangely enough, he felt quite safe from exposure, after all, as his mother had pointed out, they all had secrets to hide. He toyed with the idea of calling her, while his mother was on the phone chatting to her new friend, the foreign secretary.

"The Russian government are denying all knowledge of the hack that led to the CCTV going down," Lady Golding announced as she swept into the drawing room. "He's calling it a 'domestic issue,' whatever that means," she said.

"It means they know it wasn't government versus government," Oscar explained. "They realise it was a personal grudge against Darius, not a reason to declare World War Three."

"Maybe they knew what he was like," his mother suggested. She picked up the teapot that Jones had left out and poured them both a cup, arranging two biscuits on Oscar's saucer, just as he liked it. She handed it to him. Absent-mindedly, he dunked his biscuit in his tea and popped it in his mouth. He chewed thoughtfully.

"That was the impression I got from the Chief Whip. Apparently none of his old colleagues are terribly keen to launch a full investigation, preferring to leave it to the plods. That Penfold woman has been released from custody too, they've even paid for her to have a stay in the Priory."

"That's an admission of guilt if ever I heard one," Lady Golding snorted. "What you need to understand though, is that Elle and Ivan may well think you ordered the hit. I'm not certain how we reassure them that you didn't. The downside of that is your own safety, whether you're next on the hit-list."

It had never failed to amaze Oscar how astute his mother could be. Even at over sixty years old, her political antennae were perfectly tuned. In another era, she'd have been a politician, no doubt in the cabinet or higher. "I warned her that the car was rigged," he reminded her.

"But you didn't stop them rigging it," she replied. He frowned. "Now you can say till you're blue in the face that you didn't know he was doing it, but they won't believe you. They won't accept that you had no power over Darius at all, that he acted alone, without your consent or involvement." She paused. "Kyle's killing shows you that."

"So what do you suggest I do?" He asked.

"Nothing, I'll talk to her," his mother said, "She won't feel threatened by me."

He sagged back into his chair. His life turned from harmonious good order into a chain reaction of one nightmare after another within less than a week. Kyle's girlfriend, Amber, one of the garden apprentices, had been to see him that afternoon, tearfully defending Kyle's reputation. It had been excruciating listening to her, especially when he knew that the weed in Kyle's pocket had been for him. He hadn't even confessed that one to his mother.

Lady Golding was shocked when Elle answered her mobile, she'd expected her to have it switched off while in the hospital. Elle didn't want to explain that she'd gone home, at Ivan's insistence, to get some sleep and see the girls. When Lady Golding's number flashed up, curiosity alone prompted Elle to pick up.

"I'm so glad that you're alright," Lady Golding said. Elle was quite relieved too, realising that Kristov hadn't bumped her off, but she didn't say that.

"Are you?" She asked rather coldly, making Lady Golding sigh inwardly. This wasn't going to be easy.

"Of course I am," she replied. "I never wanted any of this to happen, neither did Oscar."

Elle snorted. She was exhausted, both mentally and physically and was having rather a sense of humour failure about the whole situation. "You expect me to believe that, when he ordered a hit on us? Or did he not tell you that bit?" She went straight for the jugular. Elle had fought people like them her whole life, people who regarded her as a common little upstart, someone who didn't belong in their closed-off, snotty club. She knew exactly what Lady Golding and Oscar stood for, how they regarded her and Ivan as classless nouveau-riche barbarians.

"He told me everything, and I mean everything. I'm as appalled by it all as you are," Lady Golding told her.

"Appalled at Ivan being gassed by the stuff used to kill six million of your kind?" Elle spat. It was the one thing in the whole sorry event that she found most horrific. "It was only sheer bloody luck that we weren't all in the same car. Well, lucky for us, not for Oscar."

"He was gassed?" Lady Golding couldn't disguise the horror in her voice. Her Aunt had died in the gas chambers during the war. She closed her eyes briefly, trying to take in the enormity of what she'd just been told. It was worse than she'd imagined.

"Oh yes. Zyklon B was pumped into the car. Kill the occupants to make it crash. We lost Nico, Ivan's bodyguard. Ivan made it out by the skin of his teeth thanks to my guard being willing to put his own life on the line to pull him out. Did Oscar tell you about all that?"

"I didn't know," Lady Golding admitted. "I don't think Oscar did either. Darius did this without Oscar's involvement."

"Oscar knew about it," Elle pointed out. "I know he knew because he got cold feet at the last minute and called me. He knew the car had been tampered with, so please don't try and cover up the fact that he was part of it too. Lucy's murder as well."

"He most definitely wasn't involved in that. He begged Darius to leave Lucy alone, let you and I convince her to stay quiet. Darius just did it anyway, although he had us all fooled for a while," Lady Golding explained, "It was so slick, using that Penfold woman, knowing she had a grudge."

"How did he know about her?" Elle demanded.

"During dinner, he listened while Lucy told him about the case, pretended to be all sympathetic. In truth he was just gleaning information. He was furious about her being pregnant, of Oscar having something he didn't have."

"Sick bastard," Elle said.

"I'm glad he's dead," Lady Golding admitted, "he's been the cause of pretty much every problem Oscar's ever had."

"Lady Golding, I know you want to paint your golden boy as a perfect angel, who is as much a victim in all of this as Lucy, who's in the morgue, or Ivan who's still in hospital, but Oscar used Darius as his personal henchman on more than one occasion. Oscar knew exactly what Darius would do, what he was capable of, so let's just stick with the idea that Oscar was involved."

"Have you put a contract out on Oscar?" Lady Golding asked, she held her breath for the answer.

"Don't be ridiculous," Elle snapped. "How would I do that?"

"The Russian mafia got Darius."

"Did they?" Elle replied. "I haven't had a chance to watch the news much this week." Her lawyer training had kicked in. Never confirm or deny.

"They killed one of our gardeners too, although the police think it was a drug-linked murder," she pressed.

"Well, maybe it was, I have no idea. The thing is Lady Golding, Darius murdered Vlad and his daughter, then had a pop at Ivan and me, as well as killing our guard. The Russians look after their own. I certainly don't control them, but they're fond of Ivan, even though he's not one of them and let's face it, who wouldn't stand up for a pregnant woman?"

Elle heard a sob, which surprised her. "Oscar thought you were dead," Lady Golding said in a small voice. "He was more upset about that than anything else, even Lucy."

"We imposed a news blackout," Elle admitted. "It was a decision we took initially for business reasons. Too many sharks would be circling if they knew Ivan was out of action. Secondly, I knew it was a hit, so by letting Oscar think we were dead, well, it kept us safe for a few days. I was just drafting a press statement when you called." She fiddled with the pen in her hand, flipping it around her fingers as she waited for the reply. She heard a sniff.

"This is a dreadful situation," Lady Golding said. "You must have been so frightened."

"I was terrified," Elle admitted, "and I still am." She paused. "Ivan can't even lift his hand to feed himself at the moment." She heard a gasp. "My personal guard has both hands burnt to smithereens, and I've been left to run a conglomerate at five months pregnant, despite being too frightened to get into a car and feeling as though I should be watching over Ivan twenty-four-seven in case someone tries to finish the job." She sounded a lot cooler than she felt. Her hands shook so much that she dropped the pen. It was a mess of epic proportions.

"So... what do we need to do?" Lady Golding asked. She put the ball back in Elle's court.

Elle thought for a moment. "I think that I'll fold the company we all invested in, it's inappropriate to be in business with Oscar." She heard a sigh. "He'll be invited to resign as chairman of Beltan, and I'll wait until Ivan's better before we make any further decisions."

"But you'll all lose a fortune if you just fold that company," Lady Golding pointed out.

"We won't. Oscar will. The land was never included in the company assets, that's owned by Ivan personally under Ukrainian property law. He can develop it for another use, it doesn't need to be mined," Elle said. "Oscar only wanted it to gain leverage over the Ukrainian government for political reasons. He can go use someone else."

"But.." Lady Golding tried to interrupt.

"Oscar should read the contract. I wrote a get-out clause in section three, subsection 'a' for just this kind of scenario. You might be blind to Oscar's foibles, but I'm not."

Game, set, match, Elle thought as she ended the call.

Oscar had heard the entire conversation. He sighed and scrubbed at his face when Elle put the phone down on his mother. Any ideas that she'd be a pushover, anxious to keep the peace had dissipated. He should have known that she'd be a formidable adversary.

His mother interrupted his thoughts. "Is there anything they'd want that we could use to buy them off?" She asked. "Because if we try and fight them, they'll make your indiscretion public, and this whole sorry saga will have been for nothing. Elle's not owning up to either of those murders, and I think we'd have a hard time linking them to anything."

"He'll ask for Conniscliffe, I know he will," Oscar said. "You told me yourself that he's a greedy man and now that he owns all the land on both sides of us, he'll want it as a grand, vast estate."

Lady Golding's face went white. She knew he was right, having seen the covetous envy on Ivan's face when he'd been shown around during his first visit. "How much did you invest in that mining company?" She asked.

"Two hundred and fifty million," Oscar replied. "If giving up Conniscliffe saves the deal, it'll be well worth it. Besides, if hostilities don't cease, do you really want to be living slap bang in the middle of their land, knowing they could pick us off one-by-one over the fence?"

"I really thought I'd die here," his mother said quietly. "Could you not threaten exposure for the money you laundered for him? The dodgy deals you helped with?"

He shook his head. "They'd damage me more than him. One thing you have to understand about someone like Ivan is that he doesn't care about public opinion, doesn't give a toss about public shame, besides, he's the poster boy for every hotshot wannabe out there. They'd probably toast his ability to get one over on the taxman while screaming for my head on a spike." He grabbed his mobile. "I'm going to talk to Elle myself." He scrolled through his contacts till he found her number, then taking a deep breath, tapped the screen.

"Oscar. I wondered how long it would take before I heard from you," Elle said. He could hear the sarcasm and hostility in her voice.

"I need to talk to you, to properly talk. We need to put an end to this," Oscar said.

"I agree," said Elle. His stomach jumped. "I think Ivan and I have suffered enough for a situation that we never brought about in the first place. Did your mother tell you I'm folding the mining company? Sorry about your quarter of a billion, but, you know, trust is an important part of any business relationship, isn't it?"

"Before you do anything, can we meet? There must be a better way to resolve this. I really didn't want any of this to happen, you must believe me."

Elle thought about how frantic he'd been, screaming at her to get out of the car. She did believe that he hadn't ordered the hit himself. "I need some sleep and time to think," she admitted. "Let's make it tomorrow, but on neutral ground in a public place."

"How about the Koffee Tavern in Derwent High Street at ten?" He asked.

"Yeah, ok."

"You won't do anything or make any decisions until after we've spoken?" He held his breath.

"Only the press release I'm working on, just saying that Ivan and I are fine, and our sadness at Nico's death. I need to get that out there, convince our staff and clients that all's well. Beyond that, I'll just sleep, eat, and reassure the dogs that they won't be taken back to prison again," she said.

He frowned. "Why were the dogs in prison?"

"Long story. I'll tell you tomorrow," she said, trying to stifle a yawn. "Now if you'll excuse me, I have a million things to take care of."

CHAPTER EIGHTEEN

"He's running scared," Ivan said when she went back to the hospital that night. "He'll try and buy you off, I bet you what you like. He'll give you anything to make this all go away, the pillock." He was sitting up in bed looking far happier and a lot pinker again, due to another blood transfusion that afternoon while Elle had been catching up on sleep with the dogs tightly pressed up against her.

"I'll wait and see what he has to say tomorrow," Elle replied. "Now, Jo sends her love and has prepared a bed picnic for you in case the food isn't up to much. I warned her it needed to be soft and cold, so she did some blinis with cream cheese and caviar for you, as well as whipping you up some of her salmon mousse and a banana custard that she said she made for her kids when they were poorly." She took various Tupperware boxes out of a cool bag and placed them on his wheely-table.

He eyed the contents greedily, his appetite starting to return. "I sent out a press release saying we were both fine, but grieving Nico, sending our condolences to his family etcetera," she went on, "and the dogs are fine, missing you though I think. Jo said that Bella weed in the conservatory and Tania stole one of your jumpers to sleep with."

"Poor baby girls," Ivan said, smiling indulgently. "Dr Mullins was in earlier, apparently my red blood cells are almost back to normal. My legs still hurt like a bitch though."

"You look much better," Elle told him. "Did that catheter hole close up ok?"

"There's been people in and out all day, I've not had a chance to check," Ivan said rather prissily. Elle laughed and dived under the blanket covering him.

"Looks OK to me," he heard her muffled voice say.

He cupped himself with his hands, "Leave it alone, I've not showered." She emerged from the covers.

"Spoilsport. I'm so horny I could jump you here and now. The books said that in the second trimester this could happen."

Ivan rolled his eyes. "I wouldn't normally turn you down, but..." He saw her pout and laughed, which hurt his throat and ended in a cough. He took a sip of water. "Doctor says I might be able to go home in a couple of days. I was thinking of asking Galina to courier over some work. I've got quite a few reports that I could be reading while I'm laying here."

"She can email them. I'll print them off and get one of the guards to bring them over in the morning. James was asking about the Datatrax negotiations."

"We're quite a way along the process. I'm still not a hundred percent sure how they're going to use the data that they get, but they're willing to pay a hefty amount for it. If the app takes off, it'll make James a very wealthy man indeed." Ivan spoke in between bites of blini. "I can get that all tied up next week, I'll make it a priority." He licked some caviar off his fingers.

"You think you're going to work next week?" Elle asked, surprised. "I spoke to Galina earlier, everything's fine, and she cleared your diary for the next two weeks."

"We could always go to France," he said, "get a bit of R and R."

"Great idea." She paused, "How do I get the plane organised?"

Ivan blinked at her. They normally relied on Nico for stuff like that, in fact they'd relied on Nico to run a lot of their life. "Give Andrei a call, see if he knows," he muttered. Elle pulled a notepad and pen out of her bag and started making a list. "Oh, and call Kristov. Tell him I'd like to see him." He wanted to thank him personally as well as find out how much he owed him for all his services. "Give Andrea Mills a call, see if she can find us a new Assistant Head of Security. Tell Roger he's in charge, once his hands are better." He watched as she made notes in her neat, small handwriting. "Might be an idea to get that dog psychologist back in, make sure the girls are over the shock." He looked up to see that her mouth had settled into a thin, rather grumpy line. "What?" He asked.

She put down the notepad and pen. "Rather than being back to barking your orders at me, wouldn't it be a better idea to ask how I'm holding up? I mean, I watched you get almost killed, was the intended victim of a hit, lost a couple of people who meant a lot to me, and I've turned into the sort of monster who orders hits on people." Her eyes filled with tears. "And all you worry about are the dogs."

He patted the side of the bed. Obediently, she got up from her chair and perched beside him. He wrapped his arms around her. "I'm sorry Malyshka, I just can't shake off this tendency to be a tosser. I do try, you know." She smiled through her tears, which were dripping down her face.

"I was so scared," she confided.

He kissed her wet cheek. "I know. I was too, but I'm glad it was me and not you and Ivan junior." He paused. "We're the Porenskis remember? I know you think I'm a mental billionaire, but I'm only really me when you're around. I probably don't tell you that often enough." He pressed a soft kiss onto her lips. "Now, you're going to make up with Oscar, end this nightmare once and for all, and we'll be able to go back to our lovely life together."

She pulled away to gaze at his beautiful face. Even with the cut above his eyebrow, he was still astonishingly handsome. "If I negotiate with him, will that satisfy you?"

"Of course," he said. "I will tell you now though that I recorded Lucy when she was in our house that night. You might want to use that as leverage. It's on a USB stick in my safe at the back. I marked it LG."

"What do you want me to achieve?" She asked. He shrugged.

"Put an end to it all, get the mining company secured, the rest is just gravy."

At five to ten the following morning, Oscar sat awkwardly on a hard wooden chair in the window of the Koffee Tavern in Derwent High Street, which was an ambitious name for a small row of shops containing mostly antique/junk emporiums and a few takeaways. The nearest Starbucks was at least twenty miles away, so the antiquated cafe had no competition, and the proprietors hadn't seen any reason to upgrade the place. He'd ordered a black coffee for himself and a pot of tea for Elle, having remembered that she was off coffee. Two elderly ladies shared a pot of tea at a table near the back, away from the heat of the window, apart from them and a bored-looking waitress, the place was empty. Oscar had never been there before.

"This is a world away from Smollenski's isn't it?" Said Elle as she strolled in, closely followed by a tall, dark-suited man whom Oscar had never seen before. He scanned the room and satisfied that there were no potential assassins, sat himself down at a table between them and the elderly ladies, just in case. The bored-looking waitress sauntered slowly over to him to take his order. Elle watched in astonishment as she wrote 'a black coffee' on her notepad.

"How are you?" Oscar enquired as he began to pour her tea for her.

"So-so," she replied, "you?"

"Same," Oscar said.

A silence stretched between them. Elle took a sip of her tea. Oscar watched her intently. Eventually he spoke; "I never wanted any of this, you do know that don't you?"

She shrugged. "I know that Ivan isn't your favourite person. I doubt if you'd have shed any tears over him."

"That's not true at all," Oscar said. "I'm in business with him, with you both. I've known him a long time, we were friends long before you came on the scene." He stirred his coffee for the umpteenth time, his actions betraying his nerves. "I miss Lucy," he said, staring into his spinning coffee. "I begged Darius not to hurt her, thought he'd let me sort it out, like he did with you. I didn't know he'd move so damn fast. I never got a chance to warn her."

Elle could see quite clearly that he was a man in pain. His shoulders were slumped, and a lack of sleep was etched onto his face. he seemed defeated, as though he would take any punches she chose to throw.

"They killed a young man called Kyle," he went on, "shot him through the heart, then beheaded him and left it spiked on top of the main gates. The police think it was a drug deal gone wrong."

"Oh?" Elle asked. "Maybe it was."

He shot her a 'don't be daft' look. "I met him at Narcotics Anonymous. I was helping him, you know, with a job, learn a trade, get out of London type thing."

Elle stayed silent. It wasn't what she'd had wanted at all. Kristov was far more brutal than she'd ever expected.

"It was my stupid idea of penance, for the way I'd treated you. I thought if I helped someone escape their poverty, somehow it would make up for what I did to you."

"You did it to make yourself feel better," Elle pointed out. "It had no bearing on me whatsoever." She leaned in closer. "In case you haven't noticed, I've not been a pauper for quite a while now." She sat back. "I'm still of the peasant class though, and that's what's important to you." He shook his head, but she went on; "Lucy was a lady, everything you ever could have wanted. She was beautiful, charming, easy going. I could carry on forever saying how perfect she was for you, but you still had to do what you did." Her cornflower blue eyes burned into his.

"I'm an addict, not just coke, in almost everything I've ever done. I gave up Darius after you, well, for a long, long time. Then I needed a favour and that was his price. Before I knew it, I was in thrall to him again, like the addict I am." He paused. "My mother's delighted that he's dead. She always disliked him, said he was a sociopath, that he'd always been able to manipulate me."

"How's Arabella?" Elle asked.

Oscar shrugged, "She's ok. I think her parents are quite relieved really. I gather her father never liked him that much."

"I'm sure not many people did," Elle said.

"No. I spoke to someone in government who let on that even his colleagues aren't too fussed. They've left it to Scotland Yard to investigate. Apparently, they think it was the Israelis who assassinated him, pretending to be Russians, so it's all been hushed up and quietly dropped in case they offend Mossad."

"I'm sure none of them wanted to venture down that particular rabbit hole," Elle agreed. "You know that Ivan and Nico were gassed in the car?"

He nodded. My mother told me. She lost her aunt, my great aunt, to the gas chambers. She was horrified and so am I."

"It was the same way that he killed Vlad and Dascha, ordered by you," she pointed out.

"To keep you safe," he countered. "Not that it counts for much now, but I didn't know it was how they did it. I didn't ask, and Darius never volunteered that sort of information." He took a sip of his coffee, wincing at how dreadful it was and met her gaze. "I asked you once, what was the price of your silence and you let me off scot free. This time Ivan's involved. I know his silence will come at a cost."

"He recorded Lucy when she turned up at our house," Elle told him. Oscar went pale, "so I can pretty much guarantee that he'll want his pound of flesh. He's also missing his man Friday and is currently in a lot of pain. Now, I suggested that we close down the mining operation and cease all contact with you. You'll take a quarter of a billion pound hit, but I'm sure that won't dent your fortune too badly. It will, however, scupper your geo-political ambitions in that area."

"And what did Ivan want?" Oscar asked. He knew, just knew he'd ask for Conniscliffe.

"Well at first he said he wanted your castle, but, well, I think that would be too unfair. Plus I'm excited about the house he's building for me at Maytrees, The Bonnington-Carter estate," she clarified. "I couldn't take Conniscliffe from you, I know how much it means." The truth of the matter is that neither of them had wanted the old place. Elle had pointed out to Ivan that Oscar spent most of his time patching it up. The two of them were rather looking forward to their sleek new indoor pool and media room. Damp dungeons and perilous turrets just didn't compare.

"Thank you," Oscar breathed. He wanted to kiss her.

"That said, I'd be prepared to swap the recording and Ivan's silence in return for the Fabergé eggs."

Is that all? Oscar thought. He stayed silent. He knew it was a fair trade. She could've taken him for far more. They both knew that he was desperate. He'd never been able to fool Elle.

"I know they're nowhere near the value of the castle or the mining operation, but this isn't about monetary value, this is about keeping all of us happy," Elle pointed out, "and those eggs would mean a great deal to Ivan, more so than to you and I."

"Then it's a fair trade," Oscar said. "I'll get them shipped over to you this afternoon."

"And I'll give you the memory stick," Elle promised. She was relieved it was all over. "How is your mother?" She asked politely.

"I think she's aged about ten years this week," Oscar admitted. "She cried so much over Lucy, then you, that I thought she'd descend back into depression again. It was so nice seeing her so happy before, even Stella was surprised. She ended up staying for a whole week after the wedding."

"And what are you going to do?" Elle asked.

Oscar sighed. "I can't get my head around the fact that I'm a widower. I'm so angry at what Darius stole from me: my wife, my unborn child. It's just too much to take in really. Her parents get back from Tuscany tomorrow, then we have the funeral to plan. After that... I don't know. I'll just go back to work and carry on I suppose." His eyes glossed over as he thought of going back to his apartment alone. Elle reached across the table and grasped his hand. It felt strangely familiar to both of them. After all the bad blood that had passed, they still cared about each other. "You will come to the funeral won't you?" She nodded.

"You'll survive. You're stronger than you think," she said, her mind flashing back to the time they were together. "Now that you're free of Darius, you can be your own man."

"It's funny, but I always used to think it was my father who bullied me. It's only now that I understand that it was Darius all along. My father tried to get me away from him. The stuff my mother's told me this week has been quite a revelation." He smiled at Elle, in no rush to pull his hand away. "And for your information, I'm glad Ivan survived this, because if he hadn't, there'd have been no way back and I'd hate to make a permanent enemy of you." He gazed at her with his bright blue eyes, full of sincerity.

"Only me?" Elle quipped.

"Don't think I haven't seen all the mafia oiks crawling around your estate this week," he pointed out, smiling, "They're goose-stepping around the fences like the bloody Gestapo."

"I went a bit overboard with the security guards. They're lining the corridor outside Ivan's room in the hospital too, getting in the way and leering at the nurses. They think I haven't noticed," she said, returning his smile.

"You mentioned that the dogs were in prison," he said, "what was that all about?" They shared another pot of tea, as Oscar had given up on the coffee, while Elle regaled him with the story, including how the police vet had declared the girls 'seriously overweight.'

"I wish I could have helped you," he said at the end, "even if it was just lifts to the hospital and moral support."

"The team have been great," she told him. "I'm just glad that I'm not looking over my shoulder all the time."

Kristov sat beside Ivan's bed and filled him in on what had been done and what had been discovered while he was out cold. The device that had been found underneath his car had been examined, then sold to the KGB for a large sum, so that they could reverse engineer it. Kristov informed Ivan that the money agreed would more than pay for the expenses that Elle had incurred, so they were all square. "You've been a great friend

Kristov," Ivan said. "You looked after Elle very well, thank you."

"Least I could do," Kristov announced, "anyway, it was quite a joy to have a pop at the establishment, get revenge for Vlad and his daughter. Makes a nice change from fighting over drug deals." His phone buzzed in his pocket, he pulled it out and glanced at the screen. "Your wife," he said to Ivan as he answered it. A few minutes later, he prodded the screen and slipped it back into his inside pocket. "Apparently she's struck some kind of a deal with Lord Golding and won't require any more warnings to be sent."

Ivan raised his eyebrows. "Did she say what sort of a deal?" Kristov shook his head. Elle hadn't elaborated on what had transpired, and in his opinion, had been a bit cagey. "Have you seen Karl lately?" Ivan asked, changing the subject onto more neutral ground.

"He's in New York, some sort of deal going on."

"He says that when he wants to spend some time with his mistress," Ivan pointed out. Kristov laughed.

"More likely that his wife wanted him out of the way so that she could spend time with hers," he said. It was Ivan's turn to chuckle, which led to another coughing fit. Kristov handed him his bottle of water. "Talking of perverts, I looked in on Nico's apartment, did you know he had a fully equipped torture room? It was just like the one Dascha had at her father's place." He shook his head. "He would've been such a good enforcer for the firm, it was such a shame that he wanted to waste his talents as a mere Head of Security. He could've had such a bright future." The old man sighed loudly and patted Ivan's shoulder, not seeing him roll his eyes behind his back.

"Have you any other up-and-coming young men who are interested in electronics and security systems?" Ivan asked, "Preferably ones who are multi-lingual too?"

Kristov thought for a moment. "There is one, his name is Ilya. He's an enforcer at the moment, but his heart's not in it. He's a clever boy, well educated, from Volgograd in the South and a good hard worker. I'll send him to see you." With that, he slipped his suit jacket back on over his pristine white shirt and bade Ivan goodbye, telling him that he'd see him at Nico's funeral.

Dr Mullins discharged Ivan on Saturday morning. With Viktor and his assistant's help, he managed to walk at a snail's pace to Elle's Bentley. They drove home slowly and carefully. Elle kept the girls on their leashes until Ivan was brought in and settled onto the sofa in the drawing room. The two spaniels went crazy, mobbing him with their entire bodies until he was laughing and begging them to calm down. Bella insisted on licking his face extremely enthusiastically, as though she couldn't quite believe he was real. Tania, who was always the more sensible of the two, simply squashed herself as tightly to Ivan's body as she could, planting her little feet so firmly onto his thighs that not even an earthquake could have moved her.

"You missed me girls?" Ivan teased, "You have? Aw, I missed you too. Paws up who wants their tummy rubbed." Elle stuck her hand up while the two girls ignored her in order to present their round little tummies to Ivan for fuss. Bella nearly slid off the sofa as she was wriggling so much. He noticed Elle had her hand up and gestured for her to come and join them on the sofa. Elle lifted Bella onto her lap so that she could sit next to Ivan. He sank back into the soft cushions gratefully, slinging his arm around Elle's shoulder.

"How're your legs feeling?" She asked. She'd taken him in a pair of shorts to put on so there was no fabric rubbing.

"Not too bad," he said, just enjoying the sensation of being in their lovely home, with all his best girls around him. There'd been a time in the hospital, when he'd genuinely feared he'd never see it again, especially when he'd heard the fear in Elle's voice, piercing through his strange dreams as he lay unable to move. Now that he was back, with his familiar things all in place, like the TV remote on the table and the dog beds by the fireplace, he gave thanks that he'd made it home in one piece.

Jo came in bearing a tray of drinks and snacks. "Thanks for coming in on a Saturday," Ivan said as she placed it on the coffee table in front of them.

"Oh, I haven't been home this week, I stayed here so that the girls didn't get lonely," she told him, "and the men needed a lot of catering. I've not cooked so much in years." Elle guessed, correctly, that she'd rather enjoyed herself in that strange way that Brits do in a crisis. As a race, they love rolling their sleeves up and mucking in when things are bad. It's a peculiarity that Ivan wouldn't have understood.

"Thank you very much," Ivan said, his voice full of warmth. He'd been pleased at the way his staff had rallied around, taking care of both Elle and the dogs. He was also looking forward to a proper cup of coffee, made with his favourite Jamaican Blue Mountain beans. The hospital stuff had been like watered-down piss. Jo smiled happily as she handed him a cup and saucer, before waving them both goodbye and going home to see what carnage was in her own kitchen after leaving her husband to take care of everything for a week.

"Alone at last," Elle murmured, her hand straying to Ivan's chest. She flicked his nipple, which immediately hardened into a tight bead.

"Yes, and I want to know what this surprise is." He raised his eyebrows at her. "It's driven me mad all yesterday, you looking so pleased with yourself."

"Come with me, it's in your study," she said, jumping up from the sofa. She placed his drink back on the table and held out her hand to help him up. Together they walked slowly back out to the grand central hall, past the kitchen and down the corridor to Ivan's office.

She'd refused to tell him the outcome of her meeting with Oscar, just that everything was sorted and there would be no more hostilities. He was a little sad that they'd passed up the chance to grab Conniscliffe, but he was delighted that Elle had said that she'd rather have HIS Conniscliffe, the house that he'd design and build for her and their family, with his heart and soul contained in every brick.

Ivan's study was a large room, which had been chosen because it overlooked the garden at the rear of the house. It had been fitted out in light oak, with a huge desk, a cleverly-concealed filing cabinet and drawers, as well as miles of bookshelves, which he'd filled, and a glass display cabinet, which housed a few vases and knick-knacks that the interior designer had chosen. He wondered if Oscar had given Elle one of his paintings. There'd been a Turner that he'd admired the first time he'd been to the castle. It wouldn't really fit the modern decor in the room, but he'd have displayed it regardless, just because he could.

"Close your eyes," Elle said when they reached the door. Obediently, he did as he was told, letting her guide him inside. They came to a halt in the centre of the room. "You can open them now," Elle said. She kept tight hold of his hand.

His eyes sprang open. He was facing the glass cabinet. Straightaway he saw the bright, jewel colours of the six perfectly-formed Fabergè eggs. He gasped, his free hand flying up to cover his mouth, which had fallen open in shock. "How the hell?" He managed to say as he moved closer to the cabinet to get a proper look. They were exquisite, perfect representations of the skill and craftsmanship of the Russian race during the reign of the Tsars. To own something so precious and rare was beyond anything the 'poor boy from the slums,' who lived inside him, could have ever imagined.

"It's the price Oscar was willing to pay for your silence," Elle told him. "If you use your information against him, I'll give them back." She paused. "I thought they'd go beautifully in Maytrees, away from little fingers of course."

"Or careless tails," he reminded her.

"Those as well."

He gazed down the line of eggs. "My favourite is the deep red one," he said. "Do you know what's inside it?" He didn't trust himself to touch them, fearing that he'd suddenly become clumsy.

"A posy of flowers in a diamond basket, if I remember correctly," Elle said. She'd briefly opened them all up when they'd arrived the previous afternoon, dropped off by the Conniscliffe Collection curator, who looked like he'd been crying.

"Beautiful," he breathed. "I can't believe you managed to get these off him."

"I told him you wanted Conniscliffe, but I thought that was unfair and too much," she said, as he turned his attention to the next egg in the line, a teal blue one. "He knew you'd want something, so I suggested these."

"He can shag who he wants, hell, I'd have even shagged him myself to get these," Ivan said.

"Don't tell him that," Elle said, laughing. "There's every chance he'd take you up on that, and I don't share nicely. Besides," she said, an impish expression on her face, "one taste of your lovely big cock would have him hooked for life."

"Would it now?" He asked, turning his attention back to her. He pulled her into his arms and kissed her deeply, tasting her properly again. He felt her body soften as he pressed up against her. Elle's hands roamed his back, feeling the strong, solid muscles of his shoulders and waist. His tight, slender torso never failed to excite her, the way the muscles flexed as he moved, his golden skin taut and flawless.

"Well, I've barely seen it for almost a week and that's driven me crazy," she admitted. She could feel his erection pressing up against her. She couldn't stop her hand sliding round to clasp it through his shorts. It felt unbearably hard and thick.

"I won't last long," Ivan admitted as he pulled her vest top over her head, freeing her tits, which bounced beautifully for him as she dropped her arms back down to slide his shorts down carefully, making sure that they didn't scrape his shins.

"Don't care," she panted as his erection bobbed in front of her face. She captured the head between her lips and lightly sucked the tip, running her tongue over the tight, shiny skin. She could taste his pre-cum, which made her so horny that her clit actually hurt from throbbing so much. She wrapped her fingers around the base and sucked hard, cramming as much of his cock into her mouth as she could. She was rewarded with a huge stream of cum, which pumped into her mouth and down her throat.

"Fuck," he shouted. There'd been no way he could've held back. "Sorry," he mewled as he felt her swallow. "I couldn't stop myself."

"It's been almost a week," Elle said after licking him clean. They never went more than a day without sex. She'd known he wouldn't have much control, but had reasoned that it would make way for a longer session and she really needed an orgasm.

She pulled down her shorts and stood naked in front of him. "I'm sure I'll get a reward for getting you those eggs," she murmured. His eyes swept up and down her delicious body, made even sexier, in his opinion, by her neat bump. Her breasts had grown bigger with her pregnancy, making them luscious and juicy. He sucked lightly on her nipple, making her cry out. His fingers slid between her legs, feeling how wet and horny she was. "Oh, you are so ready for this," he said, as he swept the papers on his desk to one side. She hopped onto the desk and spread her legs wide, planting her feet wide apart on the edge. She shivered with excitement, knowing what was to come. Ivan leaned down and kissed the tip of her swollen clit softly. He just wanted to taste her, just to keep her at the edge of her orgasm while her scent would make him hard again almost instantly.

He planted tiny kisses around the lips, inside her thighs, her pubis, avoiding the most sensitive parts. It was an exquisite tease, watching her skin glisten and hearing her pant with desire. "Please Ivan, I need to come," she begged as he drew his tongue down the crease where her thigh met her most intimate parts.

In one smooth motion, he pulled her forward to the edge of the desk and slammed his cock into her. He held her thighs in his iron grip as he thrust into her again and again, feeling her wetness flood over him as he pumped repeatedly. The only sound in the room was their bodies crashing together, his pubic bone slapping her clit over and over until she shouted that she was coming. He could feel the quivering inside that announced her imminent orgasm, and he pressed in deep and let go of his own. "Jesus Christ," she called out as hers hit. It was a deep, bone-shaking climax, the type only achieved when the body's been denied for a while. It went on and on for ages, her insides pulling in tight and releasing spasmodically.

"Oh God, I needed that," Elle said once he'd softened and slipped out.

**

In the Garden room at Conniscliffe Castle, Kenneth, the curator of the Golding art collection, carefully dusted the glass shelves in the cabinet where the six eggs used to be. He'd considered it a sacrilege to simply give them away as a gift to the Russian that Lady Golding had always insisted was a Podunk. Satisfied that not a speck of dust remained, he turned his attention to the six wooden boxes that he'd pulled out of the vault beneath the castle that morning. Carefully, with a museum worker's skill, he opened the first box to uncover it's contents, a perfect white egg, decorated with gold filigree and in his opinion one of the finest eggs that Fabergé had ever created. Carefully, he delicately brushed it with his soft-bristled brush and checked it over before placing it into the cabinet. He repeated the exercise another five times, until the space had all been filled. He stood back, assessing the placement, before tweaking one of the eggs until it was precisely centred and showing its artwork to best effect.

Happy with his handiwork, he closed the cabinet and locked it, wondering why Lady Golding had insisted that they never had more than six eggs out on show at any one time.

CHAPTER NINETEEN

It was decided during a rather tearful family meeting that Lucy's funeral would be held at Conniscliffe, with her remains buried in the picturesque cemetery in nearby Holway Village. Oscar had told her parents that he would let them choose, feeling as though he shouldn't really have much say. The coroner had released her body for burial two weeks after she was killed. Her parents decided that they didn't want to wait any longer than necessary, so it was agreed that Conniscliffe would be the best venue. It also gave Lady Golding plenty to do, which took her mind off of recent events.

The evening before the service, the undertakers brought her coffin into the synagogue and placed it on a trestle in the centre. It would stay there the night, until after the service the following morning, when they would take her to her final resting place and inter her into the ground. Afterwards, there would be a wake held in the ballroom, the only room large enough to hold the expected numbers of people who wished to show their last respects.

That night, when the castle had gone to sleep, Oscar crept downstairs, through the white garden, which he was glad his mother had saved, and through to the synagogue. He pushed through the large door, into the main room, lit only by the full moon which shone through the stained glass windows, casting a colourful glow over both the floor and Lucy's coffin. He glanced around, and satisfied that he was alone, walked over to the casket and laid his hand on it.

"I'm sorry," he said out loud, "for all the things that were done to you. You never deserved them, or this." He stroked his hand along the smooth wood. "I just wanted to be a good husband to you, to be a good father for our children. I truly didn't realise the devil was in our midst, and I'm so very sorry that I didn't protect you." He choked back the lump in his throat, but to no avail, his eyes filled with tears as he recalled the last time they'd been in the synagogue, when she'd been so beautiful, so elegant as she'd walked back down the aisle on his arm.

"I was a better man for being married to you," he told her, "and I'll keep that going, in your memory. I'll always make sure I've got change in my pocket, just like you did," he promised. "You were a great wife and would've been a wonderful mother. I'm just so sorry that you never had the chance." His tears were falling freely, splashing onto her coffin as the dam burst and he allowed his feelings to pour out.

Oscar stood there another ten minutes, leaning onto her coffin, weeping for the woman who gave herself completely to him, whom he'd allowed the Judas in his midst to snuff out. Eventually, he wiped his eyes and crept back out. He needed to try and get some sleep so that he could face the funeral.

The day itself was overcast and cloudy, quite normal for September, but a bit of a surprise after the late summer that they'd enjoyed. Oscar woke early and lay for a moment to brace himself for the day ahead. He was dreading it, all the concerned faces asking how he was in hushed tones, all the small talk he'd have to make in order to try and make the guests feel at ease around such a painful and harsh reality.

His mother was already in the breakfast room when he arrived. She was working her way through her Eggs Benedict while watching the morning news on her iPad. "You ready for this?" She asked as he heaped some scrambled eggs and toast on his plate.

"It's got to be done," he replied grumpily. "Besides, funerals aren't meant to be fun."

"Very true," his mother replied. "Solemn and dignified, that's what we aim for."

He sat down opposite her. "Can I ask you something?" She nodded. "When did you realise that there was something wrong with Darius?"

Lady Golding placed her knife and fork down and swallowed. "When we got Trudy."

Trudy was a small dachshund that they'd got as a puppy when Oscar was eight. She'd been his birthday present.

"You were over the moon with her, wouldn't stop playing with her, teaching her tricks."

Oscar smiled as he recalled the little dog, he'd loved her beyond all reason and had been heartbroken when she'd died aged fifteen.

"Darius was jealous of you. I caught him kicking her." Oscar's eyes widened. "If I hadn't caught him and stopped him, he'd have killed her. As it was she was like a little frightened rabbit for weeks afterwards." Lady Golding picked up her knife and fork to resume eating.

"I always wondered why she refused to go near him," Oscar said quietly.

"You should always trust a dog, they're the best judge of character around," his mother said. "I still miss having a dog around the place, they're good company."

Later that morning, Oscar stood with Lucy's parents, her brother, and Lady Golding to welcome the mourners as they arrived, shaking hands with everyone while their chauffeurs and drivers sorted out the flower arrangements that people had brought. Ivan and Elle stood in line behind a statuesque woman, who was wearing an immaculate black Chanel suit, black tights, and shoes and bore a completely black handbag. Elle watched as Oscar did a double take.

"Lucinda?" He asked. He sounded incredulous.

"Oscar," she said in a cut glass accent. "My father sends his condolences and apologies that he's unable to make it. My mother isn't well, as you may have heard. I'm here to represent the family."

"It's been ages since I've seen you," Oscar said, "You look well." He wanted to say 'you discovered moustache waxing,' but he stopped himself in time.

"Been in Africa for a while, building an orphanage with Harry Wales. There's no Patisserie Valerie in Zimbabwe. Anyway, I won't hold the line up. We'll talk more later." She moved down the line. Elle watched Lady Golding greet her enthusiastically, kissing her on both cheeks. She also saw Oscar catch a glance at her bottom.

"Ivan, Elle, glad you could make it," Oscar said, shaking Ivan's hand.

"Glad we could come," Ivan replied, before moving down the line to shake Lucy's father's hand and mutter his condolences.

"Was that Shrek?" Elle whispered in Oscar's ear. He nodded. Elle raised her eyebrows and moved along the line. She was held up again by Lady Golding checking Ivan over and generally fussing over him, until he graced her with his movie-star smile and pecked both her cheeks. By the time it was Elle's turn to shake her hand, she was flushed pink.

"So glad that you're ok dear, you gave us all a terrible fright," Lady Golding said, as she pecked Elle's cheek. "Bump looks as though it's growing nicely."

"Getting bigger by the day," Elle said, "and kicking a lot too. I think we might be having a footballer."

"We must have a proper catch-up soon," said Lady Golding. "I want to hear all about it." Elle moved on as Lady Golding turned her attention to the next person in the queue.

They followed the stream of people through the white garden and into the synagogue. As they took their seats, Ivan whispered that he was glad she hadn't pushed for the place, as he'd spotted a load of scaffolding up around the north wing. "All this old stone," he said, "it's too ugly, all covered in mould."

Elle didn't bother to point out that it wasn't mould on the walls. She was too busy taking in the magnificent flowers covering every available surface in the old chapel, spilling onto the floor as well. The scent of lilies assaulted her nostrils, sweet and pungent, their perfume mingled with that of the dozens upon dozens of white roses that Oscar had ordered to be made into displays in memory of Lucy's bridal bouquet. The overall effect was breathtaking.

When everyone had filed in, Oscar, his mother, and the Elliot family took their seats on the front row. A hush descended as the Chief Rabbi took to the lectern to deliver his sermon. After leading a prayer, the Rabbi talked about Lucy, stressing her sense of charity, her desire to help people through the administration of the law, plus of course, her happiness at being married to the love of her life. It was a heartfelt eulogy, woven together by the Rabbi himself. Oscar sat directly in front of him, his face devoid of expression, a skill that had taken the public school system many years to achieve.

After another prayer, for which everyone had to stand, the pallbearers came in to take the coffin and put it in the hearse. The family followed behind, all the men similarly grim-faced. The mourners began to file out behind them.

At the graveside, Ivan and Elle stood near the back, not wanting to impinge on the family, who took it in turns to throw a little earth onto the coffin while the Rabbi conducted another ceremony. When it was Oscar's turn, he threw his clod of soil, and also a white rose, which Elle found terribly poignant. She let out a sob, which prompted Ivan to gently place an arm around her and plant a soft kiss on her temple. She fished around in her pocket for a tissue and blew her nose as the sheer unfairness of Lucy's death hit her.

"Every word the Rabbi said about her was true," she told Ivan when they got into the car on the way back to the castle for the wake. "She was a genuinely kind person. It's just so unfair. She wasn't even twenty-six."

"Murder is never fair," Ivan said. "In Russia, we believe that if you murder a pregnant woman, you go straight to the very deepest pit of Hell, a bit like Dante's seventh circle if you will. We also believe that a pregnant woman who dies becomes an angel."

"That's lovely," Elle said. Ivan rested his hand on her bump.

"I just kept thinking it so easily could've been you. I couldn't have sat silently like Oscar did. I swear that man has no emotions." The baby kicked at his hand, making him smile.

"That's the upper classes for you. They see it as a strength. I remember when Diana died, and they all walked behind the gun carriage. Those two sons were the same. I cried like a baby just watching the funeral On TV."

"And that, Malyshka, is why I love you so much," he said, kissing first her cheek, then her bump.

Oscar stood by the graveside until everyone had left, just thinking about their life together, their good times, and how happy Lucy had been. He couldn't allow thoughts of how she died to even enter his head— it was just too painful. Eventually, he pulled himself together and left after seeing a man standing nearby with a shovel, waiting to fill in the remainder of the soil.

It seemed strange, Lucy's wake being held in the same place as their wedding only a few months before, but practicality had won the day, and it would've been impossible to house all the people who showed up to pay their respects anywhere else. Caterers had laid on a buffet at one end of the ballroom and were serving cups of tea and glasses of sherry, as was traditional. It was, Elle thought, a world away from her mother's wake. She chatted briefly to Minty, agreeing that it had been a lovely service, while Ivan seemed to be mobbed by various business associates who wanted to assure themselves that Ivan was indeed fine and not at death's door. Unfortunately, the funeral had scuppered their ideas of having a cheeky holiday in France, but that was life.

Oscar felt as though he was having a bad dream. He was saying and doing all the right things— his good manners had been deeply ingrained, but he did it on autopilot and would have preferred to lock himself away and just be on his own. "Hello Oscar, are you alright? You look like little boy lost." Lucinda smiled at him. "I'm sorry I missed your wedding, I'd have loved to have met Lucy."

"Yes, I'm ok, just a bit..." He trailed off. "You're looking very well."

"You said earlier. It's just a bit of weight loss, due mainly to running away after splitting with Theo. I just couldn't stay in London with everyone feeling sorry for me and thinking that I'd never get a man again."

"So you built an orphanage?"

"Yes, good for the conscience. I've just become the patron of an animal charity too. It takes ex-breeding dogs out of puppy mills, rehabilitates and re-homes them."

"I was thinking of getting mother a dog, she was talking about Trudy earlier," Oscar said.

"Your little dachshund? She was a character. I remember her stealing anything she could get her paws on. Used to sit under the table during dinner and woe betide anyone who slipped a shoe off."

"Oh God, yes, and couldn't she move fast?" Oscar laughed as he recalled her skidding around on her tiny little legs. He was grateful for Lucinda's presence, she'd always been fun and nice. Their families had been close when they were all growing up and Lucinda had been Stella's best friend at prep.

"I could just see your mother with a pretty little Bichon, or a Maltese. She'd be putting bows in its fur and getting the butler to feed it off of bone china," Lucinda quipped. Oscar laughed.

"If you get one come into the sanctuary..." He said.

"We have plenty of them. I'll find one for your mother if you want."

"That'd be great." He paused. "Are you going to Darius' funeral next week?"

She shook her head. "I'm no hypocrite. He was vile to me, made everyone call me Shrek when that movie came out. Never missed a chance to be cruel. As much as I like Arabella, I won't be pretending to mourn him." She saw the look of shock on Oscar's face. "I know he was your friend."

"Your honesty is rather refreshing," Oscar admitted. "The truth is that we fell out just before he died." He realised how that sounded. "Not that I had anything to do with his murder," he added quickly. Lucinda giggled.

"I don't think you'd be capable of murdering anybody. Didn't you set up a worm hospital once? Or am I dreaming that?"

Oscar smiled. "I set it up in the dungeon. My mother went nuts when Stella ratted me out. Talking of Stella, she's here somewhere." He scanned the room, searching for his sister.

"I'm sure I'll come across her. Truth is that we grew apart rather quickly when I discovered boys and she didn't," Lucinda confessed. They were interrupted by Minty, who bowled over.

"Cindy! I didn't recognise you! Your hair looks fab, love the highlights."

"Just the African sun," Lucinda replied as she pecked the air on both sides of Minty. "How's Thomas? Is he still playing ruggers?"

Oscar watched the two of them chat. It struck him that he thought Lucinda was quite pretty. Her slightly lazy eye barely showed and whether it had been surgically fixed or was just cleverly made up, he couldn't work out. His mother sidled up to him, "Now that nobody's whispering how ugly she is in your ear, maybe you can see her properly."

He thought for a moment. Darius had bullied her, called her ugly, picked out her flaws, and magnified them a thousand fold. There was every possibility that it was borne out of envy, that Oscar could be matched with a Rothschild, in particular one who was fun and good-hearted. He wondered if Lucinda still had a crush on him.

Elle had watched the whole encounter with a wry smile. Oscar's whole demeanour had changed when he'd spoken to Lucinda. His shoulders had dropped, his face had softened, and his hands had relaxed. She had to hand it to Lady Golding, she'd known all along exactly who'd have been right for her son.

The following morning, Oscar, Stella, and Lady Golding sat having breakfast. "Where'd you disappear to last night?" Stella asked Oscar.

"Went to bed early. I was shattered and I needed to be alone," he replied. "I forgot to thank you for flying over. I do appreciate it."

"I liked Lucy, a lot," she said, waving her hand airily as though that explained her willingness to drop everything and hurtle back to Conniscliffe. She'd been pleased to have been included in the family again, and her mother had been wonderful company when she'd stayed the week after the wedding. It had been no hardship to come back to support them in a difficult time, and it had been fantastic bumping into Cindy again.

They'd ended up hiding out in the sculpture garden, drinking wine, giggling, and rather naughtily smoking the cigarettes that Stella liked to hide from her mother. It had been just like old times.

"I was looking for you when everyone was leaving," her mother told her.

"Cindy and I were demolishing a couple of bottles of her uncle's wine," Stella told her. "I got tired of sherry. Hope you don't mind Osc, it was the sixty-six vintage."

"Help yourself," he replied, smiling at her. "So you and Lucinda made friends again?"

"Oh, we never fell out," Stella told him. "I just got sick of her always wanting to hang around you like a lovesick puppy, desperate to see your winkie, especially since it held absolutely no fascination for me." She grinned at Oscar's discomfort. "Anyway, she's mentioned that they need adoptees for the poor dogs at her charity. She's bringing someone over later to check us out, make sure mother's a suitable parent for a new pooch."

"Hold on," Lady Golding said, "I didn't say yes to a new dog."

"Yes, you did," Oscar insisted. "Anyway, it would be good company..." He was inordinately pleased that Lucinda would be over again.

His mother rolled her eyes at him. "Nothing changes does it? I recall the pair of you ganging up on me to get Trudy. Well, let's wait and see. They may think that the castle isn't a suitable environment for a puppy." She knew of course that it wouldn't be the case, but just didn't want to be seen to give in without a pretend fight.

That afternoon, Lucinda arrived, accompanied by a rather Bohemian-looking older lady, whom she introduced as Selena. Selena was one of the home-checkers that volunteered at the charity, she explained, and would make sure that the grounds were large enough to accommodate a dog as well as ensure that the animal wouldn't be left alone all day without company.

"The poor things have already been rescued once," Selena said. "We wouldn't want to put them into a situation where they'd need rescuing again."

As she chatted to Stella and their mother, Oscar wasn't paying attention. He was too busy staring at Lucinda. She was dressed in a knee-length cream skirt, with a silky cream blouse, which emphasised her full bust and nipped-in waist. Best of all were her long, slender, tanned legs, finished off with a pair of cream Ralph and Russo heels, impossibly high and garnished with gold filigree around the heel. Oscar could barely rip his eyes away from them. Stella spotted him and allowed herself a smug smile. She was glad she'd tipped off Cindy to wear them.

**

Ivan sat in his study poring over some spreadsheets sent to him by Gail. They were projections of the sales expected by the Frogs Agogo app, plus the increased cost of server space required if the app took off. The sheer number of terabytes of data that the app was predicted to generate was astonishing. While the in-app purchases were expected to generate a very good income for James, the real money lay in the game's data-mining abilities. He worked out that if only half of the Furious Frogs loyal fans downloaded and played, James's pay would be in the multi-millions at a conservative estimate. Excited, he picked up the phone to fix up a meeting with both the Datatrax executives and James. Ten minutes later, he ticked it off his 'To-do' list. Next was a call to the Allans to organise a meeting. He needed to add a secure gallery room to Maytrees. As he sat waiting for them to pick up, his gaze fell on the eggs. He'd already spent hours looking at them, carefully opening each one up to discover the delightful works of art inside. Just examining them had filled his heart with pride at his Russian heritage and brought a lump to his throat.

They were simply the best things he'd ever possessed. The rest of the world could remain owned by someone else, he didn't care anymore.

CHAPTER TWENTY

Two years later

Ivan plonked himself down on one of the woven sofas beside their vast indoor pool. He watched Elle power along, slicing through the water, deep in concentration. It was early, only six-thirty, but Nicolai had woken them both up at six, as usual. He sat beside Ivan, enthralled at the sight of his mummy streaking through the water like the dolphins they'd met on holiday in the Bahamas the previous month.

"Mummy wimming?" He asked.

"Yes, your mummy's swimming."

"I want to wim," he announced, jumping down from the sofa. Ivan just captured him in time to prevent him flinging himself in the pool after Elle.

"You can swim later. We agreed we'd take Bella and Tania out for their walk after breakfast, didn't we?" The little boy nodded. "Because after that we've got Uncle James coming over. You know what that means?"

"Cake!" Nicolai exclaimed, flapping his arms in excitement. Ivan smiled.

Catching sight of the two of them, Elle swam to the side of the pool, resting her elbows on the tiled edge. "Hey guys, how's my two favourite boys?"

"He wanted to get in there with you a minute ago. I grabbed him just before he launched," Ivan told her.

Elle grinned. "He's gonna be a little fish by the time he grows up." She'd already taught him to doggy paddle in the shallow end, assisted by Tania, who'd decided to join them. Bella wasn't so keen on water any more.

"I just showered and dressed him, so he'll have to be a fish another day," Ivan growled. "Breakfast is ready, then I promised we'd take the dogs out." He sat as Elle climbed out of the pool, her bump already visible despite being only four months gone. He handed her a towel to dry herself off.

"You go ahead. I'm gonna get a quick shower before I eat," she said.

Ivan carried Nicolai through the vast atrium in the centre of the house and through to the kitchen, where their chef had prepared their meal. He'd had to give in and have round-the-clock staff as Elle's pregnancy had progressed and she'd needed more help, plus Maytrees was way too vast for Mrs Ballard to take care of by herself. These days she was in charge of a team of cleaners, chefs, and gardeners.

Carefully, he sat Nicolai in his high chair and began to feed him his scrambled eggs, toast cut into soldiers, and a small amount of bacon, occasionally taking bites of his own meal as he waited for the little boy to chew. The dogs sat at his feet, having already inhaled their own breakfasts. They'd worked out early on that Nicolai was a good source of dropped food.

Eventually Elle appeared, her hair still wet from the shower. She took her plate from the chef and joined them at the kitchen table. "I love Saturday mornings," she announced. He had to agree. Their lives revolved around fitting work and business around caring for little Nicolai and the girls. Their weekends were definitely the best part of the week. He'd made sure everything he needed to do in London was fitted into his work week, as the weekends were always spent in Sussex. He loved Maytrees, the house he'd had built from just a hole in the ground. It was enormous, probably too big really, but it was beautiful and was equipped for everything they could ever possibly need. It was also safe. Ivan had learnt from his mistake two years prior and the ring of steel around the property also extended underneath the fences in the form of metal stakes driven deep into the ground every foot of the perimeter. Ilya had also set up an alarm system for the garages where their cars were stored every night. Roger had been delighted with his new protégé.

"James said he'd pop round about nine-ish," Elle said, deftly stopping Nicolai from feeding his toast soldier to

Bella, who was on a strict diet. "He said he's been experimenting with pastry, so we should expect choux buns."

"Did his partner get that job at Sussex General?" Ivan asked, spooning more egg into Nicolai's mouth, which he promptly spat out.

Elle nodded. As soon as Maytrees had been completed, they'd moved in and sold their old property to James, who'd wanted somewhere quieter and less stressful than the docklands. He and Lynzi loved it and were busy decorating it to their own taste. They'd both taken the entire summer off, thanks to Frogs Agogo making James a multi-millionaire. It had netted Ivan a fair whack too. "I don't know why she even wants to work," Ivan mused.

"I do," Elle said. "It takes such a long time to break into a profession that you feel guilty for not pursuing it. I still feel bad if I take a day off, especially if we're in the middle of a big deal." She picked up the teapot and poured herself a cup.

"That's madness," Ivan said, "You don't need to work. That's why we employ people, although to be fair, they're not you." He smiled at her, thinking, not for the first time, how lucky he'd been to capture her. Elle had proved herself worthy time and time again, not least in providing him with a son and heir, plus she was incubating his next one. He was confident he wouldn't panic so much at the birth of baby number two.

She rolled her eyes at him. "Pot calling kettle. Have you checked how much you're worth lately?" She knew fine well that he added it up every Friday. "You could retire, never work another day in your life and still have enough in the pot for several generations of Porenskis."

"I can't retire," he said, "who'd run the company?"

"Float it, take the money and run," Elle said. "If you floated it on the stock exchange, you could stay as chairman if you wanted, and let the board appoint a new CEO."

"Beltan must be worth billions," Ivan mused. The idea would have been unthinkable a couple of years ago, but now that Nicolai was on the scene, it could be quite appealing.

"I worked it out at about forty billion," Elle said, "but that was in a bear market. In a strong stock market it would be significantly higher than that." She paused. "Think about it."

Ivan rolled the thought around his head. "It would be complicated, all the different companies."

Elle shook her head. "I incorporated all of them into Beltan when I set it up, if we floated that, it would include all the component parts. We made them all compatible with payroll, reporting, etcetera, and I did that so we could lump them together if you ever wanted to sell up." She took a sip of her tea and grinned at Nicolai, who was drawing shapes in the scrambled egg on the tray of his high chair.

"Or we just have tons of child geniuses like Nicolai to take it over..." Ivan said.

Elle patted her bump, "It was always the plan A, just wanted to throw a plan B out there, just in case." They were interrupted by the baby, who wanted to get down from his chair. Ivan lifted him out, then grabbed an ever-present baby wipe to clean him down, marvelling at how quickly he could go from squeaky clean to having egg in his hair and be coated in crumbs.

"Talking of chairmen, I need to speak to Oscar on Monday about that Ukrainian finance minister's request. I take it he's back from honeymoon?"

"Yes, I spoke to him yesterday. He's over at Eythrope this weekend visiting Cindy's folks."

"Remind me on Monday that I need to call him."

"Yes sir," she gave a mock salute, which Nicolai immediately copied. Ivan sighed. His son was learning snarkiness early on in life.

Ivan and Oscar had made their peace early on after the incident, however Ivan had never discussed the conversation he'd had with Lucy regarding Oscar's conduct with Darius. It remained an unspoken knowledge between them. In one respect, he wished he'd asked Oscar why he'd felt the need to be shagged by a man, especially since he had Elle at the time, a woman that Ivan regarded as the sexiest he'd ever met. He'd stayed off the subject, worried that if he mentioned it, Oscar might regard it as a come-on, which it most definitely wasn't. He hoped for Cindy's sake that Oscar had given up his predilection, especially as he'd liked her from the moment Oscar had introduced them.

Ivan found Lucinda to be a rather interesting woman, widely-travelled and well-read and although she was as 'establishment' as Oscar, she seemed to have a slightly more common touch. She'd held the baby and asked about the birth, an event which Ivan had found extremely traumatic.

Elle had been determined to have a natural birth, but the moment she'd begun yelling in pain, Ivan had panicked and tried to demand a cesarean, thinking that it would be less difficult, prompting accusations of being a tosser, and a few other choice names, from Elle and a long-winded explanation from the doctor when she should've been attending to Elle.

The moment he'd held his son in his arms had been magical, a real life Porenski, the only blood relative he had. As he gazed down at the soft dark brown fuzz on the top of his son's head, he felt the planets shift, aligning themselves to continue his good fortune. "We are going to have such a good life together," he whispered to the sleeping infant. "You're going to grow up having the best of everything, I promise you. You'll have the best education in the world, the best health, and you'll be really lucky, because you've got the best mummy you could ever have hoped for." He kissed the baby's forehead. "And I promise that you'll have every advantage it's in our power to give you." He glanced up to see that Elle had tears in her eyes.

"You forgot to tell him he has the best daddy in the world," she said.

**

A week after Lucy's funeral, Lucinda drove Lady Golding down to Lewes for the 'meet and greet' of the foster carer who'd taken the poor unfortunate breeding dog and her litter of puppies. The mother dog would need to be kept in foster for intensive rehabilitation, it was explained, but the puppies were available to good homes for a small donation to the 'Many Tears Rescue Centre.' There was only one puppy not reserved, a tiny, white fluffy girl, who, knowing which side her bread was buttered, made a bee-line for Lady Golding, snuggling into the crook of her arm and licking her fingers. It was a done deal.

"I shall call her Petula," Lady Golding announced as Lucinda drove her back to Conniscliffe with the puppy safely ensconced in a cat basket on the back seat. "I've always liked Petula Clarke," she explained, "although I'm quite glad that my husband forbade me to use the name for our daughter."

"Stella suits Stella," Lucinda agreed, "But Petula Golding has quite a nice ring to it, very suitable for someone small, white, and fluffy."

Both Oscar and Jones the butler fell in love with Petula. The puppy soon learned that it had landed on its paws and ended up refusing to eat anything that wasn't served on bone china, or by a butler. It tolerated the pink bows that Lady Golding used to tie its fringe back, to keep the fur out of its eyes, but nipped at anyone who attempted to restrict its access to the damask-covered sofas. Petula most definitely ruled Conniscliffe with an iron paw.

If Lady Golding hadn't loved Lucinda before, introducing Petula into her life lifted Lucinda up to 'can never do any wrong' status.

To thank Lucinda for brightening his mother's life, Oscar invited her for lunch at Claridge's. They chatted so easily, and he had such a good time, that he was disappointed when it was time to leave. They set a lunch date for the following week.

They'd played it slow at first. Lucinda had held back, mindful that Oscar had just lost his wife, she was anxious that she'd become his rebound girlfriend, so had held him at arms length for the first six months, even though it had killed her to do so.

For Oscar it had been different. He'd known from the start that Lucinda was the type of woman he'd want to marry. He made sure not to play with her emotions, to wait until he was totally sure, and not leave her broken-hearted like Theo had done.

There'd been lots of lunches, then dinner dates, before they moved on to attending functions together.

They felt comfortable in each other's worlds and both families had been delighted with the turn of events.

For Lucinda, it was the moment she'd waited her whole life for. Her crush on Oscar had begun when she was around ten. She'd crept around Conniscliffe at night with Stella on pretence of ghost hunting, but secretly hoping to see Oscar in a state of undress. Stella had teased her about it, stating that Oscar looked 'gross' in the nude. Lucinda wasn't convinced.

Her relationship with Theo had been a monumental mistake borne out of the belief that no man would ever want her. She'd been bullied both by Darius and their friends, and at school, often because of what she represented, who her family was. Theo had started off saying that he didn't mind her being a bit heavy, he convinced her that he loved her for her mind.

Unfortunately she caught him with a skinny, bimbo type in their bed and angry that he wasn't going to be married into such a wealthy family, he'd blamed her, telling her it was her ugliness that had driven him into another woman's arms. She'd been devastated, blamed herself, and had run away to hide from London society in a rural backwater of Africa. Thankfully, spending time with the bouncy, Tigger-like Harry Wales had eased the pain, and helping truly underprivileged orphans had restored her self belief. Losing a couple of stone in the process had helped too.

Oscar and Lucinda eventually became a couple after a function at the House of Lords one night. Lucinda had known almost everyone and charmed the mostly-elderly peers, while Oscar had been in awe of her subtle coercion to get them all voting in favour of the new banking bill, which he'd had more than a hand in drafting. Of course, it benefitted her family as well, but while she didn't actively work for her family firm, he realised that she was almost as well-schooled in the minutiae of the banking world as he himself was. It was quite the aphrodisiac.

When he discovered that she had more 'sensible' taste in underwear, the deal was sealed.

This time, he planned his proposal properly, first having a ring made from a large pear-shaped diamond he purchased from De Beers, then taking her to Venice, where he asked her to marry him as they strolled across the Bridge of Sighs. It was so perfect and so romantic that Lucinda had burst into tears as she accepted. They found a little bistro to sit for a glass of wine to toast their engagement. "Can we get married at Eythrope?" Lucinda asked him. "Only you know what my father's like, me being his only daughter and all that." She examined the ring, holding her hand out to view it properly.

Oscar felt a wave of relief wash over him. The last thing he wanted was a carbon copy of his previous wedding day. As much as he loved Conniscliffe, he didn't want the pain of Lucy's murder encroaching on their special day together. "We can get married anywhere you like," he assured her.

"It'll be like a who's who of finance," she warned him. "You know what my father's like. He'll want the banking world to know that close links are being forged between Goldings and Rothschilds."

"The main merchant bank and the central bank," Oscar mused out loud.

Lucinda laughed. "I never thought of it like that, but I suppose it is really."

The Eythrope estate reminded Oscar a lot of Conniscliffe, albeit being a lot newer and built with red brick instead of ancient stone. The gardens were a particular feature however and could rival Conniscliffe in size and scope. The Rothschilds had owned properties in the area for centuries, although they'd built this particular mansion in the eighteen hundreds and furnished it in the French style, paying particular attention to the exterior of the property.

They'd married in the rose garden on a beautiful sunny day, not unlike the weather on his first wedding. The scent of roses filled the air, while birds sang, and the wind gently rustled the nearby trees, lending an informal feel to the large event.

He'd chosen Hartey to be his best man this time, and beyond the actual service itself, there were few similarities with his first marriage. The main difference was Lucinda herself, plus the fact that Oscar was absolutely, totally head over heels in love with her.

She hoped that Theo had seen the pictures of her wedding which were released to the press. She'd loved her dress, the way it had accentuated her curves. Most of all she'd loved the way that Oscar's eyes had shone when he saw her walk into the Rose Garden on her father's arm. He'd been worth waiting for.

They'd had an amazing honeymoon, flying over to the Rothschild estate in France by private jet, then on to Oscar's estate in Tuscany before spending a week on the Amalfi Coast in a hotel owned by one of Lucinda's friends. Oscar could barely keep his hands off her, needing to be inside her at every opportunity. He'd never met a woman, including Elle, who turned him on quite as much as Lucinda. She was like a ripe, juicy peach, sweet and soft, and with the solid core of a Rothschild. Although she was slender, her flesh was softly luxurious and unlike Elle's muscular body, or Lucy's skinny, lithe frame, Lucinda was entirely devoid of bony protuberances. Oscar thought she was perfect, totally, utterly perfect.

For the first time since he was eight years old, Oscar could be his own man and finally experience real happiness and peace.

ALSO BY D A LATHAM

A VERY CORPORATE AFFAIR BOOK 1-CLIMBING THE LADDER
A VERY CORPORATE AFFAIR BOOK 2-A RED DRESS AND RUBIES
A VERY CORPORATE AFFAIR BOOK 3-LORDS AND COMMONERS
A VERY CORPORATE AFFAIR-THE TAMING OF THE OLIGARCH
SALON AFFAIR
THE BEAUTY AND THE BLONDE
THE WHORE OF BABYLON CAY
THE DEBT
THE FIXER

ALL AVAILABLE FROM ALL GOOD E-RETAILERS AND IN PAPERBACK

FIND OUT MORE AT:
FACEBOOK: THE NOVELS OF D A LATHAM
TWITTER: @DALATHAM1
DALATHAM.WORDPRESS.COM

PLEASE CONSIDER LEAVING A REVIEW FOR THIS BOOK ON THE SITE YOU PURCHASED IT, OR ON GOODREADS. REVIEWS HELP OTHERS DISCOVER NEW BOOKS.

DO STICK AROUND FOR A BONUS CHAPTER FROM THE FIXER

CHAPTER ONE
THE FIXER

Sarah

The days which irrevocably change a person's life rarely announce their arrival with much fanfare. Sarah's day began badly, with her alarm clock failing to wake her at six a.m. in order for her to get herself properly together and ready for work. It normally took two coffees and at least an hour of preparation to present herself as a polished professional. That morning she had just fifteen minutes.

She stood in front of the mirror, cursing. She knew that if she didn't get a move on, she'd be late, which wouldn't go down well with Mr Hitchcock, her manager, who was a stickler for punctuality. She was starting a new project that Monday morning, so she really needed to be on time and playing her "A" game. Unfortunately, Having chosen that morning to oversleep, it meant she'd have no time for coffee. Irritated, Sarah yanked her hair into a ponytail and grabbed her bag, flinging it over her shoulder before racing out of the door. Of all people, she should be the most organised, given that she was a fixer, or rather, a glorified nanny for the top talent at Laker Brothers, the biggest film studio in the world. Her real job title was Executive Assistant: a rather prim, corporate moniker for what could essentially be a rather dirty, immoral job.

She was the person who sorted hotel rooms, found the stuff requested in stars' riders, and generally wiped their noses. She was a mixture of PA, mummy, and often pimp, catering to the whims and desires of overpaid, spoilt, and largely egotistical actors. It was actually a great job, her dream job, and she never had two days the same. Her previous charge had thankfully flown back to LA two days before into the safe care of her LA equivalent. It had left her just one day to get her laundry up to date, see her poor, neglected friends, and clean her little house in Fulham before her next assignment arrived. The last one had been a twenty four/seven job, a spoilt and demanding actress whom Sarah had been glad to see the back of.

In the grand scheme of things, it didn't sound like a particularly important way to earn a living, but it was extraordinarily well paid, with great perks, and fixers wielded a certain amount of power within their worlds due to their budgets, plus the lure of providing celebrity clients to the various businesses around London. Backhanders and bribes were commonplace, depending on the star level of the celebrity involved and the size of the fandom which followed them. Sarah was a particularly well-connected fixer and usually looked after "A" listers.

Clive Hitchcock was already in the spacious, open-plan office by the time she got there. "Morning Sarah. Looking forward to meeting your new charge?" He smirked as she rolled her eyes. She regarded all the stars she looked after as pretty ordinary, although usually bearing extraordinary self-confidence. Sarah had never met anyone that she'd want to be best friends with.

"You know the answer to that one Clive. So who have I been assigned this week?" She asked, pleased that he hadn't mentioned the fact that it was five past nine. She knew that they had at least five actors arriving, but casting was often a last-minute affair, so things often changed at the last moment.

"Actually you've got him for the next three months. He's filming here, and in Italy, all this summer. His name's James Morell. Played the lead in Cosmic Warriors. You must know who he is."

"Rings a bell," she said nonchalantly. "From what I know, he's just a pretty boy. At least I get a bit of eye candy while I'm working." She knew from bitter experience that film stars were pains in the butt; no matter how nice the outer packaging, it often concealed narcissistic personalities. Still, she reasoned that it was better to have a nice view if this James Morell was going to treat her like a dogsbody.

Clive sent the file over with Mr Morell's requirements. Sarah printed it off and flicked through it. She was to get his London home ready, to get it cleaned and stocked. She needed to sort him a car and driver for the duration of his stay, all of which was easy enough. "Where's the rest of the file?" She asked. "There's no rider, no special requirements, doesn't even say what household staff he wants." The LA fixer was clearly getting lazy, not sending through the normal reams of instructions, detailing the myriad obscure requests that most stars required.

Clive glanced up from his screen, "I don't think he wants any, but he might change his mind when he finds out what's on offer. Just work with what you have. His flight arrives tomorrow morning at eight. Don't forget to tip off the paps."

Part of Sarah's job was to liaise with PR and the publicists to make sure stars were always kept in the public eye and presented in the best possible light. She had one day to get everything ready, which was not a lot of time, but she'd managed worse deadlines with far more detailed riders. She picked up the phone to start on her list of calls. She started with a call to the estate agent holding the keys to his house in Kensington, which had been rented out while Mr Morell had been contracted to film for almost a year in the States. Sarah discovered that he was, in fact, British and had lived in London while travelling regularly to LA in order to audition and eventually break into the closed world of Hollywood. Her day ended up a whirlwind of phone calls, taxi rides, and organising the interns to run myriad errands. She fell into bed at midnight and was up again at four to get herself ready and over to the airport to do the meet and greet.

James Morell stared at his watch yet again, willing the time to pass. He hated flying alone. He had nobody to talk to, nobody to settle his anxiety at hurtling through the air in a metal cigar, and nobody to share his death if it crashed. He took another sip of champagne and tried to watch a film. He was ensconced in the luxury of first class, on a comfy flat-bed, surrounded by top-of-the-range entertainment, food, and drink. He barely noticed it all, having become accustomed to the finer side of life. He debated whether or not he should shower and get changed before dismissing the idea. He was landing early in the morning, so didn't expect any fuss. He just hoped that Laker Brothers had arranged for him to be met at the airport, otherwise he'd have to schlepp over to the taxi rank and get a cab home. His fixer had told him that someone called Sarah would be there to meet him. He hoped there were no screw-ups, although with his LA fixer's track record, anything was possible.

By the time James landed, his house was prepared, his fridge filled, his measurements sent to the various designers who wanted to dress him, clothes collected and hung in his wardrobe, a car and driver, and security sorted. Sarah was to meet him at the first class area of Heathrow at eight and brief him on the way back to his Kensington home.

Now, she was used to the various actors that Laker Brothers employed. They were usually handsome, charismatic, and fit. She liked to think she was immune to pretty faces. In her opinion they usually just covered up an asshole personality. She'd looked after quite a few in the past, and after a moment to get over their looks, Sarah was perfectly capable of being the professional around them.

She got there a little early and sat reading through her notes as she waited. She hoped his plane wouldn't be late, as there were a load of paparazzi waiting outside, which would quickly attract a large crowd of onlookers, curious as to who would be arriving.

Nothing prepared Sarah for the first sight of James in the flesh, striding down the corridor. His masculine beauty simply took her breath away. She stood frozen, clipboard in hand, just drinking in the sight of him. *'I am so screwed,'* she thought, as he beamed a devastating smile and halted in front of her. "Are you Sarah?" He asked, surprised that Laker employed such a pretty fixer. Most of the ones he'd come across had been middle-aged and rather grizzled, prized for their abilities to magic up even the most outrageous requests and deal with the most disastrous calamities. "Pleased to meet you, I'm James Morell."

He didn't really mean to use his "sexy" voice, but this gorgeous brunette with the liquid brown eyes was just too mesmerising to bark at in a businesslike way.

Sarah just stared at him for a moment before eventually mentally slapping herself, closing her slack jaw, and forcing herself back to the job at hand. "Yes, I'm Sarah. Nice to meet you. Your car's this way. Please follow me. There are photographers at the entrance." She quickly turned on her heels, desperate to hide the fact that she was blushing furiously. He trotted along beside her as they strode towards the exit, both reeling from their initial reactions to each other.

They headed through a walkway towards the exit, where Sarah had stationed a battalion of paparazzi ready to snap his arrival in the UK. James caught sight of himself in the mirrored glass running along the wall. His skin looked grey, and his dark, curly hair was wayward and bouffant, not his usual well-groomed appearance and not how he wanted to look in pictures that would be shared across the net. "I look like shit after the flight," he groaned before his brain had gone into gear. He could've kicked himself for sounding so vain in front of her.

She braved a glance at him, fully aware that she'd blush again and feel stupid for being such a sap. "You look OK to me," she muttered, turning away so he wouldn't see the pink flush rising from her neck.

Flashbulbs started going off the moment they stepped outside. Sarah steered him through the mass of paparazzi, then had to wait while he posed for pictures with a few fans who had gathered. He began signing autographs, secretly rather pleased that so many people had turned out to catch sight of him. It didn't occur to him that they'd been sent there specifically.

"We really need to get going," she huffed. Reluctantly, he said goodbye to the people screaming out his name and followed her out of the concourse and into the VIP car park. "Bob will be your driver and security," she told him. He smiled and shook Bob's hand, taking the burly, cynical driver by surprise. He was used to the asshole stars too. Most looked straight through him.

During the drive to his house, she ran through all the services he could request that would be accommodated by the studio. To her surprise, he refused most of them, only saying yes to a personal trainer. James had no desire to be stifled by a houseful of staff, as he'd experienced it in LA and had hated both the loss of privacy as well as the lack of autonomy that having housekeepers and butlers inflicted. He also didn't want to appear helpless in front of such an obviously bright young woman.

When he declined the services of a personal stylist, she smiled at his comment that he could manage to dress himself. He stared at her, trying to fathom why her smile made him glad to be back home and why she was affecting him so much. James was used to beautiful women around him, used to the way they reacted to his face and physique. Sometimes they were a welcome diversion, sometimes an irritant that his security needed to deal with, but very few actually held his interest. Sarah somehow seemed different. She wasn't like the tall, thin models and actresses he usually met, being petite and curvy. As she loosened her jacket, he caught sight of the swell of a decent-sized cleavage. This instantly captured his interest, but it was more than that, it was her confidence, her quiet capability. She was clearly...different.

She interrupted his musing. "I can arrange some company for you, either female or male, whichever you prefer." It was all part of the normal spiel that she had to give each of the stars she looked after. With the abundance of camera phones, the studio couldn't allow less-than-discreet liaisons for their charges. For some reason, those words coming out of her mouth sounded almost offensive. When his LA fixer had offered the same "service," he hadn't been the slightest bit bothered.

"Certainly not," he bit back, startling her. "Sorry, but I won't be needing anything like that. I prefer my relationships to be a little more...traditional." He fixed her with his intense gaze, trying to see into her psyche, which she found a little disconcerting, as was his intense focus on everything she had to say. Generally stars treated Sarah as though she was part of the furniture, so she wasn't used to dealing with such rapt attention. She took a deep breath to steady herself.

"Oh, OK. Will you be having anyone joining you during your stay?"

His face betrayed a sadness. "No. No, I won't." She decided to drop the subject, moving on to his itinerary and travel dates. "So will you be babysitting me all summer?" He asked, smiling. It was at that moment that Sarah began to suspect that he might be flirting with her.

"Yes. I've been assigned to you for your entire stay in London and while you're travelling to Italy," she told him, while praying that she could get over his extraordinary good looks and get her professional composure back. Her palms were sweaty, and her body was responding just sitting next to him. She breathed in his lovely scent and felt another blush rise up her already overheated neck, which James noticed immediately and was gratified to see. He decided to take charge.

"Well, we'll just have to get to know each other, Sarah, seeing as we'll be in close quarters for the next three months. I'll take you out to dinner tonight." It wasn't really a request, more a statement, but coming from him, it didn't sound impertinent. She told herself it was perfectly normal for stars to dine with their fixers, even though she knew it was highly unusual. Something told her he wasn't a man who'd take "no" for an answer. Besides, she found him unusually appealing.

"OK."

He beamed his film-star smile and settled back in his seat, while she attempted to recover her professional composure by running through his schedule for the following few days. He groaned when she told him about a photo shoot his agents had signed him up for. "I hate those things. I know they're important, but I always feel awkward," he confided.

Sarah laughed. "You're probably the most photogenic person on the planet. How'd ya think the rest of us mere mortals feel?"

"Oh, I don't know, a beautiful woman like you must take an amazing picture."

'A charmer too. I'm really screwed here,' she thought. "Thank you for the compliment, but I assure you I don't," she told him, rather primly.

"Now, I don't believe that for one moment," he said, "with your cheekbones and flawless skin, not to mention those big brown eyes, I'd expect the camera to adore you." He stared at her, drinking in her startled features, waiting for her reaction.

"I have no desire to be on your side of the camera," she told him. "I've seen enough screwed-up starlets to know it's not a life I'd aspire to."

He didn't answer. She wondered if she'd offended him.

He gazed out of the window for a while, as they sped towards Kensington, "I miss London. As much as I love LA, there's no place like home is there?"

"Even on a grey, miserable day like today?" Sarah laughed. It was forecast to rain, and the whole sky was blanketed by dark clouds, giving everything a grey, dingy appearance. James wondered if all his sweaters were still in storage. He hadn't needed them in LA.

"Especially on a day like today," he grinned. "Bright blue skies every day become tedious after a while. Everything in LA conforms, you know: perfect weather, perfect houses, and all the women look like models with the ubiquitous long blonde hair and fake bodies." He thought for a moment, "Yeah, I've missed London."

They arrived before Sarah could question him further as to why he'd got fed up with gorgeous people, weather, and homes. His house was on a small residential street in Kensington. It was white, stucco fronted, with glossy, black railings marking the perimeter. She rummaged around in her handbag to hand him his keys, but he fished a set out of his jacket pocket and hopped out of the car, clearly eager to get inside. He'd missed his home more than he'd care to admit. It had been his only significant purchase after his first blockbuster, and to James, it was a solid embodiment of his success in a way that plaudits or awards could never compete with. He'd always reasoned with himself that in the fickle world of acting, his career could end at any time, but he'd always have his house.

Sarah thought his home was lovely, modern, and nicely furnished. Bob placed his bags in the hall, and asked if James wanted them taken upstairs. "No thanks, just there's great. I'll sort them out in a bit." He turned to Sarah, "The first thing is some English tea. I've missed it more than you'd believe. Join me?" It was an effective but gentle way of dismissing Bob, who smiled thinly before turning to leave.

Sarah followed James through the long hallway, waving goodbye to Bob. She watched as James moved around his luxurious kitchen with a practiced ease, filling the kettle, and pulling out cups. It was a large room, taking up the entire rear half of his house and fitted out with off-white units and granite worktops. It was the type of kitchen beloved of moderately successful stockbroker's wives, managing to be both slick and traditional at the same time. He opened the fridge and examined the contents, noting that there was a terrific selection. "I take it you filled it up?" She nodded, nervous, praying she'd not forgotten milk. "You've done a great job, thought of everything by the looks of it." Sarah breathed a sigh of relief, then mentally slapped herself for caring so much.

He beamed a knicker-combusting smile. "Sorry, I shouldn't be surprised. You do this type of thing all the time don't you?"

"Yes. Yes I do." It was a struggle to get the words out; she was so mesmerised by the perfect planes of his jawline that she could barely concentrate. To try and regain control, she pulled his file out of her bag, to run through some of the PR requests.

Fixers work closely with the PR department. They make sure that their stars are seen in the right places, with the right people, and wearing the right clothes. Every detail is planned and scrutinised so that they're one step ahead of the celeb sites. It would probably surprise people how meticulously everything is organised so they never see the stars wearing the same outfit twice, or in the company of non-entities. Laker Brother's PR department was widely acknowledged as being one of the best and most detailed in the business. It was also the department that Sarah had cut her teeth in, so she was generally "on message" without too much of their involvement.

"They want to see you out and about in London. They'd like you to go out with your co-stars, maybe a family meet-up, and have requested that you get papped being a man-about-town. Think you can manage that?" She glanced up to see him frowning.

"Am I really controlled that much?" He asked. "I don't mind meeting my brothers or going out for dinner with Harry, my co-star, and his wife, but the rest of it, is it really necessary?"

"You have an image to keep up," she explained. "PR monitors public opinion, and they want to see more of you, preferably in a less formal setting. Don't worry, you'll have security." She wondered what his problem was.

"It's not that it's just..." He paused, "It's so false. I'm going to be catching up with friends while I'm here, so I'll make sure we go somewhere public. Should satisfy the pimps at PR." James knew the game, he'd been around long enough to understand how stardom was created and maintained, but this "businesslike" Sarah was… disappointing. He wondered how to get her to snap out of PR mode and get her blushing again. He was also falling asleep, having been unable to sleep on the flight due to a rather selfish businessman tapping away at his keyboard half the night, then a couple having an argument during the remainder. He drained his cup, savouring the taste of fresh, hot, British tea made with good, hard London water.

"Hmm," she said, non committal. "Now, Tom Ford and Giorgio Armani will be dressing you. Their people sent over a selection. I hung it all in your wardrobe. Please don't wear anything else in public. Your workout clothing will be Nike and nothing else. They've sent over a large selection." Sarah ticked stuff off her list as she went. She was just about to run through his shooting schedule, when he interrupted her.

"I don't want to be rude, but I need a shower and some sleep. Can I pick you up around seven?"

Embarrassed at bombarding him when he was clearly jet-lagged, she nodded her assent.

"Where shall I pick you up?" He asked. Sarah scribbled down her address on the back of her contact card and handed it to him.

"Shall I book a restaurant?" she asked, rightly figuring he'd be asleep fairly quickly. Besides, she could get a table in just about any restaurant in London at short notice.

"Yes, please. Wherever you like, I don't mind," he said, before yawning loudly. Sarah smiled and said her goodbyes before letting herself out.

Back outside, she took a deep breath. She was hot, flustered, and affected by that man, all very unusual behaviour for her. Inside the house, James sat and scrubbed his hands over his face, trying to work out what it was about her, and wondering if it was the jet lag that'd rendered him so vulnerable. As he let the hot water of the shower pour over him, he couldn't shake the image of her out of his head, nor the sensation that he'd found *her,* his mythical Aphrodite.

Back at the office, Clive didn't even look up. "You're back early."

"He's jet-lagged. I'll meet up with him again later. I've got some admin and calls I can be getting on with." Sarah pulled out her phone and booked a table at The Ivy. She liked it there, and the lure of being able to put it on expenses meant she couldn't resist. Glancing over, she could see Clive's eyebrows had shot up.

"If he's going to The Ivy tonight, make sure the paps know. It's a prime opportunity. Who's he going with?"

"Only with me. We've still got stuff to run through."

"Make sure you tip off the paps then, and Sarah? Try and look your best. The fans won't know that you're his babysitter, so we might as well get some mileage."

She tried not to be horribly offended at the suggestion that she wouldn't pass muster as a celebrity girlfriend. Just to make sure, she booked a blowdry at the salon down the road that afternoon. If she was gonna be papped, she'd make damn sure she looked her best.

It took five changes of outfits to decide what Sarah would wear to dinner that night. As much as she tried to keep running the mantra "It's not a date, it's a client" through her head, she knew full well that she found him extraordinarily attractive. As she stared at her reflection in the mirror, she could see that she looked polished, even glamorous, but no amount of clever dressing could disguise the fact that she was petite and a bit curvy. The little voice in her head told her that he couldn't possibly be interested, and that she shouldn't get her hopes up as he was way out of her league. The worst thing she could do would be to flirt and make a fool of herself.

Meanwhile, James was digging around in his wardrobe full of unfamiliar clothes, wondering what he should wear as he had no idea where they'd be going. *'Just another example of why I hate not doing things for myself,'* he thought, as he called Bob to pick him up, the irony of which was rather lost on him.

He arrived dead on time that evening. Sarah's breath caught as she opened the door. He was fresh from the shower and dressed in a simple, fitted black shirt and black trousers. "Hey Sarah, you look amazing," he murmured, taking in the sight of her in a lace-covered, fitted black dress, which showed off her curves to perfection. Smiling, she grabbed her bag and followed him to the car.

"There might be photographers, so I thought I'd better scrub up," she told him. "I booked a table at the Ivy. Hope that's OK?"

"Great. I've not been there for ages, and I really want some English food," he said, flashing her that devastating smile, "and you scrub up beautifully. We can convince them that you're my new girlfriend. Get the studio off my back."

Sarah should have been pleased, but inside she was a little disappointed, wondering why he needed a fake girlfriend when he could take his pick of real ones. She stared out of the window while she tried to phrase the question she needed to ask. "If you're gay, James, you can tell me. I won't be shocked or surprised. I do this for a living you know, so I often deal with closeted film stars." There'd been at least three of her charges that she'd had to cover for, carefully constructing fake relationships for their public personas. It wasn't an approach that she personally agreed with, as she had seen the intense pressure it had put the "stars" under, but she understood why they did it.

"I'm not gay," he snapped, startling her. "Everyone seems to think I am, and I'm not."

"So why do you need a fake girlfriend then?" She challenged.

He thought for a moment and was just about to start speaking, when they arrived at the restaurant. The moment they got out of the car, the flashbulbs went off, momentarily blinding them both. Sarah felt his arm snake around her waist, his hand gripping her hip firmly, forming an instant physical connection. For James, it had been a primal, instinctive reaction; a desire to protect her from the aggressive photographers. His response even took him by surprise.

Sarah's body reacted instantly. Everything south of her waist tightened viciously. She leaned into him, closing the gap between them as they posed for pictures. He felt warm and solid, a strong, steadfast man. He also smelt adorable, a mixture of citrus notes and fresh mint. She breathed in deeply as the paps yelled questions at them. James didn't say a word, just steered her round and into the lobby, where he stopped again for more pictures.

After a few moments, they made their way into the restaurant, both a bit dazzled by the flashes. "You OK?" he asked her.

"A bit blind, but otherwise alright. You?"

"All in a day's work for me."

They were shown to a quiet little table at the back of the room. Sitting down, Sarah glanced around, recognising a couple of famous faces, but nobody as "A" list as James. She turned her attention back to him. He was reading the wine list, seemingly not remotely interested in star spotting.

"Red or white?" He asked, not taking his eyes off the list.

"I prefer red, but I'm not fussed, if you prefer white," she replied.

He ordered a bottle of Merlot, and sat back to read the menu. "You were about to tell me why you needed a fake girlfriend," Sarah asked. In a normal setting, it wouldn't be any of her business, but as his handler, she needed to know. She wondered if he had "quirks" she'd have to organise someone to accommodate. She'd had to source a dominatrix for a client before, and finding prostitutes was a fairly normal occurrence.

He groaned, "OK, here's how it is. You imagine having this so-called pretty face," he pointed at himself, "and a good job, paying great money. Women fling themselves at you all day every day. Only here's the thing, Sarah, they all want the image, the outer packaging. None of them have any idea about the man inside. I question their agendas constantly. You know, whether they're gonna sell their stories, spill to the press."

"What Titanium Rod's really like in bed..." she said. He laughed.

"Exactly. You imagine if I'd had too much to drink one night."

"Titanium Rod was anything but," she was catching on. He roared with laughter.

"It's never happened yet, but yeah, you get the picture."

"That's why we offer discreet escorts to our stars, so that kind of thing doesn't happen. They all sign watertight NDAs."

"I really don't want to use prostitutes, thank you," he snapped. Sarah wondered if she'd offended him. "I'll find the woman I'm looking for one day. Until then, I'd rather not settle for second best."

"If you don't let anyone in, or assume all women have ulterior motives, then it's never gonna happen," she snapped back, annoyed that he assumed all women would be after his fame or money. It was a bit rude, and made him sound like a typical pompous star. Up until that point, she'd thought he was different.

They were interrupted by the waiter. After they'd ordered, she fully intended to start going through the work stuff that she'd brought, as there was still quite a bit to do.

"I don't think all women are after my money or fame," he said quietly. "That didn't really come out right."

"Clearly," she replied. "Anyway, we need to run though your diary for the next three months. I need to organise a hotel in Rome while you're filming. You have a choice of three." She handed him the printouts. He barely glanced at them.

"I really don't mind where I stay. Will you be coming out there?"

"Yep. I'm assigned to you for the next three months."

"In which case, you can choose where we stay. Pick the best one."

Sarah laughed, "I'll be at the Italian version of a Travelodge. Only the actors get the five-star treatment."

"Well in which case, one of my requirements is that you're in the same hotel as me, preferably on the same floor." He smiled tentatively. She scribbled a note in her pad, fully intending to book the Grande Vizente, which had an award-winning spa and a rooftop restaurant. She'd already pored over TripAdvisor to find the top three hotels. With the studio paying, it'd be rude not to indulge. She prayed that they'd have two rooms available. Sarah was about to move onto discussing his workout regime when he interrupted.

"So you know all about me, down to what shoe size I am. It's only fair for me to know about you. Where are you from Sarah?"

"I'm from Hertfordshire originally. I moved to London after uni. Mainly because I'd got the job at Laker Brothers."

"What uni did you attend?"

She paused, before replying "Cambridge. I studied psychology. I interned at the head office, in the PR department, and was offered a job. A few promotions later, here I am."

He looked shocked. "A Cambridge degree? And you're wiping actor's noses for a living?"

"I'm paid a hell of a lot more than I'd get working in the NHS," she pointed out.

"Even so. Wouldn't you prefer a job that actually utilised your degree?"

"Not if it meant living in poverty, I wouldn't, no." She was getting a little annoyed. "Anyway, this isn't about me. We need to sort your diary, if you don't mind?"

He ignored her. "Are you single, married?"

She ignored the question. "Rod McDowell has been assigned as your personal trainer while you're in London. He operates from Equinox in Kensington Church Street. Bob will pick you up at 7 a.m. each morning to take you there." He groaned. "He'll be back from his holiday in a day or two, but I arranged for one of the gym employees to look after you starting tomorrow."

"I asked if you were single or married. Don't dodge the question." His voice had changed to being playful, teasing.

"I'm single, at the moment." Sarah admitted. She was always single, primarily because she worked strange hours, often in the bubble that surrounded the "A" list actors and actresses in her care. It was almost impossible to meet nice men, let alone sustain a relationship. Her last boyfriend had dumped her almost a year previously, fed up with constantly being dropped to run around after a particularly difficult actress, who'd had a fairly serious psychological issue and didn't like being alone.

"That's good to know," he said, before smiling a sphinx-like smile.

The food was exquisite, and they both ate heartily. James seemed to relax and regaled Sarah with funny stories from the Cosmic Warriors set. In turn, she made him laugh with some of the tales she often told about fun experiences she'd had while working on various shoots. The evening seemed to flash by, and all too soon it was time to go. He couldn't remember when he'd last enjoyed a woman's company so much.

The paps got them again as they were leaving. James immediately grabbed her waist, and held her close as the flashbulbs blinded them. "Who's your girlfriend?" One of them yelled. James didn't answer, he just flashed his film-star smile and steered Sarah towards the waiting car. They jumped in and slammed the door. Within seconds, Bob had pulled away into the traffic.

Sarah lay back into the leather seat, slightly blinded by the flashes. James squeezed her hand, an affectionate gesture meant to reassure her. "You OK?" he whispered, before he slid up the privacy screen, cutting them off from their driver. He desperately wanted to be alone with her, to try and gauge whether he could make a move or not. She was difficult to read, having not flung herself at him or flirted outrageously like most women did.

"I'm fine," she told him. Inside, she was a bit shaky, whether from the paparazzi or the fact he was holding her hand, she couldn't be certain.

"You did amazingly well. You're clearly a natural," he mused. She could see him smiling in the glow that the street lamps cast through the car windows. It struck her that he hadn't taken his eyes off her all evening and was again staring at her. It should've put her on her guard, or even made her uncomfortable, but she sensed that there was something genuinely kind about him. She could tell that he was as normal and decent a man as one could ever find in Hollywood. At that point, she'd even have gone far enough to say that he stood out amongst the stars she'd previously met as probably the most well adjusted.

"We've certainly put the cat amongst the pigeons," she remarked. Sarah just hoped she wouldn't be waking up to a mass rally of his fans deeming her too ugly for their god. James's fans were well known for being a bit extreme in their devotion to their idol.

"They'll all be wondering who the beautiful woman is," he said kindly.

It only took fifteen minutes to get to Sarah's place. She was almost sad to get home so quickly, as she'd enjoyed James's company and found him to be a lot more fun than she'd expected. As they pulled up outside, she reminded him that Bob would pick him up at seven.

"So when will I see you again?" He asked. Inside he was having a furious debate with himself as to whether or not to make his move. It reminded him of how he was aged fifteen, taking his date home from the school disco in the back of a taxi. The thought amused him.

"Tomorrow. I'll be accompanying you to the Heat interview," she told him. She was just about to hop out of the car, when his arm snaked around her waist, and he pulled her close, crushing her to his chest. His eyes bored into hers, asking for permission before his lips met hers, softly, slowly, before he deepened the kiss. His tongue grazed her lips, before pushing in to meet hers, shyly at first, then becoming bolder, more demanding. It went against every rule in the book, but at that precise moment, Sarah didn't care.

She softened into him, lightly holding his waist, feeling the firm ripples of his precisely-toned muscles. Eventually he pulled away and stroked his hand down her cheek. "You have no idea how lovely you are, do you?"

She shook her head, mute. Everything about the man screamed perfection. He looked, tasted, and smelt divine, as though the gods had listened to a woman's pleas and created the most exquisite male specimen.

He planted another, chaste kiss on her lips before pulling back. "Until tomorrow Sarah, and I honestly can't wait."

"Tomorrow," she parroted, breathless. In a dream state, she opened the car door and got out, testing her legs before standing upright. She took one last glance at him. He blew her a kiss.

Sarah walked up to her front door in a daze, questioning herself as to whether or not that had actually happened. As his car pulled away, she touched her tingling lips, and came to only one conclusion; she was totally, utterly screwed.

James felt triumphant as the car sped over to Kensington. Easy lays and hungry starlets held no fascination compared to the bright, intelligent woman who'd made him feel like a schoolboy again. He would have Sarah, he decided.

I hope you enjoyed this taster chapter from The Fixer, by D A Latham, which is available from all good e-retailers and in paperback.

Printed in Great Britain
by Amazon